Skin Deep

Mark of the Least

KENDRA MERRITT

BLUE FYRE PRESS

This one's for Mom, who was the first one to introduce me to fantasy.

If there's anything good in here, you can thank her. Everything else you can blame on me.

CHAPTER ONE

S neaking into a chapel at midnight could get me lynched by a mob, but then I'd had worse days. Including the one when I'd become a bear, complete with fur and claws and the most useless stub of a tail.

A full moon cast too much light as I stalked across the narrow street, my paws leaving platter-sized prints in the snow. I moved as quickly and quietly as my massive form would allow. Anyone peering out their window would have seen a giant brown bear, scruffy in the winter cold, not a baron with a family as old as the mountain.

When I reached the stone wall of the Refuge, I glared at the sleeping houses. But no torches flared and no cries of "Monster!" disturbed the little hamlet.

My lip lifted over my yellowed teeth, but I didn't let myself growl. It was humiliating enough to have to sneak through the village my family had protected for the last four hundred years. It'd be worse if I was caught.

But sometimes it was worth risking the mob just to prove

to myself nineteen-year-old Léon still lived under the fur. To remind myself I had thoughts and dreams that didn't belong to the bear.

I paced along the front of the sturdy stone building before I raised my paw and tried the latch. The big double doors swung open, and I stepped inside.

The Refuge, dedicated to the Saint of Craftsmen, had been built in my grandfather's time, a concession for the men who worked the quarry the town had been built around. But a new addition drew me out of the safety of my manor.

My claws scraped against the flagstones, but the noise barely disturbed the empty chapel. Then I misjudged my bulk and nudged a bench, sending it screeching across the floor.

I snapped my teeth in frustration and froze, heart in my throat, but the west wing where the Disciples slept remained silent. I shuffled the last fifteen feet to the north wall of the building where I stopped before the window.

The rumble of the bear's thoughts lapped at the edges of my mind, threatening to pull me down into instinct and beasthood. I fought against it, trying to hold onto my human thoughts by concentrating on human things.

So I stood in the chapel and stared up at the stained glass window, hoping the beauty and the danger would bring me back to myself.

Colors filled the spaces between the dark lead, drawing my eyes from reds to oranges and blues to greens. Black lines and milky crystal formed graceful wings and heavenly armor glinted silver and gold. My paws itched for a brush and a sheet of parchment. If only I could see the window during the day when the sun would light the glass angel from outside as he pointed the way toward paradise.

I had to make do with the two pitiful candles that had been left to light the chapel for any late-night pilgrims and cursed lords.

It was enough. The window's beauty would shine even in the darkest night.

The heat in my thoughts slipped away, leaving my chest hollow, and I drew a shaky breath. Without the anger, the only thing left to fill the empty spaces inside me was shame. Reminding me I'd earned my curse fair and square.

The window stood as a testament to all I'd lost and all I'd give to have it back.

I sniffed, fighting the tightness in my throat. Could a beast cry? Almighty save me, I hated the fur and longed for my paintbrushes with an indecent hunger, but I'd never thought I'd miss the ability to weep.

I tried to recall my anger. It was more comfortable than the shame that ate my gut.

But the angel stared down at me, and I could only hang my head in the dark.

Almighty, save me, I prayed. *Please, save me. I promise I'll be good. Better than I was, if only I can be a man again.*

My father would be spinning in his distant grave to see Lord Léon Beauregard praying in a chapel for workmen. But he wasn't here, and I was out of options.

A draft from behind made the candles flicker and die.

I raised my head and snorted, hackles rising. I whirled, my flank hitting another bench to send it crashing against the wall.

Two figures stood in the shadows by the door, and I squinted. My poor eyesight barely made out the sweep of long cloaks.

A growl started low in my throat and I didn't bother controlling it. It was hard enough to hold onto my human thoughts, and these two had interrupted the only moment of humanity I'd managed to steal in months.

I snarled and huffed and reared up onto my back legs, but my display did nothing to move them. In fact, one stepped forward, hand outstretched as if to offer mercy.

My lip lifted to show my teeth. Didn't they realize I could rip them in two without a second thought?

I'd done it before.

Guilt stirred, reminding me of the man beneath, and I came crashing down to all fours.

Well, muck on that. It's not like I wanted a fight. But Almighty, they stood between me and the only way out. The door to the dormitory looked too small.

Another option stood behind me: the window, fragile and wide enough for my bulk.

No.

The beast's instincts threatened to overrun the rest of me, but nothing would induce me to destroy that masterpiece, the one thing that helped me cling to my humanity.

I took a deep breath, braced my claws against the flagstones, and launched myself toward the dormitory. The latch burst and my momentum got me past a doorway.

Almighty save me, I'd left half my fur behind on the doorframe, but I was through, racing down the aisle between the cots. Wide-eyed Disciples bolted from their beds as I focused on another door at the end of the hall.

The wood shattered as I barged through the doorframe. Mortar crumbled around me and a couple stones crunched and shifted.

I landed in a spray of snow and shook my head to clear the slush from my eyes. The building opened onto a small yard before the ground dropped away into the quarry. I backpedaled away from the cliff and rushed toward the street.

And slid to a halt when I saw the torches and pickaxes and pitchforks. Not again.

Maybe they'd been waiting for me this time. Maybe they had some sort of primitive instinct that told them when a monster roamed. Whatever it was, no one could form an angry mob faster than Georg the blacksmith, and he stood on the frontlines of this particular nighttime gathering of concerned citizens. You could really only hold a pitchfork two ways. The way it was meant to be held, and the way that said, "I'm fully prepared to fork you where you really don't want to be forked." These guys were very good at the latter.

My lips peeled back and I lowered my head. The men in front tightened their grips.

"Wait." The quiet voice demanded our attention without resorting to volume or ire, and I turned to see one of the intruders from the chapel step onto the street. A young woman. Her gait faltered in the snow, but she pushed ahead and came to a halt between Georg and me. A huge white cat with black markings stalked beside her, and a man as bald as the mountaintop followed her.

The young woman observed me and then turned back to

Georg and his mob. "Do you mind?" she said and made a shooing motion toward the press of men.

They grumbled, exchanged dark looks, and stepped aside, forming an aisle.

She met my eyes and tilted her head at the cleared space, offering me an escape route.

I glanced between her and the path of trampled snow. What was the catch?

She folded her arms, and torchlight rippled across her as her cloak flared. For the first time my weak eyes registered the color.

She wore blue. Like an enchanter. And the last enchanter I'd encountered had waved her hand and stolen my humanity.

My breath stuttered in my chest, and I launched myself toward freedom, instinct seizing the man inside me and burying him under the panic of the bear.

Anwen waited until the bear's stubby tail had disappeared into the trees before turning back to the gathered villagers. They muttered and the tall man in the lead eyed her up and down. He stood straight and thin as a tree but a blacksmith's apron hung from his neck and his skin was rough from standing over a forge all day.

The man snorted and turned toward the woods, gesturing for the group to follow him. "Come on," he said. "His tracks will be easy to follow in the snow."

Anwen shot a worried glance at her patriarch, expecting

him to take over, but Justin just gave her a look that said, "Go ahead."

She frowned, then squared her shoulders and turned back to the mob that prepared to follow the bear. "No," she said, putting a little power beneath the word to ensure every man there heard it in his bones.

The blacksmith turned back, eyebrows raised under his dark shaggy hair. His gaze settled on her face and Anwen fought the urge to touch the scars that crisscrossed her cheeks and forehead. Instead she stared back, raising her chin.

"Begging your pardon, miss, but this is our business," he said.

"Your business is hunting bears?"

"No. We're defending our home."

"What of your lord? It's his duty to protect these lands. Your village included."

The man scowled. "Our lord sits silent in his manor. Maybe he's lazy. Maybe he's dead. But if he won't do his job, we will. The beast is dangerous."

"Because he's strange?"

"Because it's sick." The man ran his hand through his hair. "Creeps around where no animal has a right. Scares the children. Makes our women nervous."

Not just the women, Anwen thought as their grips tightened on makeshift weapons.

She crossed her arms. "And you think pickaxes will solve your problem?"

"What else can we do?"

"You can let us handle it."

The blacksmith's gaze traveled from her, where she stood

skinny and shivering under her cloak, to her patriarche. Justin had knelt to touch the bear's tracks. His bald head glinted in the torchlight, and his dark blue eyes remained fixed on the ground.

Anwen winced. Justin had led their Family for decades and had taught her to accept and control her power, but he'd also spent the last fifteen years in the Refuge, teaching new enchanters. Even at eighteen she had more experience with the real world than he did.

The blacksmith laughed, a harsh sound that rang against the front of the Refuge, and the others chuckled and nudged each other.

"Go home, girl," he said. "This'll take more than a wave of your hand."

Her eyes narrowed. He'd seen her cloak. Was he so dense he doubted the power of an enchanter, or just her youth? Both were easily addressed.

Justin stood, blue eyes flashing in his pale face, but before he could act, Anwen crooked her finger, and Brann slipped out from behind her. His black-and-white coloring made him blend in with the snow and the shadows until he chose to remind people he was there. Like now.

The blacksmith's gaze locked on the hundred-pound cat as he sat beside Anwen, his head even with her waist. Brann's thick tail lashed once, twice.

The man's eyes followed the movement.

Brann yawned, showing all his teeth, then rubbed his head against Anwen's hip and purred.

Anwen fought not to roll her eyes at the display.

The act worked on the blacksmith, though. "Mistress," he said with far more respect.

"I'm sorry," she said with a smile. "I assumed you knew what my cloak meant. I take it you have no trouble leaving the rest to us, now?"

The blacksmith's eyes flickered from Brann to the scars on her face. "Had a lot of experience with beasts, have you?" he said, coming to the wrong conclusion.

Anwen shrugged, letting him think what he would. "Enchanters are often called on to sort out local disturbances," she said, stroking Brann's head. "Or didn't you wonder why two of them had climbed your mountain?"

"Don't normally care what you lot do, so long as you don't do it near us."

Anwen's smile fell but the blacksmith didn't give her time to respond.

"I'll keep my lads out of your way if you keep yours out of ours."

Anwen sighed. Neither the cat nor Patriarche Justin were hers to command, but the blacksmith jerked his head at the disgruntled mob and led them off down the street before she could think of a way to explain her complicated relationship with the man who'd practically raised her or the cat that had chosen to follow her.

When the would-be hunters disappeared into their homes, Anwen turned toward her patriarch, who hovered at the edge of the forest.

"That could have gone better," she said.

Justin gave her a warm smile. "I think you did well. You've always had a gift with people. Catrin would have just knocked them all off their feet and started another incident on top of the one we're here to investigate."

Her shoulders relaxed under his encouragement, and she limped across the snow so he could put his arm around her. Justin had no eyebrows. In fact, he had no hair at all, giving him a perpetually quizzical look, but his strangeness was more familiar to her than her own face. Especially after the accident that had left her scarred.

"Why didn't you take over?" Anwen said carefully. She didn't want to offend him, but he'd been acting strange since they'd left the capital. "You outrank me."

"I thought you could handle one grumpy blacksmith," he said.

Anwen squinted at him suspiciously, but he didn't say any more.

Brann paced to the edge of the trees and back again. Then he sat back on his haunches and opened his mouth. "I'm not sure I trust him." The cat's voice was a pleasant tenor even when he was disgruntled. He raised his right fore-paw and examined it with narrow blue eyes before he started to wash it. "Why would a man smell of fire and burning metal?"

"He's a craftsman," Justin said. "The village respects him." He stood and shook the snow out of the folds of his blue cloak, the thick gold trim along the edge flashing. Anwen's cloak seemed stark in comparison with only its thin geometric embroidery.

Anwen bit her lip as Justin frowned at the tracks again.

"Do you think you can follow the trail?" she said.

He'd said he was here to watch her but Justin's strength

lay in his compassion, not his hunting prowess. Matrona Catrin was the one who still traveled with Enfani and looked after them.

He must have heard the hesitation in her voice. He tilted an eyebrow in her direction, as if he knew her thoughts. "In this snow it will be no problem."

"Why did we let the monster get away?" Brann said. "We had it cornered there in the chapel."

Anwen exchanged an indulgent look with Justin.

"We didn't want anyone to be caught in the middle," she explained. The Zevryn had been traveling with her for nearly a year, but nuances of human behavior still baffled him. "Whether we're dealing with a mad bear or...something else, it could get messy. Better to track him and find a safe place for an ambush."

Justin shot her a look. "Something else? What are you thinking?"

She flushed and turned to trudge back toward the Refuge, following the bear's tracks backwards. "I don't really know yet. I just got this feeling while we were in the chapel that we weren't looking at a wild animal."

Justin followed her. "What else would it be? The rumors said a monster terrorized Whitecliff, but I'm sure it's just this bear. Nothing out of the DierRealms would look so ordinary. No offense," he said to Brann.

"I take it as a compliment," the Zevryn said.

Anwen faltered before stopping at the edge of the cliff that sloped down toward the quarry. Pieces of the Refuge's door littered the snow, and inside the building, the Disciples worked to cover the opening with blankets.

"I know, and I bet we've found our monster but..." She frowned. "How many bears sneak into a building just to stare at a stained glass window?"

"He could have been looking for shelter," Brann said, pacing up to sit beside her.

"And the weeping?"

Both Justin and the cat gaped at her. "What?"

"Before he noticed us. He was...sniffling."

"Maybe because it's cold out," Justin said, but his voice lost its conviction.

Anwen stared out over the empty space. The darkness hid the piles of rock and gravel she knew lay below on the quarry floor and the scaffolding disappeared against the shadows of the cutting walls, making it seem like they stood on the edge of the world.

"I think you're imagining things," Brann said. "He was about to eat you."

"He was posturing."

"Which means he was showing you he could eat you. How is that better?" Brann's gaze fixed on the darkness in front of them.

"Monster, bear, or whatever else he is," Justin said, shaking his head and breaking their reverie. "He needs to be dealt with."

He turned away from the precipice to head back toward the edge of the forest. Anwen struggled to turn and follow him, the snow dragging at her bad leg. "All right, what do you want to do?"

She'd grown used to being alone, discussing her plans only with Brann. But when the patriarche who had raised you since you were six said he wanted to get out of the capital and get some fresh air, you said "Mountain or seaside?"

"I'm going to go find his lair," Justin said. "I'll come back when I've figured out what we're dealing with. You should rest. I want to make sure you've recovered fully."

Anwen's mouth fell open as she realized what he was getting at and why he wouldn't quite meet her eyes.

"Is that what this is?" she said, her voice rising. "Some sort of test to make sure I'm back in fighting form? Is that why you insisted on coming?"

He raised his hands as if to ward off her anger. "You have to admit, you've had a bad couple of years."

Anwen fumed. "This was Matrona's idea, wasn't it?"

"Matrona Catrin may have suggested it, but I agreed. Besides, I hardly get to see you anymore. I wanted to spend this time with you and make sure you were all right after... after everything with Adrien de Fay."

She still glared.

"Come on, Enfan," he said, invoking her title and place below him in the hierarchy of their Family. "This will be good for both of us. And if you let me go first, you don't have to climb the mountain twice."

Anwen wanted to scowl and argue, but he had a point. Her leg already ached. It made more sense to wait until they had a clear way forward.

"You should take Brann," she said. "If you have trouble tracking him, he can always change into a bloodhound."

"Is that all right with you, Master Zevryn?" Justin asked.

Brann sniffed and leaped to the thatched roof of the mayor's house, showering Anwen with snow as she passed under the eaves. "Just as long as it's clear I'm on loan. I travel with Anwen."

Anwen flushed but Justin didn't seem to take offense the same way Matrona Catrin would. He chuckled as Brann dropped from the roof to join them on the street.

"What are you supposed to be this time, anyway?"

"Luce ancano," he said. "On the steppes of Galadon it means 'snow stalker.'"

"Have you been there?"

Brann's gaze flicked away. "Well no, but I've seen drawings."

Anwen hid her smile. Sometimes she forgot how young Brann was and how little time he'd spent in their Realm.

Justin stopped to look down at the tracks again as if memorizing any irregularities. He rubbed his arms in the cold and wrapped his cloak tighter around himself.

Anwen bit her lip.

"Don't worry, boss," Brann said softly so Justin couldn't hear. "I'll watch out for him."

Anwen sighed and looked down at the white cat whose black smudges made her think of shadows on snow. "Must you call me that?"

Brann grinned, showing off a set of neat sharp teeth. "Would you prefer pumpkin?"

"No."

"Honeypie?"

"Brann."

"All right, you can be the Fang. I was saving that one for myself but I love you too much to fight over it."

CHAPTER TWO

Couldn't stop. Had to run. Cold froze his breath. Made him shiver under the fur.

His heart pounded and he glanced behind. No one followed. No blue fabric on the white snow.

Safety above. One foot in front of the other. Closer and closer to the smells that said 'home.' Over great clumps of snow, up the steep hill.

Something blocked his way. Worked metal stretched across the road. It burned in the cold. It meant safety. It meant home. There was a word for it. A human word. With human ideas of security and defense.

Gate.

Finally, my thoughts cleared out the instincts of the beast, and I settled back into my own head.

I leaned my shaggy head against the gate post and heaved a sigh that frosted in the air.

The beast had grown unsatisfied with owning my shape

and reached more and more for my thoughts now as well. Anytime I felt frightened or hungry or enraged his instincts seized control, and his short sharp thoughts dominated until he'd retreated to whatever dark, primitive portion of my mind he called home.

And my plan to focus on very human things, like art and beauty, to cling to the remnants of my humanity, was clearly flawed.

I stared down the white, winding road, but the enchanter that had sent me fleeing wasn't waiting there to finish the job. My fear felt silly now. She couldn't have known what I'd done just by looking at me. And I was safe here at the top of my mountain. No one, not even a wandering enchanter, would look at my sanctuary and assume a bear lord lived there.

With a sigh, I pushed through the wrought iron gate that hung at an angle across the overgrown road.

When my parents were still alive, the manor had bustled, even at this time of night. Torches had shed flickering light across the cleared cobbles of the courtyard and grooms had rushed to greet anyone coming down the carriageway. My family's armorial banner had flown from the peak of the lead roof, proud and certain in its place in the world.

Tonight, the manor stood dark and silent. Empty, too— except for one know-it-all manservant too stubborn to flee with the rest. He didn't bother with the banner anymore so the peaked roof stood bare against the dark sky.

A grim scene, but it was my sanctuary nonetheless. Nothing could touch me here.

I wedged the heavy wooden door open with my shoulder, knocking big flakes of old whitewash from the lintel above me. Giles always insisted on closing the doors after I went out, trying to maintain some semblance of civilized behavior.

Darkness and an echoing great hall greeted me. The sconces stood empty, their candles long since gone, and the empty floor cried out for the long table I'd smashed in that first awful day as a bear.

I nudged the door shut and my shoulders relaxed. The villagers were convinced a monster roamed the woods, so they stayed down by the quarry. And why would an enchanter climb the mountain to an abandoned manor?

I hurried through the hall as if I could escape the condemning emptiness and shuffled up the steps at the end of the long room. If I was lucky, Giles would already be asleep. I didn't need a lecture on top of the near disaster with the mob.

A single candle burned in its sconce outside my room and I squeezed inside. Sleep tugged at my mind, but I turned to the alcove just inside my door where a leather-bound book laid open on a carved stand.

It was more than habit now to stop and stare at the book for a few minutes before bed. It was ritual. I didn't need light to know what page was displayed. My namesake, Leonides, raised his broadsword to slay the sea serpent which twined through the big letter M at the top of the page. Below the neatly spaced text, a woman lay dressed in white, chained as a sacrifice and awaiting rescue.

Yasmina, the most beautiful woman in the world,

Leonides's destiny. I'd labored on the page for days, Brother Warren hanging over my shoulder to watch my brushstrokes through a magnifying lens. The manuscript itself was more precious to me than all of my family's squandered wealth.

Which was why it was kept here in a space I was too big to enter so I couldn't destroy it with carelessness or clumsiness.

I backed away, pushing aside the mingled pride and pain that filled me when I thought about holding a brush again. Why did I insist on reminding myself every time?

For the same reason I insisted on sleeping in the master bedroom rather than the stables. And the same reason I crept into the Refuge to see the new stained glass window.

To remind myself I was human. To convince myself the fur didn't matter.

Too bad it wasn't working.

Summer heat beat down on my golden head, and I blinked in the familiar sunlight. I whirled, searching the bright garden for the stand of roses that always grew at the far edge. I grinned and raced across the manicured grass for the bier. Blood red blooms and deep peach blossoms climbed the lattice of the gazebo. I pushed through the branches, thorns pricking my hands.

Where was she?

A laugh drifted through the roses, taunting me, encouraging me.

I broke through into the center of the gazebo only to see a

trim figure dart through an opening opposite me, her slender fingers grazing the painted wood.

I followed. Her green tunic fluttered at her heels, and a pale pink veil covered her hair. She laughed again, turning to reveal the curve of a cheek and the dark ends of her eyelashes.

I put on a burst of speed and caught her elbow at the garden gate. She spun into my arms—

And I woke. Dust and hair tickled my nose and made me sneeze.

I groaned, the noise rumbling deep in my throat and oversized chest.

Yasmina. My Yasmina. The most beautiful girl in the world. I'd dreamed of her since I'd first heard the tale of Leonides and thought we might share more than a name. He'd found his equal, and somewhere out there, my Yasmina waited for me to rescue her. I knew she was mine even if I'd never met her, even if I'd never seen her face.

I rubbed my eyes. But I couldn't go find her while I looked like this. As the night before attested, my mind wasn't entirely my own.

I needed something to anchor me in my humanity. Something more tactile and tangible than a stained glass window.

Right on cue I heard Giles putter down the hall outside my room. He dropped something with a clatter, paused, probably to pick it up, and then he resumed his errand toward my mother's solar. The bear's eyesight might have been fuzzy, but his nose could pick up the earthy burnt smell of ochre and several other pigments underneath.

I rolled and lurched to my feet, then stepped off the filthy furs and blankets Giles had cobbled together in place of my parents' antique bed frame which I'd broken three years ago. Most bears hibernated in the winter, and I was always sleepier when it snowed, but that didn't seem to be enough to keep me in bed. Something—an itch, a sneeze, a dream—always woke me up. A piece of me wished I could sleep through this curse, but I'd likely wake as the bear and never remember myself again.

At the end of the hall a wide flight of stone steps led up to my mother's solar. I climbed toward the large open room my mother and her ladies had used for their sewing. It had been closed up dark and empty since her death, but Giles had opened it up a week ago when I'd started pawing at the door like a housebroken dog.

This morning the double door hung open a fraction.

"Good afternoon, my lord," Giles said before I'd even pushed my way inside. He bustled across the wood floor, doing something mysterious with a broom and some clean dustcloths. His movements pulled at the worn patches of his livery, which he'd sported since my parents had died, and his thick white hair glinted in the wan light coming through the dirty windows.

Bowls of fresh paint lined the windowsill, and I grunted in approval.

The noise made Giles look up, censure crinkling the skin around his brown eyes. "My lord, how late were you out last night?"

If I hadn't been absolutely certain of his pedigree, I'd have thought he had some bloodhound in his ancestry. He certainly had the long nose and the uncanny ability to make me feel hunted.

I glared at him from under my thick hairy brow. He knew I couldn't answer and yet he insisted on asking stupid questions.

"You really should be careful, my lord. More outings like this and your tenants will surely guess something is amiss. Do you want them amassed outside the gate, demanding an explanation?"

I snorted and rolled my eyes. Bears weren't built for sarcasm so I had to rock my whole head to get the point across.

Giles pursed his lips.

Almighty, it had just been a little mishap. After a good night's sleep and a dream of Yasmina my stealthy outing and subsequent escape from the mob seemed long ago and even a little humorous. I mean, I'd admired some artwork and managed to give an enchanter the slip, all in one day. My lips pulled back in what would have been a grin if I'd had my old face.

Giles folded his arms. "It was the window that made you go, wasn't it?" he said. "I wish I'd never told you of the blasted thing."

I nudged his shoulder, trying to tell him it was worth it. It didn't work.

"Why would you risk your life to go sightseeing?"

I did it for the same reason I'd had him clear out the solar and bring my paints up here, but I had no voice to tell him that.

I swung away from him and sniffed the bowl of red ochre.

I could no longer use a finger to test the paints for dryness and texture, but I'd found my nose worked almost as well. The blue smelled off and I nudged it out of line.

Giles sighed and took the bowl. "Do you really think painting is going to bring back your humanity?" he said while he dipped out a spoonful of spun egg whites to stir into the blue. The sticky substance would help bind the paint to the surface of the wall.

I grunted and jerked my head to indicate he should continue.

Painting wouldn't break the curse, but I couldn't go look for my Yasmina while I was losing my mind to the beast. He'd wander off and leave everything important behind. So I needed something to anchor me when the bear's instincts threatened to take over.

When I was sure Giles would do as I directed, I shifted to squint at the room. Afternoon sunlight poured through the diamond-paned windows. A large fireplace sprawled across the opposite wall and delicate woodwork adorned the ceiling.

I could imagine Yasmina—my Yasmina—sitting in this room. One day I'd find her and marry her, and I wanted her to have a beautiful space to call her own.

Giles transferred the bowls to the floor by the wall with a scowl. I'd already moved on to the only solution I could think of, but he was still obviously mired in last night's mistake.

"You're not taking this seriously, my lord. People hunt bears that get too close to towns and the curse didn't make you immortal. Just hairy. One stray arrow is all it takes to change a life. You know that well."

I growled low in my throat. He had to remind me?

If I'd been my true self, he wouldn't have dared speak to me so. Everyone else had fled days after my transformation, but my teeth and fur and claws had only made Giles bolder. I'd chase him out, if I didn't need him for one humiliating reason.

My stomach growled, loud enough to coax a reluctant smile from the stubbornest of manservants.

"There's a couple fish in the larder, my lord," he said. "I'll bring them up here for you, shall I?"

I hung my head and grunted. Were it not for Giles I would have starved three years ago. Who ever heard of a predator that couldn't hunt? But I'd lost my stomach for the chase the day before my transformation and now I could only shamble after bunnies half-heartedly.

Even without words he'd anticipated my needs. Again. Insufferable man.

Hours later, diamonds of light crawled across the floor as rows of painted briars climbed the walls between the windows. Green leaves peeked through the blossoms as they opened under my careful ministrations. Red and white flowers grew, each one better than the last. No pigment came close to the peach in my mind's eye, so I had to be content with the bastard child of red and yellow for the rest of the blooms.

Yasmina had always hidden among the roses in my dreams, so it seemed fitting the walls of her solar would be covered in them. And they were big enough that even my clumsiness could manage them.

I gripped the block of wood strapped to my paintbrush in my teeth and added one more stroke to the wall. The bear's mouth made the movement jerky, but this solved the problem of trying to hold something so narrow in my giant teeth. Or trying to paint without thumbs.

I dipped the brush into the bowl of red and huffed in frustration when it scraped the bottom. I turned to send Giles for more before I remembered I'd already sent him to the village for more green. Whitecliff was too small to warrant anything like an artist, but it lay close enough to the road from Gwynmont that merchants and travelers often stayed the night, trading dried plants and minerals I could use for pigments.

No more red, no more green. The ochre had gone into the flowers, red and pink and orange, while tender green buds and leaves balanced the warmer colors.

I still needed something blue. Not roses. There were no blue roses in Yasmina's bier. But the garden needed butterflies and maybe a bird.

I couldn't tell yet if painting helped me keep a better hold on my human mind. But it certainly kept me calmer. My heart slowed, my breathing evened out as I painted, the wall and the roses filling my entire focus. My father had called it a frivolous hobby, but painting was the only thing I had that wasn't wrapped up in being a baron or a bear.

I dipped my brush into the blue and squinted at the wall. My tongue poked out in concentration, an embarrassing habit I'd never grown out of. Good thing no one lingered here to see.

"Almighty, she was right," a deep voice said behind me.

My heart leapt and I jumped, smearing blue paint across

one of the better orange blooms. I stared at the ruined flower, heat surging hard and tight in my gut.

Worse than a mob, worse than the shape and thoughts of a bear was a mucked up painting. Yasmina's painting.

I dropped the brush and spun, bowls scattering away from my paws. A piece of my mind wailed at the mess and the waste, but I shoved it down under the rage that surged hot and hard in my gut.

A stranger stood tall in the open door, the light reflecting from his bald head. He had no eyebrows, and his eyes went wide in his white face as his hands came up in paltry defense.

The beast's instincts reached for the edges of my mind, clouding my thoughts and whispering violence. A growl grew in my chest, rumbling the floorboards beneath my massive feet.

The man stepped back and lowered his hands so his blue cloak fell over his shoulders and swirled around his feet.

Heat drained from my gut and cold poured in. How many enchanters roamed the mountains of Valeria that I would encounter two in as many days? My heart pounded and my mouth went dry. Why was he here? Would he kill me or just take the last of my humanity until nothing of Léon remained?

For the bear, panic translated to anger.

I lunged forward, jaws outstretched.

Only to come up short as something grabbed me from behind and lifted me by the scruff of my neck.

The enchanter had raised his hands again, his brow furrowed, and I hung in the air like an angry kitten, only far less cute.

I roared.

The enchanter's eyes narrowed and he closed his fists.

My roar turned into a gasp as heat flared under my skin, burning from the outside in.

Almighty, he would finish the job the other enchanter had started three years ago. Light seared my eyes, and I winced away. My back feet scrabbled against the floorboards, seeking purchase as heat burned through my fur. The blood boiled in my veins and my bones twisted and cracked.

I panted, too spent to raise my voice in pain and terror as his power took hold of my limbs and pulled. I wrapped my arms around my body, trying to hold myself together, but instead of fur, my fingers brushed smooth skin.

My eyes snapped open and I raised my hand in front of my face. My hand, not my paw.

I looked down. Naked legs stretched toward the floor and knobby toes brushed the wood planks.

My fingers curled in front of my eyes in gratifying precision, and a breath huffed between my lips. A laugh of wonder or a sigh of awe, I wasn't sure. A steady tingle flowed through my veins, making me feel light and bouncy. The weight and worry of the bear had disappeared, leaving nothing but a memory.

As my feet hit the floor, I straightened to heap the first of many praises on my savior. But I stopped. The blood drained from the enchanter's face, then his eyes rolled back, and he collapsed onto the floorboards.

I stepped forward, hands outstretched, but burning pain caught me mid-step. I gasped and doubled over. Fire spread beneath my skin, this time from the inside out.

"No," I wanted to shout but the word came out a strained whisper.

Fur sprouted from my arms again, and I screamed. My cry deepened and roughened into a familiar roar.

The fire rose as quickly as it had the first time, and my legs went out from under me. My fall shook the floor, but I didn't care. My thoughts fuzzed and faded as the bear took over.

CHAPTER THREE

P ain. *Always led to fear. Always led to fury. He tried to stand. Too tired, too hurt. Too riled. He lifted his head and growled. Lips curled back. Something lay on the floor beside him. Too close. He lurched to his feet. Ready to defend. Ignored the pain.*

Red and orange and green caught his eye. He turned. Impossible roses climbed white walls.

The blue. Good color, but not there. Ruined something. Anger gnawed his insides. Anger and something else.

Regret.

With a deep shudder and a trace of irritation, I slipped back into my own head.

I groaned and slumped down to bury my nose in my furry forearm.

To fight for my own thoughts, to be so close to freedom, only to have it snatched away...it was too much. My throat closed up and for the second time in two days I wished a beast could weep.

A weak groan made me jump and spin.

The enchanter lay where he'd crumpled, his blue cloak twisted around his long frame. He lay still, eyes shut, breath coming in short, shallow gasps. He must have been unconscious, moaning with pain and instinct, not by choice.

Fear warred with the hope swelling in my chest.

Three years ago an enchanter had pronounced me beyond saving and then changed my life forever. Every day since I'd fought for survival just like she'd said I would. I hunted like a beast, hid like a beast, and ran like a beast.

Her cloak had been so vivid against the fall leaves. I'd never wanted to see that color again. Even when painting I mixed my blues to be darker, avoiding the lighter cornflower shade the enchanters wore.

But this man hadn't tried to hurt me. He'd tried to free me, something I hadn't even hoped for. Yes, he'd failed to transform me back into a man, but he was the first one to even try.

For the first time in three years, hope won out over fear.

I'd never considered an enchanter as a solution to my problem before. I'd assumed they'd all be on the same side. The side against me. But maybe I'd been wrong.

I tilted my head to get a better look at him. He didn't look much like a savior. With no eyebrows he looked surprised, even with his forehead creased with pain. But gold embroidery edged his cloak which I seemed to remember had something to do with rank.

Whatever his abilities, he couldn't do anything for me while he laid on my floor like a dead fish.

I stepped closer to the prone enchanter and used my

broad nose to nudge him. Then I sprang back and waited for a response.

Nothing.

I tried again, this time hard enough he rolled.

I jerked back and tilted my head. Was he supposed to be that hot? It had been a long time since I'd been human, but Giles occasionally reached out to grab a tuft of fur and he was never that warm. I could practically see steam rising from the enchanter in the sun streaming through the windows.

Whatever magic he'd been trying to do—or undo—it hadn't worked, obviously. But also, he'd collapsed halfway through. Maybe unfinished magic damaged an enchanter's health.

I snuffled his face worriedly. I couldn't let my only hope die on the floorboards of my mother's solar before he'd had a chance to free me. How could I cool him off? The cold air coming off the windows clearly wasn't enough.

As gently as a well-meaning saw blade, I gathered the back of his cloak in my teeth and started walking backwards. My clumsy brutish body made me an unlikely nursemaid, but then whose fault was that? I still managed to drag the enchanter to the door and down the stairs. His head only clunked a little with every step.

I huffed in pride. We'd make it to the cellar, probably before he died of fever. And once he'd recovered, he could set about freeing me of my curse for real this time.

If I could have chuckled, I would have. In a few hours I would be free. Then I'd find Yasmina.

Wouldn't Giles be surprised?

Anwen hurried up the snow-covered road as fast as her bad leg would go, concentrating on the ground in front of her. "Why did he go alone?" she said, trying not to sound like she blamed Brann, who bounded along beside her.

"He told me to check the other side of the manor. He said he was just going to scout the situation."

The snow cat leapt from drift to drift, so fast he left her behind and had to double back. He'd offered to carry her up the mountain, but she was supposed to be proving she could handle herself as well as she had before the accident. Riding around on Brann's back would only prove the opposite.

"And you didn't argue?" she said.

"I'm a guest in your Realm. It's not my place to disagree with my elders."

Anwen snorted and gave him a disbelieving look.

He rolled his eyes. "Of course I argued. He insisted. What was I supposed to say? That I didn't trust a grown enchanter to take care of himself?"

Anwen bit her lip. She hadn't been brave enough to say that very thing, so she couldn't blame Brann for not doing so either.

"I wish I had, now," Brann said, quietly.

Anwen stopped beside a frozen waterfall hanging from the cliff lining the road. She leaned on her knees to catch her breath. Brann circled back to brace her.

"Tell me what happened," she said. "I need to know what I'm heading into."

"Let's just say you were right," he said. "We knew we had

more of a problem than a rogue bear almost right away. We followed him, expecting to find his cave or a den."

"Well, then, what did you find?"

Brann shifted around and jerked his head toward the overgrown road that wound up the side of the mountain. Anwen followed his gaze and gasped, the air chilling her lungs. The road stretched smooth and white to a break in the trees at the crest of the hill. Between the trunks swung a broken gate and behind it, stone walls soared into the crisp blue sky.

A castle perched on the side of the mountain overlooking Whitecliff. Almighty, there was even a tower edged with crenelations. Behind it, the mountain loomed as if to anchor the fortress in strength and history. The road ended at the gate. Nothing beyond the castle was worth getting to, apparently.

"You know that silent lord the blacksmith talked about?" Brann said at her feet. "I don't think he's all that silent. It's just maybe he's better at growling than ruling now."

Anwen straightened, eyes focused on the edifice at the end of the road. "Patriarch Justin is in there? The bear attacked him?"

"I saw it dragging him down into the cellars. Storing him away to eat later, maybe," Brann said, his voice lowered ominously.

"You couldn't go after them?"

Brann's ears flattened. "I might be able to change my shape, but even I will need help against a bear his size."

Anwen squared her shoulders and blew out her breath decisively. "All right," she said, more to herself than to Brann.

She stepped back onto the road and used a bit of power to clear each step of snow so she didn't have to push her way through.

"What are you going to do?" Brann said, bounding around her.

"What we came here to do," she said. "I'm going to take care of a monster. Whatever the state of his mind."

"I want you to be careful," Brann said. "He smells wrong."

"I'm always careful."

"No, you always care. There's a difference."

All right, maybe it would have been better to wait for Giles.

My breath frosted in the deepest root cellar where I'd tucked the enchanter into a corner. I'd managed to work his cloak off, but his skin still burned when I stuck my nose against his hand.

I scanned the narrow stone-lined room buried under my family's historic home, looking for more ideas to bring the man's temperature down. If he died now, I'd have murdered an innocent man. Not to mention I'd lose my best chance of ever being free. But short of shoveling snow down the steps, I couldn't see any other options. Maybe I should drag him outside and bury him in a snowbank. I'd just wanted to be able to close a door on his escape route in case he woke up frightened. I didn't want him running off before he freed me.

I paced from one end of the cellar to the other. It was a short trip, appropriate for the tiny circle of my thoughts. I could drag the man to the village and leave him on the steps of the Refuge. The Disciples of Saint Innovate were quarry workers and craftsmen, not healers, but the Disciples cared for those who had been hurt in the quarry. Some of their patients even survived.

But I could imagine the reactions if a bear dragged an unconscious body into the village, and it wouldn't matter if the enchanter lived only to find I'd been run through with a pickaxe or some other unlikely instrument of death.

But I also couldn't watch my only hope die.

Back and forth with no answer.

"In here?" a voice asked from the top of the cellar steps, making me jump and snort.

Before I could rush to defend my territory from yet another intruder a woman limped down the stairs, backlit by the light streaming down behind her. She blinked and squinted in the dark before she raised her hand and summoned a small sun to rest on her palm.

Another enchanter? Saints, this was getting ridiculous.

I shook the stars from my eyes, and when I could see again, I found her staring at me. I stared back. This wasn't a different enchanter. She was the same one I'd seen in the village the night before. With thick red-brown hair and clear eyes, I could tell she was much younger than I'd taken her for in the dark. Probably about my age. Scars crisscrossed her face, hinting at a past filled with violence.

A pity. Without them she could have been quite pretty. Her marred beauty gave me an unpleasant jolt, like a remembered shame.

My shoulders heaved in relief when her gaze finally left

me to search the dark cellar. She was the intruder here. So why did her eyes accuse me?

She gasped when she found the enchanter crumpled in the corner. "Justin."

She stepped forward. Toward my prize.

I bared my teeth and growled. I wouldn't let her steal away my only hope.

A huge black-and-white mottled cat sprang out of the darkness and landed between us, claws and teeth bared, ready for a fight.

"Back off, monster," it said, eyes narrowed.

I blinked in surprise. Yes, the mouth had moved and the cat had spoken, but knowing it was true didn't make it easier to accept. I'd heard many enchanters traveled with magical companions but I'd always thought that was just an exaggeration.

The girl placed a hand on the cat's back, but she looked at me as she said, "Please. He's my patriarche. Let me help him."

It wasn't the words that made me hesitate. It was the way she spoke to me, not at me or around me. Like she knew a man with a mind lay under the fur. It shocked me enough that I stood frozen while she slipped by and knelt in jerky movements beside her companion.

The cat braced her, glaring at me all the while. I grumbled to myself but what could she possibly do to steal him away? Even enchanters couldn't disappear into thin air. Could they?

Her hands moved over the man's pale face. He would be a head and shoulders taller than her when they stood together, but crumpled in a heap he seemed frail and ethereal.

"Backlash," the girl murmured. "He must have tried a complicated casting and been blocked." She glanced at me so briefly I almost missed it. "The vytl reflected back through him and now it's burning him from the inside out. If it wasn't for the cold, he'd be dead by now."

The man stirred for the first time since he'd collapsed. "Anwen?" he whispered through cracked lips.

"I'm here," she said, bending toward him.

"You were right."

Her gaze flicked up to me again. "I know," she said.

The man's eyes closed before he could explain his cryptic remark.

"Can you help him?" the cat asked.

"Not here. Myrddin is his best chance now." She used the wall to lever herself to her feet and reached down as if to drag the man back to town.

She was taking him away from me. My claws gouged the dirt floor. I didn't even stop to think how ridiculous that was. The man was at least twice her weight and not easily moved, but I only saw my hope being ripped away from me moments after I'd found it.

I shoved myself between the girl and the man, and she stumbled back and fell to the packed dirt floor.

"Hey," the cat shouted, but I swung my head around and bowled him over before he could get between me and my prize. I could take care of one paltry cat and this slip of a girl if it came to a fight.

I crouched, ready to defend my claim.

The girl contemplated me from the floor, a crease forming between her eyebrows. "What do you want with him? Is he some kind of prisoner?" she said, voice sharp. Again, she spoke as if I could answer.

I'd never wanted my voice back more than in that moment.

How to tell her what I wanted—no—needed? Could I gouge words into the dirt floor? I'd never had to do that with Giles, who always seemed to understand me. But my claws were unwieldy and that would take too long while the man lay dying.

I peered into the shadows at the base of the wall and, without budging from my position, reached out a huge paw to snag the enchanter's discarded cloak. I dragged it into the light and nudged it with my nose.

The girl stared at it, brow furrowed, before her expression cleared, confusion replaced with something else.

"You want an enchanter to free you." Her gaze softened.

My hackles rose as I recognized her expression. This pitiful creature dared pity me. I may have been cursed, but I still held enough power to get what I wanted. I placed a giant paw on the man's chest, my claws pricking the skin of his throat. Maybe now she'd understand the situation. The enchanter was mine.

Her gaze followed my movement. Her lips tightened and her hands fluttered like she was about to protest. But then she clasped them together in her lap and said calmly, "Do you specifically want Patriarche Justin? Or will any old enchanter do?"

She shifted forward, and I found her face level with

mine. Hazel eyes pierced me with understanding, crinkling with good-natured amusement.

Was she teasing me? Even with her patriarche lying under my claws?

I wanted to be angry, but her confidence made me shiver under all my fur. She didn't look at me like I was a monster. She looked at me like I was a man. In the last three years only Giles had done that, and I wasn't exactly in the habit of staring deeply into his eyes.

She nodded as if she'd seen something important when we'd locked eyes. "Very well." She struggled to her feet once again. "Will you accept me in his place?"

"What?" the cat said, hair standing on end.

I snorted my own surprise.

"My patriarche needs help," she said directly to me. "He won't be any good to you in this state. I, however, am more than capable. I will stay here until I free you of this curse."

I looked between her and the man beneath my massive paw. A conscious enchanter in exchange for an unconscious one? Could it be a trick? Or a trap? Or maybe this trust was just the price of my freedom.

Slowly, very slowly, I let my paw drop back to the dirt floor.

"Thank you," she said.

She stepped back and a stab of panic threatened my human mind, bringing the bear's instincts surging to the surface. I knew she couldn't escape, but the bear only saw her retreating and reacted. I grabbed the edge of her cloak in my teeth and growled.

The cat hissed. "Watch it," it said.

She lifted her hand and, after a moment's hesitation, placed it on my head.

Warmth spread from her touch and I tried to tell myself it was her magic that made me shiver again. I met her eyes. Green and gold streaks highlighted the brown. It was really too bad about the scars. With eyes like those, she'd have been any painter's dream.

"I'm not leaving. I meant what I said. One prisoner in exchange for another."

Prisoner sounded a little extreme, sure, but it also made it sound like I was in charge. Though shouldn't she look more frightened if she thought she was going to be imprisoned? The mixture of humor and compassion and worry in her eyes rushed through me, leaving me hollow and disoriented.

I let go of her cloak and stepped back, shaking my head. Her words agreed with me, that was all I should care about.

She took the discarded cloak and tucked it around her patriarche.

"Anwen," the cat said, voice suspicious. He eyed me with a bright blue gaze that saw more than I liked.

"Take Justin to the village," she said, ignoring his look. "I'll tell Myrddin to meet you there. He can take Justin back to Namerre on the Byways."

"I don't want to leave you alone with this monster. He's been terrorizing the village for months."

The girl glanced at me. "He's no more a monster than you."

"That's what I'm afraid of," the cat grumbled, just loud enough for me to hear.

The enchanter at her feet stirred. "Anwen?"

"It's all right, Patriarche, you're going to be fine," she said.

"Be careful," he whispered.

"I'll be fine. I'm just staying to finish what we started."

"No, Anwen, the casting on the bear. Something's wrong with it. It rebounded."

She knelt and smoothed the sweat from his brow. "I promise I'll take every precaution you taught me." She turned her gaze on the cat. "Go, Brann," she said. "Now."

The cat pushed itself up to stand on its hind legs and... grew. Its edges fuzzed and it swelled to the vague height and shape of a man but with misty lines and limbs and two blue eyes, glowing bright as the heart of a flame.

I pushed down a terrified understanding. Before, I'd challenged what I'd thought was a normal cat. What would it have become if I'd actually pushed the issue and tried to attack?

The creature stooped to gather the prone enchanter in its misty arms, then paused. It glared at me. "Anwen," it said.

"Go."

It went, spurred only by the power of her voice, leaving me alone with my prisoner.

CHAPTER FOUR

This wasn't exactly what I'd imagined when I'd predicted Giles would be surprised. He returned that night to find his lord playing host to an unexpected guest. He took one look at me standing awkwardly by the front door, then glanced at the enchanter where she sat on the steps of the great hall, and he came to all the right conclusions.

"I leave for a couple hours and you manage to capture an enchanter?" he said. "Just so she can turn you human again? What happened to painting? That's a nice pastime that doesn't require hostages."

I grumbled and wouldn't meet his eyes. On the steps, the enchanter covered her mouth with her hand as if to hide a smile.

She might have been my prisoner but I didn't feel in control of her or anything else, for that matter.

Giles shot me an exasperated look before turning to the girl in the blue cloak and giving her a respectful bow.

"There are still some decent beds in the servants' quarters, mistress," he said. "You are welcome to sleep there."

"Thank you," she said with a regal nod and struggled to her feet as if that was all she'd been waiting for. "What is your name?"

"Giles," the manservant answered.

"And your lord?"

Giles threw back his shoulders and raised his chin like a herald in the royal palace. "Lord Léon Beauregard, Baron of Whitecliff."

"Léon," she said, locking eyes with me. "I am Anwen." And she let Giles show her to her room.

The moment she disappeared, I collapsed in a heap on the flagstones, tension pouring out of me. Well, Léon, you have yourself a personal enchanter. Now what?

I groaned and would have buried my head in my hands if I could. What was I thinking?

My nose twitched with the unfamiliar scent of soap and lavender that must have come from the enchanter. It made my claws flex against the flagstones.

I'd been thinking I wanted to be human again. Right. To get rid of the claws, and the nose, and the stupid fuzzy tail. To be able to paint, and talk, and live again.

To find my own version of Yasmina.

I lurched to my feet.

The enchanter, Anwen, was my only chance at all of that. I couldn't risk her getting away. If that meant she was truly a prisoner here...so be it.

✦

Early the next morning a weight settled on Anwen's legs over the blankets, waking her.

"'Prisoner' was right," Brann's voice said. "I guess you're lucky he gave you a room at all instead of making you sleep in the cellar."

Anwen grinned and opened her eyes. She lifted her head from the straw mattress to see Brann shaped like a house cat, prodding the coarse coverlet.

"I'm glad you found me," she said. "This place is huge."

Brann snorted, glancing around at the bare whitewashed stone and the sparse furnishings. "You can't tell by looking at this room."

"This is where the housekeeper slept." Anwen sat up and stretched. If Brann had returned, it had to be near dawn. "And believe me, it's a far cry from where I grew up. Look." She dislodged Brann to swing her legs over the edge of the mattress. "A real bed frame." There was even a washstand in the corner, though Anwen couldn't imagine breaking the thin sheet of ice to actually wash her face.

"He's a baron," she said to the cat as she bent to tie her boots. "Even his servants have their own rooms."

"If he had any," Brann said. "This place is empty. Hollow. Like it's rotten inside."

"Don't be melodramatic. I take it you're back because Myrddin came for Justin."

"He'd already reached the village by the time Justin and I got there. Myrddin was going to let Justin recover a bit before he took him back to the capital."

"Then they should be there soon."

As if to emphasize her words, fiery lines began scrawling

across the wall opposite her. Like jewels on a LongNight festival tree they hung there, lines forming letters, letters forming words, and words forming familiar handwriting gone jagged with irritation.

I can't believe you managed to get yourself and our patriarche into trouble. And then I couldn't even come see you. I wanted to watch you put this bear-monster in his place.

The words turned to ash and Anwen stepped closer to wipe them away. She grinned as she wrote against the wall, fire trailing from the end of her finger. Then, with a flick of vytl, they sped across the distance between her and Myrddin.

There was nothing to see. And Justin got himself into trouble, not me, thank you very much. I take it you're back in Namerre?

Yes, he made the trip well.

"If enchanters have a way to travel such vast distances in one night, why did we walk here?" Brann grumbled at her feet.

Anwen raised an eyebrow, finger still poised to write. "One day I'll take you on the Byways and you'll see why it's not something we want to do every day."

She turned back to the wall. *Justin will be all right, then?*

He's already raging that he left you there with that thing.

That thing is the one who saved him, Anwen wrote. *Léon dragged him to the coldest part of the manor so he didn't overheat.*

Forgive me if I don't sing his praises. He's still keeping you captive. Let me know if you want a knight in shining armor.

Anwen made a face. *Spare me. I promise I'll be back as soon as I figure out what's wrong with Léon's curse.*

Speaking of, she wanted to do some poking around to see if she could learn why Justin's casting had reflected back on him. She swiped the rest of the ash from the wall and brushed off her hands.

She opened the door of her room and stumbled back in surprise.

Léon raised his huge head and snorted. The shaggy brown bear lay across her threshold, an effective and smelly barricade.

"Did you sleep there?" she asked, her eyes crinkling in amusement. "Saints, that can't have been comfortable."

He grunted and lumbered to his feet in the cramped hallway.

"See?" Brann said. "Even he thinks of this room as a prison."

The bear glared at the house cat who sauntered under his nose, tail erect.

Anwen started to follow Brann but the bear huffed and blocked her way. His defensiveness might have been amusing, but she needed to show him it was unnecessary.

"I was just going for a walk." She tilted her head at him. "Would you like to come?"

He jerked a little as if he hadn't expected that, and Anwen suppressed a laugh. She could get used to surprising him.

Reluctantly, Léon moved aside enough for her to slip out into the hallway. Then he followed a couple steps behind as she made her way out of the manor.

Anwen had always needed to move in order to think. But since the accident, movement had been a lot harder. Her leg ached in the cold and the snow ate at her gait until she felt like she pushed through a sea of stone. More often than not she had to settle for fresh air and hope her thoughts would clear up in a few steps.

Gray sky stretched overhead and errant white flakes drifted through the air, threatening another layer of powder to hide the wide tracks trailing behind them.

There wasn't much to see in the snowbound garden. The only thing that thrived were the hedges, grown tall and unruly. But the barren paths were mostly clear of snow and a great place to pace.

Léon lumbered beside her, slowing his gait to match hers. Every now and then he threw her a look. She didn't consort with many bears, but with his eyes narrowed under his furry brows, he looked distinctly suspicious. Like a vigilant guard waiting for her to run away.

The thought made her smile, but she'd learned enough from Adrien not to make the mistake of laughing at him. It was kind of cute the way he really thought she was a prisoner. As if one bear could keep her anywhere she didn't want to be.

Then she thought of the empty manor and her smile fell away. How many friends and family members had abandoned him to his curse over the years, and what kind of toll had that taken on his heart? And what did that curse even look like, besides turning him into a bear?

Anwen stopped and turned to Léon. She couldn't see his curse exactly, only how the vytl eddied around him. But it was enough to show her its outline. Justin would have seen it too if he'd had the time to stop and look.

His curse should have just been a simple transformation. Every enchanter still learning control practiced transforming sticks and rocks into flowers and cakes. It was always a good lesson when they bit into their cake and found it still very rock-like on the inside. Transformation changed the surface only.

The same theory should apply to living things as well, though Anwen had only ever heard of it being done. Most enchanters avoided those kinds of transformations for that very reason. If you made a dog into a person, it was still a dog walking around in a human body.

Anwen's eyes narrowed. Léon's curse did not follow that rule. The vytl binding him into the form of a bear went past the surface, so his curse lay buried somewhere deep inside him.

Trying to change him from inside as well as out.

"He's losing himself," she said, her voice going quiet with horror.

The bear jerked.

"What?" Brann said. He had absorbed a heap of snow to make up the difference between his house cat form and his snow stalker form. Now the black-and-white mottled leopard sat back on his haunches and stared at Léon.

"Sorry, I talk out loud when I'm thinking." Anwen turned to the bear. "You're losing yourself, aren't you? Bit by bit you're turning into a bear in your head, too."

His eyes widened and he glanced to the side as if looking for someone to translate for him. Finally, he nodded, stiffly.

"The curse is deeper than your skin. It's wrapped up inside you somehow. It will take more than a hasty casting to break you free. I can't believe someone would do this."

Léon jerked his head sideways as if trying to say something. It was too bad she couldn't give him a voice. Or read his thoughts.

After a moment's hesitation he reached out and flipped the edge of her cloak. Anwen began to see how Giles could interpret his looks so well.

"An enchanter did it? Well, clearly no one else would have the power..." she said, tapping her lip in thought. "But why would anyone condemn another human being to this kind of erasure? What happened?"

Léon stepped back, eyes darting around the garden. Like he didn't understand her question. Or didn't want to answer it.

She lifted her hand to soothe him. "It's all right. I only want to know so I can help you."

Léon huffed, blowing the ends of her hair across her chest and whipped around to hurry back to the manor.

"I guess that answers that question," Brann said.

"How?" Anwen said, staring after Léon's rapidly disappearing form.

Brann's eyes narrowed. "Anwen, if another enchanter did this to him, there must have been a good reason."

She spun and flung out her hand toward the manor. "No reason justifies this—this atrocity. This slow murder. It's an abuse of our power. We were given these gifts by the Almighty to help Térne. Not destroy a person thought by thought."

Brann looked away, uncomfortable. "He must have done something to warrant their anger."

"Then he should have been taken to Namerre and tried for his crimes. Like every other noble. Instead, some enchanter thought they could punish him by taking away his humanity."

"That doesn't sound so bad," Brann said. "I don't think I'd like being human."

Anwen shook her head. "Transformations are surface. You can't change what something actually is." She waved a hand at him. "Unless you're a Zevryn of course. For him the bear isn't just window dressing. The curse is actually destroying him from the inside out. "

"So do you have a better plan than whatever Justin did?" Brann said.

Anwen stared around the garden. Surface and depth.

"Maybe," she said. "Maybe if we deal with the surface first..."

Coward. Moron. My head rang with silent admonishments. Maybe if I ever got my voice back, I'd be able to convince Anwen I hadn't been running from her. No really, mistress. I had a pressing engagement with the Whitecliff Bear Association. The Society of Fur Concerns was discussing the dwindling options for decent dens.

Some jailer I turned out to be. If she wanted, she could slip out the gate now and I'd be stuck as a bear forever.

Why had I run anyway? Because she wanted to know

what had happened that miserable, awful day? I was a bear with no voice. I couldn't tell her even if she somehow forced me to.

I rushed up the stairs to my room, telling myself a tactical retreat was completely different from hiding.

Would it be so terrible for Anwen to know the truth? She was just one young woman who would be gone from my life the moment she broke the curse.

A piece of me balked at telling her anything. She was an enchanter. Same as that Emrys woman who had bound me to claws and fur. Anwen could just as easily condemn me to my fate, and I couldn't risk that.

But I'd known her for less than a day and already I could see the only true similarity was the hue of her cloak. This Anwen carried so much compassion it spilled out in her words and deeds. She wouldn't leave my mind to rot in the cage others had devised for me.

I could tell her about the girl.

I threw myself down on my furs and shifted to get comfortable. Agitated thoughts circled my head like crows.

I would never be able to beg forgiveness from the one person I'd hurt the most, but I could at least hear Anwen say it wasn't my fault. It was a mistake. A careless mistake.

I groaned and buried my face in my furs. I'd missed my voice for years, and here I wanted to use it to confess my sins. To an enchanter no less.

I must have dozed off for a few moments because the next

thing I heard was Brann's voice beside my ear.

"Rise and shine, Beauregard. I'm pretty sure you're going to want to be awake for this."

I opened my eyes and growled, angry the cat had caught me napping.

He sat on his haunches and tilted his head, gazing at the walls covered in crooked murals. My first attempts at painting after I'd turned into the bear.

Almighty help me, he was in my room. I surged to my feet, my gaze going to my manuscript in its alcove. It looked all right from here, but that wasn't the point. He'd still trespassed in my space.

"What's this?" he said, following my gaze. His eyes lit up, and he stepped toward my manuscript.

My teeth snapped shut inches from his flank.

He sprang back, muscles bunching beneath his mottled fur. "Relax, Beauregard. Anyone would think you'd woken on the wrong side of the bear."

He chuckled as Giles pushed through the curtain across my doorway. "I asked you to wait for me," the manservant said.

I growled. Was nowhere safe?

"Make all the noise you want," Brann said. "You're still getting your wish. Anwen said to tell you to brace yourself."

I jerked back. What? What was he talking ab—?

Fire lanced through me. A familiar fire, seeing as I'd felt it twice now. I roared as my skin rippled and stretched before I clenched my teeth shut on the pain.

I focused on my swirling thoughts, ignoring the pain racing under my fur. I'd wanted this. This had to be Anwen's power gathering to release me. What else would hurt so much?

My joints crackled and I screamed and arched my back. This couldn't be freedom. It had to be the end. Her casting had gone wrong and I was dying. Or she'd lied and my death had been her goal all along.

I shut my eyes and buried myself beneath the bear's thoughts and instincts.

But soon even those were stripped away. His unhappy grumblings quieted, and I was alone behind my eyelids. The fire faded, leaving my skin stinging in its wake. Cold seeped through my limbs, shocking after the heat.

I couldn't do this anymore. Remaining a bear had to be better than living through that pain even once more.

"Is he all right?" Giles's voice came to me like sunlight through water, rippling and angled differently. "Where is Mistress Anwen?"

"She said she had to cast from outside. She didn't know how long it would take."

A breeze brushed my back, eliciting a shiver. No fur dulled its bite.

I opened my eyes. Fingers curved in front of my nose. I flexed my claws and the fingers moved in perfect time. Dark, stringy hair I remembered as gold obscured my vision.

"My lord?" Giles's voice broke.

Almighty, it was a dream. Or a nightmare.

I sucked in a breath, waiting for the fire to return.

"How is he?" Anwen's soft voice reached my ears, but I couldn't find the muscles to swivel them toward the sound.

"Well, the screaming's stopped, so that's something at

least," Brann said.

"Unfortunately, I can't help the pain. We're not built for shape-changing like you. I wanted to be here but the casting is on the castle, not him."

"Will he be all right?" Giles said. "Is he hurt?"

I couldn't stop staring at my fingers.

"His eyes are open but it doesn't look like anyone's home," Brann said.

A tide of embarrassing emotion climbed up my throat, making every breath feel like a sob, and when Brann's unwelcome face appeared in my field of view, much clearer than it ever had been to the bear, I found my vocal cords.

"Grrrrr."

Well that wasn't what I wanted to say.

"Oh dear," Brann said. "Looks like the beast's still in there."

"Maybe I should have asked Myrddin for help," Anwen said. "He could be here within the day."

And have one more person mucking up my sanctuary while I struggled with wonder and relief and a strange sort of sadness? Over my dead body.

The growl leaked between my teeth and I coerced it into a word. "Grrrrr—et...ooout."

"Léon?" Anwen knelt awkwardly beside my mattress. "How do you feel?"

My muscles didn't work the way I expected them to, and I mashed my face into the floor once before I managed to push myself onto my elbows. I looked down and figured out why I was so cold.

Naked, clumsy, and dumb from the change, I was not in

the mood to meet Anwen's compassion. Or Brann's ridicule. Almighty, I needed space.

"Geeeet. Out." Before I started crying.

"He's fine," Giles said. The fear had left his voice, replaced by a sort of exasperated relief. "Come, mistress."

He helped her to her feet.

I'd used up my vocabulary and could only moan as I collapsed against the mattress.

Brann sauntered out the door ahead of Anwen. She stopped at the threshold and turned, her cloak swirling across the wood floor. "Léon?" she said. "The magic on you is very strong."

Part of my mind was occupied with getting my arms under me and away from the cold air, but the other part noticed she said "is." Not "was."

"I couldn't change what's inside you. Only the outside. You will remain human as long as you stay in the ca— manor. Outside you will revert to the animal."

Her eyes searched my face but who knew what she saw. I didn't have control of anything yet, let alone my expression.

A nod. I could manage a nod as a bear, it shouldn't be so hard as a man.

She saw the movement and nodded back, before turning to leave me blessedly alone.

Only halfway free. I hadn't even begun to relish my freedom before it had been snatched it away again. I was still trapped. Leashed.

But if I followed that train of thought my brain might come out my ears. One thing at a time. And right now, words were a very big thing.

CHAPTER FIVE

Until now, I'd never appreciated the work I'd done as a baby learning to walk. None of my limbs wanted to obey and habit kept urging me to drop to all fours and amble across the floor. The third time my knees refused to hold my weight and I ended up on my butt, I roared in frustration.

The sound of my human voice raised in the beast's anger stopped me cold. Was this what Anwen had meant by not changing my insides? Was the animal still waiting to take over?

It took the rest of the day to force my legs to hold me and my back to straighten, and I spent the entire time with my teeth clenched on any sound I might make.

Propped upright against one of my walls, I finally brushed the matted hair from my eyes and peered around. Without my bulk to crowd the space the room looked...empty was the kindest word I could come up with.

My first transformation had left the furniture in shambles. I didn't know how much had been destroyed while I flailed in pain and shock and how much had gone to pieces when I'd spent days in a towering rage, but the result was the same. What hadn't been smashed had been removed to make way for my huge body. Only the nest of blankets and furs remained, lying on the bare floor, and my manuscript sat safe on its stand.

But faithful Giles thought of everything and outside my door lay a basin of water growing tepid, a comb, and a pile of clothing including underclothes, a linen shirt, and a doublet and hose in the green and brown of the Beauregard household.

A bath was impossible without the bronze tub stored in a forgotten closet and an army of maids to heat the water to fill it, but the comb and the basin of wash water served me better than three years of dust baths. By the time I finished, the color of my skin had lightened and my shoulder length hair had returned to the gold I'd remembered.

Scrubbed and dressed, and at least resembling a human even if my skin felt tight and ill-fitting, I crept along the hall, using the wall for support. The stairs in the great hall presented a problem, my knees going every which way so I had to cling to the banister. But there was no one to see as I wobbled my way to the ground floor.

Voices came from the kitchen, and I pushed the door open, gripping the doorframe with my other hand.

Two figures sat by the hearth, backlit by the fire. They looked up as I stepped into the room. Giles sprang from his chair as expected, but Anwen remained seated, the firelight flickering over her scarred features. Her steady regard made me flush for no good reason, and I concentrated on Giles instead.

"My lord, you look well," he said, beaming as though words weren't enough to convey his relief. He stopped short of embracing me, which would have mortified us both, but he did give me his formal bow, head even with his waist.

"Are you hungry?" he said when he'd straightened. "There's stew."

My stomach had been rumbling since I'd woken up with Brann's nose in my face, but two hours ago I'd barely managed to hold a comb and drag it through my tangled hair. I frowned at my uncooperative fingers and couldn't imagine them trying to manage a spoon.

"Or there's bread you could dip," Giles said, noting my hesitation.

Sometimes the man was far too perceptive. But he was right. I could wrap my hands around a loaf easily enough.

I nodded and Giles hummed happily while he filled my request. I grabbed the trestle table for balance and shuffled all the way into the kitchen. I was probably the first Beauregard to set foot in the place since the manor had been built from the ancient keep. But it was one of the only rooms that still had furniture in it. And after the hike from my room, I had an unhealthy desire for a chair.

I couldn't see my feet in the dim light, and I tripped on the edge of a rush mat halfway across the flagstones. I caught myself against the hard edge of a table, and clamped my teeth shut on a curse. With my luck, any profanity would come out a growl. When I'd righted myself, I smoothed my hair back and tugged down the hem of my doublet, glancing around to see who had witnessed my clumsiness.

Giles bustled away in the corner, but Anwen watched from her seat by the fire. I gritted my teeth and tried to ignore her scrutiny as I made my way to the chair Giles had vacated and twisted around until my butt safely hit the seat.

The corners of Anwen's mouth lifted, and my lips pulled back in a snarl. Was I that amusing?

Words, Léon. You have words now. If I could manage the precarious route downstairs, I could wrestle my recalcitrant tongue into obedience.

"Laugh," I said, glaring at her from behind my disheveled hair. "Dare you." The *L* tripped me up, and the back of my tongue didn't know when to finish a vowel, but I'd made myself understood and that's what mattered.

Anwen shook her head, but her smile didn't fade. "I would be the last person to laugh at your difficulties, Léon."

She shifted her tunic over her knees, and I remembered the limp. She knew very well what it was like to be clumsy but she remained serene and confident.

My shoulders hunched and heat beat in my cheeks. I could hear my mother's voice in my head saying, "That's no way to treat your rescuer."

"Sorry," I said. Then I reached out and caught one of her hands in mine. I raised her knuckles to my lips and gave her a small lopsided grin. "Wanted...to thank you."

She cleared her throat and avoided my gaze as she reclaimed her hand. "You're welcome."

I smiled to myself.

I'd had most of the day to think about my situation and how Anwen fit into it.

I couldn't remain trapped in the manor for the rest of my life no matter what shape I was in. So I needed my imprisoned enchanter to deliver more than a half-broken curse. And to do that I needed her to like me.

I needed to convince her I was worth saving.

That shouldn't be too hard. I'd once had charm enough for three lords.

I touched my cheek then gestured to her scars. "What—?" I tried for "happened" but it came out more like "hambuded." I winced. Maybe I'd better stay away from longer words until I'd regained my old eloquence.

Anwen had understood anyway. Her mouth pulled tight as her toe traced the outline of a flagstone. "An accident a few years ago. I'm sorry if it bothers you."

Dolt. That was no way to charm her. "Doesn't," I said. How to express the idea in as few words as possible? "I'm monster." I gestured to myself, then pointed at her. "You're angel."

She flushed, the scars standing out stark white against the red, and her mouth fell open.

Muck, that wasn't—I'd only meant she'd saved me from the beast inside.

Giles stepped up beside us, and I took the bowl he held out to keep my hands busy. Maybe if I stuffed my mouth with food, I'd stop putting my foot in it.

The bowl contained a slab of coarse bread and some venison stew. I wouldn't have to wield fork, knife, or spoon this way. And given how I could barely clutch the bowl, I couldn't imagine how many fingers I'd lose trying to use a knife.

If I was careful, I could eat without spilling on the first clothes I'd worn in three years.

Giles was no cook—I'd scared ours off the second day after my transformation—so that first bite shouldn't have been heavenly. More grease than meat and too much salt, but I'd never lost the craving for cooked food. I finished the bowl before I realized I'd wolfed it down faster than any wild animal.

When I raised my head, Anwen watched with an amused smile. One of her scars slashed through the corner of her mouth, giving her a lopsided grin. Almighty, did the girl do anything but smile?

I tried it myself, lifting the corners of my mouth, ignoring the way it felt like I bared my teeth.

The huge cat sprang from the shadows, landing next to Anwen, and I fumbled my bowl in surprise. I growled and licked grease from my fingers. If the damned cat had made me spill on my clothes...

"Ratcatcher," I mumbled.

Anwen laughed, the sound filling the room with warmth. Her mirth infected me, and I found my lips curving into a true grin.

"Brann is a Zevryn and he's been my companion for almost a year," she said. "He can be anything he wants, but he seems partial to cats."

"Snow leopard, currently," it said.

"And it talks," I said.

The cat lowered a pointed blue glare at me. "The correct

phrase would be 'he talks.' Not it. Please don't make that mistake again."

I waved a hand. "It, he. Matters not. Still cat."

I got the distinct impression the animal raised its eyebrows, even though I was pretty sure cats didn't have eyebrows. "Of course, you're right," it said. "Gender doesn't matter at all." It turned to Anwen and jerked its head at me. "It seemed smarter as a bear."

I growled.

It snarled.

Anwen gripped the loose skin over the cat's shoulders. "Brann, Léon. Be nice. We'll be here for the foreseeable future, and I'm not treating any claw marks you two give each other."

My mother had been dead for three years but her censure was alive and well in Anwen's rebuke. I dropped my gaze in contrition. Even the snow leopard hunched its shoulders. Who knew a cat could look sheepish?

Then Anwen's words sunk in.

"You'll stay?" I said, pushing my hair out of my eyes to see. Time to find a strap to tie it back.

She blinked in surprise. "Of course," she said. "My work isn't done. I'm sorry it's taking me so long. The enchanter who designed the curse must have really hated you." She raised her eyebrows, inviting me to speak.

This was my chance for redemption. I could barely wait to hear her soft voice telling me it wasn't my fault, it was just a stupid mistake, the enchanter had taken her punishment too far.

I opened my mouth, my confession tumbling out in a jumble of mangled words, relief making them incoherent.

My fists clenched and I stopped talking to snarl in frustration.

Anwen's eyes widened and she leaned forward to touch my hand. "It's all right, Léon. Stick to simple ideas for now." She smoothed down the front of her tunic. "We'll work on it and have you speaking like an orator before long." Her eyes narrowed at Brann. "But that means we all need to be friends."

The cat shook off her hand and sat up straight, meeting my eyes with its bright blue ones.

"Very well. I apologize, Léon."

I ground my teeth. I couldn't refuse to apologize in front of Anwen. I would seem like the lesser man. Beast. Whatever. I twisted my lips in what I hoped Anwen would consider a smile, though it felt more like a sneer. "Sorry too, Brann. Friends?"

I extended my hand, letting some of my hostility and irony creep into my expression. Let's see how he managed to shake hands with a paw.

He slipped his massive paw across my palm and flexed his claws, drawing the barest pinpricks of blood. I held his gaze and didn't wince away in pain.

"Yes," he said. "Friends." His grin showed off fangs as he let go of my hand.

I'd get him back later. I just needed to make Anwen like me. The cat didn't need any of my goodwill and I didn't plan to give him any.

"You free many lords?" I said, working some of my old grin into my stiff smile.

"Just you, so far."

"How long have you been an enchanter?" Giles said, coming to stand at the end of the trestle table to work.

"I've been a member of the Emrys Family for eight years."

The name rang in my ears and made my jaw clench. Giles's hands stilled and he drew a breath that sounded like a gasp. Did the sound of her name make his gut roil, too? He'd been there the day my life had been ruined. The day I'd ruined a life.

Brann's eyes narrowed when neither of us said anything. I turned as if to set my bowl down, keeping my back to her. Anwen de Emrys. Emrys. I'd cursed the name for three years. And now I knew why Anwen's scars seemed so familiar.

I caught Giles's eye and shook my head. She couldn't know. If I was ever to be completely free, she couldn't know the part I'd played that day. I'd come so close to telling her without knowing what my words would do. They would have stolen my last chance.

I turned back to her, preparing the lies that would keep her from running, preparing the false smile that would charm her into helping me. One day I'd be free and Anwen would never have to know why her Family had cursed me three years before.

CHAPTER SIX

I hadn't been up this early since Giles had been my tutor instead of my valet, and even then I'd only gotten out of bed to find a place to hide from his lessons and nap until noon. The sun was barely up, so maybe the rest of the household would still be asleep. That would be a relief after Anwen and Brann's constant presence the last two days.

There was something I had to do now that I was human again. It was awkward, but a promise was a promise, and I'd made this one to the Almighty. But making a Pledge to one of the Saints would be even worse with Anwen and her forthright cat watching.

The chapel was at the other end of the second floor but to get there I had to traverse the balcony above the great hall. I poked my head around the corner. The space looked empty.

I hurried down the corridor, using the railing for balance, but when I was only halfway across the kitchen door creaked open. Anwen slipped into the great hall, followed by Giles and Brann. She glimpsed me on the balcony, and I froze. Damn, I was caught.

"Ah, Léon. You're just in time." She relieved Giles of the brooms he'd been carrying.

I resisted the urge to bolt and straightened my shoulders. Hopefully the Almighty would understand my delay.

I altered my course for the stairs, my hand white-knuckled on the banister. "For what?" My tongue seemed less thick today, but it was probably wise to stick to shorter words and sentences for now.

"We're cleaning up," she said.

I sighed in relief. "Good," I said as I stepped off the stairs onto the dusty flagstones. "Smells bad. Couldn't sleep."

I'd gotten used to the musk and dirt over the years, but I was a lord again, with standards, and I'd found it extremely difficult to sleep and hold my breath at the same time.

Anwen wrinkled her nose. "I can imagine."

"We don't have to imagine," Brann said, sauntering up the stairs beside me. "Our noses work just fine."

As I reached the ground floor, Anwen held out one of the brooms.

I couldn't have been more surprised if she'd handed me a tambourine and asked me to dance. She expected me to sweep? That's what servants were for. I glanced at Giles but he was no help. He had his head down, his broom gliding industriously across the flagstones. He deliberately avoided my gaze.

Anwen's eyebrows went up and challenge filled her hazel eyes.

I blew out my breath. Charming, I reminded myself. I

was charming and polite and...and what else would she like? Humble?

Besides, it couldn't take that long to sweep a couple rooms, could it?

"All right," I said, taking the broom. At least my hands cooperated and folded neatly around the thick handle. "But I'll need help. Lots of help."

"Truer words were never spoken, Lord Bear," Brann said above us. The large cat had draped himself on the balcony railing, his tail curling and uncurling.

I had to pick between glaring at the cat and impressing Anwen, so I pushed the broom around the floor and gave her a sheepish grin, the one that said, "Isn't it sweet how hard I'm trying?" It had worked on plenty of maids.

Anwen, however, shook her head with a tolerant curve to her lips and bent to concentrate on her own sweeping.

I frowned. That wasn't how it was supposed to go. Had I lost my touch? Surely three years wasn't long enough to forget everything one knew of women. Better try again.

"Where are you from, Anwen?" I said carefully, staring at the bristles of my broom.

"I was born in Gwynmont." She named a town just south of the pass to Ballaslav.

"Funny," I said. "Heard of their coal mines, but not their beautiful women." I chuckled triumphantly and waited for her reaction.

She narrowed her eyes and Brann snorted from the balcony. Even Giles paused in his sweeping to roll his eyes at me.

Muck, it had to be this slow tongue stealing my effectiveness.

Anwen returned to her work. "Well, I left when I was six. Must not have rubbed off on me," she said, graciously.

I glanced at the doors to the outside and wondered if transforming back into a bear on the doorstep would be as painful as this conversation. Probably. Escape was impossible so I just had to persevere.

"Keep going, Beauregard," Brann said. "This is the best entertainment around."

Anwen put her hands on her hips. "Are you just going to watch?" she said.

"It's what I'm here for." Brann licked his paw nonchalantly.

"Brann."

She only had to speak his name in that tone of voice and the cat stood up. Though he stretched and yawned first as if to make it clear he was still his own cat. "Oh, all right. But only to make this go faster so you can move on to something more interesting to observe."

Anwen rolled her eyes as he leaped down from his perch and joined us on the ground floor.

"Interesting?" I asked Anwen.

"His kind feed off of new experiences," she said. "He's gathering them to take back to his Realm."

Without blinking, Brann stood in the pile of dust, fur, and leaves Anwen had made, and suddenly both dirt and cat were replaced by a small bear. The bear smirked at me with Brann's bright blue eyes as he sauntered past, and Anwen unbarred the door for him.

In the driveway the bear turned and vanished, the cat reappearing in its place. The wind scattered a flurry of debris around him.

I blinked. Was that the pile he'd absorbed? My eyes narrowed as Brann returned to the great hall and repeated the exercise with Giles's pile.

"What's he doing?" I asked.

"He's doing a better job of moving dirt and dust around than you are," Anwen said, gesturing to my idle broom.

I bent my head to my work.

"Brann's race, the Zevryn, are shape-changers," Anwen said, watching her companion dump the second pile outdoors. "He can manipulate his form into anything you can imagine. But if he wants to become bigger, he needs more material to work with. So he absorbs inanimate objects to give him bulk. And when he's done, he expels it to get rid of the excess material." She shrugged. "That's how he explained it to me. I don't fully understand it though."

Whether we understood it or not, the shape-changer made short work of the little we'd swept up around the hall and returned to his perch with a smirk.

Silence fell again, and I recalled my task. "So after you left home, where did you go?" Girls liked it when you asked questions and showed interest in them, right?

"The Refuge of Saint Redemption," she said.

I hadn't made a study of the different Saints, but even I knew ordinary people went into the Refuge of Redemption and came out enchanters.

"So young?" Enchanters were made not born, but six seemed a little early to choose such a career. Maybe it was like being a Disciple. Some of them were sent to their Refuges as young as that.

"We don't really get to choose when we go."

"Why not?"

She stopped sweeping to look at me. "Do you know how we become enchanters?"

"Training?" I said.

"That is where our control comes from," she said. "But the ability to reach out and manipulate vytl comes from something far more basic and primal."

I shook my head in confusion. "Like what?"

"The need to survive. Every enchanter has gone through some life-changing—and in most cases a life-threatening—event. And in the process, something inside them snapped, giving them the ability to touch vytl. That's the energy we draw from Térne that gives us our power."

I blinked. Enchanters came out of trauma? In some circles, Redemption was known as the Saint of Suffering, but I'd never thought to wonder why.

"But the world is full of pain," I said. "Why are there so few of you?"

"Not everyone who lives through something horrible develops the ability. And not everyone who goes to the Refuge develops the control to leave again."

The white lines crossing her face caught the light. "What did you live through?" I said, voice soft.

She glanced at me out of the corner of her eye, sighing. "That is a very personal question."

Without my consent my hand lifted to brush her cheek.

She leaned back before I could make contact and looked

away. "This came later," she said, touching a thick scar that ran across her chin and down her neck. "I was already an enchanter; I'd already lived through suffering. I like to think I handled it better the second time."

I opened my mouth, but Brann spoke up. "She could ask you something you'd rather not remember," he said. "Make it fair."

My teeth clicked as I snapped my mouth shut, and I fought the flush that crept up my cheeks. The comment was so pointed, as if Brann knew my secret. But he couldn't. He would have told Anwen.

She concentrated on sweeping, not meeting my eyes.

I bit my lip. I'd really offended her this time. Great job, Léon. That's the opposite of getting her to like you, in case you didn't know. What could I say to make her smile again? Nothing that came naturally seemed to work with her. Could she really be that different from all the other girls I'd charmed in my life?

She must like subtlety. It had never been my strong suit, but surely, I could manage it if I tried. Especially since my freedom depended on it.

Anwen swept another pile of fur and debris out the open door. The wind threw it into the air, the sun catching sparks in the dust.

It whirled in spirals for a moment before being carried away on the breeze. When it had cleared, a figure stood at the end of the driveway.

Anwen shaded her eyes against the sun, and her heart sank as she realized the visitor wore a blue cloak like her own. She didn't have to see the silver embroidery trimming the garment to recognize her matrona.

The woman tilted her chin and raised an imperious hand. A command, not an invitation.

Anwen blew out her breath. She'd hoped to get through the day without an argument.

Brann poked his head out the door to see what was taking her so long. "Anwen?"

She turned so he could see the figure as well.

"Oh," he said, his tone going flat and lifeless. "I will come with you."

Anwen checked to make sure Léon was still looking for mops before she and Brann walked side by side down the driveway. The light fluffy snow dragged at Anwen's feet.

The woman they approached wore her dark hair in a crown of braids, and her smile grew sharp edges as they closed the distance between them.

"Matrona Catrin," Anwen said. They were related by talent, not blood, but the woman before her felt more like her mother than the peasant woman who had actually birthed her. Few parents appreciated finding out their child had developed the dangerous ability to use vytl, and Anwen's mother and father had been no different. It had only taken one "episode" for them to send her to the Refuge for the Disciples of Saint Redemption to deal with.

"Enfan," Catrin said, the corners of her eyes crinkling as she folded Anwen into an embrace. "You are well?"

Anwen saw a trace of fear flicker through her matrona's

expression as she pulled away. What would make Catrin worry about her safety out here?

"Very well," she said. "What brings you here?"

Please don't say just checking up on you. Please don't say just checking up on you.

"I was in the area and I just thought I'd check up on you."

Anwen ground her teeth. She accepted a certain amount of protectiveness from Justin, especially after the accident three years ago. But the same concern from Catrin always managed to come off as condescending.

A cough sounded at their feet and Catrin looked down, her smile going rigid. "And how are you enjoying your visit to our Realm, Niobrann?"

"It is very educational," Brann said. "I hope my fellow Zevryn will appreciate my efforts here."

"Many of us did think you'd do better with a more experienced enchanter, but if your companionship is suiting you, I will not complain."

That sure sounded like complaining, Anwen thought to herself. "Matrona," she said instead. "I'm glad to see you, but I'm perfectly capable of handling myself."

"Did I say otherwise?" Catrin said, raising dark eyebrows in offense. "You can't blame me for worrying, enfan, when your patriarche returned to the Refuge half dead. He said you'd found a lord transformed by an enchanter." Catrin turned and squinted at the manor and the large open doors.

"Yes, Léon has been a bear for the last three years."

"Léon...Beauregard?" she asked.

Anwen's eyes narrowed. "You know him?"

Catrin hesitated. "Our paths crossed once. It wasn't an auspicious meeting."

Anwen's brow contracted. "What do you mean?"

"He was not a...kind boy."

"He is a little conceited," Anwen said. "But who wouldn't be, if they became a baron so young."

Catrin's eyes widened. "You've spoken to him, then?"

"I managed to undo his transformation to a certain extent yesterday. He is restricted to the manor but he has regained his human form."

"And has he said anything?"

Anwen suppressed an unprofessional giggle. "A little. Though it's hard to hear around the foot in his mouth."

Brann snorted. "You'd think he'd get tired of the taste."

Catrin's lips thinned. "I meant anything about the enchanter who placed the curse on him."

"No." Anwen didn't meet her gaze. "He seems reluctant to talk about it, and I don't blame him. I thought I would give him a day or two to get adjusted before I pressed the issue."

"Maybe it would be better to leave it alone. From what I know of the boy, he probably deserved his time as a beast."

Anwen drew a sharp breath. "No one deserves to lose their humanity."

Catrin opened her mouth as if to condemn Léon again but Anwen interrupted.

"The one who should be punished here is the enchanter who did this." She slashed her hand through the air. "No matter what Lord Beauregard did, nothing is as bad as stealing someone's life. It's murder."

Catrin snapped her mouth shut on whatever she was going to say.

Anwen tried to control her reaction, but she knew she was glaring at the woman who was supposed to be her respected elder.

Catrin crossed her arms. "There is no law against an enchanter punishing a criminal."

Anwen's teeth clenched. "No. But maybe there should be. People already fear us for what we can do. Why give them more to fear?"

Catrin shook her head and touched Anwen's cheek. "Oh, my little idealist. You're still the same girl who wanted to cure all the suffering in the Refuge. But the world will not right itself at your command."

"Maybe not," Anwen said, raising her chin. "But I can fight against this one thing."

"You should leave that to the enchanters' Moot. They are the only authority we should answer to."

Anwen thought about praying for patience. She'd never been as close to her matrona as some of the other enfani. She'd been so young when she'd first come to the Refuge that she'd spent most of her time with Justin, who stayed put to help those who were hurting. By the time she'd been old enough to travel with Catrin, she already saw the world with the understanding her gentle patriarche had given her.

Now she and Catrin seemed to disagree more and more. Anwen respected the older woman and wanted her respect in return. But no middle ground existed in this particular argument.

"Besides, you should be concentrating on your wedding,"

Catrin said with a conciliatory smirk. "Isn't that what all girls dream about?"

Anwen unclenched her hands, prepared to accept the peace offering. Even if this subject was almost as awkward as the last.

"There's time," she said. "I don't want to rush it."

"Have you even seen Myrddin recently? Maybe some alone time with your betrothed would give you some inspiration."

Heat rushed to Anwen's face, and she shot a glance at Brann. But the shape-changer was no help, turning his twitching nose to sniff the frigid breeze.

The thought of seeing Myrddin, her best friend and childhood companion, gave her a warm feeling inside but not for the same reason Catrin insinuated. Their arrangement was comfortable, like an old pair of boots, worn to the perfect fit. Nothing new or exciting about it.

"Yes, perhaps," she said.

The angles of Catrin's face softened and she held out her hand. "Come with me," she said. "We don't get to spend a lot of time together. We can talk about men and choose what you'll wear."

Wasn't this what she wanted? A chance for her matrona to understand her better? Anwen glanced at the manor behind her. Yes, but not at the cost of her other responsibilities. Maybe she'd have considered it if it didn't sound like Catrin was desperately trying to manipulate her.

"I'm staying here," she said, with as much respect as she could. "Maybe when I'm done with Léon we can talk about the wedding."

Catrin's expression soured, but she took it with grace.

"Of course, Enfan. Just remember what I said. Someone wanted to punish him for a reason."

Anwen nodded.

"I'm serious, Anwen. Promise me you'll think about it."

"I will, Matrona."

"Be safe, Enfan."

She almost stopped Catrin to ask for her help with Léon's curse. She'd risen to the position of Matrona by being clever as well as powerful and respected and Anwen hadn't managed to do more than trap the lord in his own manor.

But a bit of misplaced pride kept her silent. She could figure this out without her matrona's help. And if she did, perhaps she would earn Catrin's respect in the process.

CHAPTER SEVEN

B listers. I had actual blisters. From a broom. And that was only from an hour's work. I'd never experienced such an affront to my dignity. Well, except for the tail. Apparently there was a technique to sweeping and all I'd been doing was flinging dirt around. I was so useless that Anwen had shooed me off to find soap and water for mopping.

Was mopping as bad as sweeping? The thought made me grimace and give up my search perhaps a little too quickly.

Back in the great hall, the main doors stood open, letting in the streaming sunlight and an errant breeze. Temptation curled in my belly, and I shivered as I stepped across the flagstones to close them. I'd called Anwen my prisoner, but really she'd been the one to trap me here. I tried not to think about it, but after spending three years alone on my mountain, the stone walls of the manor seemed to be sagging, pressing me into the flagstones.

Anwen had said I couldn't leave the manor. Could I step across the threshold or would the change grab me the moment my foot landed on the other side? Would it be permanent this time? I couldn't feel anything as I drew closer, no tingle, no burning beneath my skin. But it was better to be safe than sorry so I stayed as far away from the outside as I could, reaching for the edge of the door.

"My lord."

Giles's voice from behind me made me jump.

"My lord, what do you plan to do?"

"About what?" I turned to give him an arch look, enjoying the feel of sunshine and free air on my skin.

"About Mistress Anwen. It's her. She's the reason you're cursed."

"You think I don't know that?"

"You have to tell her."

I jerked back and shook my head, hard enough to rattle my brains. "She'd leave." My jaw clenched. "She can't leave."

"At least then she'd have heard it from you." Giles's white eyebrows drew together in a disapproving line. "What if she learns about it some other way?"

A flash of blue at the end of the driveway caught my gaze. I raised my hand to shield my eyes from the bright sun shining off the white snow. Anwen stood with Brann at her feet.

Another person looked up and I got the impression of dark hair and smooth pale skin.

Even from this distance I recognized the shape of her face and the way she stood. My mouth went dry. Her features had been burned into my memory three years ago.

"Look," I said around the tightness in my throat, gesturing down the driveway.

Giles's eyes narrowed as he followed my finger. "Is that—?"

"The one who changed me."

He paled as the blood drained from his face. He'd remember her as well as I did.

The woman peered over Anwen's shoulder, directly at me. I couldn't see her eyes, but I could feel them settle on my form in the shadows of the doorway.

My heart skipped in my chest. What was the woman telling Anwen? Would the next expression under her scars be pain and disgust? I strained to run out to them, but my feet stayed stuck to the threshold as surely as if Anwen had glued them there by magic.

I would not become the bear again. If I had a choice in anything in the next five minutes, that would be it.

A spark at the corner of my eye made me turn. My mouth fell open and Giles gasped behind me.

Letters made of bright blue fire scrawled across the door under my hand, words forming as we watched. I stepped back, snatching my hand away.

"Loose tongues make former friends," it read in soft round handwriting. Below it, a signature formed line by line with a hiss. Catrin de Emrys.

"What does it mean?" Giles whispered.

I'd wondered the same thing when I was a child. The proverb hadn't made any sense to a ten-year-old who didn't have any friends. It wasn't until later I'd learned you could lose so much more than friends.

I gulped and straightened. "I think it means she doesn't want Anwen knowing the truth any more than we do."

Which was interesting. Was the Emrys woman somehow ashamed of her actions? Or maybe she'd be in trouble if other enchanters found out what she'd done.

"That seems reason enough to tell Mistress Anwen," Giles said.

"No." My fist thumped the door. "We tell her nothing about that day. I can't risk her leaving me like this."

Giles's disapproving eyes did nothing to sway me. I'd play along with Mistress Emrys this once, if our purposes lined up.

Anwen turned back and trudged through the snow as the woman behind her disappeared beyond the gate. The words on my door faded to black and fell away as ash. As Anwen grew closer, Giles leaned across and brushed away the remaining soot with his broom without meeting my gaze.

I shrugged off his censure with a pang of guilt. Ignoring Giles had never done me any good but it was habit by now.

As Anwen drew nearer, I turned my grin on her. Other girls would have blushed; she just gave me a placid look as she labored up the steps.

"Visitor?" I said.

"The matrona of my Family," she said and stopped on the top step. "She was in the area and thought she'd drop by."

"She didn't want to come in?" I said, reckless with relief that the woman hadn't given away my secret.

Giles raised his eyebrows but didn't say anything.

Anwen tilted her head and narrowed her eyes. "You're acting very odd. Why are you standing on the doorstep like this?"

I frowned. "Well, I can't go outside, can I?"

"Why not?"

I crossed my arms. "I spent long enough as a bear, and I'd rather not undo all your hard work in a matter of hours."

Her eyes widened as if this was news. "Oh, I thought I explained. Léon, the boundary I set is along the outer wall. From the gate, around the tree line." She pointed out beyond the outbuildings and driveway.

I blinked. I could step outside? Breathe?

"I didn't think it would be good to bind you to the house entirely, in case you needed fresh air. Or there was a fire. And if you do have to cross the line, it won't be the end of your humanity forever."

I tore my gaze from the bright sunshine outdoors. "What do you mean?"

"The magic keeping you in bear form is tied deeply inside you. But I found a loophole. I placed my magic around the manor. Inside the circle my casting is dominant, keeping you human. Outside, the opposite is true. If you want to change back, all you have to do is step back over the line."

It proved hard to concentrate on her words when my gaze kept straying toward the crystalline sky.

"You'll be able to feel the edge easily enough," she said. "But if you'd like I'll show it to you."

She glanced behind her at the league of snow she'd already covered that day and her brow drew down.

"No, don't worry," I said without waiting to think about it. "I'm sure I'll find it when I need to." Which was never. I had no intention of crossing that line until I could do so without experiencing that unmaking and remaking.

She turned to go inside and I balked.

"I think I'll take a walk though," I said. "It's been years since anyone's checked the outbuildings."

"All right. I thought we could start mopping next."

"This will only take a few moments." And it would give me some much needed space.

She gave me an indulgent smile, the scar pulling at its edges, and I flushed. If she wanted to believe I was ducking out of the whole cleaning thing, that was fine by me. Better that than she guess how much her quiet presence crowded me.

Giles held out a cloak I hadn't seen him leave to fetch, and I snatched it from his hands and darted outside. With the door shut behind me, I took a deep breath of the cold air and let out a cloud of steam in relief. There had been no burning, but I expected the bear to be lurking under the surface anyway.

I wiggled my toes in my boots. No claws. Just hose-clad legs and boots.

I threw back the cloak, leaving my arms free as I trudged through the thick layer of snow, feeling the icy air move across my face and hands. Every little shiver made me appreciate my skin. The world had been made new along with me, and I stared, my sharp eyesight taking in the details the bear's fuzzy gaze always missed. The rough outbuildings and the spiky branches of the bare trees stared back at me.

I tried not to see the thick tree trunks as the bars of my cage.

It wasn't that I didn't appreciate what she'd done for me so far. It was just that I'd spent three years alone except for

Giles's company. After all the company I needed a few moments to myself.

I walked around the north corner of the manor, surveying the stable yard and the surrounding area.

The outer wall had collapsed here several years ago, but my parents had never been home long enough to oversee its repair and it had made a nice back door for a bear. Fresh snow filled the gap, and I reached out to brush it from the tumbled stones.

An itch started under the skin of my fingers and I gasped as a tingle traced up the hair of my arms. I could almost feel the bear crawling up the back of my throat, shoving his way into my mind.

I snatched my hand back too quickly and overbalanced, stumbling in the snow until I fell onto my backside in a drift.

My chest heaved as I stared at my hand. Pale skin encased slim bones and no fur had sprouted as I feared. The tingle had gone the moment I'd stepped back.

Muck on you, stupid. You found the boundary. No need to act like a hen at the chopping block.

I scrambled out of the snow. Thank the Almighty Brann hadn't been there to see and mock me. Or Anwen.

Strange notion. Why did I care what she thought of me, beyond keeping her oblivious to the secret that would ruin my chance for true freedom?

When I was upright, I spared a glance back at the crumbling wall. I couldn't see anything, but I was sure Anwen's magic stretched across that gap.

Nothing would induce me to cross that line again. And

now I knew what it felt like when I got close, I could be careful. No more transformations for me.

My eyes narrowed. In the clean snow beside the wall, small indistinct footprints led away, toward the stables.

What had invaded my territory? I followed the trail to the big sturdy building. It had been abandoned for years since the horses couldn't stand my proximity while a bear.

I ducked under the snow-covered eaves and hauled the door through the drift that blocked its path. It creaked a little as I slipped in.

It wasn't as warm as I remembered, with a cold draft whipping through the building from an open window. And I wasn't greeted by the welcoming nickers of familiar horses. But it smelled much as it had the day I'd ridden out with my huntsmen and came back a cursed man. Only a trace of rot hid under the sweet scent of hay and feed.

The empty stalls gaped at me, but it wasn't as quiet as I was expecting. A rustling from the loose box in the back made me jump.

I crept down the wide aisle, my feet stirring rotten hay and who knew what else. My boot caught a stray hoof pick and sent it spinning away to jangle against a stall door.

The rustling stopped. Nothing moved for a long minute.

I sighed and straightened up. I must have scared the intruder away, through the open window in the back maybe. A rush of relief made my knees weak. What would I have done if I'd actually found an animal? All I had to defend my home with was dirty straw and a stray bucket.

My lips pursed. The mighty Lord Beauregard who had

once hunted boar and deer across the mountainside had been terrified of a noise.

"Boo!" A shape much larger than I'd imagined burst from the loose box, sending me staggering back against the wall.

I lost my footing in the slimy remnants of the stable and landed on the packed dirt floor.

It took a full thirty seconds for me to realize I hadn't died and I was still breathing. Gasping, really.

My fingers curled against the frozen dirt floor. "Almighty take you for—" I raised my eyes and stopped before I could say something foul.

A little girl stood in the middle of the stables, mussed blonde hair tumbling over her gray cloak and blue eyes gazing at me with interest. She stood no taller than my elbow.

"What are you doing here?" I said before I thought maybe I shouldn't yell.

She stood with her feet planted and head cocked. "You're not Josselin."

"Of course I'm not—"

She was gone before I could finish, darting back into the loose box with a giggle.

I groaned and hauled myself to my feet, brushing the back of my hose. But the straw stuck to the wool, making my rear end look like a hedgehog. Great.

When I stuck my head over the low wall of the box, the little girl was burrowing into the corner, grabbing handfuls of filthy straw and piling them on her head.

"What are you doing?"

"Playing hide and find," she said, giving me a gap-toothed

smile before holding a grubby finger to her lips. "Shh. Don't tell Josselin where I am. He always finds me."

I rubbed my temples. "If you're trying to hide, why did you jump out at me?"

"That's what Josselin does. He's always trying to scare me."

"Right," I said. She'd certainly succeeded there. She tossed more hay onto her head. "Hey, come out of there. It's dirty." That was something you were supposed to say to children, wasn't it?

"No!" she cried, grinding herself down into the muck. "I have a good spot this time. He always finds me."

I leaned on the wall and tallied my options.

"Emeline? Emeline where are you?" a frantic voice called from outside. Josselin, I guessed.

The little girl squealed and finished tucking herself into the straw. Pieces of it clung to her hair and smock, and she grinned out at me, her pride as visible as she was. I couldn't help the chuckle that rose in my chest.

"I take it you're Emeline," I said.

She nodded.

"It's nice to meet you Emeline, I'm Léon."

She giggled and held her finger to her lips again.

I lowered my voice. "And that's your brother? The hide and find champion, Josselin?"

She snorted. "He's not a champion," she said.

"He sounds worried."

"We've never played this far out before. But I came through the hole in the wall."

"All by yourself? Saints, you can't be more than six."

"Six and a half," she said indignantly.

Josselin called again from outside, and I heard Anwen's muffled answer.

"Tell you what," I said, cocking my head. "I can show you the best hiding spot ever."

Her eyes widened. "The best?"

It had certainly baffled Giles a time or two. "I used to be pretty good at hiding myself," I said.

Emeline thought about it a moment, her brow creasing and her tongue sticking between her teeth, before she bounded to her feet and grabbed my hand.

"Show me," she said.

I suppressed a snort and walked her to the ladder that led to the loft. I gripped it and wiggled it, making sure it was still solid, before climbing up to the second story. Hardly any moldering straw lay around but plenty of empty barrels and burlap sacks filled the space.

"Here," I said, peering into an empty barrel. "In you go."

Emeline beamed as I lifted her up and tucked her into the barrel. Almighty, she was tiny. She folded up with room to spare. I put my finger to my lips and she mimicked the gesture. A couple of burlap sacks hid her from view.

Outside I found Anwen and Brann talking to a boy of about ten. His hair had more red in it than Emeline's but the color of his eyes and the shape of his face revealed their relation.

He stood tense, hands clasped in front of him as he spoke. "Please, miss. We didn't know anyone lived here. We were just looking for somewhere to play. Safe from the monster."

"Monster?" Anwen's gaze flicked to me as I stepped out of the stable, and the corner of her mouth lifted.

"Our guardian says there's a monster in the woods. But Emmy likes hide and find and so I thought maybe here...I've told her and told her to be careful. What if it got her?"

His voice trembled and Anwen reached out to comfort him. "Oh Josselin, I'm sure the monster didn't get your sister."

"How do you know?"

"Because I'm the monster," I said. "And I don't eat children."

The boy gasped and spun to face me.

"Léon," Anwen said, exasperation leaking into her tone. "Josselin can't find his sister. I'm going to search with magic. Could you go with Brann to search the grounds?"

I crossed my arms and leaned against the corner of the stable. "No need," I said. "She found me."

"Well, then where is she?"

"I can't tell you. That would be cheating," I said. I met Josselin's eyes. "She's found a really good spot this time."

"She always says that," he said, the tension going out of his shoulders.

"I guess you'd better get started then," I said.

He looked between me and the stable door and took off.

"I didn't know you liked children," Anwen said.

Neither did I.

It took Josselin a few minutes to search each of the stalls. It wasn't until a giggle floated down from the rafters that he found the ladder to the loft. We followed up the ladder as he went from barrel to barrel calling, "Emmy? Emmy, where are you?"

He hadn't reached her barrel yet when she burst up, flinging bits of straw and burlap sacks every which way.

"Boo!"

Josselin rolled his eyes. "Emmy, you're supposed to let me find you."

"Did I scare you?"

"Only an idiot would think you're scary."

I shifted my feet. "Maybe under the right circumstances," I said.

"But I had a good spot this time, right?" Emeline said. She scrambled from the barrel and ran over to me. "My new friend showed it to me."

Josselin started forward and jerked to a stop, his eyes wary. "He says he's the monster."

I raised my chin. I didn't care what a ten-year-old boy and his sister thought of me.

Then why did my heart clench when Emeline gazed up at me, trust radiating from the grip she had on my hand?

"He's not a monster," she said. "He's Léon."

I cleared my throat and pulled on my arm, trying to dislodge it from Emeline's grip. I was not the kind of man girl-children clung to.

"Maybe it's time you ran along home," I said.

Emeline pouted and resisted my pulling. "No. I'm not done playing."

"You can't play at home?"

A shadow passed over Josselin's face and he kicked at the

snow. "Our guardian doesn't like us underfoot. So we play in the woods."

I scowled. What kind of monster did they have at home that they would brave a very real one to avoid him?

Anwen seemed to be smothering laughter. "Well, I'm sure Léon would be happy to let you play here. It's big and it's safe from the monster." She cast a sidelong glance at me, like she was daring me to disagree.

My muscles seized in panic. Give up even more of my space and my precious solitude?

Brann smirked beside Anwen, as if reading my thoughts and waiting for me to screw up. Anwen tilted her head expectantly.

I couldn't refuse with her hazel eyes steady on my face. What kind of creep kicked a pair of children off his land for playing?

"Of course," I said, unclenching my teeth and forcing a smile. I caught the cat's gaze. "And I'm sure Brann would love to play with you."

Brann's lips pulled back, revealing the tips of his fangs. "I am not a hobby horse. Nor am I a babysitter."

Emeline squealed to hear the voice come from the white fluffy cat. "Kitty," she said and knelt next to him so she could put her arms around the talking animal and snuggle against his fur. "Look Josselin, it's a talking kitty. Nice kitty."

"No, not nice kitty," Brann said, wriggling to extract himself from the girl's embrace. "Ferocious kitty. Savage kitty." He peeled his lips back and snarled at her but she giggled. His last resort was to change into a mouse and scurry away, leaving Emeline with two fistfuls of gravel. He reappeared across the loft, absorbing a barrel so he could become a cougar.

"Wow, that was so neat!" Josselin said. "Can you do it again? Can you be a dog? Oh! No, I know, a horse!"

Brann gave me a murderous look. "This is your fault, you fathead."

I grinned and twiddled my fingers at him.

"Oh, go on, Brann," Anwen said, and laughed. "The practice will be good for you."

Brann sighed and mumbled, "I'll get you for this later, Beauregard. See if I don't."

CHAPTER EIGHT

With all the people invading my space, I still hadn't made it to the chapel to make my Pledge. Late that night, after we'd managed to send the children home, I crept down the hall, one hand on the wall beside me.

It would be just my luck to trip and fall and bring Anwen to my rescue when I'd finally managed to get away from her. The woman always smiled, never snapped, and was still somehow the most draining person I'd ever met.

My charm rolled over her like mist, having no effect. Instead, she looked at me with those eyes and something inside me twisted until I was holding a broom or inviting a pair of grubby children to make use of my lands. I had to examine every word coming out of my mouth to make sure it wouldn't give away my secrets or drive Anwen off before she'd broken my curse.

The door of the chapel hadn't been used in three years and it squealed as I hauled it open. I winced and glanced behind me.

All clear.

I slipped inside and breathed a sigh in the quiet darkness. The tension in my shoulders leaked away despite the smell of dust and the air of neglect.

No leaves or fur marred the floor, but when I stepped forward, my boots left a print in the fine layer of dust.

I hadn't brought a taper to light the candles, but diamond-paned windows let in reflected moonlight, enough to see by. Simple beams stretched overhead to the low ceiling. But this room's beauty didn't lay in its architecture or furnishings.

Intricate blossoms and curling tendrils of vines climbed the wall in delicate splashes of colors. Vervain, speedwell, iris, lady's mantle, dittany. A summer's bounty grew in a fortune of paint.

Other people nurtured and harvested their Pledges from gardens, or bought them at the market during Holy Day. They placed their greenery on the altar to represent their commitment to worship the Almighty through magic, travel, service, motherhood, or scholarship. There were dozens of saints, dozens of Paths of Worship, thousands of dying plants laid on the altar in supplication and promise.

Rotting flowers had never seemed like an appropriate offering to me. Wasn't the Almighty the giver of life? So with Brother Warren's help I'd painted my Pledges. Every saint represented by a blossom, an herb, a tree. And at the far end of the room, roses covered the wall behind the altar. My constant vow. The physical representation of my commitment to Saint Createjoy's Way.

I stepped closer and reached out to touch a faded red petal. Apparently even paint wasn't permanent. A vase of dried sticks beside the altar was all that was left of someone's ancient offering. Strangely fitting for me now.

My hand fell away. After my transformation I'd ignored this room, not because it was too small, but because I couldn't live by my Pledge anymore. How could I dedicate my art to the Almighty if I couldn't hold a brush?

But every time I'd panicked or felt the bear draw close, I'd prayed.

And the Almighty deserved thanks for the answer to that prayer.

Except I still had no patron saint to follow. Nothing in my life to Pledge as my worship.

My mother had always laid lady's mantle on the altar, a sign of her worship through motherhood. I fought the urge to snort. Giles still Pledged dittany for his worship through scholarship. I would not be joining him there. And my father had ignored the tradition entirely. The man had never provided me with a role model in life, why would he start now after he'd been dead for five years?

I clenched my fingers. I'd fumbled my fork at dinner again today until I'd thrown it down and strode from the room. If it took so long to learn how to use a fork again, how long would it take to learn to use a paintbrush? No beauty would come from these fingers anytime soon, so Saint Createjoy was out.

I hung my head, my fists clenching. I may have had my humanity back, but I was as useless as I'd been with claws.

The door creaked behind me and I spun, stumbling and fighting to stay upright.

Anwen peeked in, face pale in the dim light.

My jaw tightened. Almighty, could I not be rid of the woman?

"There you are," she said, and the sound of her soft voice broke the last of my control.

"Yes, here I am," I snapped. "Can't run. Trapped by magic. Can't hide, you'll find me. God Almighty, humanity is just another kind of prison." I cut off the flow of words and kicked the vase of dry twigs so it crashed against the stone wall. Dead sticks and broken bits of crockery tumbled across the floor as I stood.

Brilliant, Léon. That will get her to like you. Shout at her. The Almighty should have ignored your prayers, you blockhead.

She had every right to turn tail and run, leaving me to my lonely spite. But she didn't leave. She stood there, gazing at me with those eyes, peeling me open. But this time, I'd shown her the muck underneath and she wasn't retreating.

I didn't feel exposed. I felt understood. I broke away from her gaze, face burning.

"I'm sorry," I said. No way to take the words back. Just had to move forward and try to mitigate my own muck up.

"No," she said. "I'm the one who should be sorry."

I blinked and my mouth gaped.

She gestured around her. "I invaded your castle with an acerbic cat. Took hold of your life and twisted it to suit my needs without consulting you. I trapped you here, assuming I knew best, but I didn't even ask you for your opinion."

I smoothed my fingers down the sides of my doublet, my

anger and frustrations draining away as I forced them to relax. "If you'd asked, I would have said yes."

"Good to know," she said. She bit her lip. "I'll speak to Brann if you like."

"He's not that bad."

"But I am?"

My eyes widened. "No. No, you're not, you're—" I looked up to see her lopsided smile. She'd been teasing. But she still deserved an explanation. "I've spent three years with no one but Giles for company. I guess I got used to it."

"You're feeling crowded," she said.

I nodded.

"I'll go," she said, turning.

"No!" There I went, shouting at her again. I didn't know if she'd meant for now, or for good, but I realized I didn't want either. I gestured to the altar and the wall of flowers behind. "You don't have to go. I can't do what I was going to do anyway."

"What were you going to do?"

"I..." I flushed. "It wasn't important."

"Léon, you snuck away from us to come stand in a chapel." She glanced around the room. "Seems pretty important to me."

What did it matter if I told her? "I wanted to thank the Almighty," I said. "For my freedom."

Her fingers tapped her chin. "Have you always been this pious?"

"No," I said without apology. "It was just habit before. Then when I was a bear, I didn't think He deserved my worship. But every time I panicked or I felt the bear rise up, I prayed. Habit again, I guess. But He answered those prayers."

"Did you really mean them?"

"Doesn't matter," I said, shaking my head. "I still spoke them. Can I ask for something in fear or desperation and then claim it doesn't count when He actually answers?"

She nodded, a small satisfied smile on her lips like she'd only asked the question because she'd been looking for the right answer. Guess I'd given her one.

"Good point," she said. "But the garden is bare. Did you dry any flowers for your Pledges during the winter?"

I hadn't even thought of that. Stupid. Most people thought ahead and planned for their piety when snow and ice kept the gardens dormant.

I shrugged sheepishly. "I used to Pledge a different way," I said, gesturing to the walls. "But I can't anymore."

Her lips parted as she gazed around her. "You did all this?"

I swallowed and turned to study the mural. "My parents were never home while I was growing up, and I always ran from Giles's lessons," I said. "So I found some other ways to spend my time."

"Giles was your tutor?" She wandered over to the shattered vase and picked one of the dried sticks out of the mess.

"He wanted to be a Disciple of Wonderment, once," I said. Wonderment was the Saint of Reason. His followers worshiped the Almighty through scholarship. "Before my parents hired him to civilize me. Once he realized how much I liked to draw, he asked a Disciple of Saint Createjoy to come teach me. I think Brother Warren was the only one who could get me to sit still for more than five minutes at a time."

She sat on one of the cushioned benches, turning the stick over and over in her hands while she stared at the walls. "It's amazing." Her bright eyes returned to my face. "Why did you say you can't paint anymore?"

I tore myself from her uncomfortable study. "Can't hold a paintbrush," I mumbled. I didn't know how to explain that I wanted this particular Pledge to be perfect. Holding a wood block between my teeth like I'd done as a bear just wouldn't cut it this time.

She focused on my hands, which I clenched and tucked into the folds of my doublet.

"It's only been two days, Léon," she said. "Your speech is better. Your dexterity will probably return."

I tensed. "And what if it doesn't?" I said, quietly, trying to hide the way my voice trembled.

She bit her lip and I turned away, taking that as my answer. Her tunic rustled as she struggled to stand, and her feet scuffed the floor unevenly as she moved away.

I turned so I wouldn't have to watch her leave.

"Earlier you asked me what I'd lived through," she said from the doorway. "To become an enchanter."

I glanced around, surprised by the change of subject.

"I fell down a mine shaft when I was six. It took them two days to get to me."

I expected bitterness or anger but only a distant sadness laced her voice.

"When they finally got me out, I could do things I couldn't do before. Move objects, heal cuts. Making light is still my favorite." A globe of glorious gold, like a piece of the sun, burst into existence over her head, then faded to a speck of starlight.

I blinked, clearing the sparks from my eyes and fighting the urge to ask her to bring it back.

"But an untrained enchanter is dangerous, especially one so young. My parents sent me to Saint Redemption's Refuge after I set our house on fire."

She met my eyes and I managed to hold my ground against the emotion there.

"Why did you tell me?" I said, without thinking and then winced.

She quirked her ragged smile at me and shrugged, but she didn't answer. She raised the stick between her hands, her brow furrowing in concentration as she stared at the space between them.

I opened my mouth to ask what she was doing when she drew her fingers along the dead shaft and a long-stemmed rose appeared between her hands. Its soft red petals were just beginning to curl open.

She grasped the thorny stem carefully and touched the blossom with one gentle finger before handing it to me.

I only hesitated a moment before I took it.

"For your Pledge," she said. "Createjoy, right? Saint of Beauty." She gestured to the wall of roses behind the altar.

"B-but I can't make beautiful things anymore," I said, and hated myself for arguing as she handed me what I'd been wishing for.

She smiled. "Worship isn't a way to earn the Almighty's grace, Léon. We can't earn something that's already been given to us. We can only thank Him for it. He doesn't care how well you paint. Only that you do."

Then she slipped out, leaving me with my mouth hanging open. The problem that had loomed so large before seemed small and manageable with her help. Was she that way about everything? Would she make my curse small and manageable, too?

CHAPTER NINE

The next morning, I tracked Anwen down in the kitchen, ready to get started on breaking my curse. We'd wasted enough time yesterday cleaning.

"It's not that I don't appreciate what you've done so far," I said, leaning my elbows on the back of a kitchen chair and giving Anwen a sidelong smirk. "I really do. I just—"

"You don't want to spend your life trapped in your manor," she finished for me. "I understand, Léon. You don't have to explain."

"I don't?"

"Sit down. The only reason I haven't tried to break your curse fully yet was to let the vytl in the area replenish itself. I used most of it to create the boundary that keeps you human, and with all this rock and snow, vytl is kind of hard to come by."

I sat in the chair she indicated and raised an eyebrow. "I don't know what that means."

She sighed and dragged another chair in front of me.

"Vytl comes from life. Plants, animals, even Térne itself gives off energy. But in the winter when the world is dormant or in rocky places like this, there is a lot less vytl to go around." She gestured out the kitchen windows, wreathed with frost even in the bright morning sunlight. Then she sat down with a wince.

I frowned. "So you can't do anything to break my curse until spring?" The thought made me itch with impatience.

"Relax," she said. "Right now, I'm still trying to get a good sense of what's keeping you bound. I just need you to sit still long enough to look inside."

Her words immediately made me want to fidget. Especially when her fingers pressed my temples, cool against my skin. With her face so close to mine, I didn't know where to rest my gaze.

Her eyes, shot with green, brown, and gold, went dark and unfocused. Huh, this close to her I barely noticed the scars.

Actually, when you ignored them, she was kind of pretty.

"Giles?" an unfamiliar voice called from the door to the yard. "Oh, I'm sorry."

Anwen's eyes snapped back into focus as I twitched out from under her grasp.

A woman stood in the doorway, her russet tunic kilted up to mid-calf to stay out of the snow, revealing a pair of worn boots. A linen kerchief covered her hair but dark strands escaped around the edges and a battered basket hung in the crook of her elbow.

Her gaze darted between Anwen and me, taking in my

fine doublet and hose and Anwen's simpler tunic, uncertainty written in the creases of her eyes and lips.

"Who are you?" I asked. "What are you doing here?"

Anwen cast me a look, her brows lowered.

Why was she annoyed with me? This stranger was the one interrupting us when I finally had Anwen concentrating on breaking my curse.

Giles stepped through the door from the great hall. "Fanny?" he said. "I wasn't expecting you until later."

The woman turned to him, her stance relaxing. "Da said his bones were complaining about a storm coming, so I decided to get here sooner rather than later."

"Giles?" I said, drawing his name out in irritation.

He blinked at me. "This is Miss Fanny, my lord. She brings the bread and the produce from the village."

"Since when?"

"Three years, my lord," he said, eyes crinkling at the corners.

My mouth fell open. She'd been supplying the manor since my transformation and I'd never even heard of the woman?

Giles rubbed his lips, hiding a smile. "You didn't think I baked the bread myself, did you?"

I flushed. I wasn't about to admit I'd never bothered to wonder where the bread came from at all.

He moved past me and gave the woman, Fanny, a smile I'd never seen on him before. "I'm glad you came early, then, if there's to be a storm," he said. "I wouldn't want you to have to trudge out here in a blizzard."

"It's not like I haven't done it before," she said. "Remember the last time?"

Giles groaned. "Too well. Three days holed up in the kitchen hoping the food would last."

She gave him a look from under her eyelashes. "At least we stayed warm."

Giles turned an amazing shade of pink.

Good heavens, were they flirting? Was this how old people flirted? I'd have laughed if I hadn't been so disturbed. Giles had no business spending a snow storm...canoodling... with some woman. And how had I missed all this? Sure, I'd spent every blizzard curled up in my room ignoring the cold outside, but was I that oblivious?

Giles cleared his throat. "Yes, well, as I said, it's good you came. I was going to ask if you could bring an extra loaf tomorrow. We have more mouths to feed, now."

"So I see," Fanny said, looking at Anwen and I sidelong.

I stood and straightened my doublet.

"Fanny, this is Lord Léon Beauregard."

The peasant woman's eyes grew round in recognition and she bobbed a curtsy.

Giles barely glanced at me before gesturing to Anwen. "And Mistress Anwen de Emrys who's been helping us this week."

Anwen's habitual cheer had reasserted itself and she limped across the smooth flagstones with her hand extended. "It's so nice to meet you, Fanny. Giles has told me so much about you."

He had? I hadn't even known the woman existed. When had Giles gotten so chatty?

Anwen wasn't wearing her blue cloak inside, but Giles had introduced her as "mistress," the honorific for an enchanter. The change on Fanny's face was immediate. The awe and respect she'd showed me faded, replaced by fear, and she stepped back to avoid Anwen's greeting. Her hand sketched the local sign against evil.

Anwen stopped, the pleasure draining from her welcoming smile, and her hand dropped back to her side.

As her face fell, my stomach twisted. How often did she face people who feared her for her power without knowing how gentle she really was? It must be lonely, standing outside the social order, scorned by the upper class and feared by the common people.

There was an awkward pause as I wondered what would bring her smile back and who was responsible for making her happy again.

Anwen took the decision out of my hands, accepting Fanny's fear with grace and continuing the aborted conversation with ease. "Are you the one who bakes the bread, Fanny?" she asked.

The woman lowered her wide-eyed gaze and shuffled her feet. "Yes, mistress."

"I never did get the hang of baking." Anwen's lips twisted ruefully as she glanced at the wide oven on the opposite wall standing cold and empty. "The last loaf of bread I tried to make came out lumpy and burnt. My freire, Myrddin, laughed and laughed. I told him he could make it next time."

Fanny eyed Anwen, curious despite herself. "What is a freire?"

"It means brother." Wistfulness pulled at the edges of

Anwen's mouth at some private memory. "Though we're related by talent and friendship instead of blood."

Fanny picked at the broken edge of her basket. "And did he try baking the bread, mistress?"

Anwen's expression soured. "Yes. And his came out far better than mine ever had."

Fanny laughed, her stance relaxing, and some genuine pleasure crept back into Anwen's expression. Had she charmed the common woman on purpose? If so, she was better at it than me, given my record with Anwen.

"Why didn't you just..." Fanny twiddled her fingers. "Magic the bread?"

Anwen rolled her eyes skyward. "My matrona would have killed me. 'Magic is a gift from the Almighty, Anwen. It is not a shortcut for your chores.'"

Anwen's version of her matrona's voice made Fanny laugh. "She sounds just like my grandmother. 'There is no shortcut for hard work.' I still always tried to find one though."

"Exactly." The enchanter sighed. "I was always too scared of Matrona to try, but Myrddin wasn't. He ended up flooding the whole house once. Patriarche Justin was taking a nap upstairs and woke up to Myrddin teaching me how to swim in the kitchen. He wasn't pleased. Especially when he had to catch his boots before they floated out the door."

Now everyone laughed. Except me. My fingers drummed on the edge of the table.

Why did I need to shift my feet so badly? The image of a soggy patriarche chasing floating boots was plenty funny, but my skin was starting to feel itchy.

My teeth ached from clenching them and something burned in my gut. Not anger, that was a familiar feeling. This was...this felt more like it had the moment Anwen had changed me human.

I doubled over, pain radiating like flames from inside. My hands twisted, changing to claws, and fur sprouted along the backs of my hands.

"Anwen!" My voice broke on her name as panic flooded me with a wash of cold. I couldn't change back now. Not with so many people nearby. What if I hurt someone?

With no warning, the pain disappeared, leaving me gasping on my knees with no memory of reaching the floor.

"Anwen?"

"I'm here." She knelt beside me, bad leg twisted under her.

"What was that?"

"The curse."

"Yes, but why?" My hands fisted against the floor. "What did you do to it?"

She shook her head. Fanny stood behind her, eyes wide. Giles had taken a step toward me but stopped.

"I didn't do anything to it, yet," she said. "I didn't even get a good look at it before we were interrupted."

"If it's coming back...if even you can't keep me human—" I gripped her hand, trying to anchor myself.

"Stop, Léon." She placed her other hand on my wrist. "Something is wrong, yes. But we'll fix it. I promise. I'll go check the boundary. Make sure it's not failing. Giles?"

Without answering, Giles left Fanny pale and shaking by

the door to kneel beside me and help me to my feet as Anwen moved to the kitchen door, calling for Brann.

While Giles settled Léon in his room, Anwen traced the boundary of vytl step by step, circling the manor. She examined each thread that wove through the stones of the wall.

Brann paced beside her, squinting as if he too could see the glowing lines and eddies. But only enchanters who had gone through trauma and come out changed could see the energy blanketing the world.

So far each strand seemed strong and intact, but she knew there had to be a weakness somewhere. Why else would Léon nearly lose his shape in the middle of the kitchen?

Unless it had something to do with the magic she couldn't see. The part woven so deeply into his heart she couldn't read the tangles and knots of it.

What kind of monster would steal a man's soul as punishment? Whatever he'd done, a man deserved a fair trial and humane treatment.

She shook her head. She wasn't free to go hunting down this rogue enchanter. Not yet. Not until she'd freed Léon.

"You have that wrinkle between your eyes again," Brann said. With each step she broke through the crust of snow, filling her boots with cold and wet, but he trotted beside her as a white fox, his weight spread lightly so he glided along the top.

"Sorry," she said and gave him a distracted smile. "I was thinking about Léon."

"He likes you," he said with a vulpine leer.

Anwen huffed a laugh at the thought. "He likes the idea of me. Maybe even as much as he likes the sound of his own voice," she said without rancor. "Not exactly what I'm looking for in a man."

Léon wielded charm like a sword, ready to cut a swathe through whoever he aimed at. But Anwen had been cut before and wasn't about to fall victim to another handsome face with a promise emptier than Léon's stables. Adrien had been enough to teach her that.

"It's amusing to watch him trip over himself trying to impress me, but that's all on the surface," she said. "It wasn't until he snapped at me that I felt like I saw the real Léon."

"A spoiled boy lord?"

She stopped at another section of wall and bent to inspect the glowing lines of vytl binding the stones. "Yes, I'll admit that's true."

"Then why are we out here in the cold trying to help him?"

"Because that's not the whole truth," she said straightening up. Nothing wrong in this section. "Léon might be spoiled and arrogant, but when he's not trying to be slick and charming, there's a whole lot more underneath. He's hurting."

Brann snorted.

"I'm serious," Anwen said. "He lost something important."

"Like what?"

"Painting."

"A hobby."

She shook her head. "That may be what it looks like to you. But it was more than that to him. How did you feel when you first lost your home?"

"That's different," Brann said, voice tight.

"Is it?" Anwen asked. "I could say what you lost doesn't really much matter since you still have a home and a family here." She regarded him pointedly. "But I wouldn't because I know what it meant to you."

He gave her the courtesy of thinking about it. "You think painting meant that much to him?"

"Go visit the chapel when you have a chance."

They came to the gate where they'd met Catrin two days before. Here the vytl lay in broken lines, frayed ends drifting without anchor.

"There's the problem," Anwen said and bent to repair the damage.

"Was it deliberate?" Brann asked, sniffing the snow by her feet.

Anwen squinted at the frayed ends. "I don't know. I think this could have just been a weak spot when I originally cast it. This is where I finished and I was in a hurry to get back to Léon." She paced two steps up the boundary and two steps back. "Or it could have been damaged when Catrin stepped onto the Byways. The transition can be violent."

She concentrated on weaving the magic stronger this time, smoothing the rough patches with a gentle touch while Brann scuffed the snow with his claws.

"She spoke to me before she left," he said.

"Catrin?" She didn't look up from the frayed strands of vytl. "What did she have to say?"

"She wanted me to convince you to leave. She couldn't persuade you to leave so she wants me to."

Her gaze strayed to him for a moment but her work continued without hesitation.

"I'm...not surprised. She's used to being obeyed. It's hard for her when her enfani develop minds of their own."

He stared at his paws. "That's why I chose not to travel with her. Back when I first came to your Realm."

Now she did stop her work to look at him. "She is the Matrona de Emrys. By all rights you should have gone with her."

He flexed his claws, gouging the snow. "I choose my own partner. And seniority is not the most important aspect of partnership."

"What is?"

"Character." He shook his head and paced to the wall and back.

She bit her lip to keep from laughing at his discomfort. Zevryn genders might have been confusing compared to humans, but when it came to talking about anything important, Brann was all male. "So what was it about mine that made you choose me?"

He mumbled.

And Anwen was all female so she had to ask, "What was that?"

"Your compassion," he said, glaring at her. "I may give you a hard time about it, but you're special. You always think the best of people. You always care about them, even when it's inconvenient or they don't deserve it." From the way he ducked his head, she didn't think he was talking about Léon. "You don't even see the ugliness in other people."

"Catrin may be tough but she cares," Anwen said. "The only reason she wants me to leave is because she doesn't want me to be hurt again."

She stood up and squinted at the new casting holding Léon's curse at bay. Everything seemed in order, but Anwen was beginning to realize that when it came to Léon nothing would be as simple as it seemed.

A shadow moved under the trees and she started. Brann spun, the fur along his spine standing up with alarm.

"What was that?" he asked, his voice a hiss in the darkness.

She strained her eyes, trying to see between the dark trunks. "I don't know," she said, her tone matching his.

"Didn't we come here because there were stories of a monster in the woods?"

"Yes." Anwen moved closer to him. "The blacksmith reported a shape roaming the edges of the village, getting dangerously close to the people. And there have been mauled animals found not far into the trees. But obviously they were talking about Léon. He's been lurking for years, and as a nobleman he's probably a brilliant hunter. But he's no longer a bear and therefore no longer a danger."

A low noise shivered through the air. Like a cross between a creak and a groan.

"Then what's out there now?" Brann said. "An animal? Your bear lord can't be the only one in these woods, right?"

"He's not my bear lord," Anwen said. Nothing else

moved beneath the bare branches, but her skin crawled as if eyes watched her.

"Can you check with magic?" Brann said. He paced back and forth in the open gate.

"Not without a link, something that connects me with the person or object—"

"All right, all right, I don't need the lecture," Brann snapped. He whipped around, ears swiveling to catch the sounds of the forest. What was creepy was that there weren't any.

Anwen blew out her breath. "This is ridiculous. We are too old to be afraid of the dark."

"Right," Brann said, straightening up. But he kept his gaze on the space between the trees. Just in case. "It was probably a squirrel. We're done out here, right?" He started toward the manor and stopped to look back at her.

"Yes." Anwen turned to follow him and hesitated. Léon was obviously the monster the villagers feared. But could there be something else out there? Something like an angry enchanter that sabotaged her castings in order to keep Léon bound to the bear?

Anwen wasn't too proud to admit when she was out of her depth. So far Léon's curse had beaten her.

Catrin had mentioned the enchanters' Moot coming up. Maybe Anwen could call in a few favors.

CHAPTER TEN

Yasmina ran through the curtain of roses as she always did, casting a playful laugh over her shoulder.

The scene hadn't changed. The sun still shone, she still teased me, but this time I wasn't smiling. I chased her with a lump in my throat and a hitch in my step. I reached out, my fingers clutching for her with desperation rather than hope.

One thought circled in my head, disturbing in its simplicity and insistence.

She had never let me catch her. In all these years, why hadn't she let me see her face?

I picked up speed and closed the distance between us, but as my hand closed on her arm, a sudden spike of uncertainty shot through me. What did she really look like? What if she wasn't what I was expecting?

The thought threw me out of the dream and into the dim morning chill.

From the streaks of pink and orange light coming through the diamond-paned windows of my room, the sun was barely over the horizon. My breath puffed white in the frigid air and I glanced at the hearth. Ash and charcoal lay dark and cold against the stones of the fireplace.

That's what I got for not banking the fire the night before.

I rolled over, pulling the fur cover tight around my shoulders. Giles had pulled the mattress out of some forgotten corner, but while it smelled better than my old nest, the unfamiliar lumps had made me toss and turn all night.

Why had the dream changed? Why did it matter so much that I hadn't seen Yasmina's face since I started dreaming of her? She would be beautiful—the most beautiful woman in the world—so worry had no place in our courtship. And the rest of the dream was the same. The only thing that had changed...was me.

I surged up from my nest of blankets and wrapped the fur around me before stumbling over to stand before my manuscript.

My fingers escaped the edge of the fur to stroke the fine parchment. I turned a page, careful not to touch the delicate paint. Yasmina was still there with her Leonides, the way I'd imagined her when I was thirteen. But imagination wasn't enough anymore. I wanted to know her. The real her.

And I needed to be free to find her.

I'd been human again for most of a week, but the bear had reappeared the other day in the kitchen, reminding me there was still a beast inside.

Anwen hadn't said much when she'd come back in from checking the boundary, and I'd gotten the impression she was formulating a plan. So I'd left her alone to work on the problem. Maybe now it was time to ask her for some answers.

Dressed in doublet and hose, I prowled towards the kitchen where I could hear voices.

I found Giles at the trestle table along the wall cutting bread and cheese. My heart sank when I saw Josselin and Emeline sitting cross-legged on the floor, playing with a couple of battered toys. I'd half hoped they'd forgotten my promise about playing on my lands.

The door creaked and Emeline beamed at me. She bounced to her feet and raced over to grab my hand. "Léon, you've been asleep forever. I wanted to come get you, but Giles said no."

Thank the Almighty for small mercies. I cast a grateful look at Giles, who merely raised an eyebrow and turned back to his cheese.

"Léon, play with me," Emeline demanded.

I gritted my teeth and searched the kitchen for Anwen, but she seemed to be the only person not in the room.

Josselin frowned. "Emmy, remember what Giles said. We have to call him 'my lord' now."

"But his name isn't my lord," she said, tilting her head. "It's Léon."

Her brother glanced at me, teeth worrying at his bottom lip. Anytime the kid thought I wasn't looking, he stared at me like I'd leap on him or Emeline with teeth and claws out. "No, it's not his name," he said. "It's his title. Because he's important."

Well, he wasn't wrong.

"That's silly," Emeline said. "I'm not calling him something that's not his name."

"Emmy..."

"Anwen calls him Léon."

"That's because Anwen is an enchanter," Josselin said.

Explaining that would take forever and I didn't have the patience to sit through it all when Anwen wasn't in sight.

"Léon is fine, Josselin," I said. "It's easier that way."

He didn't look convinced, but Emeline beamed up at me like she'd won an argument. I tried to extract my hand from her grip but she could out-cling a limpet, so I had to peel her from my arm before I could step over to speak to Giles.

"Where is Anwen?" I said. "She's usually up before me."

"She left before dawn," Giles said, gaze steady on the task before him.

My heart thumped the inside of my chest and I drew a harsh breath. "Left?"

He glanced at me. "For the enchanters' Moot. She said she was going to find some help."

She'd left the manor. She'd left me without saying anything. How could she? She was the only thing keeping me from turning back into the beast. Even now I could feel his claws against the inside of my mind, trying to get out.

An insidious voice in the back of my head whispered, "Maybe she's given up on you." All the charm I'd poured on her so far had just rolled right off. Nothing had made her want to stay and free me.

I stalked to the kitchen door and opened it to see two sets of tracks leading away toward the front gate. One human, one cat. My breath came faster as my thoughts spun in circles. She'd left. She was never coming back.

"You didn't actually mean what you said about her being a prisoner here, did you?" Giles arched his eyebrows.

I scowled. "Why wouldn't I? Everyone else has abandoned me. The only way I can get someone to stay is to trap them."

He stared at me and I shifted uncomfortably, reminded that when everyone else had fled, he had remained.

"My lord, she said she would return by nightfall." He turned back to his work.

His placid steadiness did more to calm me than his words. He had always been rock solid, more reliable than the mountainside beneath us.

I took a couple of deep breaths and tried to relax my shoulders. "Then I'll just have to believe her." She hadn't done anything to make me distrust her yet.

Emeline came over to tug on my arm again.

I suppressed a sigh. "And Brann went with her." So I couldn't foist the kids off on the cat.

"Before they left he said to have fun with the children," Giles said with what looked suspiciously like a smile.

"Of course he did," I said.

"Léon." Another particularly vicious tug on my sleeve forced my attention to Emeline. "Léon, you're going to play with me."

I frowned. "I am?" Was I supposed to take orders from a six-year-old now?

She giggled and handed me a carved wooden horse, the surface smooth from years of use. "You get to be the donkey."

If I ignored her, she would just persist. Or worse, start crying. At this point indulging her was easier. And the little tattletales would be sure to tell Anwen if I wasn't a very good playmate. I squinted at the toy, its planes and angles familiar under my fingertips. A name floated just out of reach in the mist of memory.

"Giles," I said. "Is this...?"

Giles harrumphed and wouldn't meet my eyes. "You weren't using it anymore," he said. "The baroness didn't let us throw anything away. They've been packed in the attic for years now, waiting for the next generation."

"The donkey was yours?" Emeline said, looking between me and the toy.

"It's not a donkey," I said, taking it from her. "It's a warhorse."

Her mouth twisted skeptically. "I think she's Daisy the donkey."

My brows came down in a frown. "He's a boy. And his name is Thunder." I turned to the other sensible male on the floor. "Right, Josselin?"

"Thunder is a better name for a warhorse," Josselin answered solemnly. "Much better than Daisy. Can't the doll Anwen gave you be called Daisy?"

"No." Emeline's face scrunched with distress. "She said her name was Mari. It's important."

I rubbed my forehead. Anwen had better appreciate my sacrifices when she got back. "Why?" I said.

"Because that was Anwen's mama's name."

And she'd had to leave her mother when she was no older than Emeline. Who else would recognize the importance of that connection than another orphan?

Josselin and I rushed to assure Emeline that the doll could remain Mari.

It took nearly an hour but I managed to negotiate a truce.

In the end, Mari the doll rode the warhorse Thundering Daisies and everyone was happy.

"Ignoring the way the public fears us will only lead to more problems in the future," the patriarche of the Gerard Family said, his deep voice rang around the council chamber.

"Fear of power is natural." Patriarche Cullen de Fay's red hair and beard were a blazing beacon in the center of the circle. "Our abilities are a gift from the Almighty. We are set apart. Of course they fear us."

"And you don't see that as a problem?" Matrona Lilly de Gerard threw up her hands.

Anwen sighed and dropped her chin to rest on the palm of her hand. It wasn't that she disagreed with the elders arguing against Patriarche Cullen. It was just that they'd been at it for hours already. Her rear end ached and her bad leg was minutes away from declaring mutiny against the bench she'd appropriated.

She let her gaze wander from the figures below. Since enchanters had no common home of their own except the Refuges, the King had let them borrow the council chamber while they were in the capital for the Moot.

Anwen tried not to gawk like the peasant she'd been, but she couldn't imagine living in such splendor every day.

Twelve huge armchairs with clawed feet and indigo and silver upholstery which normally supported the ruling dukes sat in a circle on the parquet floor. The Family elders sat there now, and Anwen spotted Patriarche Justin's bald head among them. He still looked pale and his hands trembled as they gripped the armrests of his chair.

Patriarche Cullen caught her attention again as he waved his arms over his head, and Anwen tried to pick up the thread of the argument. It didn't really work.

"I don't believe this," Anwen whispered. She turned to Brann, but he crouched on the desk beside her, perfectly still, his eyes fixed on the figures debating below. The tip of his tail twitched anytime someone made a particularly sound argument.

"Brann?" she said.

"This is fascinating," he said as if he hadn't heard her comment.

"What do you mean? They're just talking."

He finally turned his face enough to pin her with a glance. "What did you expect?"

"Progress."

"Is this not how your kind makes progress?"

Maybe it was. But it seemed like a waste of time to Anwen. "They're stating the same argument over and over. Nothing new has been presented in—" She craned her neck to see the hourglass and chalkboard on the table in the center of the room. "Almighty save us, three hours." She slumped in her seat and glanced at Brann, who had turned back to the debate.

A chandelier doused in gold paint holding hundreds of candles hung over them, casting light on the enchanters gathered below. Every now and then it dripped wax, as though ticking away the wasted time.

"You're enjoying this?" she asked Brann.

"It's new," he said as if that explained everything.

Which, for him, it kind of did, since the Zevryn gobbled up new experiences the way she would devour a wheel of cheese if given half a chance. He would be taking his memories of this Moot back to his people, who would feed on them for years.

Anwen cast a quick glance around her to see if anyone else was as bored and disillusioned as she was.

Benches rose in circular tiers around the central space the elders had claimed, each one placed behind a polished desk.

Twenty or so enchanters had settled themselves on the bottom tier by their elders in hopes of being helpful or having the chance to speak, but most of the enfani brave enough to attend the Moot had scattered to the outer rings, their expressions ranging from glazed to bored to overwhelmed. Hundreds of blue wool cloaks lay draped on bench seats or over the desks, softening the effect of what had to be an entire forest's worth of wood paneling and furniture.

"I'm glad you're enjoying it," she said, careful to keep her voice quiet enough so none of the others around her could hear. "But this is all just wind in the forest."

He tilted his head. "What does that mean?"

"Lots of air moving around but when the storm's done nothing has changed."

"Unless a branch breaks."

"I—well, I guess it's not a perfect metaphor." She grinned to herself.

"Every civilization since the Vemiir Empire has had rules to govern it," one of the patriarchs said.

"And who would you have regulate us? The King and his

council?" Patriarche Cullen gestured to Master Victor of the Mystric Family, who sat in the first ring of benches with his hands folded and his eyes sharp. He had not said anything yet, but everyone knew he worked closely with the King and was here as a representative of the crown.

"They do not understand us or what it takes to gain and control our power." Cullen dismissed Master Victor with an airy wave.

"Someone must protect people who are being mistreated and misused by rogue enchanters," Matrona Lilly said. "Why not some kind of regulating body? Made up of enchanters who answer to a higher authority."

Anwen's eye caught a flash of candlelight gleaming from a blonde head halfway around the circle to her left. She stiffened in recognition when she saw Nivianne de Fay, but the other girl was studiously ignoring her.

Anwen followed suit. Even unintentional eye contact would be awkward since their Families were feuding.

Cullen scoffed and rolled his eyes. "How do we even know these rumors are true? No one has come forward to confirm there are enchanters using their power to punish the masses."

If that was his argument, Anwen could end this useless meeting right here. She clambered to her feet, anxious to take the opening before someone started talking again.

"I can confirm that," she said loud enough to reach the floor. She ignored the wide-eyed looks the other enfani gave her.

Cullen spun and all the elders followed, their eyes searching the tiers for the speaker.

"I've been working with a young man, a baron, who was transformed into a bear as punishment for his transgressions."

Cullen de Fay's eyes narrowed in recognition. "Anwen de Emrys. Shouldn't you be planning your wedding?"

Anwen felt the creeping flush of humiliation sting her cheeks, no doubt sending her scars into stark relief against the red.

"Now see here." Patriarche Justin de Emrys struggled to his feet, his face white but set in angry lines. "You have no right to discredit her just because your enfan—"

"Fine," Cullen snapped, jerking his chin at Justin. "Don't strain yourself. What did you want to say, Enfan de Emrys?"

Anwen unclenched her teeth. "Only that I have seen the destructive power of a rogue enchanter firsthand. I came to ask for help breaking Lord Beauregard's curse. His transformation is deeper than the surface. The magic binding him has already damaged one of us."

Cullen turned, cutting her off as effectively as if he'd slapped a hand over her mouth. "This is not a forum for off-topic discussion."

Matrona Lilly de Gerard studied Anwen. "Wait a moment, Cullen. This might be valid."

Justin stepped forward, face red in the candlelight. "She's right. I came up against this enchanter's work myself. I felt..." He swayed on his feet and tried to catch himself against the chair next to him. He missed his grab and toppled to the floor.

"Patriarche," Anwen called, her voice lost in the confusion of noise below.

"I'm all right," Patriarche Justin said as several other elders helped him to his feet. "I just...need a moment."

"You should be resting," Matrona Lilly said, draping Justin's arm over her shoulder. "Let me help you."

The two of them exited the chamber but not before Justin cast a look up into the crowd, searching for Anwen. She tried to catch his eye but they were gone before he saw her.

Cullen sneered at her as she stood helplessly above them. "Like I said. This is not the forum for your request. If you need help with your little problem, submit a formal petition through your elders and stop wasting our time."

Anwen let her knees give out, and she plopped back on the bench, teeth clenched tight on her own defense. Cullen de Fay obviously still hated her for her part in what had happened with Adrien. And Justin hadn't recovered enough to take the brunt of his spite.

"Well, that was...interesting," Brann said as the debate continued below.

Warmth gathered under her hand and she snatched it away from the desk in time to see glowing lines of orange fire sketched across the wood. Words formed in the grain of the table and she squinted to read them.

So how complicated is this curse? Is this like a puzzle for babies or could I win a medal if I help you?

"Who?" Brann said, craning his neck to read the missive.

Anwen's lips quirked. "Who else?" She recognized Myrddin's handwriting from long lessons where they'd passed notes just like this. Myrddin had always appreciated a complicated piece of casting. He'd spent hours when they were kids coming up with the most convoluted way to finish a lesson that Anwen had managed in five simple minutes.

She leaned to the side so she could see past the elders

across the chamber. In the row behind Master Victor a young man grinned at her, his long legs stretched out in front of him and his black hair carefully tousled. She was too far to see them from here, but she could imagine his strange blue eyes crinkling at her. When he was much younger, he'd beaten up every boy who'd dared to call them violet.

He twiddled his fingers at her in hello.

She swept her hand across the surface of the wood to wipe away the words and wrote out her own message. With a thought she directed them to the tabletop in front of the young man.

Are you crazy, Myrddin? What if Cullen catches us passing notes?

Relax, he's too in love with the sound of his own voice. There was a pause in the writing. *I thought maybe you didn't want to talk to me. I'm glad it's just your conscience getting the better of you. Wow, is that really how you spell that? Concian— Conscni— Consie—*

She wiped away that fatal sidebar before he could get stuck between vowels. *I didn't even see you down there until now. Aren't you supposed to be paying attention? So you can debrief the King later.* After years of practice and familiarity it only took her a moment to scribble the words, sending each letter even as she wrote them.

You think they let me utter a word to his majesty? Victor doesn't really trust me with anything important yet and I don't think his majesty even knows my name. I'm just a glorified secretary.

Sure you are, she wrote.

Would I be stupid enough to bluff a woman who knows all my secrets?

Yes.

Oh, all right. There is one project they're thinking of giving me. Something about a noble with complaints against him. The King is thinking about revoking his title.

See, you're important.

It's far less glamorous than it sounds. Your work in the mountains is much riskier. According to some people.

What do you mean?

Matrona Catrin contacted me almost a week ago asking me to intervene. She's worried you're in danger.

Anwen ground her teeth. Muck on overprotective family, she thought and then was glad she hadn't written it. Myrddin loved it when he could get her to swear.

I guess she really doesn't like the bear lord you're determined to help, he wrote when she didn't answer.

Funny, I didn't think it was any of her business. Or yours.

Still, I told her I would talk to you.

Her handwriting became spiky with haste and agitation. *I can take care of myself without all this interference and overprotective—*

Her words disappeared in a smear as if he'd wiped them away before she could finish.

Hellooo, read my words. They're only printed in fire right in front of you. I told her I would talk to you. I never said about what.

A grin threatened her thunderous expression. Her freire could out-slink a snake. *So you aren't going to try to talk me into leaving?*

Hell no. I know better than that. And well done, sora. I thought I was the only one with the talent and the inclination to make Matrona that livid. So what's up with this Léon of yours?

Anwen rolled her eyes even though she knew he couldn't see her. *He's not my Léon.*

Oh. A long pause. *Good, because Matrona was also on me about setting a date. For the wedding.*

She bit her lip and wiped the words from the table. Then sat, mind and heart empty.

The desk in front of her remained awkwardly blank and she didn't know what to fill it with. Hey, I know we're just friends but want to marry me anyway? That had already been said. And as kind as Myrddin had been about the whole thing, it still felt like she was taking advantage of him.

Look, he finally wrote. *I'm behind you completely if you want to go through with it. But I'd understand if you don't.*

She chewed her lip.

Anwen?

Is that a boy's way of saying I don't really want to marry you?

Across the room his shoulders jerked. *Just tell me what you want and I'll make it happen.*

Anwen couldn't help glancing at Nivianne de Fay. Myrddin had once been betrothed to her the same way Anwen had been betrothed to Adrien. Until Adrien had broken their engagement. Anwen hadn't been the only one hurt by his betrayal. She and Nivianne had been friends once but now the sight of the other girl made Anwen's stomach twist, since she reminded her of Adrien.

I don't want to get hurt again, she wrote.

All right. Then this is the best thing. It will keep us both from getting hurt.

Except the only one she was protecting was herself. And Myrddin, her sweet friend and freire, wanted to protect her too, so he didn't make it worse by pointing out the truth.

For what it's worth, Myrddin wrote. *After that whole thing with Adrien, I went over there and beat the muck out of him.*

Anwen gasped. *Myrddin, you didn't. Magic is not for our personal feuds.*

What makes you think I used magic? All I needed to kick his ass was a fist in that pretty face of his. He ran away crying.

It shouldn't make her feel better. That fierce spike of satisfaction proved she was a horrible person, but she couldn't keep from replaying that vivid image over and over in her head.

She tried to make her words look as nonchalant as possible. *You probably would have kicked his butt if he'd tried using magic, too.*

Myrddin's teeth flashed in a grin. *Most definitely. And I'll do the same thing to this Léon if he hurts you.*

Anwen sputtered, making the other enchanters around her turn to look. Her shoulders hunched and she leaned over the desk to hide her next message. *Myrddin, you—you ass! You said you weren't getting involved. I don't believe you.*

Yeah, well, we both know his type, don't we?

I can handle one spoiled lordling, thank you very much.

And when you're done handling him, send him on over.

To think I was actually going to ask you to help me with his curse.

His writing grew spiky with excitement. *You mean the complicated one? You can still ask me to help.*

Nope.

Aw, come on. I promise I won't lay a finger on the lordling.

I guess you should have thought of that before. No fiddly magical puzzles for you.

You're so mean. I'm telling.

CHAPTER ELEVEN

I stood at the door to the kitchen yard, staring out at the snow turned red in the light of the sunset. Behind me Giles showed Josselin how to trim the candle wicks so he could light them for the evening.

Slowly the jagged shadows of the trees at the forest's edge crept over the break in the wall and the light faded from red to purple.

Anwen still had not returned.

Worry churned and burned in my gut until it crept up my spine and into my heart. The heat washed down my limbs and a spasm made my fingers clench on the doorframe.

Just like when I'd stood in the kitchen with Anwen, the bear grasped and grabbed the back of my mind to drag me under. The wood under my fingers splintered as claws sprouted and hair thickened to fur along the back of my hand.

"What are you looking for?" Emeline asked at my elbow.

Horror gripped my insides, and I fought the beast back

with clenched teeth. Not here. I would not transform now when Anwen wasn't here to put me back together.

The bear retreated with a dissatisfied growl.

"Nothing," I told Emeline, as I flexed my human fingers against the marred wood of the doorframe. "Shouldn't you two be heading home? It's getting late."

Emeline looked at Josselin, who hunched his shoulders and glanced outside. "It's too late to go now," he said. "It's dark. Maybe we could stay here?"

Emeline's lips curved in a tentative smile.

I frowned. "Won't your guardian be worried?" What was I? An innkeeper?

"He doesn't care about us," Josselin said. "So long as we're back in the morning."

Had the boy planned it this way so I wouldn't have a choice? I couldn't send them back in the dark and the cold no matter how manipulative they were. What would Anwen think?

"Fine," I said. "Why don't you go pick out a room you like?" There were plenty of empty ones to choose from and I had something to do. I'd made the decision in that split second between Emeline's question and my answer, but that didn't make my resolve any less firm.

Emeline tilted her head. "Right now?"

"Yes, now." Anything to get them out of the way.

Josselin was already moving toward the hall, but Emeline still stared up at me. What would it take to get her to leave me alone for two seconds? Giles wasn't in sight anymore so I couldn't get his help.

"How about I come tell you a story once you've found a room?"

Her eyes lit up. "A story?"

"You can tell stories?" Josselin said.

"Why not?" It couldn't be that hard, could it?

"Does it have heroes in it? And princesses?"

"And battles and pirates?" Emeline put in.

"Yes, yes, all of that. Now go find yourself someplace to sleep." I needed them out of the kitchen. If you stood at the door, you could see the edge of the forest, and I didn't want any witnesses.

Emeline still hesitated. "Why aren't you coming with us?"

I bit back a sharp response. "There's something I have to do first," I said, striving for patience.

"What is it?"

"Something important. I'll be right there." Really, it wouldn't take long. Anwen had only left this morning, so the Moot couldn't be far.

"You promise?" Emeline said.

I shooed her with my hands. "Yes, yes. I promise. Now go."

She rolled her eyes and took off after her brother.

I turned toward the twilit kitchen yard. The shadows had turned a deep blue.

I stepped out into the snow.

"Where do you think you're going?" Giles's voice came from behind.

I turned to see him outlined in the doorway. "I have to find Anwen. She's late."

"My lord," Giles said. "You know what will happen. She explained it to you."

"Giles, she's the only thing keeping me human. The bear's too close to the surface already. If I stay here..." I held out my hands and hoped Giles would understand my desperation. "I have to find her."

Giles nodded, holding my eyes with his. "Very well, my lord."

"Make sure the children get home first thing in the morning. In case..."

"Yes, my lord." He hesitated before he added, "Godspeed."

I took a deep breath and threw back my shoulders before heading for the broken wall.

Three steps from the door the wind hit me, cold slicing through my insufficient doublet and shirt as if I wore nothing. I forced myself on. I hadn't thought to grab a cloak but the cold wouldn't matter once I crossed the wall.

I tried to stride through the gap with my shoulders and back straight, but my feet stopped the moment my skin tingled.

Muck, I was such a coward.

I needed Anwen's calm and Anwen's magic. All I had to do was step across to go find her. I could always step back.

My feet remained fixed.

Apparently, I wasn't doing a very good job of talking myself into this.

I braced my feet, pinched myself hard, then threw myself at the gap in the wall. I cleared it with a savage cry that twisted and deepened as fire surged under my skin.

I hung in the air, burning and morphing, for ages, but it could only have been moments. When I hit the ground at the edge of the forest, I was clothed in fur and claws and fangs.

And a wiggle of my butt told me the hated tail was back.

God Almighty, but that hurt. At least the transformation had been quicker this time. Leaving more time to find Anwen.

I blinked at the surrounding trees but my fuzzy vision didn't clear. I'd have to rely on my sense of smell. I circled the outer wall, nose to the ground like an overgrown bloodhound.

Outside the gate I caught a whiff of wet wool and lavender and the foreign musk that had to be Brann. Their footprints led straight down the road. That was to be expected and I set off to follow them, but as the manor fell out of sight, I lost the trail. Anwen's scent disappeared in a stretch of pristine snow.

As if they'd stepped into thin air.

I huffed and ranged to either side of the road searching for any trace of them. Had they gone into the woods here? Or had something carried her off?

My breath came faster. Where was she? I cast about in a panic trying to find some trace of her boots or Brann's paw. Almighty, I had lost her. No! I couldn't let her get away. I could still find her, I just had to try harder, dammit.

I snuffled, trying to pick up her scent, my big clumsy feet obliterating any trace of her that might have remained.

An unfamiliar emotion clogged my throat and fogged my eyes. Saints, why was my chest tight? I lifted a huge forearm and rubbed my face with my fur. Don't wipe your nose on your sleeve, my mother had always said. I laughed. It sounded like a growl. Or a sob.

No, no. I wasn't going to cry. I was angry. Yes, that was a good emotion. Why was I out here chasing Anwen? Why hadn't she stayed at home where she belonged? She could have broken my curse by now. Instead I was out here, traipsing around looking for a nonexistent trail in a forest as a bloody bear.

I growled again. Yes, that felt good. Much better than tears. I was angry. Angry at Anwen for getting into this mess. Angry at Brann for not getting her out of it. Angry at the witch who'd made me a bear in the first place. And angry at myself for not trusting Anwen. I'd come barging out here, impulsive and impatient, hoping she was just late, and that she hadn't decided I was a lost cause.

She was out here somewhere, and I was going to find her if I had to tear apart the forest to do it.

Snow crunched beneath the bear's feet. He plowed through the forest, the memory of her voice, her scent driving him. Bare branches snapped at his face. He ignored their sting. Anger churned in his gut and kept him going, wandering blindly.

A dark shape jumped from the bush behind him. He whipped around, snarling, claws outstretched. Ready to rend anything that came out of the dark.

Anwen stepped from the air onto the snow, colors swirling

around her. She paused, waiting for her equilibrium to return before moving.

Brann leaped down beside her, his fur standing on end as he plowed into a drift and sent white clumps flying everywhere. He spat slush from his mouth and sat up. "Never again," he said, voice raw and strained. "I don't care how fast it is, I'm walking next time."

Anwen's stomach rebelled, threatening to return her dinner, but long experience told her the vertigo and nausea would pass in a few moments as long as she stood still.

"I told you it would be bad."

He glared at her, bright blue eyes narrowed to dangerous slits. "No, you said 'unpleasant.' That was a Belarkin's Leap further than unpleasant."

"Who's Belarkin?"

"One of my ancestors. The story is he jumped from the tallest cliff in our Realm in order to kill himself."

"That's terrible."

Brann's grin widened. "Not really. He had so long to think about it on the way down, he changed his mind and his shape and flew away."

Anwen's stomach had settled and the world had stopped smearing around her, so she took a tentative step.

"I think I'd rather jump off a cliff than take your Hellways again, though," Brann said, pulling himself from the drift and shaking vigorously to rid his coat of snow.

Anwen raised her arm and turned so her cloak absorbed the moisture he flung into the air. "The Byways are one of our greater achievements of this age. It's a network of vytl gathered into lines and maintained by the combined efforts of all enchanters. If you want to travel to, say, the capital in a matter of hours instead of days, you step onto the line and let it—"

"Don't tell me how it works," he said. "I've just got my stomach settled."

Anwen's grin was crooked. "Probably better you don't know, then."

He scanned the area. "And where did it drop us?"

Anwen joined his perusal. Shadows stretched under the trees and the sky had turned a deep velvety blue, and the first stars sprang into being behind the shreds of a few clouds. "Um."

"You don't know?"

"The Byways aren't always exact. The idea is to get close enough to walk, not drop you on your doorstep."

"So which way to the bear lord's doorstep?"

Anwen pointed. "That way."

"Are you sure?"

"Léon lives on the hill. We just have to go up."

"Right, because walking in the snow wasn't bad enough."

Anwen didn't say anything. He could change into a bird to stay out of the snow, but he felt disloyal by making her walk by herself. In the end, she was the one who would suffer from the snow, but a cold and wet Brann was an annoyed Brann.

"I told you we should have stayed in Namerre for the night." A shiver rippled his pelt.

"And run the risk of bumping into another enchanter?" She made sure he could see her own shudder. "The Moot was awkward enough."

"Yes," he said thoughtfully. "I'm sorry they ignored your request."

She'd meant it was awkward every time someone mentioned her and Myrddin's wedding, but yes, the rest of it had been equally humiliating. "I should have pushed harder. None of the rest of them have seen what Justin and I have seen."

"They didn't believe Justin either. If they acknowledge there's a problem, then they have to do something about it," Brann said.

She didn't answer. Justin had tried, but he'd always been underestimated and undervalued. And now he was sick on top of it.

"They can't ignore the problem forever," she finally said. "Someone will have to do something about all the people who hate and fear us. Otherwise...otherwise I'm afraid our world is going to end."

"A bit dramatic don't you think?"

She rubbed her arms. "Emotional people are violent. Maybe the Zevryn are different. But I worry about what will happen if enchanters become so alien it's easier to think, 'Let's get rid of them' instead of, 'We have to live with them.' Think of how Fanny looked at me before she got used to the idea that I was an enchanter."

Brann gave her a rueful cat grin. "Catrin was right, you know. You do want to right all the world's wrongs yourself. And you can't stand it when your hands are tied."

She rolled her eyes. "So many of our problems are the result of misunderstandings between enchanters and normal people. But how do we fix it?"

He leaped from one drift to another. "Well, when someone does something you don't understand, you normally talk to them. Get them to explain themselves."

"So we have to explain enchanters to the entire human race. Sounds practical." She huffed a despairing laugh.

He shook his head. "I change my shape based on whim, do I sound like a practical being to you?"

"I guess that's my job," she said. She paused and peered up the road. "You'd think we'd be able to see some lights by —" She tripped over something low and solid. Her breath whooshed from her lungs when she hit the ground.

"Are you all right?" Brann said, rushing to her side.

Cold soaked through her tunic as she shuffled to get her feet under her. "I tripped over something. It's hard to see in the dark."

"Tripped over what?" He peered around her as she levered herself up out of the snow.

She leaned on his back to steady herself and felt him stiffen.

"Changer's mercy." Brann's voice shook and she turned to see what had spooked him. "No, don't look," he said.

But his warning came too late, and her eyes widened as she found the legs half buried in the snow at her feet.

"God Almighty," she breathed as her gaze traveled up the legs to find the rest of the body tumbled in a drift at the side of the road.

"Is he dead?" Brann asked in a small voice.

She called up a thread of vytl and a ball of light burst into being over her shoulder, casting a harsh yellow glow on the man's face frozen in surprise and the dark spots on the snow.

"Very," she said, answering his question.

Ragged slash marks marred the man's torso, staining his smock and the snow around him red. Anwen's fingers stole to her scarred cheek. For once she was glad she couldn't remember her own accident.

"Poor man," she said and gestured to the bow laying several feet from his outflung hand. "Looks like he was hunting. But whatever he was chasing got to him first."

"Anwen," Brann said quietly. "Those are claw marks." He spread his paw in the snow beside the man and flexed his claws. "And whatever it was is bigger than me."

Anwen shivered and glanced around the dark woods. "What could it be? And is it still around?"

His head whipped up. "Isn't it obvious? The only thing big enough around here is a bear."

Her head jerked. "He couldn't have."

"Why not? He's an arrogant lord trapped in a beast's body. I know better than anyone how instincts can overcome even the best intentions."

"It's not Léon," she said, a bite in her voice. "He wouldn't do something like this."

Brann snorted and turned away. "People aren't good just because you will them to be, Anwen. You're defending someone who doesn't deserve your mercy or your pity and yet you insist on giving him both."

Anwen slashed her hand through the air. "You have no right to make that judgment."

"And you do? You barely know him."

"Why are you so set against him?"

His jaw clenched, making a muscle jump under his fur.

"One animal recognizes another. I know he's hiding something."

"Like what?"

"What if he's playing you? What if he's acting decent because he knows you are the only one who can free him from the rest of the curse? He shows you the smooth and sleek outside so you'll stay and think he's worth saving, but inside he's thinking of new ways to trick you into liking him."

Anwen raised her chin. "That's absurd. I would help him no matter who he is, or what he's done. I promised him."

"He doesn't know you'll hold to that promise."

She threw up her hands. "I'm sorry you don't like him, but the evidence you're looking for isn't there." She gestured to the body. "It's winter. This man can't have been dead for more than an hour or two if scavengers haven't gotten to him yet. And Léon hasn't been a bear since we got here. We would know." She smiled in triumph and raised her chin, daring him to contradict her.

Something crashed through the bushes at the side of the road and a tree shook, sending snow falling in a sheet. A snuffling sound made Anwen jump and take a step back. Her hands came up, ready to defend herself against whatever was out there. Brann darted in front of her, hackles up and his lips peeled back in a snarl.

A huge shape staggered through the screening bushes and stood in the middle of the road, blinking at the light over Anwen's shoulder. A bear, brown and shaggy with sharp gold eyes, froze while its chest heaved and its breath came out in white plumes in the frosty air.

The eyes fixed on her and a small whine escaped its throat.

"Léon?" Anwen whispered.

The bear shuffled forward and butted its head against her chest, sagging there as if he had crossed the entire world to find her. She reached up and settled her hand in the thick fur that covered his huge skull.

He sighed.

"You were saying?" Brann said with an ironic tilt of his eyebrow.

CHAPTER TWELVE

Anwen's touch on my furry head restored my senses but the panic still simmered under the surface, making the night hazy and unfocused. I had no memory between startling the deer out of the bush and finding Anwen and Brann on the road.

Hopefully she hadn't noticed the way I'd run to her, the way I'd buried my head against her as if she were the light and warmth in the darkness. I shied away from that thought. One naive, scarred enchanter shouldn't mean that much to me.

I couldn't make sense of Anwen and Brann's murmurs through the haze in my mind, but they argued about something as they guided me home. Anwen limped on my right, her hand in my ruff to keep me on track. Brann stalked on my left and used his teeth anytime I strayed toward his side of the road. Even the bear recognized a formidable opponent and left Brann alone.

The fire that passed along my skin when we passed

through the gate was just as bad as the first time, but the fuzz in my mind softened the experience. Only the biting cold on my bare skin startled me into wakefulness as I fell face-first and naked into the snow.

My clothes hadn't made the transformation with me. I huddled over, hiding everything important while Anwen politely averted her eyes and Brann snickered.

Fortunately for me and my dignity, Giles stood with a cloak. He must have been waiting by the door. "What happened to your clothes, my lord?"

I shook my head. Something about the magic must have stolen them. Brann absorbed matter to change shape, but I was too exhausted to speculate why I couldn't make the damn things reappear.

"We'll have to think of a better solution if you're going to make a habit of this," he said as he threw the cloak over me. "You can't be making Mistress Anwen blush every time you shed your fur."

Forget about Anwen. The heat in my face threatened to set the kitchen yard ablaze.

"Come, my lord. You need your bed."

"No, Giles," Anwen said, keeping the manservant from helping me out of the snow. "We need some answers first."

Something in her voice made Giles straighten and glance at me apprehensively.

I struggled to concentrate. "What?" I managed.

"What were you doing out there?" Anwen asked, tone serious as a funeral.

I braced my hands on my knees to lever myself to my feet and wrapped the cloak around myself. If I'd had all my faculties, I would have prevaricated. I would have joked, "Oh, I missed the fur and the claws."

But exhaustion ate at my wits and the only thing that came out was the truth.

"You were gone," I said, shoulders sagging. "You vanished without a word of goodbye. I worried. And when you were late, I worried some more. I knew your Moot couldn't have been far so I left to find you."

She blinked those thrice-damned eyes at me. "Léon, we were in the capital."

It was my turn to blink. "Namerre? But that's days away. How—?" I bit off the question.

Magic, of course. No wonder people feared enchanters if they could cross half a country in a matter of hours, or maybe minutes. I was so stupid.

"Tell him," Brann said, a growl lurking under his words.

Anwen's eyes remained fixed on me. "Léon, we found a body. Do you remember?"

My brows contracted. "Someone was killed on my lands?"

"Torn limb from limb by some animal," Brann said.

My fingers curled around the edges of the cloak, the hair on the back of my neck stirring. If I'd had my fur, my hackles would have been standing up.

Was another predator prowling my territory? Hunting the people of the village? A growl rose in my chest and my thoughts lost their clear edges, becoming dark and jagged. The bear surged beneath it all, urging me to defend my own with tooth and claw. My fingers curled around the edges of the cloak.

"Any large predators you know of in the area?"

"Wolves, mountain lions. I've never fully run them off. A mistake I'll rectify immediately."

Brann jerked his chin. "I was thinking of something a little closer to home." His voice rose on the word "home" and he raised his paw to gesture at the manor.

Cold realization rushed through me, washing away the bear's instinctual responses. "You think I did it?"

"What happened tonight?" Anwen said, the gentleness in her voice grating on my fragile state of mind. "Did you see anything? Encounter anyone?"

"Kill anyone?" Brann said.

I shook my head, trying to ignore his censure. "I don't remember."

He rolled his eyes.

"I'm serious," I said. "I left the manor at sunset. I followed your trail a ways down the road until it disappeared. After that I..."

"You?" Anwen said.

"I panicked. The bear took over. Maybe there was a deer. I don't remember anything clearly until I saw you on the road."

Anwen dropped her gaze.

"Please, you have to believe me," I said. "I'm not a killer. I couldn't even hunt rabbits as a bear. I don't remember what happened, but I wouldn't have killed a man."

I tried to take a step toward her but whether it was two transformations in one day or the thought of another sort of monster roaming my lands, the world tilted and I pitched forward to my knees. As the kitchen yard fuzzed around me, I could imagine the edge of Anwen's cloak moving away. Retreating.

Don't let her leave me. Almighty, don't let her leave.

The angle of the light coming in my window was wrong. I didn't usually sleep this late. My head pounded and my limbs took too long to respond to simple commands like "stand up" and "grab your pants."

Anwen. Was Anwen still here? Or had she decided I was a killer and given up on me?

I rubbed my eyes and groaned. The last time I'd felt like this was the day after I'd been cursed. The first time I'd woken as the bear. Trapped in a sluggish body with a splitting headache and the aching joints, I'd panicked. The furniture, including my parents' antique bed frame, had been the first victims of my fear and pain.

At least this time I remembered enough to keep myself calm. I rolled over and took stock of my human limbs and skin, sighing in relief.

Voices came from the kitchen, urging me to rise, dress, and stagger down the stairs.

"If we want any hope of finding out what happened, we need to leave now," Brann's voice said.

"Go then," Anwen said. "I'm not leaving without talking to Léon. Not after what he said last night."

Thank the Almighty, I thought as relief swept through me. She was still here. She hadn't left me. At least not yet.

"Anwen," I said as I stepped into the kitchen.

"Léon." Anwen turned, the scar making her smile of greeting look strained. "You're awake."

"Finally," Brann muttered. "You know it's rude to sleep past noon."

I ignored him and glanced at Giles who stacked plates on the sideboard. "Josselin and Emeline?" I said.

"They left just after breakfast," he said. "Mistress Anwen saw them off before waiting here."

"We're going out to find the body," she said. "See if the daylight reveals anything we missed last night. But I wanted to wait until you were awake."

So I wouldn't wake up to an empty manor again. I had a vague memory of mumbling to myself as I'd passed out last night. Almighty, don't let me have said anything out loud. Maybe it would be better if the bear took my mind and drove me from my home. It would be less embarrassing.

"If we want to find anything, we'd better leave," Brann muttered. "Scavengers have probably gotten to it by now."

Anwen shook her head. "I wish I'd thought to place a shield around the area to keep other animals away. But I was...distracted."

By getting me home. I flushed. And I hadn't even smelled the dead man frozen to the road when I'd come across them the night before. I'd been so wrapped up in Anwen's presence.

"Let me come with you," I said, moving to grab a cloak from the rack by the door.

"I don't think that's a good idea."

"Why not? I can help. These are my lands. If there's someone out there killing people, I should be the one to do something about it." Two weeks ago, I wouldn't have cared. I'd have holed myself up in my sanctuary and hoped whatever it was left me alone, not caring about the village or the hunters who lived in pockets in the mountains of the barony.

But when I thought of leaving all those people to fend for themselves, an image of Anwen's reproachful gaze spurred me to action.

She was shaking her head. "Léon, you're not coming. I can't keep you human and..."

And they couldn't trust me as the bear. Almighty, she really did think I killed that man. And she should.

I swallowed and turned away. I was perfectly capable of hurting someone.

I'd done it before.

"We'll be back before dark," she said.

A commotion at the door announced the arrival of Josselin and Emeline. They couldn't have been home for more than an hour before turning around and coming right back here.

"Léon!" Emeline flung herself at me. "You promised you'd be back. You promised us a story, but Giles said you'd gone." She glared up at me but kept her arms wrapped around my legs.

I glanced at Anwen. If she really thought I was a killer she would send them away to keep them safe.

She bit her lip but finally turned to Brann who waited at the door, leaving us alone.

Josselin stood back with his arms crossed and his eyes narrowed. He wore a long hat that drooped across his forehead, hiding half of his face, but I could still see his scowl. "He broke his promise."

"I know," I said, strangely relieved Anwen hadn't warned them away. I should have wanted them gone, but for once Emeline's hug felt good. "I'm sorry. I had something I had to do last night."

Emeline's brow wrinkled. "Was it important?"

I glanced out the open door to watch Anwen disappearing with Brann. "Yes," I said. "Very. But I'm going to make it up to you."

"How?" Josselin said, his shoulders relaxing. But his arms remained crossed.

What did I have that I could give them? I'd already given up my sanctuary and my time. But Josselin's distrust and Emeline's hurt ate at me until I found myself opening my mouth and offering the one thing I owned that would be special enough to regain their good opinion. "Have you ever heard the story about Leonides?"

"No." He drew the word out as if he wasn't sure that was worth giving up his anger for.

"Wait till I show you the pictures."

I turned to shoo Josselin toward the chapel. Then I neatly extracted Emeline from my middle and closed the door.

She'd said she was coming back. I had to believe that.

"And Leonides swooped down from the dragon's back and struck off the sea monster's head," I read in the hushed silence of the chapel. "The head landed at the chieftain's feet and he cried out with joy and declared Leonides a hero. Leonides leaped onto the rock that held Yasmina, and he broke the bonds on her wrists and ankles. She looked up at him with love in her eyes and claimed him as her husband. He hoisted her into his arms and carried her into the village where they were married."

The afternoon light filtered through the chapel windows as I turned the leather-bound manuscript carefully so Josselin and Emeline could see the illumination of the dragon and the golden-haired hero rescuing his heroine on the next page.

After a brief lecture they'd been very good about looking at but not touching the delicate paintings. Emeline even sat on her hands in case she was tempted to stroke the scarlet scales of the wyrm.

"Is that you?" she asked in a hushed voice, nodding to the last page where Leonides stood with his arms around the dark-haired Yasmina. The princess's face was an amalgam of all my immature ideals and fantasies, but Leonides's features bore an embarrassing resemblance to me. I'd only been thirteen and a little obsessed with the story when Brother Warren had helped me illuminate the manuscript.

"I'm named after him," I said, hoping she wouldn't ask any more awkward questions.

"Did Leonides really do all those things?" Josselin leaned closer to peer at the hero in his leather armor, his sword a slash of silver paint at his waist. It was the first time today he'd forgotten himself enough to get close to me. He'd spent the whole story angled away.

"Supposedly," I said, reluctantly closing the book and stroking the cover. "It was a very long time ago when the

Vemiir Empire still existed, so most of the details are probably made up. But there really was a man named Leonides and he did great things."

"I liked Yasmina," Emeline said. "She was my favorite."

"Of course she was," Josselin said, rolling his eyes. "You're a girl."

"That doesn't mean anything. I liked her 'cause she was the best. Wasn't she the best, Anwen?"

I whipped around on my bench to find Anwen standing in the doorway of the chapel watching us.

"I'm sorry," she said, limping into the room. "I didn't hear the story. Maybe Léon will read it to me some other time."

I flushed and tucked the manuscript under my arm. If Emeline had been perceptive enough to see me in Leonides, I was terrified to think what Anwen would read into it when she saw my interpretation of the story.

Her eyes darted to the leather-bound parchment in my grasp. "Giles says you're very careful about who gets to see that manuscript," she said as the children continued their argument across from us.

"Yes, well, I did break a promise," I said. "I figured they deserved something special."

She opened her mouth again, but I interrupted before she could ask me to show her my heart and soul.

"What did you find?"

Her eyes searched my face before she sighed and turned away. "Nothing," she said and gestured for me to follow her. We moved into the doorway out of earshot of the children.

"I'm not—I haven't had a lot of practice with dead bodies," she said. "We met the magistrate and had him take the victim back to town for burial, but he didn't have any more insight than us."

"So we have a phantom killer," I said. "Something that can murder and disappear back into the woods."

She didn't answer me right away. "Léon," she said. "Why did the enchanter turn you into a bear?"

My mouth went dry and my stomach clenched in a cold, hard knot. I couldn't help rocking back from her.

She noticed my reaction and looked away. "I've been meaning to ask, but I wanted to give you some time to adjust. Now..."

"Now you need to know if I was violent." It made sense, with bodies showing up in the snow around my sanctuary.

Her lips thinned. "I'm glad you understand."

I'd been expecting the question for a while, and I had my answer prepared. If I played the part well enough, she wouldn't have to look any deeper. She wouldn't have to know the truth.

I gripped my hands together and met her eyes. "I was rude to the wrong person."

"Rude?" she said. "To an enchanter?"

It wasn't even a lie. More like half a lie. "You have to remember I was fifteen. I know now it was a mistake." A mistake that grew harder and harder to live with every day. Might have had something to do with the victim who wouldn't stop trying to redeem me.

"That's all?" Her brows drew down. "They condemned you to a slow death for something so trivial?"

"Why does that bother you so much?" I said with a glare. "This morning you believed I was a murderer."

She planted her fists on her hips. "I haven't decided what I believe yet. But even a murderer deserves a chance for redemption."

Faced with her idealistic conviction the lie struggled in my chest. "Maybe I did deserve my curse," I said. "I wasn't nice, Anwen."

Finally, she gave me her lopsided smile and it felt like spring had come early. "Yes, but why would you tell me that if you didn't have at least a little nice in you?"

Because when I looked into her eyes, I wanted her to know the truth as much as I needed to hide it. I swallowed hard and clamped my teeth shut before I lost control of myself.

"Where's Brann?" I said, deliberately changing the subject. Her constant fluffy shadow was nowhere to be seen.

"He insisted on staying out to search some more. I think he's hoping to catch a rabbit."

I scowled. "To prove he's a better hunter than me?"

"He is rather competitive." She studied me through her lashes. "I thought most noblemen were hunters."

I looked away from her scars. "I used to be."

Giles appeared at the end of the hallway and approached the door of the chapel. "Excuse me, my lord. I thought perhaps the children would like supper before they head home."

Josselin and Emeline had been sitting on the floor debating the merits of princesses versus heroes but they bounced to their feet as soon as I called them. Anwen stepped aside to let them through.

I caught her arm. "I'm not a killer, Anwen," I said quietly.

She paused, looking down at my hand. "I want to believe you," she said. But the sad smile she cast over her shoulder as she left said she didn't, yet.

Emeline watched as Anwen left with Josselin and Giles before she came back to take my hand and haul me away from the door.

"What were you talking about?" she said. "You look funny."

"Monsters," I said, wondering how much a little girl could pick up on.

"Josselin says you could be a monster."

I winced. "And what do you believe?"

"If you are, you're not the kind of monster that hurts people."

That knocked the wind out of me. "Is there another kind of monster?" I said.

"You let us play where it's safe." She snuggled against my arm. "You're the kind of monster that protects people from the bad monsters."

CHAPTER THIRTEEN

In the door of the kitchen Emeline raced past me to sit beside Anwen at the fire. But Josselin walked at a more sedate pace, the late afternoon sun coming through the window and lighting up the side of his face. He'd taken off his floppy cap.

Without thinking, I reached out and took his arm, stopping him in the middle of the room. My fingers reached for his chin and he flinched away.

I wasn't surprised. Given the bruise spreading across his cheekbone, he was used to blows, not curious fingers.

"What happened?" I said.

Anwen heard the anger in my voice and looked up.

Josselin pulled his arm from my grasp and mumbled something that ended with, "Our guardian."

My jaw clenched. "He wasn't happy when you didn't come home last night."

Emeline waited at the hearth, eyes wide.

Josselin shrugged. "It's not the first time," he said. "Georg hits when we're too slow fetching his tools at the forge."

My lips twisted as the rush of my blood raised the hair along my arms. Georg. The blacksmith who made it his job to run me out of town anytime he saw me anywhere close. No wonder he'd told the children there was a monster in the woods.

"That anvil-faced louse is your guardian?" I said.

"He took us in when our da died last year." Josselin glanced up at me, then away. "It's okay, so long as he doesn't hit Emmy."

How many times had he put himself in the way of the man's fists in order to protect his sister?

Underneath my skin the bear lurched awake and clawed my insides, wanting out. He wanted to tear. He wanted to rend.

Josselin stepped toward Giles, face turned away, leaving my fingers clenching on empty air. I felt Anwen's gaze on me, her eyes taking in the struggle written across my face, but she waited.

I took a deep breath, focusing on calm, nonviolent images. A paintbrush between my fingertips, smooth strokes with thick paint. There was nothing I could do for Josselin right now, except maintain my humanity.

The bear grumbled and fidgeted, like a dog circling his bed before sleep. Then he sank down beneath my thoughts and I breathed freely.

Across the way, Anwen nodded once and turned back to Emeline. She braced a poker between her feet and speared a piece of bread on the end. A chunk of cheese followed it and finally she held the whole thing over the glowing coals.

I took a moment to uncurl my clenched fingers and make sure my face remained quiet if not serene before I stepped across the kitchen to join them. I needed a distraction, something normal and boring. If I thought too hard about Josselin, I'd get angry again and who knew if I could contain the bear twice in so little time.

"What are you doing?" I asked Anwen.

She glanced up at me, her expression carefully neutral, but there was a shadow behind her soft eyes, as if she saw the shape of a killer instead of me.

"Making toast," Emeline said, beaming.

A smoky savory smell wafted up from the hearth as the cheese pierced on the end of her poker started to turn brown. Anwen pulled the whole thing away from the coals and deftly smeared the cheese over the bread with her knife.

"Here." She held the hunk of bread out to me and raised her eyebrows.

I found myself flushing for no reason.

Muck, I must have stopped too near the fire. I shook my head. "That's yours."

Her eyes smiled at me, even if her mouth didn't. "Then I guess you'll have to make one for me next."

How could she tease me when she thought I'd murdered someone the night before? Maybe that was just part of the magic of Anwen. She believed the best in people despite the evidence.

"All right, fine." I held out my hand for the poker and sat myself beside her. "Although I'm not a very good cook."

"I want one, too," Emeline said.

Anwen folded her hands politely in her lap as I shoved a piece of bread down the point and speared some cheese on the end. I thrust it over the fire and watched the flames lick up and catch the bread until suddenly I was holding a flaming firebrand.

"Hey!" I said and tried to blow out the fire.

Anwen burst out laughing and nearly fell off her stool.

I shook the poker, thinking that might extinguish the flames, but I only succeeded in flinging burnt bits of cheese into the coals, where they smoked and stank. Finally, I stomped on the flames to put them out.

I stared at the blackened chunks that smoldered on the poker.

"I don't want that one," Emeline said, her light brows lowered in consternation.

Giles raised his attention from the table and sniffed. "What's burning?"

"My pride," I said.

"Here," Emeline said, holding out an imperious hand for the poker. "I'll show you."

I handed it over without argument and the little girl deftly speared a piece of bread and a hunk of cheese and held them over the flames.

Anwen rubbed her mouth but I could still see the hint of her grin behind her hand.

"So I'm a terrible cook," I said.

"That's all right," she said. "I can teach you."

"I look forward to it, lady."

"What are you talking about?" Emeline said, looking up from the fire. "She was showing you right now."

"That's called flirting," Giles said, walking behind us.

I sputtered and choked. "Giles! That's not—" I turned to Anwen. "I promise, I wasn't—" I shut up before I could lie outright. That's exactly what I was doing, but you weren't supposed to point it out. It ruined the effect.

Anwen sat back with a placid look, completely untouched by the awkwardness.

"That's good," she said. "Because technically I'm betrothed."

It was a second before I realized my mouth hung open. Betrothed? She was getting married? To who? And why the hell did that thought make my stomach twist?

I forced my lips into something just short of a grimace. "And who's the lucky man?"

She smiled at her hands. "Myrddin."

I didn't like that smile. "Myrddin, your brother?" Myrddin the floater of boots?

"Freire is more of a title. We're not really related."

I covered my confusion with the only thing I was really good at: more flirting. "So I still have a chance."

"What?" she said, looking up at me with wide eyes.

"You're only technically betrothed."

She gave me a less than graceful look out of the corner of her eye. "I meant really betrothed."

"But you said 'technically.'"

"Léon," she said, her tone warning me to back off.

"Well, if you love him..." I said and shrugged.

But instead of beaming and telling me exactly how great

he was, she avoided my eyes, her cheeks turning pink under her scars.

"Our relationship isn't really like that."

"Like what? You don't love him?" I held my breath.

She threw me an exasperated look. "We're best friends."

"But?"

"But our arrangement is just that. An arrangement."

"Then why?" Did enchanters arrange marriages like nobles?

She hesitated, and I thought she would refuse to tell me, but then she spoke. "I was...betrothed once before. It didn't go well. Myrddin suggested this and I agreed it was the best thing."

More didn't seem to be forthcoming and I chewed my lip, thinking up my response.

"So I do still have a chance," I said with a grin. In all the charm I'd piled on her, in all the flirting and manipulation, this was the truest thing I'd said to her.

She sighed. "Léon—"

At my feet, Emeline shrieked and I leapt forward, grabbing the poker from her. But my clumsy hands fumbled the tool and I only managed to throw it back into the fire. I whirled and took the little girl's hands, looking for burns.

"What happened?" I said. "Did you hurt yourself?"

Emeline sniffled. "No. I dropped cheese on my smock."

A messy yellow-black smudge had smeared her garment.

"That's all?" I said as my heart rate returned to normal.

"It's ruined," she said, just this side of a wail.

"It's all right, Emmy," Josselin said. "It's just cheese. It'll wash out."

"I broke through the ice on the well in the kitchen yard this afternoon," Giles said. "Should still be clear."

"Think you can take your sister out and get her cleaned up?" I asked Josselin.

He nodded and took Emeline's hand to lead her into the kitchen yard.

The sun threw orange and pink streaks through the door, heralding twilight. They'd have to hurry if they were going to get home before dark. I couldn't keep them late again if Georg was going to punish them for it.

Anwen watched as I sat back down, a smirk playing on her lips.

"What?" I said.

"Nothing." She glanced away, lips pressed together in secret mirth.

Was this how she looked at every possible murderer she encountered?

"Are all enchanters as nice as you?" I said without thinking.

She turned back to me, with a sober look. "You should know better than anyone that some are not."

I shook my head, not because she was wrong, but because I'd only been thinking of her in that moment. I hadn't even thought about her matrona or the day I'd changed both our lives forever.

"We're just people," she said. "Some good. Some bad. I've been trying to figure out how to explain that to the world. So enchanters won't be so feared."

I blinked.

She laughed. "I know it's silly. Little Anwen de Emrys trying to fix everything again."

That last part sounded like a quote, and I wondered who had mocked her that way in the past. Could it have been Myrddin the freire? And could I punch him for it?

"It's not silly. It's brilliant."

Her eyebrows went up and I kicked myself for my vehemence. But I couldn't stand the way she'd said that. As if her compassion was something to make fun of when it had been my salvation.

"I mean—It's going to be hard. And you're never going to reach everyone. And some people won't believe you no matter how you explain things to them, but is that a good reason not to try?"

"But try what?" she said, tilting her head. "I can't just stand on a street corner preaching the virtues of enchanters."

"I...don't know." I shrugged sheepishly. "I'm partial to painting. And that's not all that helpful."

She sat up, eyes shining. "Not painting. Writing. Like that book you won't show me."

I snapped my fingers. "Yes, I mean, no. I mean of course you can see it. But you could write a history—"

"Of the enchanters. Where we come from—"

"How you're trained. What you believe."

"I can write about what's happening now. So people in the future can understand what's going on."

"You'll be a chronicler."

"And you can help."

"Wait, what?" I pulled myself back from the enormity of the idea. Writing history.

"You can teach me how to make books. Like yours. I can write, but I don't know the first thing about parchment or binding. Or illumination."

My jaw clenched. "You know I can't do that anymore."

She crossed her arms. "Have you tried?"

I gestured to the plates on the table. "I don't have to. You've seen how I am with a fork."

"Do you have to be that precise?"

"I told you before. If it's going to be my Pledge, it needs to be perfect."

She crossed her arms. "Says who? Who are you painting for, Léon? You or the Almighty?"

"I—" I stopped. Brother Warren had shown me that I was closest to the Almighty when I was doing something I loved. Creating beauty. If the perfectionist in me said it wasn't worth it if it wasn't perfect, I was punishing the Almighty as much as I was punishing myself.

I opened my mouth to reply but Emeline's scream tore through the open door.

I bolted from my chair, leaving Anwen struggling to her feet behind me. The kitchen door crashed into the wall as I sped past, and I skidded to a stop in the snow.

Georg, the blacksmith, backhanded Josselin, who fell to the ground. But the boy scrambled to his feet and launched himself at the tall man again, yelling incoherently.

"Hey!" I said as Georg brought his fist back again. "What the hell do you think you're doing?" The bear rose up and simmered just under my skin, making my lips pull back from my teeth and a growl gather in the back of my throat.

The blacksmith stopped and peered at me, eyes narrowed under the black fringe of his hair, ragged from years of scorching at the forge. His broad hand clenched Josselin's arm and he swung the boy around as he straightened to face me.

"Who're you?" he said.

"He's the lord of Whitecliff," Josselin said. Blood ran from his nose, but he still struggled against the blacksmith's grip. "And he can send you to jail for what you did to Emmy. He'll send you to the King. And the King'll cut off your head."

I doubted the King would care what I had to say if I was saying it as a bear, but Josselin's confidence touched me.

Georg eyed me up and down. "You're the baron, eh? Skinny bugger, aren't you?"

I turned from him to the boy. "Josselin, where's Emeline?"

The boy rubbed at his nose with his free hand. "I told her to run and she did."

A glance told me little footprints disappeared over the broken wall into the forest.

Georg gave Josselin a strong shake so his head snapped back. "And you'll get to find her before I let you back into my home. I've lost enough work tracking you down. You'll spend all night in those woods if you have to."

I wanted to rush forward and snatch the boy from Georg's cursed hands, but the man was half a foot taller than

I was. He might not have been bulky, but he had spent years wielding a hammer.

"Take your hands off him," I said in my best baron voice.

His free fist clenched, and I couldn't help wondering what it would be like to have my nose broken.

"You can't tell me what to do with my own brats." He glanced behind me. "Neither can you, mistress. So just keep your magic to yourself."

I glanced back at Anwen who stood in the doorway, her brows drawn and lips tight. "As much as I hate to agree with him, Léon..."

She couldn't use magic to separate a man from his rightful ward. If she did, she'd be as bad as the enchanter who'd transformed me. Worse even, since the law was on his side.

I turned back to the blacksmith and raised my chin. "Beating them takes away any right or responsibility you have to them."

He pointed a thick finger at me. "You talk about responsibility when you've been shirking your own? Where've you been for years when we've been defending your land from monsters?"

The setting sun cast sharp, accusing shadows across the man's face.

I swallowed. "I was away. But I'm back now. Things are going to be different."

He drew himself up and laughed at me. "You're gonna start with interfering in how I run my house? The kids belong to me."

My jaw ached as I clenched it, and I shook with more

than cold, but I could do next to nothing against him. My education had included boxing and sword work, but I'd never had a chance to use either against another person before.

And of course, Brann was gone when I needed another large predator to back me. Stupid cat.

I couldn't back down, though. Not with Josselin and Emeline's safety in the balance. If things were going to be different, it had to start here.

"They don't belong to you. Not anymore," I said. "I—I'm confiscating them from you. As Lord Beauregard of White-cliff I relieve you of your rights to see them."

He blinked and his grip loosened enough for Josselin to stomp on his instep and wrench his arm free.

Josselin ran back toward the manor, and Georg lurched after him. I jumped between them. Georg yelled and planted his fist in my gut. Pain exploded in my belly, and I doubled up, gasping. The bear reared up, demanding violence. I was happy to oblige him, so I growled and launched myself at the man. Georg outweighed me and knew it, but the move caught him by surprise and he stumbled back. I followed, my feet slipping in the slush beneath us.

The broken wall hit him in the back of the knees, and he tumbled over it, dragging me with him.

A fiery ripple passed over me, making me yell. My skin stretched and split, my bones cracked, and my joints shifted.

I landed on my face in the snow, then surged to my feet and roared.

Georg scrambled back with his hands, his eyes round, seeing a bear where a skinny lord had been a moment before. I shook the slush from my shaggy fur and loomed over him, my lips drawing back in a snarl that revealed my impressive set of teeth.

I wished I could talk, so I could say something heroic and fitting. Like "Never darken my doorway again" or "Eat snow."

Probably better that I couldn't if that was the best I could do.

My low menacing growl still got the point across.

"Léon." Anwen didn't have to raise her voice. Her tone told me to be careful. I had teeth and claws and the temper to use both against the man in front of me.

But that was a luxury I couldn't afford with the suspicion already hanging over my head.

I let my displeasure rumble through my chest one more time before I stepped back and jerked my head at Georg. I might not have had words, but the gesture was clear enough.

Get out. Before I eat you.

Georg lurched to his feet, his breath coming in white puffs between his pale lips. I watched with satisfaction as he darted away through the trees, snow flying behind him from his haste.

I turned back, my chuckle coming out as a grunt. Anwen stood on the other side of the wall with Giles, holding out a cloak to me. Despite my victory, her brow furrowed in concern.

"Come back now, Léon," she said, voice tight.

I stepped toward her and stopped.

Tiny footprints dashed away into the darkening shadows under the snow-laden branches, disappearing from my blurry sight far too quickly.

Emeline.

She'd run into the forest where Georg couldn't find her. Where it was cold and dark and she didn't know her way home.

Where someone or something was murdering people.

"Léon?" Anwen said.

I shook my head and refused to step across the boundary. I could explain myself better as a human, but I would lose precious time and energy.

Anwen stepped up to the wall and reached across to sink her fingers into my ruff. My big body shivered. Could she feel my reaction to her touch? Almighty, please let her think I was cold.

"Léon?" Her inquisitive voice swept across me like a caress, and I turned my head to meet her green flecked eyes.

I grunted and jerked my head at the small footprints that stretched out into the forest.

"You want to find Emeline?" she said.

I nodded.

"I don't think you should be out there alone. Not as a bear."

I jerked away from her touch. How could she waste time worrying about me when a real killer could be stalking Emeline?

I stepped out of her reach and turned, ready to stalk into the forest, whether she wanted me to or not. She was just one young woman. She couldn't stop me.

"Just..." she started behind me. "Just be careful."

I snorted. I weighed hundreds of pounds and carried a full set of claws and teeth. What could hurt me?

"As soon as Brann gets back, I'll send him out after you. He'll help."

For anything else I'd have insisted the cat stay away, but for Emeline's sake I'd accept help even from Brann.

I turned to go, and as I did I caught a glimpse of Josselin and my heart sank. He stared at me with wide eyes in a face pale with fear.

My throat bobbed as I swallowed. He'd never really seen Léon the monster before today.

I tried to smile, to reassure him, but the bear's mouth didn't cooperate. Josselin gasped and stumbled back into the kitchen.

I just kept myself from going after him. This wasn't something I could fix. Not like this.

Anwen's lips thinned, and she crossed her arms over her chest as I turned my back on them and headed into the forest.

CHAPTER FOURTEEN

I left a trail of craters in the snow as I followed the small footprints carefully between the trees. My nostrils flared and grim satisfaction washed through me when I caught a trace of burnt cheese. At least I was on the right track.

The last streaks of orange and pink disappeared between the trees and the trunks threw blue and purple shadows across the snow. The bear's sense of smell outstripped my human nose, but I still wouldn't be able to follow Emeline's trail through the trees on scent alone. I had to be able to see her footprints. I quickened my pace, racing the shadows.

The tracks led up the mountain, away from both the manor and Whitecliff. I'd been walking for a good twenty minutes when I realized the prints in the snow were getting closer together and more scuffed. Emeline had dragged her feet when she made these. My own legs were starting to burn from the constant uphill climb.

I scoured each bush and mound of snow, searching for signs of the little girl.

A soft whumphing noise made me stop in my tracks and prick my ears. Then I shook my head.

Just snow falling from a branch. I moved on.

A darker shadow flicked between the trees on my left.

I skidded to a stop again, my head swinging to face the mystery.

Nothing moved in the empty space between the trunks.

Almighty take you for a fool, Léon. You're literally jumping at shadows.

I started moving again, but the skin along the back of my neck and spine prickled as if I was being watched. My hackles rose, and I moved faster.

The bear shivered beneath the surface of my skin.

He writhed and scratched at the inside of my mind, grumbling and fighting. I gasped and my vision smeared until the shadows ran together into one thick darkness. I shook my head and growled back at him.

He surged and I fell to my hairy knees and forearms. It would be so easy to let him take over so he could run or defend us from the creeping panic. But I knew my eyes played tricks on me, taking the shadows and twisting them.

And the bear couldn't rescue Emeline. Only I could.

I shut my eyes and called up thoughts that would remind me of humanity. The feel of Anwen's hand on my shoulder. The scent of bread and stew and burnt cheese. Answered prayers and eternal hope.

It felt like hours before I was able to raise my head and draw in a shuddering breath, but the length of the shadows beneath the trees said it had only been minutes. I shook my great head and moved on.

Emeline's footprints grew more indistinct and the dark covered the last of her trail, but up the hill I caught a glimpse of a crumbling stone wall and I sighed in relief.

Even a little girl of six would have recognized shelter in the rambling ruins.

I surged forward on a burst of energy, approaching the cluster of tumbling walls and fallen towers.

Hundreds of years ago the Vemiir Empire had collapsed violently in the three months of darkness no one could explain. As a child, the idea of a ruined Empire intrigued me and I'd begged Giles for stories about the way they'd built their entire civilization on magic, and when the Darkness had taken magic for those three months, the entire empire had crumbled.

As a child I'd clambered over these walls pretending I was Leonides battling the sea monster, so I knew all the best hiding spots.

Still, I almost missed the small form huddled in the remains of the octagonal tower that had once housed Vemiir troops.

A small gasp arrested me, and my head snapped around to find a red splotched face staring up into my furry one. Her gold curls fell in a tangled clump along the side of her tear-streaked face.

I held my breath, waiting for her reaction. Waiting for the scream, waiting for the terror.

Neither came.

"Léon," Emeline breathed before she flung herself at me.

Her arms closed around my neck, her fingers gripping my fur as she sobbed in relief.

My heart swelled. She recognized me even covered in fur and claws, and she wasn't afraid. Suddenly I knew what Leonides must have felt rescuing the seaside village.

She whispered my name over and over again, her small high voice echoing responsibility in my ear. Her violent shivers vibrated against my fur, and she looked up long enough to reveal a split bottom lip.

I held in a growl. No wonder Josselin had attacked a man three times his size. I wished now I hadn't let Georg off so easy.

"Léon, I was scared," she said into the fur on my chest. Her teeth chattered, fracturing her words. "Josselin said to run and I did, but I didn't know where to go and then I didn't know where I was or how to find home."

She burrowed further into my broad chest and clutched my fur between her white knuckled fingers. I made soothing noises against the top of her bright head as I thought to myself: home. She thought of the manor as home.

Some of my warmth must have seeped into her because her shivers tapered off and her split lip turned its normal shade of pink instead of blue.

I nuzzled her away from my chest and lay down on the ground in front of her. I jerked my head over my shoulder with a grunt, trying to indicate she should get on my back. She looked baffled for a moment and then her eyes cleared. With a giggle she clambered onto my broad back, hiking her smock up so she could sit astride. Her hands gripped my ruff and I lumbered awkwardly to my feet.

I felt her shift and lay herself down along my spine, instinctively seeking the warmth.

I set myself in the right direction without hesitation. The bear lay quietly docile under the surface now I'd found Emeline, though I still had to make my way over and around the lengthy ruins with her stretched along my back.

Which was why I didn't see the body until I'd lumbered over a low wall and nearly stepped on it.

Emeline didn't make a sound from above me and I realized she must be dozing with her hands buried in my fur.

I stepped closer to the body, hoping to examine it without waking her.

Anwen had described the poor fellow they'd found before, but I hadn't appreciated the full horror until now. Hard to believe this mess had once been a human being.

My nostrils flared at the smell of blood and death and my eyes narrowed. A hint of animal musk wove through the rest.

My heart thumped, and I backed away from the scene of carnage. Whatever had killed the young man had done so only moments before.

My hackles rose. Something stalked my territory, invading my space and my home. Threatening my people. Threatening Emeline and Josselin. Threatening Anwen.

A rumble started deep in my belly and rose through my chest and into my throat. I clamped down on the bear, willing him to stay quiet and hidden. I had to get Emeline home and safe.

This threat had to wait. I turned from the body and started back toward the manor. I hadn't gone two steps before I became aware of another presence. Eyes tracked me through the trees and my wide nostrils picked up an unfamiliar scent. I slowed and swung my head around in a menacing arc, ready to defend.

A smudged shape stalked us through the trees. Dim moonlight glinted from reflective eyes and heavy paws padded through the snow. I pulled my lips back in a low snarl.

"Léon?"

My breath puffed out in a relieved cloud.

Brann. Almighty save me, I never thought I'd be relieved to hear his voice.

I grunted in acknowledgment, and he came through the trees, blue eyes blinking at me in the dim moonlight.

"Any luck?" he said.

I turned so he could see Emeline asleep on my back.

His shoulders relaxed and his eyes crinkled in what was probably a smile. "Good. Let's get her back to warmth."

He turned.

I hesitated.

If I left with Brann, I could pretend I hadn't seen the body. The others would never find out, and we could go on as if it hadn't happened.

But whatever was killing these people threatened me and my own. And Brann was a powerful ally. Walking away wouldn't win his trust.

I grunted and jerked my head back the way I'd come. In moments I was back at the scene, staring down into the dark lifeless eyes of the young man. Brann stood beside me, silently.

Finally, he looked up from the body and straight at me. "Did you do this?"

I should have braced myself for the question, but for some reason I'd thought showing him would prove my innocence. If I'd done it, I'd be doing my best to hide it, not confess it.

"Léon, don't bite me for saying so, but this looks really bad," he said.

I growled low in my throat.

"Anything with claws could have made these wounds," he said, stalking carefully around the body. "And you've been alone this whole time."

I shook my head, careful not to dislodge Emeline but anxious to get my point across. I didn't do this.

"The simplest explanation is usually the likeliest," he said, damning me with his logic. "And we only have your word that you didn't do it."

I peeled my lips back from my teeth. My word wasn't good enough? I walked right up to him, crowding him with my body and my teeth.

His form shifted and stretched until he stood in roughly the shape of a man. He'd looked this way once before, when he'd taken Justin out of my cellar. His body seemed misty and ethereal but his feet pressed the snow down the way it always did. Was this his actual shape? The one he wore in his home Realm?

He snarled back, not budging. "I know your kind, Léon. You can't hide your true nature from me."

I stepped back, startled. What the hell did that mean?

He sighed and shifted back into his familiar cat shape. "Enough. I'm not arguing about this now. I can't prove you did it and you can't prove you didn't. I will not condemn you tonight. But I'm watching you."

It was more than I'd expected from him. I turned away from the carnage with my precious burden.

We walked back to the manor in silence. I pretended not to notice the suspicious looks Brann cast me, and he pretended he wasn't casting me suspicious looks.

We came to the broken wall into the kitchen yard, and I stopped short; the change rippled under my skin but didn't take hold yet. I didn't want it to with Emeline still clinging to my back. Something in my movement woke the little girl and she sat up.

Brann called out and the kitchen door opened. Light and people spilled out into the snow. Giles carried a heavy blanket, and Josselin searched anxiously for his sister. Anwen stepped out behind them, lifting the edge of her tunic free of the clinging snow.

A stranger followed her, fuzzy in the bear's eyesight. My lips pulled back from my teeth.

But Anwen limped forward, drawing my gaze to her worried face. Her eyes darted between Brann and me and then Emeline, and the lines etched in her forehead smoothed away.

"Emmy," Josselin called, relief clear in his voice.

Emeline swung her leg over my back, and I crouched before she jumped down. She made it safely with a soft thump and scrambled over the wall to embrace her brother.

Josselin put his arms around her and glanced at me warily out of the corner of his eye. I turned away from his fear and suspicion toward Giles, who waited beside the wall.

"Come, my lord," he said. "You've done well."

Now Emeline was safe, exhaustion swept through me and it was all I could do to clamber over the low stones of the wall and stumble to the other side.

Fire raced along my skin but I bore it silently. The frigid air stole what little energy I had left, and I stumbled in the snow, catching myself with my hands.

Giles settled the thick blanket across my shoulders, and I dragged my heavy head up to meet Anwen's eyes. Her proud smile reached inside and warmed all the dark corners of my heart.

Behind her the tall stranger with dark hair studied me.

I wanted to snap, "What are you looking at?" But it wasn't hard to guess what made him stare. A naked lord kneeling in the kitchen yard, his privates far too close to the snow.

I flushed and dropped my head again, long blond hair hiding my face from the light that shone from the kitchen door. I gathered my strength and tried to stand, but my knees wobbled and I drooped again.

"Léon?" Emeline said, and she dashed back to me. "What's wrong?"

"Emeline, no!"

I glanced up and saw Josselin reach out to grab his sister's arm before she reached me.

"Don't touch him," he said. The fear and revulsion in his voice stabbed at me and I dropped my eyes, clutching the blanket closer around my shoulders.

Brann stepped around me. "There's another body," he said quietly to Anwen. He kept his voice low, but the words were clear in the cold kitchen yard. Anwen's face crumpled and her anguished eyes sought mine.

I was cold and tired, the chill of the snow biting into my knees and feet where I knelt and the exhaustion dragging my limbs down as if it could bury me in a drift, but I clutched the edges of the blanket and raised my chin.

"It wasn't me," I said, my voice hoarse from everything that had happened in the last few hours. "I found him on my way back with Emeline. I showed Brann because I thought you all should know, not because I was feeling guilty."

"It looked pretty bad," Brann said, as if I hadn't even spoken.

"I didn't do it," I growled, my voice dropping into a menacing octave.

"I'm not passing judgment," Brann said. "I'm just saying what I saw."

"What about the bear?" Anwen said, quietly.

I shook my head. "He didn't take over. I didn't let him."

"So you were aware the whole time?"

I opened my mouth to say yes. But there had been that moment when I'd fought him. It had only been a moment for me but how long had it taken me to beat him back? And what could have happened in the meantime?

They saw my hesitation and the adults all exchanged a look. Even Giles bit his lip.

Emeline followed their telling glances, her brow furrowed. She broke free from her brother's grasp and ran the couple steps to me.

"Stop it," she said, throwing her arms around my neck. "He hasn't done anything wrong. Léon is good, I know it."

Anwen's face softened. "That isn't really the issue, Emeline."

"I don't care," she said, shaking her head. "He's good and that's all that matters, so stop yelling at him."

Her defense sent warmth rolling through my chilled limbs. I lifted my hand and squeezed her arm where she embraced me. "They're not yelling at me, Emeline."

"Maybe not yet, but they want to. You can always tell with voices."

Well, she had me there.

Anwen clasped her hands in front of her. I didn't know how to erase the doubt in her eyes. I could say I didn't do it as many times as I wanted but it wouldn't mean anything until I could prove it and Anwen believed me. I wanted to put my arms around her and protect her from the world. But that was stupid so I kept the thought to myself.

Giles lowered his gaze to the snow. "I will fetch the magistrate and we will take the body back to town."

I staggered to my feet, clutching the cloak closed around my bare form. My feet and legs had gone numb with cold.

"I don't care anymore," I said. "I'm going inside."

Josselin's eyes widened and he looked up at Anwen. "What about us?" he said. "We can't go home."

Emeline shivered in her wet smock, eyes huge and blue in her pale face. Josselin stood next to her, arms crossed, gaze fixed on the worn toes of his boots.

My mind filled with images of them tearing down the halls of my ancestral home, shrieks ringing from the stones of my coveted sanctuary, and I winced. But the knot in my gut didn't go away.

"You can stay here," I said, jerking my head at the manor behind me. "You're not going back to that man." They'd stayed in the manor before and hadn't destroyed it yet. I'd just have to broaden my definition of sanctuary until it included Josselin and Emeline. Shouldn't be hard. Anwen had already snuck in there somehow.

Emeline beamed at me before she raced into the kitchen. Josselin started after her, stopped short, and cast a nervous glance at me before shaking his head and following her.

Anwen nodded to me with a distracted frown.

I had to make her smile at me again. Or at least not look at me like I was a murderer. I had one last argument, and I stepped up next to her as she turned to follow Brann into the manor.

"You know, I'm not the only large predator in the area," I said. I jerked my head at Brann, who swiveled his ears back to tell me he'd heard. I didn't want to accuse her trusted companion, but Brann had shown up right after I'd found the body.

A voice I didn't recognize rose behind us. "Brann was with me until I left him at the ruins to find you."

I kept myself from jumping. I had forgotten the stranger.

I raised my chin and twitched an eyebrow. "And you are?"

"Myrddin de Emrys."

Of course he was. Anwen's freire and technical betrothed would be starkly handsome, with artfully tousled black hair, cheekbones sharp enough to cut, and eyes so vivid they were nearly purple.

"And you are Lord Léon Beauregard," he said, holding me with his gaze.

"Of Whitecliff," I said and winced. Could I sound any more defensive? Say something pleasant, Léon. Impress Anwen's kinsman even if you can't impress Anwen. "What brings you here?"

"His majesty sent me as his representative. To determine if you are fit to retain lordship of this barony."

I stumbled to a halt on the kitchen threshold. Fit? When I'd just lumbered in here as a smelly bear, complete with fur and tail, and there was a murderer wandering my lands who could quite possibly be me?

"Brilliant," I said. "Perfect timing."

CHAPTER FIFTEEN

The next morning I skulked down the corridor, hoping I didn't run into any of the veritable army I had quartered in the manor now. After the night I'd had, I needed the morning to myself. At least Myrddin wasn't lurking around any corners.

My fingers clenched on the leather case in my hand as I remembered the tall handsome man who claimed kinship with Anwen.

Myrddin had looked at me like a hawk eyes a pigeon just before it stoops.

"His majesty received a report that the lord of this area was not fulfilling his duties the way his majesty expects," he'd said.

Maybe his majesty should mind his own business, I'd thought to myself. "A report?" was all I said out loud.

Myrddin tilted his head. "An anonymous report," he said.

Anonymous, my ass. The only one who had that kind of initiative and authority was Georg. I could well believe he had sent a message to the capital detailing my absence. Although he'd probably left out the part about me turning into a bear for fear of sounding ridiculous.

The worst part was I couldn't even be mad at him, since it was well within his rights to do so. As the Baron of Whitecliff I owed protection to my people and fealty to the Duke of Woodshire, as well as the King. I'd been lucky that the Duke hadn't demanded an explanation from me personally before this.

I'd stood there clutching the blanket, making sure it covered me from neck to foot. I was already comparing myself to tall, dark, and powerful. I didn't need Myrddin making his own comparisons to my naked form.

"Of course I'll stand by his majesty's decision," I said, pointedly. I gritted my teeth and added, "And if you need a place to stay..." I started to gesture to the manor and then thought better of it, keeping my grip on the blanket.

"I'll be staying in the village," he said. "It's more neutral."

As neutral as a troop of loyal Valerian soldiers, I thought. Didn't you figure that's where your "anonymous" tip came from, you prat?

He'd left after having a quiet word with Anwen. Whatever he'd said had made her smile at him.

Could you hate a man after five minutes of conversation?

I pushed open the chapel door and breathed a sigh of relief in the still morning. I wasn't up to dealing with anyone yet today. Not after meeting Myrddin and worrying I might be a killer.

I couldn't do anything about either problem, which made me itch. Like the bear scratching to get out. Only painting had ever been enough to distract me from the responsibilities I'd been too young or too lazy to face. And later it had distracted me from the people who had abandoned me. Mother and Father, Brother Warren, every servant I'd ever known.

I set my leather case down on the altar and flipped it open. Brushes of all shapes and sizes lay nestled in the folds. My fingers slid down the edge of one, and I set a jar of red pigment beside it.

Giles usually mixed my paints for me in the little closet we'd converted into a workshop many years before. But I hadn't wanted to tell him what I was doing this morning so I'd snuck down to mix up the ochre myself.

Anwen's rose still lay on the altar. It remained as lush and radiant as it had the night she'd handed it to me. Some magic of hers? Yasmina's rose bower was ever-blooming as well, but that only existed in my head.

I selected a brush, opened the jar, and stood behind the altar to stare at the wall of roses.

Anwen's words rang in my head. "The Almighty doesn't care how well you paint, only that you do."

Was that true? I'd always used painting as an act of worship, but I'd been preoccupied with making sure it was perfect. I didn't want to offer Him an inferior product. But if what she said was true and I couldn't earn the grace He'd given me anyway, then giving Him my best would be enough, even if my best was only an imperfect, splotchy reflection of my former skill. He wanted the best my heart could give, not the best my hands could give.

I trembled as I dipped the bristles of the brush into the

red paint and my fingers fumbled, thick and clumsy on the wood.

I said a short prayer and set the brush against the wall.

I felt like whistling while I walked down the hall later that morning to check on Josselin and Emeline, only my lips wouldn't cooperate.

But who cared about lips when I could paint?

Sure, anyone and their dog could fill in flowers I had outlined and painted years ago, but I'd held a brush and I hadn't ruined the roses with my clumsiness.

I wouldn't think about illumination. For now, a rudimentary control over my fingers was enough.

I poked my head in the room where Josselin and Emeline had slept. A pair of maids had shared this one once upon a time; now the two rumpled beds on either wall held the toys Giles and Anwen had given them plus a couple extra I strongly suspected they'd smuggled from home over the last couple days.

"Good morning," I said from the doorway.

Josselin jumped and looked up from his bed with wide eyes.

My good mood soured.

Emeline bounced up, wielding her doll like a jousting lance.

"Look, Léon," she said. "I made Mari a dress just like Anwen's."

She held up the doll, who now wore an assortment of blue scraps Giles must have found in the laundry.

"Pretty," I said. I'd learned enough by now to know that was the appropriate response.

"Come play with us."

Josselin's limbs drew in as if to protect himself, but Emeline lunged for my hand. And found them both full.

"What's that?" she said.

Reminded of my success that morning in the chapel, my cheeks warmed. "My painting supplies."

Emeline's mouth dropped open and Josselin's jaw slackened across the room.

"Really?" Emeline said. "Can we see?"

I surveyed the room. The walls had been whitewashed once upon a time and the blank space plucked at me.

"You want to paint in here?" I said. "We'll have to mix up some more colors, but I think this place could use a good mural. Don't you?"

Emeline squealed and tossed the doll on her bed before darting out the door.

I dipped my head at Josselin. "You want to come?"

He bit his lip and thought about it. But finally he shook his head and huddled on his bed.

I stifled my disappointment and followed Emeline out. Apparently I'd have to work harder if I wanted the boy to trust me again.

"So I thought the King didn't even know your name?" Anwen

said with a sideways smirk at her freire as they walked down the main street of the village.

Myrddin grinned. "I guess all the errand running paid off," he said. "He picked me specifically to come check up on your lord."

She sighed. "He's not my lord."

Myrddin kicked at the snow as she and Brann trudged along. "No, but you're working with him pretty closely." He caught her eye. "Anwen, this is my chance. If I do well with this assignment, I'll be assigned to serve the King as his personal healer."

"What do you want me to do?" she said. Her eyes narrowed. "I'm not going to lie just so you can impress the King."

"You think I would ask you to?" he said, his mouth drawing down at the corners. "I'm here to find out the truth. Whatever that is."

She consciously relaxed her shoulders. "Then what can I do to help?"

"Tell me about Léon." He stopped in the middle of the road and turned to her. "What kind of man is he? How does he manage his lands? Is he fair? Just?"

Anwen blinked. "Myrddin, he's been a bear for three years. I imagine it's hard to manage your lands when people run you off for getting too close to the village."

She gestured across the street where the Refuge of Saint Innovate stood, the first place she'd encountered Léon. Icicles hung from the edge of the peaked roof, throwing off points of sunlight.

Myrddin sighed, his breath coming out in a cloud. "Good point. What about the rest?"

"He's..." She chewed her lip. "Arrogant. Self-absorbed."

"And hiding something," Brann added from beside her. His whiskers twitched. "I can tell."

Anwen gave him a look. "He's also impulsively sweet. And a brilliant artist."

Myrddin knew her well enough to know she wasn't done. "And?" he said.

Her chin came up and she fixed him with a glare. "And I wish I knew him better. He might be a killer. But he is also very protective of the people he values. Look at the way he treats Josselin and Emeline."

Fire flashed in the corner of her eye, and she turned to catch the writing scrawled across the stone facade of the Refuge.

Anwen, meet me at the quarry.

There was no signature, but she and Myrddin both knew the handwriting well enough.

Myrddin groaned. "See you later," he said and spun on his heel fast enough to send snow flying.

"Myrddin!"

"She doesn't need to know I'm here," he said over his shoulder.

"Coward."

He waved his hand as he raced across the street. "Good luck."

The snow leopard apparently felt the same way because he shed a bunch of weight as a shower of snow and gravel and leapt into the air as a crow.

"Brann!"

Anwen stood alone in the street, a couple of villagers casting curious looks her way. She grumbled under her breath as she turned beside the Refuge and made her way to the edge of the quarry. The door Léon had burst through on the night they'd met was boarded over. The Disciples hadn't replaced it yet.

She stopped at the edge of the cliff and peered down. Most of the men in the district worked below her, wielding pickaxes and sledges. A hundred paces to her right a long ramp cut into the cliff, sloping from the village to the working floor.

"Enfan," a voice said behind her.

Anwen kept herself from jumping. She should have felt it when Catrin stepped from the Byways, but not even a whisper of power had crossed her flesh.

She turned and pasted a smile on her face. "Matrona," she said.

"Thank Redemption he didn't get you too," Catrin said before grabbing Anwen's shoulders and pulling her into a rough hug.

"What are you talking about?" Anwen said.

"Your bear lord." Catrin drew back and stared into her face. Her brows drew down. "You don't know? Two people have been killed, Anwen. Torn apart by a wild animal. Or a desperate man. You must come away before he decides to take his vengeance on you."

Anwen's eyes went wide. "How did you know that?"

"The villagers have been talking. There was one brought back last night."

Anwen's teeth clenched. Clearly her matrona had been hanging around the area, even after she'd agreed to leave Anwen at the manor.

Catrin pulled Anwen's arm through hers and Anwen felt her reach for the vytl that would allow them to step onto the Byways together.

Anger swept through her and she tore herself away. "You'd force me to leave?" she said. "Just like that? What happened to trusting me to take care of myself?"

"Your Family wants to keep you safe right now."

Anwen crossed her arms. "Patriarche Justin agreed to this?"

Catrin lifted her eyes skyward as if asking for patience. "Patriarche Justin is missing."

Anwen jerked upright and dropped her defensive stance. "What?"

"The healer said he was fully recovered and the next day he was gone."

Anwen smoothed trembling hands down her tunic, forcing herself to think through Catrin's words. Gone wasn't the same as missing. Justin normally stayed in the capital, but that didn't mean he wasn't allowed to leave on some errand only he knew about.

"You can help me look for him," Catrin said. "That's more important than staying to protect a murderer."

Anwen gave Catrin an exasperated look. "We don't know that it's Léon." Just a moment ago she'd told Myrddin he might be a killer, but Catrin's high-handed way of assuming things irked her, making her obstinate.

"We know an enchanter cursed him. Perhaps he's taking his revenge. Perhaps he's trying to kill you."

"Then he's doing a damn poor job of it."

Catrin gasped.

Anwen turned her head so Catrin wouldn't see her roll her eyes. "I won't condemn him without proof, and I won't abandon him when I promised him freedom. And even if I did, I wouldn't go without saying goodbye, without telling him why I was leaving." Not after what he'd said that night after the Moot. Sprawled in the snow, delirious from exhaustion with the cloak covering only the important parts. He'd gazed up at her with eyes the color of cornflowers and begged her not to leave. "Like everyone else," he'd added as his eyes closed.

"I had no idea he was so charming," Catrin said, lips thin and white. "Or that you'd fall for those pretty lies the same way you did last time."

Heat suffused Anwen's face, quickly followed by the chill of pain. If Catrin had thought to shame her into leaving, she'd picked the wrong tactic.

"Goodbye, Matrona," she said and turned away, heading toward the hill and the road that led to the manor. Arguing that she'd kept her heart locked securely away from Léon's smooth flirtation and awkward sincerity would only convince Catrin of the opposite.

"You don't want to know why you can't break the magic binding him?" Catrin called after her, voice desperate.

Anwen fumed at the obvious tactic. She wouldn't stop. She wouldn't look. She wouldn't ask. She could figure it out herself.

She blew out her breath in frustration. Almighty take her for a fool. She stopped and turned. "What do you mean?"

"The curse goes too deep," Catrin said. As if she'd studied him alongside Anwen. "You can't break it from the outside."

"Then how—?"

"Only from the inside. Destroy what it's connected to and you destroy the curse."

Anwen gasped. "But it's connected to his heart."

Catrin spread her hands. "Then you know the worst of it."

Anwen turned, burying the cold hard pit in her stomach under a layer of hot fury. Almighty help her, a death curse?

"Anwen," Catrin called as she trudged away. "Someone wanted to punish him."

She ignored the sharpness in her matrona's tone. "I don't care what he did," she said over her shoulder. "He doesn't deserve death."

I'd always had the utmost respect for Brother Warren, who had taught me to wield my brush and pen with loving and precise movements. It couldn't be easy to teach someone to create life from paint and ink.

But then, his student had actually cared about being good.

I'd just pointed Emeline at the wall and stood back.

Precision was not a term I would apply to the way she filled in the big pink flowers I'd drawn on the wall for her.

But she seemed to be having as much fun smearing paint on the walls as I had detailing the clothes on a two-inch-tall paper man, so, who was I to judge.

Josselin glowered from his bed, but every now and then he forgot that he was scared and angry, and he bit his lip with envy.

I sauntered over to a bare wall on his side of the room and contemplated it. With my charcoal stick I sketched a couple curving lines, frowned, and started again. My clumsy fingers couldn't manage anything small, but if I started large enough...

"What are you doing?" Josselin said. He'd scooched closer to the end of his bed so he could peer over my shoulder.

"Drawing," I said, deliberately withholding details.

He rolled his eyes. "Drawing what?"

"What does it look like?"

He squinted at my picture. "A blob."

So much for my pride. "What if I add a line here, and here?"

His eyes widened. "It's a horse."

"Oh good. I was worried you were going to think it was a cow."

"It needs barding," he said and leaped down from his bed to snatch up an extra charcoal stick. "And a rider." His tongue stuck out between his teeth as he concentrated on adding the horse's tack.

I smiled, being careful to keep my sigh of relief inside. I'd worried he'd never speak to me again without that trace of fear behind his eyes.

The boy had a steady hand. At least I could tell the rider was supposed to be male. And after a few minutes he produced some credible leather armor for his knight.

Across the room Emeline had abandoned even trying to stay within the lines of the flower blossoms she insisted were poppies. Now she was just spreading paint around in bright swathes of color. It was a good thing I made my own pigments and I was rich enough to afford all the ingredients. I'd be out of red in no time.

I handed Josselin a brush and a palette and showed him how to hold both. He still avoided touching me, but he'd stopped glaring and he listened carefully to my instructions.

"Short strokes give you the most control," I said. "They'll make your painting look crisper and more defined."

Josselin glanced over his shoulder and frowned at his sister.

"I see what you mean. It doesn't look like flowers anymore," he said. "It looks like blood. Something died over there."

I winced. His words reminded me of blood on snow and dead hunters.

"What are you making, Josselin?" Emeline said, finally turning to see her brother's efforts.

"A hero," he said.

"Like Leonides?"

"Yeah."

"Léon, I want a princess. Can you draw Yasmina for me?" She grasped my hand with her red-smeared fingers and dragged me toward her side of the room and the one stretch of white left untouched by red.

I glanced back at Josselin's wall. I'd barely managed a recognizable horse with the lingering talent in my clumsy fingers. "I don't—"

"Please?"

It couldn't hurt to try. If she turned out all horrible and wobbly, I could always whitewash over her again.

I busied myself with her vague outlines, remembering to start big. But when it came to her face I paused.

I'd chased Yasmina in my dreams for years, but I'd never seen her face. I'd imagined one for her when I was thirteen and learning to illuminate, but since then I hadn't dared, fearing my imagination couldn't come close to the radiance of my Yasmina.

How should she look? What colors would achieve the sunlit highlights of her hair?

"Relax, stop thinking. Let your heart tell your hands what to paint." Brother Warren had used those words anytime I'd been frozen with indecision.

I'd always thought they were stupid. A heart couldn't reason, couldn't instruct. But maybe that was his point.

I closed my eyes and steadied my hands.

When I opened them, I set my charcoal against the wall and sketched.

The shape of her face formed under my hands, her cheekbones, and lips. Her chin and the line of her eyebrows. The curling hair that fell around her face as if she'd pulled it free from a clasp. I had to rub out her eyes twice before they felt right.

I needed color. I snagged a paintbrush and the palette from Josselin, who had stopped to watch me work.

Brown with streaks of green. I frowned and dipped my brush again to add the faintest bit of gold to spark in her eyes.

I finished and uncurled my back, my eyes meeting the amused gaze of my painted princess. The brush fell from my startled grip, clattering against the stone floor, and I choked on a breath.

This was Yasmina? My Yasmina?

"Léon?" Emeline said, looking between me and the painting. "What's wrong? You didn't finish her."

I forced a smile to my numb lips and bent to retrieve the brush. "I thought you'd like to color her in."

Thank Createjoy she set to with relish, leaving me to stumble to my feet and back away. I caught myself at the door and risked one last look back at the wall.

Anwen's eyes laughed at me from Yasmina's portrait. Anwen's smile tugged at Yasmina's lips. My head had told my hands to draw Yasmina. My heart had told my hands to draw Anwen.

Emeline puttered below the image, humming under her breath, completely oblivious to the revelation beneath her paint-spattered fingers. Josselin returned to his hero. Neither recognized the woman without her scars, but I couldn't escape the truth in those eyes.

I turned and slid out the door.

CHAPTER SIXTEEN

Three years. It had been three years, but I remembered that day clearer than anything that had happened while I was a bear.

I had urged my horse faster, ducking branches that threatened to take off my head as dead leaves flew around us. Would it be so bad to run headlong into a tree and never wake up again? Never have to face Giles's disappointed look. Never have to remember Brother Warren's anger as he stomped from the manor's great hall into the autumn twilight.

No, I wasn't thinking of that.

But the image was there. He hadn't even waited to change out of his paint-spattered robe before he'd packed his things and told me he was resigning as my tutor. The red and orange pigments staining his skin had only emphasized his blazing face.

"I will not teach you anymore. Someone who willfully destroys anything is not worthy to follow Saint Createjoy."

I kicked my horse, taking my anger out on the mare.

I hadn't meant to destroy his work. I'd been angry and sad, and I hadn't been thinking clearly when I'd thrown the paint at his artwork. With my parents gone, I'd been Lord Beauregard for two weeks and I was starting to realize that the title might have made me important, but it wouldn't make me any friends. Or bring back my family.

I sniffed. It didn't matter. I couldn't get rid of the title. Not with generations of Beauregards behind it. It didn't matter that I'd driven Brother Warren away. A lord didn't have time to paint, anyway.

It didn't matter that I'd have to return to a manor full of worthless people and empty of the ones who mattered most.

Maybe Brother Warren would catch the plague. Like my parents. It would serve him right. They'd left me alone and had never come back. Now he would, too.

A flash of brown caught my eye from ahead and to the right of me.

"There," I called to Giles, who struggled to keep up with my headlong pace. "There is our quarry. I told you we'd have venison tonight."

"Be careful, my lord," he said behind me. "People travel these woods as a shortcut to Whitecliff."

I gritted my teeth and leaned low over my horse's neck, searching for another sign of the frightened deer.

That fated flash of brown appeared again, drawing me deeper into the forest. I hurried after it as if I could outrun Giles's censure and Brother Warren's abandonment. The huntsmen kept pace around me, and the hounds flowed along beside the horses, baying their pleasure. My father had trained them to hunt criminals in these same woods, but they were just as good at bringing down a deer.

"There it is," I called and brought my bow to bear. My arrow flew straight in the still air, and I cried out in triumph as my quarry stumbled and fell.

The huntsman next to me sounded his horn and the hounds converged on the downed prey, their snarls and barks echoing back to us.

A high-pitched scream split the air.

Creeping dread settled like a weight in my limbs. "That's no deer," I whispered and spurred my horse through the trees. The dogs had grounded our quarry beneath a huge boulder shaped like a horse's head.

A girl dressed in a brown smock struggled under the snapping jaws of the hounds.

I sat frozen atop my horse, jaw slack in shock, breath coming in short sharp gasps.

"Call them off," Giles shouted. He slid off his horse and ran to the girl, grabbing the dogs by the scruff of their necks and hauling them away from her. The huntsman whistled, his eyes wide with horror, and the dogs immediately left their prey to circle around him.

Giles gathered the girl in his arms, her blood staining his tunic.

I swallowed down the bile that soured the back of my throat and swung down off my horse. I fisted my hands to keep them from trembling and strode over to them. Her face was a clawed mess, but I could tell her eyes were closed. It was a mercy she'd passed out.

My arrow had struck above her knee, hamstringing her

and causing her to stumble. I knelt down and snapped the head off and pulled the shaft from her leg.

I swiped my sleeve across my mouth to keep from gagging. I had done this. I'd been angry and hasty and I'd killed this girl.

I stumbled backward, shaking my head.

"My lord, she needs help," Giles said, pressing the wound in her leg to staunch the bleeding. There was nothing he could do for her face. "We should take her to the village, see if there is a healer."

I turned away from the mess I'd made and clutched my horse's saddle. "No," I whispered into its shoulder. I couldn't spend another moment looking at the blood. I couldn't spend another moment with the evidence of what I'd done.

"She will be dead within the hour," I said, working some heat into my tone. "There's nothing we can do for her. We're going home." Home where I could hide from every mistake I'd made.

I didn't turn around. I couldn't face the disappointment and condemnation in Giles's eyes either, and I was running out of distractions for all the awful things in my life.

He made a noise as if to protest.

"Now, Giles," I snapped.

"Enfan!" A voice shouted through the trees, and I spun to face it.

A woman sprinted into the clearing, checking herself when she saw me. Her eyes went to the bleeding girl, and the woman gasped with horror.

"Saints take you, what have you done?" she said. "Your

dogs have nearly killed her," she said, wrestling her from Giles's arms.

"You should know better than to bring children into the woods while men are hunting."

She drew in a sharp breath, her mouth going thin and white.

I shook my head. "I don't have time for this." My blood beat in my ears, urging me away. I turned and took hold of my saddle to avoid her accusing blue eyes.

"You'd turn your back on an enchanter?"

I glanced back, taking in her cloak with its silver braid. "Why should I care?" I said with the weight of a barony in my voice. "I'm Léon Beauregard, lord of Whitecliff."

"Please, it was an accident," Giles said. "My lord mistook her for his quarry."

"Then your lord is a fool. Girl or deer, they are all the same to him."

I spun, ready to throw her off my lands for her insults.

She surged to her feet and raised her hands as if to stop me. I waited for her to strike me—then she'd really be in trouble—but she just stood there.

"Listen well, Léon Beauregard. You are an animal. A beast fit only to scrounge for food and struggle for existence. Until you learn the value of human life, that is all you are good for. I condemn you to that fate until your own life is counted as naught."

A tingle settled under my skin and I shivered, but nothing worse happened.

I snorted. "Your words are empty," I said. "Get out of my

forest and off my land." Then I wouldn't have to look at either of them anymore.

I put my foot in the stirrup and heaved myself into the saddle.

The woman knelt to gather up the girl, and I held down my nausea long enough to notice how small and pale she looked under all the blood. Her dark hair hung loose over the woman's arm. The enchanter didn't seem worried by my threat. She glared at me from her place in the leaves.

"Remember us tomorrow, when you wake," she said. "Remember the name Emrys. And curse it."

Her scowl ground at my anger until I could no longer contain it. I spurred my horse forward. She waited without flinching until I lost my nerve and jerked my horse around her.

I did not look back. It didn't even occur to me. Now I wondered what I would have seen. The woman's words meant nothing to me then. They seemed like leaves on the wind, fluttering hopelessly against the inevitable. I would remember them, though. Just like she said. In the morning, I would wake and curse the name Emrys.

Anwen was Yasmina.

And I was the monster. I wasn't the hero coming to rescue her.

I shook my head, thoughts circling like vultures over some dead thing. She couldn't be Yasmina. My Yasmina was supposed to be beautiful and Anwen was...Anwen was scarred.

But when I'd painted her, my fingers had seen past the scars. Which was the real Anwen? The inside or the outside?

And even if she was Yasmina, she would never love me, never forgive me because I was the hunter who had ruined her life.

I wasn't sure which bothered me more.

I staggered down the hall, steadying myself against the stone blocks of the wall. *Almighty, please make my head stop spinning.*

My Yasmina was here. I'd found her.

She was Anwen.

Yasmina wasn't beautiful.

Anwen would never forgive me.

Voices inside the kitchen stopped my feet on the worn flagstones, and I held my breath to listen. Had Anwen returned from her walk with Myrddin?

"What do you mean?" No, that wasn't Anwen's voice. It was Fanny's.

"We are not promised," Giles said, and from his tone he was pretty upset about it. "If you wish to find another..."

"Another? I've never even looked—Giles, what are you talking about?"

"I'm just telling you I understand. If coming out here every day is too hard..."

"Why do you think I come?" Fanny said, exasperation leaking into her voice. Then quieter. "My heart has not changed."

"You deserve a life," Giles said. "A husband. One who is not bound elsewhere."

"Yes." She dragged the word out. "I want those things. But I want them with you."

"Fanny."

"I know you don't want to leave him alone. But my nephew is looking for a position. He could come and take care of the baron while we get married."

"What then?" Giles said. "I've never been anything other than a tutor and a valet."

"Benevere isn't far." Fanny's voice grew coaxing. "You could go back to the Refuge of Saint Wonderment and finish becoming a Disciple like you wanted before..."

Before he'd given up his life to teach a spoiled brat turned bear lord. With his stark white hair, I'd always thought of Giles as old. He'd held himself with such maturity and I'd seen his disapproval as that of a man past his prime. But his face was remarkably smooth and free of wrinkles, and now I wondered how old the man really was. Obviously young enough to fall in love.

Giles didn't answer, and I drew in a painful breath. Almighty, he was thinking about it. He was actually thinking about leaving the manor. And why shouldn't he? I was old enough to take care of myself. I wasn't a bear anymore. I didn't need a reluctant manservant with a penchant for disapproving looks.

Pain spiked my chest, but I ignored it and pushed into the kitchen, startling both parties. Giles jumped away from Fanny, staring at me with wide guilty eyes.

"My lord," he said and then stopped as if he couldn't think of anything else to say.

"Contemplating desertion, Giles?" I said, acid burning my throat until I swallowed it down.

Giles's face went red then white as he realized I'd overheard their conversation. Fanny faded back against a wall but I didn't care about her.

That one moment of unwitting hesitation had told me what I needed to know. That somewhere under the competence and loyalty Giles imagined a life away from the manor. Away from me.

I could give him what he wanted.

"It's all right," I said, fixing my gaze over his left shoulder. "You really should go." I nearly choked on the words.

"My lord, I didn't—"

I cut him off with a wave. I could give him what he wanted, but I couldn't let him see how much it hurt. "It's not like I'll miss you."

His eyes flashed and he drew himself up.

"Of course not, my lord," he said. "Because you've always managed to find your own dinner."

I flushed. A low blow for a low blow. "Right. Don't trip on your way out," I said and rushed for the great hall before he could respond. I retreated mindlessly until I found myself standing in the snowy driveway clutching my cloak.

Brilliant, Léon, fantastic. You just threw away the one relationship that kept you sane when the cracks in your mind threatened to eat everything important.

I considered going back to hide in my room, but that retreat would be even worse than the one that had brought me out here. And I didn't want to witness Giles's furious departure. There was no doubt he would depart. In the ten years I'd known him, Giles had never once snapped back at me. Reprimanded, yes. Raised a sardonic eyebrow, yes. But snapped? Never.

My eyes burned and I squeezed them shut, willing the moisture and the clog in my throat away.

"Léon?"

I jumped and ran a hasty hand over my nose and eyes. When I could focus, I found Anwen standing in the driveway not twenty feet away, staring at me.

"What's wrong?"

The sight of her brought back the flood of conflicting emotion I'd felt after painting her. Although some of the dismay had retreated, leaving more room for the shame and the joy.

How many times had I dreamed of Yasmina, and now that she was standing in front of me, I had nothing to say to her?

"Giles is leaving." It was the only thing I could say that didn't pour out every ugly thought. And even that made my voice tremble.

Her eyes widened. "Giles?" she said, and I couldn't interpret the way her lip twitched. "Leaving? Are you sure?"

"He wants to be with Fanny." I choked, then added, "And I might have yelled at him."

The twitch became a smile. "I imagine if you apologize you can head him off before he gets too far."

How could she laugh when the foundation of my life was crumbling under my feet? And really, it was her fault. I wouldn't have said what I'd said to Giles if I hadn't been so off balance about Anwen. Yasmina. Whoever she was.

"You don't understand. He's leaving." I drew out the word since she hadn't understood the first time.

She lost the smile and her eyes turned serious. "I think I do understand. Giles has been with you for years. Through tantrums and transformation. He is your anchor. When things went bad, he was your constant. And without him you feel lost."

My mouth opened and closed before I nodded. How did she know?

"But Léon, think about everything he's been through with you. All he's put up with and given up for you. You think he'd just up and leave after a fight? You dishonor him by questioning his loyalty to you."

I'd lost track of how many times that day I'd flushed with shame. She was right. Even if I'd pushed Giles far enough to make him leave, he wouldn't do so without saying goodbye, without tidying up and putting everything in its place before closing the door behind him. I had time to right my wrong.

"I—I should tell him..." I turned to go back inside but stopped. I gave Anwen a small sincere bow. "Thank you, lady."

She blushed and as I turned away, she held out her hand. "Wait, Léon. There's something..." Her face fell. "There's something important I must tell you."

My eyebrows drew together.

She wouldn't look at me.

If she was right, Giles would wait, and I had time to see why she avoided my gaze. I gestured toward the cleared path to the gardens. "Walk with me?"

Without thinking, I extended my arm for her to hold, and had to catch my breath when she took it. Her hand fit perfectly in the crook of my elbow, steadying me even as I helped her move around the side of the manor. Back here, the afternoon sun warmed the air enough that staying outside to talk wasn't such a hardship.

"It's so beautiful," she said as we passed the low wall that separated the kitchen yard from the garden. She regarded the bare facade of the manor. "I still can't stop thinking of it as a castle."

My lips twisted; she was stalling. "You should see it all lit up for LongNight," I said, playing along for now. "It's...well it's even more beautiful." That sounded phenomenally stupid. I could probably paint it but words failed me.

"That's less than a week away," she said, eyes crinkling. "Maybe you can show me."

My mouth went dry, and I forced my thoughts back to the path they'd been headed down before she distracted me with dreams of the future. "Why are you stalling?" I said.

She sighed. "I learned something today," she said. "About your curse."

I raised an eyebrow, but she looked away. We stopped in front of a bench. From here you could look over the whole garden with its winding paths and overgrown bowers.

"My matrona actually pointed it out."

I stiffened. Almighty, save me, Catrin had told her the truth.

"I managed to change your curse, manipulate it. But since then I've been stumped, Léon," she said. "And now I might know why."

The knot in my gut released. Maybe not the truth that would condemn me then. Her expression remained pensive, not accusatory.

"What do you remember about that day?"

"I've already told you—"

She shook her head, taking both my hands in hers. "No, not about your actions. What do you remember about the enchanter? What did they say? What did they do?"

Carefully now. A slip would reveal all and I still hadn't decided what I was willing to risk in light of my convicting painting.

"She said I was an animal," I said slowly. "That I was fit only to struggle for existence. Then she raised her hands, like you do when you're casting, but nothing happened." I shrugged uncomfortably. "Not then anyway."

"Do you remember how she worded it?"

"She said I didn't value life." My brow furrowed. "She said her punishment would hold until my life was counted as 'naught.'"

Anwen sat on the bench as if her legs had gone out from under her. Her hand crept to her chest.

"Anwen?" I reached out to touch her shoulder before I jerked back. "What is it?"

"Almighty, she was right."

"Who was right? Catrin?"

Her hazel eyes were brighter than usual and her mouth twisted in pain. "I'm sorry, Léon."

The breath froze in my chest. "For what?" I forced myself to say.

"It's a death curse."

"A-a what?" I didn't really need her to repeat it, but those words made my stomach curl into a painful ball.

"That's why I haven't been able to do more than modify the magic on you. The vytl binding your form isn't linked to your skin. It's linked to your heart. The only way to break the curse is to destroy it completely."

I collapsed beside her. My thoughts skittered in all directions, only one remaining clear.

"My heart has to stop," I grated out.

She stared out at the gardens, but I got the impression she didn't actually see them. "Or change itself so much the curse no longer recognizes it."

"How do you change someone's heart?"

Anwen raised her hands palms up then let them fall back to her lap. "I think that's the point. You can't change someone that deeply. If I try to break it now without addressing that, it would kill you. It allows for a very final redemption," Anwen said, staring at her hands. "You would be buried as a human."

"But death isn't freedom."

"Not the kind you're looking for, no. Whoever did this to you was angry. They wanted you to suffer until the end of your life."

Suffer was right. And as Anwen slipped to her knees in front of me, I couldn't help agreeing with them. I lifted my hand to touch the scar that lined her jaw. I'd done this to her and death was a fitting punishment.

But it wasn't the only way to freedom. She'd mentioned another.

I had earned my punishment with my selfish and careless treatment of Anwen's life. In order to earn my freedom, my heart had to change. I had to become the opposite of the boy who had selfishly damaged another human being. What would that look like?

To love someone selflessly.

I could see why Catrin had thought death would be easier.

She caught my fingers with hers. "Léon, I'm not giving up. I will not leave until you're free."

I'd flirted and cajoled and manipulated, desperate to keep her by me, never knowing she'd given her word, set her mind. Lovely, loyal Anwen. I couldn't shake her loose now if I tried.

That's why I loved her.

I stopped short, probing at that thought, testing it for truth.

Ye Saints, I loved her. Loved her compassion, her humor, her grace. She wasn't physically graceful. She couldn't be with that limp. But she was full of grace and mercy.

If she was full of mercy, would she forgive me for the role I'd had in her past?

No. If she knew, I lost all chance of winning her at all. And suddenly that was far more important than just keeping her here. But if loving someone was the key to my freedom, why was I still cursed? Even sitting in the slushy garden I could feel the bear lurking under the surface. Maybe there was more I was missing. Maybe she had to love me back.

I'd always thought love would feel like flying. But my chest tightened and my heart sank into a small hard ball, protecting this new feeling, keeping it safe and locked away from the truth that would threaten it.

She still knelt before me, oblivious to the slush soaking through her tunic, her hazel eyes intent on my face. Almighty, if I wasn't careful I'd fall into them and never surface.

I raised my other hand to tilt her chin and leaned forward. My lips parted and my breath stopped.

Her eyes narrowed. "Léon, what are you doing?"

"Nothing." I jerked back, cold washing over me followed by a burning that rivaled my transformations.

I surged to my feet, leaving her blinking up at me. I might have found my Yasmina. I might have realized I loved the woman behind the scars. But obviously she wasn't there with me. She hadn't made that leap.

Yet.

I had a new task now. I'd never courted anyone before, but if Giles could do it, so could I.

CHAPTER SEVENTEEN

There was only one person in the world who could help me convince Anwen I was worth loving. Which meant I had an apology to make.

I clambered through a forgotten attic, between the wall and the inner slanting beams of the roof, cursing all dust and damp. My ankle twisted and I caught myself on the inside of the lead roof, a stream of cold air freezing me through a crack.

What on Térne was Giles doing up here? It wouldn't be a safe place to store anything with rain and weather coming through the cracks between the slate tiles. Some of the boxes I'd tripped over showed signs of water damage. Almighty, if I had to spend a minute more in this forgotten attic, I'd have a few choice words for—

"My lord?"

I started, lost my balance, and fell on a moldering box. The top collapsed, dropping me into a pile of rotting furs. I didn't want to think about how long they'd been up here and what vermin could have made their home in them. However, the fleeting thought that neither my father nor my grandfather had been avid hunters crossed my mind.

Great. Century-old animal parts. Just what I was hoping to encounter this morning.

I hauled myself upright and swiped my rear end clean.

Giles regarded me with his brows raised, cool and collected as always. Had he come to check the storage room before leaving forever?

"Can I help you find something?" The words were innocuous enough, but I could hear the distance beneath them. He was already preparing himself to abandon me.

I shuffled my feet. Just speak, Léon.

"I..." I glanced around at the cramped space and the scraps of broken, rotting wood and winced. The words I needed weren't there.

He started to turn away, hurt sliding across what little of his expression I could see.

"I'm trying to find my old manuscript supplies," I said careful not to catch his eye. "Anwen wants to learn. I thought I'd teach her."

"And you thought they'd be up here?" He hesitated, then turned to face me. His brow furrowed just as a particularly sharp draft swept through the attic, making me shiver.

I couldn't tell him I was up here looking for him.

Muck on me, I was such a coward. That was exactly why I was up here, and I couldn't manage to own up to it at least once in my life.

His face fell and he began to turn away again.

"I'm sorry," I blurted.

He stopped, his mouth falling open. "You what?" He'd probably never expected to hear those words in his life.

I flushed. "I'm sorry," I said again and realized I'd say it as many times as he needed to hear it. "I'm sorry I yelled at you. I'm sorry I said those awful things. Please don't go because your lord is an ass."

Giles blinked, the corner of his lip twitching.

Almighty, if he laughed at me...

"My lord, I appreciate the apology." He paused, as if savoring the word. He really hadn't thought I'd ever stoop to apologizing. "But I wasn't planning on going anywhere."

"But," I said, struggling to keep from gaping. "But Fanny..."

He lowered his eyes. "Fanny has been asking me to leave with her for years. It is an old discussion."

Something about the way he said it made me think the discussion had ended a little differently this time. "You argued," I said.

"We did." The tips of his ears went red. "Though my decision should not have come as a surprise to her. It has always been the same."

Because he always chose me. Almighty, Catrin should have turned me into a donkey because I really was an ass. I stared at my feet with nothing to say. No words to stem the tide of emotion between us.

"I think it's admirable that you want to teach Anwen," Giles said, avoiding my gaze equally. "But they're in one of the storage rooms on the ground floor. I don't put anything valuable up here. It's too damp."

I stared at the intruder sitting cross-legged on the floor, listening patiently while Emeline flooded the great hall with her chatter. Almighty, I couldn't go a day now without tripping over Myrddin somewhere. The tall enchanter seemed as at home with his long legs folded on my flagstones as he had been standing in the snowy courtyard. Didn't the man ever look awkward or ruffled or uncomfortable?

Anwen sat on the steps, her chin in her hand, while Brann lay along the railing above them, tail curling in interest.

Emeline, the little traitor, was showing off Thundering Daisies and telling Myrddin how the warhorse had gotten his name. Josselin sat quietly beside her, eyes wary behind his polite expression. At least one of them was resisting Myrddin's easy charm.

"So you live here now?" Myrddin said, turning the carved horse over and over in his hands. "Alone?"

I bristled and stepped forward. Enchanter or not, I wouldn't let him imply anything inappropriate where Josselin and Emeline were concerned.

"Not alone," Emeline said with an indignant huff. "There's Léon, and Giles, and Anwen."

"You think Anwen will always want to live here with Léon?"

I froze, foot halfway to the floor, but Myrddin cast a playful look at Anwen. She rolled her eyes in response.

"Of course," Emeline said, looking over at Anwen. "And Léon will probably let her paint her own room, too."

A vision of Yasmina's solar flashed through my head. No need, I'd already done it for her.

Myrddin gave me a long look. "Will you let me paint my own room?"

My eyes narrowed. "You didn't want to stay here."

Myrddin shrugged. "True. Too bad. I could have brushed up on my painting skills." His face lit up and he beamed at Anwen. "Get it? Brushed up?"

"Almighty save me from your sense of humor," she said, but she was laughing.

"You paint?" I said, my brows drawing together. Muck, how could I compete with Myrddin the betrothed?

"Once," Anwen said. "He's painted once. The effect was..."

"Spectacular," Myrddin said when she hesitated.

"I was going to say crude."

I opened my mouth to ask what the hell that meant, but Anwen saw my look.

"It was a practical joke," she said. "Stick figures painted in the sky with fire making rude gestures to tick off our matrona."

Myrddin grinned. "To be fair I was thirteen. Everything I did ticked off Matrona."

"It was appalling. One of them was—"

Myrddin leaped from where he was sitting to cover her mouth. He at least had the grace to blush. "Now, now, loose tongues make former friends."

Anwen pushed his hand away. "Do you promise?"

"Ha ha," he said. "You're not getting rid of me that easy."

Anwen sighed dramatically. "Easy. He calls a lifetime of work easy." But her smile spread across her face again.

Their banter tugged at my stomach. They shared history and humor, jokes and stories I would never be a part of. The same feeling had twisted in my gut every time my parents had set off in their carriage, leaving me behind.

I wanted history with Anwen. I wanted jokes we could chuckle over privately. I wanted her to roll her eyes at me and smile at the same time.

Myrddin stood and brushed off the seat of his pants before heading for the kitchen.

I caught his arm in my grip. I couldn't say anything about the jealousy that steamed below the surface, but I could bring up a legitimate problem.

"What do you think you're doing?" I said to him, low and reasonable.

His brows went up. "My job," he said. "My royally appointed job."

I jerked my head at Josselin and Emeline. "I don't see how questioning a couple of children will help you determine if I'm fit to retain my title."

"It gives me a sense of the man behind the title. Why? Do you have a problem with that?"

I struggled to put words to the distress pounding through my limbs. It wasn't just jealousy over his looks and his easy camaraderie with Anwen. It was a new feeling and hard to pin down.

"I'd rather you didn't speak to them without me," I said.

He studied me as if he could see every dark corner of my

mind. "You think by being present you can suppress the dirty laundry you don't want found?"

My chin jerked up. "Do you think anything could suppress Emeline?"

He chuckled.

I ran a hand through my hair. "It's just...they've been hurt by adults before. I won't let it happen again."

Instead of insisting he wasn't interested in hurting them at all, he paused then nodded. "I understand. Next time I interview them, I'll make sure you're present."

Giles came through the door behind me with the box we'd spent the morning searching for, and Myrddin's gaze lit up.

"Ah, Giles," he said. "Could I ask you a few questions?"

I let go of his arm, and he moved on to my manservant.

Giles shot a look at me.

I raised one shoulder.

"Not at all," he said, then handed off the box to me.

Myrddin gestured him toward the kitchen but turned back to me as an afterthought. "Would you like to come along? To be sure I don't abuse him?"

Under the joking was a real question. I could insist on overseeing the interview like with the children, but I couldn't afford to appear that defensive.

I gritted my teeth and shook my head. "Giles doesn't need my protection." I couldn't help adding, "If you upset him, he'll kill you with a look."

Giles raised a mild eyebrow at me before he followed the chuckling Myrddin away.

I shuddered. The enchanter could laugh all he liked but

Giles spoke volumes with those eyebrows. Usually loud and disappointed volumes.

Emeline bounced up before I had yanked my mind away from Myrddin and his blasted interviews.

"Léon, can we play outside in the snow?"

"Huh? Yeah, sure, but don't forget your cloaks."

Josselin and Emeline shot through the door into the kitchen, the same door Myrddin and Giles had used.

I couldn't snarl at the enchanter. He had the power to take away my lands and title, which had been in my family five generations already.

I took a deep breath and shook away the worry, then approached Anwen.

"What's that?" she said, nodding at the box.

A wave of misplaced shyness caused my smile to wobble. "A present," I said and set it down beside her.

She gave me a puzzled look before lifting the lid and peering inside. Her eyes widened.

She pulled out a stack of pale, smooth skins, cut to size.

"Parchment," I said, crouching beside her. "There are some quills in there, too, but we'll mix up some new ink in the workroom."

She blinked at me, her mouth parted. I had to turn away, hiding the way her lips made my blood creep up my neck.

"You mean you'll teach me?"

I shrugged. "I think you're right about having someone to explain enchanters. And I think you're the best one to do it. You were the one who convinced me to start painting again, so this is repayment."

"Thank you," she said.

I avoided the power of her gaze by rummaging through the box until I found a wood board, sanded smooth and whitewashed.

"You can practice on this. Layout your pages so you make mistakes here and not on precious parchment. Then when you're ready, you line the pages and ink your words. If you want illumination, and let's face it, who doesn't want illumination, you'll have to find a Disciple of Createjoy. My fingers can't manage it now."

I kept the bitterness out of my voice while I sketched a couple of broad lines with a stick of charcoal and wiped it clean with a cloth to demonstrate.

"Now you try."

I winced at the way she grasped the charcoal, her fingers eclipsing the stick as they curled around it. I didn't want to be constantly correcting her. If I left her at it long enough, she'd figure out the best way for herself, but it pained me to see such a fine instrument held so clumsily.

She worried at her lower lip as she studied the board in front of her and pressed down to start writing. The tip broke under the pressure of her hand. She scowled.

"Blast," she said. "That's harder than it looks."

Brann snorted and Anwen shot a quelling look at him.

I frowned. "I...I thought you knew how to write."

"I do." She glanced up with a peculiar mix of annoyance and shame. "But I've only ever done it with my finger." She demonstrated, tracing her name then mine in lines of fire on the flagstones before sweeping away the ash with her hand. "The only people I've ever corresponded with are enchanters, and I'm not sure any of us have ever written a real physical letter."

I took the charcoal from her and sharpened the end again with the knife I found in the box. I gave her an encouraging smile and handed it back to her.

"Here," I said. "Try it like this." I wrapped her fingers around the pencil, arranging them so they held the tip delicately and nimbly. I looked up into her hazel eyes. Even after painting them, I wondered at the colors that made up the whole. Streaks of brown and gold offset the gray-green that lurked behind.

Did Myrddin appreciate her eyes? Did he love the way they sparked, wide and wondering? No, not wondering. They were at their best when she was smiling. When her lips turned up and the skin at the corners of her eyes crinkled. Like they were doing now.

"Léon," she said.

I blinked. "What?" What had she been saying? I'd missed it.

"Are you going to let go so I can try again?"

I looked down at where my fingers were still wrapped around hers. A flush ran through me, making my skin prickle, and I drew my hand away. "Right, yes. Great."

She chuckled low in her throat, and I had to swallow.

Anwen leaned forward, her teeth clenched on her lower lip as she concentrated, tracing crooked letters onto the board. My eyes fixated on her lips.

"Put your tongue back in your mouth, Beauregard," Brann said not so quietly from the railing.

Anwen looked up in question, and I shot to my feet. "I

should go check on Josselin and Emeline."

I raced from the Great Hall, Anwen's puzzled gaze and Brann's laughing eyes following me.

Small footprints disappeared at the end of the driveway. I stood, my arms crossed and my breath huffing white before my face. I spun on my heel and walked back toward the manor a few paces, spun again and stopped in front of the gate.

The footprints still went through the gate and off down the road.

I swore.

"You think their guardian came back to take them?" Myrddin said behind me.

He, and everyone else, had come running when I'd yelled through the manor that Josselin and Emeline were missing.

I shook my head. "It's just their footprints. They didn't meet anyone else. At least not here." I spun around and paced again.

"Léon," Anwen said, putting a hand on my arm as I passed her. "I'm sure they're all right."

"They wanted to play outside," I said, the bear growling under the surface. "I told them they could. I didn't tell them to stay on the grounds. I didn't tell them to be careful."

When I looked up, Myrddin was watching me with that assessing expression, and I shut up. No reason to give him more fodder for his report. Almighty, I was no better a guardian than the one that had beaten them.

"My lord, we'll find them," Giles said.

"Damn right." I stopped digging a trench with my pacing and stripped off my cloak and doublet.

"What are you doing?" Anwen said.

"I can't afford to lose any more clothes."

Brann snorted. "I doubt that."

I gritted my teeth, ignoring the cat. My hands went to the hem of my shirt. Almighty, this was just like last time. What had prompted them to run?

The bear surged up, scratching at the inside of my skin, demanding release and the chance to tear apart his enemies. And I was half a minute away from letting him loose.

I had my shirt over my head when I heard them. The linen became a prison as I struggled to pull it back down so I could turn and see.

Josselin leaped over the gap in the wall forty yards away, and Emeline tumbled after him. They laughed, their faces glowing from the cold.

I snatched my doublet and cloak from Giles's hands and strode toward the children, the bear subsiding in the face of my relief.

Josselin noticed my approach before his sister did and jumped in front of her, arms spread. I forced down my first instinct to yell and settled for planting myself in front of him, hands on my hips.

"Where have you been?" I said.

Josselin gulped. "You said we could play."

I fought to keep from shouting. "Here on the grounds. I don't want you gallivanting through the woods."

Had I just used the word gallivanting? Saints, I sounded

like Giles. A glance behind me showed he and the rest of them had followed. Great, now I had an audience.

"Why not?" Josselin said

"Because it's dangerous."

"We've always been fine before. And if you're the monster, then it's safe, right?"

They didn't know about the killings. And I wasn't about to tell them there was another monster for them to worry about.

"Look, just stay on the grounds when you play, all right? And I want to know where you are at all times."

"Even if we promise to stay inside the wall?"

"Yes."

"Why?"

Good question. Why did I care so much? Before, I'd just wanted them to stay out of my way.

"Because I'm responsible for you. And I care about what happens to you," I said. I hadn't realized what that meant when I took them in. I'd thought giving them a safe home would be enough, but I'd been letting them run wild, too. And was that really what was best for them?

Josselin had lost his fear and defiance and was looking at me in puzzlement. Emeline sagged, her smock wet below the knees. I had to make my decision soon.

"Giles?" I said, my voice thoughtful. "How would you feel about being a tutor again?"

"My lord?"

I looked at him over my shoulder, raising an eyebrow. "I haven't been doing my job as their guardian. It's more than giving them a bed and letting them paint their room. If you don't mind, I'd like you to teach Josselin and Emeline."

"What would you like me to teach them?" His head tilted and there was a definite gleam in his eyes. Was that interest or approval?

"I—" I hadn't thought that far. "Start where you started with me."

I turned back and found Josselin's brows lowered. "That's not fair. No one in the village takes lessons," he said.

I shrugged. "Children living with me will learn what Giles wants to teach. And when they play, they'll stay on the grounds and not go wandering."

"Anything else, my lord?" Giles said, the corner of his mouth quirked in what would be a smirk on anyone else.

Saints, what did he expect? I was making this up as I went. "And they'll eat all their dinner and go to bed on time."

Josselin's mouth opened and closed but nothing came out. Finally he smiled and said, "All right," before he took Emeline's hand and led her into the kitchen.

I blinked and cast a glance back at the others. "Did I win or lose that? Could anyone tell?"

Anwen laughed and stepped forward to lay her hand on my shoulder.

I shivered under her touch.

"Poor Papa Léon," she said. "Come inside by the fire. You must be freezing."

My skin had goosebumps from the icy air, but my shoulder burned where her hand had rested. I rubbed it surreptitiously, turning away from Myrddin and Giles who looked thoughtful and proud, respectively.

CHAPTER EIGHTEEN

These days it felt like all I did was stand in the snow and strip naked.

"My lord, you don't have to do this," Giles said as I handed him my doublet and cloak. He folded both over his arm, his lips tight with disapproval.

"I'm aware of that." I yanked my boots off, bracing myself for the cold. That morning, letters of fire had spread across my wall, safely in my bedroom where Anwen couldn't see. They'd said, "Beauregard, I would speak with you today." The terse missive was signed C. Emrys.

"She can't mean you any good," Giles said.

"She can't mean me any bad either. Not if she wants to keep Anwen's good opinion." It felt good to reassure Giles, even if I didn't entirely believe the words myself. The Emrys matrona probably just wanted to talk, and I kind of wanted to hear what she had to say.

Unless it was just, "Die, you pig."

"If anything happens to me," I said, "you'll tell Anwen

where I went and who I was supposed to meet. Catrin knows that."

A muscle in his jaw jumped as I handed him my boots and stripped off my hose.

"Muck, that's cold."

"Be careful, my lord."

"If Anwen or Myrddin ask, I'm inspecting my lands." I paused. "Maybe tell Myrddin that even if he doesn't ask." It might be a point in my favor.

I didn't wait for his answer but stepped across the dividing line and accepted the fiery shiver that left me with fur on the other side.

It took me a little more than an hour to reach the meeting. Her message hadn't specified a location, but there was only one place on my lands where Catrin would want to see me.

The barony was littered with rocks named for animals the rain and weather had beaten them to resemble, and I stopped beside the arching boulder called Horse Head. Even as a bear, it was twice my height. My breath came a little faster. I tried to ignore it but my eyes were drawn to the cleared area before the boulder where Anwen had lain bleeding three years ago. I jerked my gaze away, chasing the memory from my mind's eye.

What was I even doing here? It's not like I could actually talk to Catrin, not shaped as a bear. And what would I say anyway? Sorry I ruined your enfan's life?

Maybe Giles was right. Maybe she did mean to harm me, and I, the trusting idiot, had walked right into her trap.

Familiar pain raced up and down my limbs, making me yelp in surprise. I should have expected it. How else would she talk to me? I clenched my teeth shut, waiting for the pain to pass as it always did.

When I opened my eyes, Catrin stood three feet away, staring down where I knelt in the snow, my human arms hugging my torso.

"Matrona Catrin," I said, teeth chattering.

"Lord Beauregard." Her bright blue eyes narrowed and she tossed a blanket at me. "Cover yourself."

I wrapped the blanket around my shoulders, making sure it was long enough to conceal everything before I stood. "If the details of my transformation bother you, you have only yourself to blame."

She jerked her chin up as I brushed the snow off a ledge of the boulder and sat down to save my feet from the freezing slush.

I held my breath, my heart pounding against my rib cage as I waited for her to speak. I wanted to hate her, but the feelings that had been so clear before now fuzzed and twisted in my mind into something far more confusing. I couldn't actually blame her for what she'd done, now.

Finally, Catrin tired of waiting for me and rolled her eyes. "Well?"

I raised an eyebrow. "You were the one who invited me here, Matrona."

She clenched her jaw. "What have you told her?"

"Anwen?" I suppressed a chuckle when she ground her teeth.

"Yes, Anwen. Who else would I mean? Saint Redemption?"

I shrugged, enjoying her frustration. I might not blame

her for her actions but I didn't have to make things easy on her. I spread my hands. "What would I tell Anwen, Matrona? Would I tell her how you transformed me? Would I tell her how I cursed your name for three years?"

She made an impatient gesture, and her blue cloak swirled from her elbows to her feet.

I immediately sobered. Angering this enchanter was what had gotten me into this mess in the first place. She could just as easily kill me as turn me into a bear this time.

"No, Matrona," I said quietly. "I haven't told her about you."

Her shoulders relaxed enough for me to notice the change.

"Just as I know you haven't told her about me."

She glowered. "I could," she said. "I could tell her it was your disregard, your arrogance that ruined her life. She would leave you to your fate. The fate I designed for you."

I winced away. "Then why haven't you told her the truth?" I said.

She examined her fingernails. "Why haven't you?"

I opened my mouth to spit out a retort, but then I stopped to consider her question. Before, I'd wanted to keep Anwen here with me. I'd been afraid to lose her. I was still afraid to lose her. But now there was something stronger holding me back. Something less selfish.

"I don't want to hurt her," I said.

She spread her hands to indicate her answer was the same as mine.

My eyes narrowed. "But you were protecting her three years ago. I deserved what you did to me."

She raised her eyebrows, and I flushed.

"Yes," she said. "At least we agree on that. But Anwen would see my actions that day as a betrayal of the power we both keep in trust." She dropped her gaze, cheeks turning pink.

Catrin hid a monster under her skin as much as I did. I remembered the way Anwen had spoken of the enchanter who'd cursed me, the way her eyes had blazed and her fists had clenched. My graceful, merciful Anwen, who believed everyone deserved a chance, would never look at her the same way again if she knew what her matrona had done that day.

"So neither of us can tell her the truth," I said.

A precarious balance. We were only safe as long as the other agreed to keep quiet. The moment one of us broke and told Anwen the truth, our entire tower of lies would come crashing down, crushing all of us under its weight.

Catrin ground her teeth again. "It appears we're agreed on that as well. Where does that leave us, Lord Beauregard?"

I rubbed my hands down my shins, under the blanket, trying to decide how likely it was she'd betray me. "Exactly where we were, I guess." I thought again before speaking. "I'm not going to hurt her, Matrona."

She sneered. "Forgive me if I don't believe you."

She was right, I'd already hurt Anwen. But how could I explain I would die before I hurt her again?

The fact that I was still cursed proved that I hadn't changed as much as I wanted to think I had.

I opened my mouth, but she spoke over me. "She doesn't deserve to be stuck here with her tormentor. I won't hurt her, but I will convince her to leave while her pride and her feelings are intact."

She raised her hands.

I leaped from my seat on the boulder, shedding the blanket. "Wait. No!" I scrambled toward her, but as I moved, fire seared my limbs and dropped me to all fours.

When I finally lumbered to my feet as a bear, she was gone.

I cursed under my breath but it came out as growls and snorts. Hardly satisfying.

I turned and headed back toward the manor, making no effort to keep my movements quiet.

I'd only gone a few paces when I caught a whiff of something unfamiliar. I whipped my head up, nostrils flaring. It was musky, like an animal, but there was an undercurrent that reminded me of the village.

I snorted. The old tang of blood overlaid it all, indicating a predator.

The bear reared inside me, readying himself to defend his territory. For once I agreed with him. I reached out to tap his instincts, accepting his defensiveness. And he let me hold him at the edges of my mind. My humanity remained unclouded.

Was that the key to taming the beast? Let him have his portion of my reactions, give him his space and he'd give me mine?

I would have pondered the idea, but I caught another whiff of the unknown predator and surged forward. Something hunted my lands and I wanted to know what.

Someone screamed and I put on a burst of speed, hurtling through a line of trees and underbrush.

Branches lashed my face and my eyes shut in defense.

Right before I crashed into something low and solid.

A snarl came close and instinct prompted me to react, but my teeth snapped shut on empty air.

I opened my eyes but the space between the trees was empty. The sharp scent of blood made me turn. A woman crouched between a tree and a lip of ground that formed a waist-high cliff. I hadn't even noticed the dip when I'd sailed over it.

She clutched her arm, marred by bloody gashes. Like the ones we'd found on each body so far. She whimpered and stared up at me.

I stepped closer, and she flinched and screamed.

I fought down a surge of frustration. Of course she'd be frightened of me. I was a bear first and her savior second. And she wasn't anything like brave little Emeline.

I shifted from foot to foot. Should I abandon the woman to her fear and seek out the monster?

No, no. If I left, whatever it was might come back for her.

I backed away, assessing her for any other hidden damage while keeping my distance. As far as I could tell, it was only her arm and the shock of the attack that kept her locked in her hiding place. I grumbled and retreated even farther, until she couldn't see me through the trees.

Finally she crept out, glanced around and bolted through the forest. Toward Whitecliff.

I followed at a discreet distance trying to keep my steps

muffled. I couldn't smell whatever it was that had attacked her, but I still wanted to be sure she got home all right.

I stopped at the edge of the trees as the woman stumbled between the buildings. People swarmed down the street to greet her. Georg the blacksmith led the pack.

I couldn't hear, but I could make out her frantic gestures back toward the forest.

Time to make myself scarce.

I was certain now. Something else was out there. Something else was killing my people.

It wasn't me. Thank the Almighty it wasn't me.

The sun had tipped over its crest toward afternoon by the time I made it back to the manor. I nudged open the gate and stepped over the dividing line, letting the fire burn away the bear. This time I was almost sorry to see him go. He'd helped me in the forest, and it seemed impolite to shed him like a fur cloak.

When I rose to my human feet, I found a stack of clothes beside the gate. I pulled my underclothes and hose on as quickly as I could.

Did I search for Giles first or Anwen?

The decision was taken out of my hands when a low rumble drew my attention to the road behind me. What the...

Figures carrying pickaxes and hammers came marching up to the gate, their angry voices rising to a roar that echoed off the front of the manor. Muck on it all, a couple of people carried torches even though it was bright afternoon.

Not again.

They must have seen me near the village and followed me home.

The noise of the mob brought Anwen to the door of the great hall. She stood there, brow furrowed with consternation as Myrddin slid out beside her. Brann followed, shaped like an ordinary house cat.

I scrambled to join them on the steps as the angry villagers came up the carriageway and stopped in front of the manor.

Surprise, surprise, Georg led the pack.

"What is the meaning of this...invasion force?" I said, drawing myself up. I'd assumed the responsibility of being a noble, I might as well look the part.

"We've come to demand justice," Georg said, except he wasn't looking at me. He glared at Anwen and Myrddin. "This...lord..." He spit across the snow. "Isn't a lord at all. He's a beast and we've come to put him down like one. That's what you're here for, isn't it?" He jerked his head at Myrddin.

"I'm here for the truth," Myrddin said.

"Well, that man is a murderer," Georg said, pointing at me. "There's your truth. A woman came into the village today, mauled by a monster. A bear, she said."

Myrddin and Anwen peered at me with twin expressions of concern.

"Léon?" Anwen said.

I didn't flinch. "I know," I said. "I saw her."

Myrddin's expression didn't change, but Anwen bit her lip. "You did...?" she said.

I turned to her, unable to keep the triumphant smile from my face any longer. "I saved her," I said. "This—this thing attacked her, and I saved her. I watched over her all the way to the village."

"A thing?" Anwen said. "You didn't see what it was?"

I opened my mouth to respond, then stopped. Almighty, I couldn't tell them I'd closed my eyes.

"Come on, Beauregard," Brann said. "Your imagination has to be better than that."

"I mean it," I said, refusing to let Brann's sniping bother me. "Something strange is out there. I smelled it."

"And then you found the woman," Myrddin said as if he was leading me toward something. Probably a cliff.

"Yes," I said.

"He's killing us," Georg said, brandishing his torch. "And you two are letting him."

Myrddin glared at the blacksmith, but Anwen just studied me with sad eyes.

I couldn't blame the village woman for not being able to distinguish between monsters, but I'd thought Anwen at least would believe me.

"I saved her," I said.

"Did the bear take over?" Anwen said softly.

"No," I growled. I took a deep breath and fought for the control I'd had in the woods. "I...partnered with him. We worked together, but I was always aware and in control."

Myrddin and Anwen exchanged a glance.

"I saved her," I repeated but no one was listening.

"If you won't do anything," Georg said, lowering his chin. "We will." He started forward. Whether he intended to burn down the manor or just set me on fire I didn't find out because Anwen stepped between us.

"No," she said quietly.

Georg didn't stop.

Anwen closed her eyes and the ground rumbled. The snow rolled and soil broke through, painting the white with slashes of brown and black. The road itself reached up to grab Georg's feet and bind him to the earth. The rest of the villagers stumbled and cried out as waves of rock and dirt sent them to their knees.

"I promise we will learn the truth," Anwen said over the men's alarm. "And when we do, the perpetrator will be punished according to the law. But we will not tolerate this violence."

She glared at each man in turn, then said, "Go home."

They picked themselves up out of the churned snow and ran.

Georg glowered from under his ragged eyebrows, and I met his gaze without flinching. Anwen shook her head and the earth released his feet. The blacksmith bent and brushed the mud from his hose before turning to follow his men.

Anwen's shoulders drooped, and she looked downcast before she retreated back into the manor.

I stared after her, my eyes wide and my breath heavy. I hadn't seen Anwen's power firsthand before. Not arrayed against an enemy like this. Almighty, she'd stopped an angry mob in full stride without breaking a sweat.

Maybe ordinary people really did have something to fear from enchanters.

Myrddin gave me a look as he headed inside as well.

I'd joked about Anwen being my prisoner but I hadn't realized how much of a joke it was. Anwen would never be held anywhere against her will. The only reason she was still here was because she'd chosen to be.

Yet another reason to love her.

Inside the manor, an argument blazed.

"I can't do it alone," Anwen said.

"That's why I'm suggesting we do it together," Myrddin said. "Do you really want to wait any longer? I think that mob was proof we need to get this solved now."

Anwen sighed.

I stopped in the middle of the great hall, watching them warily. "What's this?" I said.

"We have something we want to try," Myrddin said. "It might free you."

My eyes narrowed. "You think I'm a killer," I said. "Why would you want to help?" Anwen would help a thief steal the crown jewels if she thought it was the right thing to do. But I didn't understand her freire nearly as well.

Myrddin raised an eyebrow. "I'd rather people stopped dying," he said. "And I think his majesty would agree with me."

I clenched my jaw.

He rolled his eyes. "And it's the fastest way to clear your name if you're not the killer, all right?"

I crossed my arms. "I thought you said there was nothing you could do?" I asked Anwen.

"I also said I would never stop trying," she said, a bit of heat entering her voice.

"Now that we know we're dealing with a death curse, there are certain things we can try," Myrddin said. "Between the two of us we might be able to keep the curse from killing you."

"Comforting," I said.

Myrddin grinned unpleasantly.

Anwen sighed in exasperation. "Myrddin is one of the best healers the Emrys Family has trained," she said. "Since the curse is so intricately woven into your heart, I thought he might be able to figure out how to unwind it."

My gaze drifted between Anwen's frank expression and Myrddin's grin. "Are you sure about this?"

"Positive," Myrddin said at the same time Anwen said, "Well, we can't be entirely sure about any of it."

They glared at each other with identical expressions of annoyance.

"Brilliant," I muttered. Possible death or unbroken curse. Pick one, Léon.

"I guess my life is in your hands," I said, and bowed to them.

I'd thought the words were symbolic, but later when I was lying on a bed in one of the guest rooms I realized how literal they'd been. They'd decided the nest on the floor of my room was too awkward to work with, so Anwen sat on one side of the bed and Myrddin stood on the other while I lay like a corpse between them.

I shuddered. Best not to think of corpses for now.

"Léon?" Anwen said. "Are you all right?"

"Fine," I said. "I just have to lie here, right? Easy."

Myrddin snorted, and I shot a glance at him. His face was open and serious. The consummate professional. A spike of relief shot through me. Thank the Almighty it was him standing there and not his matrona. Catrin would let me die for my sins. But Myrddin didn't know the truth and would therefore do everything he could to keep me alive.

"Ready?" Anwen said.

I nodded, then realized she'd been speaking to Myrddin.

She smiled at me. "Close your eyes."

Nothing in my life to this point had been as terrifying as lying there with my eyes closed listening to them murmur cryptic things like "Carefully now. Watch the—" and "I see it. You just keep that stuff out of my way."

I'd expected to feel something when their magic coursed through me. Hot or cold, some kind of tingle. Even the fire I felt every time I transformed.

But there was nothing.

I cracked an eyelid hoping to get some idea of what they were doing.

"Léon," Anwen said before I'd even focused on her blurry face.

I snapped it shut. "Sorry."

"I know it's boring," she said. "But I think I've found—"

Agony ripped through my chest, radiating out from my heart. I arched against the bed and screamed.

"Myrddin!"

"Muck, it slipped right under me."

"Hold him—"

Almighty, I couldn't breathe. I gasped, drawing short

gusts of air into my tortured lungs as my stomach roiled. I clamped my mouth shut and breathed through my nose. If I was sick now, I'd end up drowning in my own vomit.

"Redemption's mercy, what is that?"

"Who cares? We're losing him."

My muscles clenched as if I could hold onto life by sheer will. It felt like someone had stuck their hand through my chest and took hold of my heart. The hand squeezed, and I went silent, teeth clenched, too focused inside to voice my pain.

A cold palm pressed against my burning chest. Numbness spread through me, calming the storm. My muscles unlocked and I took a clear breath.

The pain in my chest faded though I kept my eyes clenched shut, preparing for it to return.

"Léon?" Anwen's voice trembled.

I couldn't bear to hear her that upset. I opened my eyes and took another breath. Anwen leaned over me, beautiful eyes wide. Something around my hand unclenched, and I realized she'd been crushing my fingers in her grip.

Myrddin loomed only inches behind Anwen, his face white and his left palm against my chest as if he also was preparing for the pain to come back, too.

"What happened?" I said, though my tongue felt thick and unwieldy.

"Um," Anwen said, eyes flicking between me and Myrddin.

Myrddin sat back, withdrawing his hand. "We almost killed you," he said. His voice shook as much as Anwen's.

"Felt that," I said. I thought I'd put enough effort into the words but my voice came out wispy and breathless.

"I tried to sever the vytl binding you," Myrddin said, rubbing his left hand with his right. "And it...it tried to hold on."

"I've never seen vytl react that way. Normally it's happy to return to the world."

"This was like it had grown into you."

I would have asked him to explain but I didn't think I could understand longer words at that moment.

"S'all right," I said. "Next time we'll know better."

His lips thinned. "I wouldn't recommend trying this again, my lord," he said. "I don't think your heart can take it."

Considering that organ pumped feebly against my chest, I wasn't going to argue with him.

CHAPTER NINETEEN

Being an invalid had its advantages, as I found out the next morning when Giles brought me breakfast in the guest room where I'd spent the night.

"Feeling better, my lord?" Giles said, holding out a tray full of bread and cheese and two dried apples he must have been hoarding since autumn.

I pushed myself up carefully in the bed and felt no twinges in my chest. I briefly considered milking my injuries for everything they'd get me, but the worry behind Giles's cheerful expression made me reconsider.

"I think so," I said.

Anwen walked in behind Giles carrying a steaming mug, and I pulled myself up even straighter, grabbing the covers and tweaking them up my torso. I'd stood in front of her in nothing but my skin and a cloak every time I transformed, but it was different lying here under the covers while she examined me with her gaze.

Brann, shaped like his usual snow leopard, slunk in beside her and took up a guarding position by the door.

My nose wrinkled and I sniffed. I'd accused Brann of killing the second victim mostly as a wild alternative to my own possible guilt, but now I looked at the possibility seriously. He had more freedom of movement than I and the same claws to rend flesh. I sniffed again. But my human nose couldn't tell me anything except that he smelled like fur and musk and Anwen. I didn't think he had the tang of old blood hanging around him telling me he'd killed something recently. Since the Zevryn fed on memories and experiences, not meat, that made sense.

I sat back. Brann probably wasn't the monster, but there was something similar in their scents.

"Myrddin said to drink this." Anwen handed me the mug.

"What is it?" I said. A potion? A poison?

Probably not the latter. Myrddin had seemed sheepish and apologetic after our scare the night before.

"An infusion of willow bark and witchhazel with some vytl thrown in for potency," she said. She cocked her head. "I told you he was one our best healers."

I gagged down the mess—potent was right—and set the mug on the floor beside the bed. Then I collapsed back against the pillows.

"My lord?" Giles said, moving to my side.

I waved him away. "I'm all right," I said. "Just a little tired still. How are Josselin and Emeline?"

"Anxious to see you're all right," he said. He turned to Anwen. "Can he have visitors?"

Anwen stepped closer and laid her hand against my chest. I sucked in a breath at her touch. Could she feel me tremble under her fingers?

"Are you a healer, too?" I said to distract myself.

She chuckled ruefully. "Not really. But I know enough to be able to call Myrddin if something's really wrong."

"And your verdict?"

"Your heart is fine and strong," she said, pulling back and tapping my chest. "If you promise to rest today, I might let you out of bed tomorrow."

If my heart was fine, why did it thump every time she turned those eyes on me?

Out of the corner of my eye, Giles sagged in relief, then straightened his spine. "I'll tell the children to wait till then." He left the tray and retreated through the door.

Anwen fussed with the edge of my blankets, like she didn't want to leave just yet.

My fingers twisted together before I finally found the courage to bring up what was on my mind. "You can't try again, can you?"

She stopped fiddling with the covers and met my eyes. "Myrddin is afraid we could cause permanent damage."

I lifted my chin and clenched my jaw. "Then, will you be going back to the capital with him? Since there's nothing left for you to try."

Her mouth opened and closed. Finally she said, "You... seem very preoccupied with whether I'm leaving or not."

I winced. "I'm sorry. It's just that people tend to leave me."

She sank down on the edge of the bed. "Who?" she said.

"All the servants, Brother Warren, and my parents before him. They wanted an heir but they weren't really interested in raising a son. I never saw them much. Then one day they left and never came back. They died somewhere far away."

She paused. "And Brother Warren?"

"He..." Almighty, did I really want to tell this story? It skirted so close to hers. But the words were there and her eyes were so understanding. "He taught me to paint. He taught me to make beautiful things. But no matter how much beauty came from my fingers, I was still filled with so much ugliness. When we found out my parents were gone...something broke inside me. Brother Warren tried to walk me through my pain, but I just wanted everyone to hurt as much as I hurt." I flushed and clenched my fists in the blanket. "I destroyed a painting he'd worked on for years. His masterpiece. I ruined it and he left. That's why I was cursed."

Her brow furrowed. "I thought you were rude to an enchanter..."

"I was. But that's why. I was upset and lonely and I didn't want to think about how it was my fault." I huffed a laugh. "Then there was the transformation and all the servants refused to serve a bear and I ended up lonelier than before." I shook my head. "People leave me because I drive them away."

I raised a hand and brushed the edge of one of her scars.

She put her hand on mine, trapping my fingers. Her mouth creased as she thought. "You weren't the nicest person, that's true. But you didn't drive your parents away. And the servants were only frightened. That was the curse, not you. It was the enchanter's fault."

She was truly amazing. Even after hearing my story, knowing the awful things I'd done, she still believed the best of me.

I shook my head. "Sometimes people deserve to be punished." I dropped my hand and my eyes. "Sometimes they don't deserve forgiveness."

Her gaze remained steady. "Do you remember the saint I serve?"

"Of course," I said, brows drawing together.

"What is her name?"

"Redemption," I said quietly.

"Yes, Saint Redemption. She takes our pain. She takes our loneliness, our anger, our suffering and changes it into something useful. Something beautiful."

"She makes you into enchanters," I said. "But I'm not an enchanter."

"No, but that doesn't mean your pain can't be redeemed. The Almighty makes our suffering mean something more."

"How?"

"We allow Him to change us." She tilted her head. "How do you feel when you think about Brother Warren now?"

I snorted. That was an easy one. "Ashamed," I said. "I wish I could apologize to him. I was awful to a man who didn't deserve it and—and I'm sorry." I couldn't apologize to Brother Warren, at least not with an unbroken curse, but the other victim of my arrogance and selfishness sat in front of me. Did she hear my apology to her as well? Did my words affect her?

The bear still simmered under my skin. I was still cursed.

So the answer was no. I hadn't learned to love her enough yet to get her to love me back.

She patted my hands where they rested on the blanket. "You don't have to worry about me leaving," she said. She didn't see the deeper meaning of my words. "I made you a promise and I'm not going anywhere until I see you free."

She stood to go and I let her fingers slide from my grip. "Besides, I want to see the manor lit up for LongNight. Since you told me how beautiful it is."

My eyes stayed on the door long after she had disappeared through it.

Almighty help me, I'd trade any possibility of freedom if it meant I could keep Anwen by my side forever.

She was my goal. She was the end of my curse. She was my Yasmina, destined to be my bride in a bower full of roses.

But did she feel the same? She smiled at me, but muck, she smiled at everyone. What else could I do to win her heart? I gave her the means to teach the world about enchanters. I told her things I'd never told anyone. I shared my life with her. What was left?

Giles came in to take away my half-eaten tray, giving me one of his looks, but I was too busy thinking.

"Giles," I said as he was leaving. He stopped and turned. "What would it take to get the manor ready for LongNight?"

He tipped his head. "My lord?"

I threw back the covers. "LongNight," I said again. "I know it's only a couple of days away, but we have people to celebrate with this year. And I think you might secretly be a miracle worker. If anyone can make this place glow, you can."

He put the tray down and stopped me from leaping to my

feet with a hand on my shoulder. "Mistress Anwen did not say you could get up."

He pushed me back down while I sputtered.

"The candles and lanterns are all in a closet," he said and I subsided. "The children can help me collect fresh pine boughs, and I'm sure we can find the quilts we used when you were a child."

"I suppose it's probably too late to hire entertainment the way my parents did."

Giles crossed his arms. "A troop of jongleurs is staying in the village. They're on their way to Gwynmont, so they won't be here for LongNight, but they did agree to perform their pantomime in the village square the night before."

I let out a laugh. "Oh, Josselin and Emeline will love that. I won't be able to go, but I've seen the LongNight panto before." Hopefully Anwen would like it, too.

And that reminded me...

I glanced at Giles. "Does Fanny still bring the bread every day?"

His lips thinned and I almost wished I hadn't asked. "Yes, my lord."

"Perhaps she'd be willing to do some extra cakes and treats."

He drew himself up. "I will ask her."

I waved a hand as if I wasn't rounding out a fantastic idea in my head. "No, no. I'll speak to her."

Giles narrowed his eyes, but I returned his gaze with a bland look. "Is that all, my lord?" he finally said.

"Can you think of anything I've missed?"

He shook his head. "I'll handle the preparations, my lord. You should rest if you want to be part of the celebrations."

"All right," I said as meekly as I could manage. "But would you bring me some charcoal and the writing board? Just to pass the time," I added when he shot me a suspicious look.

His look would have been more than suspicious if he'd known what I was planning.

LongNight was supposed to be celebrated in fellowship with family and friends, the ones who meant the most to you, the ones who brought metaphorical light to your darkest night. I couldn't imagine sitting vigil in the candlelight without Anwen.

And I was pretty sure Giles felt the same way about Fanny. I just had to get them to start talking to each other again.

My perfect symmetrical handwriting had devolved into something that resembled Anwen's unpracticed scrawl, but at least it was legible as long as I was careful to write large enough.

The next morning I tried not to play with the board in my hands and smudge the words I'd agonized over as I waited in the kitchen yard.

A gasp behind me made me whirl, but I relaxed when I realized it was just Anwen.

"Léon, what are you doing?" she said, voice raised in ire.

"Shh," I said. "I don't want Giles knowing I'm out here."

"When I said you could get out of bed today, I didn't mean you could go stand in the cold."

She took hold of my arm, and I had to pull away from her

even though I longed for the contact. "Please, Anwen. I'm making something right. I probably won't have to wait long."

"What are you waiting for?" She'd lowered her voice but her eyes were narrow and wary.

"Fanny," I said. "I have to get to her before—Oh good, here she is."

I strode across the packed snow of the yard, my cloak swinging from my shoulders.

"Miss Fanny," I said. "I have a message for you from Giles." I swept her a bow that belonged in court, not in the kitchen yard.

Fanny stopped short and stared at me as if I'd dropped my pants and started dancing the Ballaslavian polka.

"This ought to be good," Brann said, appearing in the kitchen doorway.

I ignored him and held out the writing board. I'd wanted to get the whole thing down on parchment, but when I'd seen my handwriting, I'd decided not to waste precious supplies.

She didn't reach for the board. She just kept looking between it and me and the doorway.

"I can't read," she said.

Stupid. Of course she couldn't read. Fanny was a peasant. A tenant of her lord.

I faltered for a moment. "He must have meant for me to read it to you."

And I had an audience. Oh joy. Anwen crossed her arms and tapped her fingers. Brann made a show of finding a comfortable spot on the wall of the well.

I cleared my throat and held up the board.

"My dearest Fanny, my light and
     shining star.
I miss your lilting voice, I pine for you
     from afar.
Your clear blue eyes invade my
     dreams.
And nothing in the world is as
     it seems.
I serve an oaf, a trick of fate.
Save me with your love before it's
     too late."

When I glanced up, Fanny's face was bright red, and she'd raised her hand to her mouth.

Not exactly the reaction I was going for. And I'd worked so hard to find something that rhymed with star besides mar and tar.

"Fanny?" Giles said behind me.

I stifled a groan. I'd had worse ideas before but none came to mind right now.

I spun, thinking of how to head them off before Fanny ran and Giles killed me. "I was just reading her your letter," I said.

"You were?" Giles said.

What did that tone of voice mean? He sounded like he was choking.

I nodded. Fanny nodded. Anwen nodded.

Brann snickered.

"It was quite lurid," the cat said. "Like watching a public execution."

"Hey," I said. "I wor—I mean—Giles worked hard on that."

"I'm sure he did. So he can have all the credit."

"Well, yes, of course." I shuffled my feet.

"Especially when it goes badly."

My mouth opened and closed but no sound came out. My voice was too embarrassed.

Giles turned to Fanny. "Should I apologize...again?"

"No," Fanny said—a little too quickly I thought. "No, no." She raced across the kitchen yard to take his hands in hers. "You're forgiven."

Giles's face softened and he opened his mouth to respond.

"As long as you never try to write me poetry again," Fanny added.

Giles cast me a look over her shoulder I couldn't interpret. Some kind of mix of exasperation and relief. "No fear of that," he said. "I'm pretty sure my soul only has the one poem in it."

CHAPTER TWENTY

Emeline, Josselin, Anwen, and Giles formed an unlikely parade as they traipsed down the road toward White-cliff. Brann draped Anwen's shoulder disguised as a white house cat, and I followed at a distance, keeping watch over them without letting them see me. Anwen had forbidden me from leaving the manor. She'd cited my near death the day before, but Myrddin's concoction had restored me to normal, and I had a feeling Anwen was more worried about the killings than my heart. If another body was found tonight, she didn't want me to be blamed.

But it was exactly because of the killings that I had defied her wishes. I couldn't let them travel through the woods to Whitecliff alone when there was something prowling my lands looking for blood.

I would make sure they'd arrived safe and then I'd hunker out of sight until they were ready to return to the manor. No harm done.

My charges broke through the trees as the sun set behind

the village, the last rays sending elongated shadows across the pale walls of the quarry. The troop of jongleurs had built a large bonfire on the village green and the women of White-cliff had swept the bare earth free of snow. Benches of rough-cut logs circled the fire, surrounded by milling village people.

I faded into the trees at the edge of the village, watching through the buildings. Myrddin joined Anwen, and Fanny stepped up to Giles as the adults herded the children to one of the benches and made sure they were appropriately bundled for a night performance in the winter. It was freezing, but that was part of the tradition.

As the last of the villagers settled into their seats the lead jongleur stood in front of the fire. He wore a red and blue parti-colored doublet and matching hose.

"Good folk of Whitecliff," he said in a voice pitched to carry even into the trees where I hid. "'Tis the eve before LongNight and the shadows stretch their fingers, seeking our despair and our fear."

I shivered, the familiar words taking me back to my own childhood when I'd huddled against Giles in the great hall in past years.

"Let us revel in light and laughter to keep the dark at bay."

The revels were supposed to happen on LongNight, to ease the way into a candlelit vigil. But the jongleurs would be gone before then. I don't think anyone minded the switch as they laughed at the juggler, gasped with the storyteller, and sighed at the love songs.

I kept my eyes on my people in the middle of the throng, gauging their reactions to the festivities. I couldn't hear the stories or the songs very well and the juggler was hidden behind the corner of a house, but I saw it all in the delight on Emeline's face and the thrill in Josselin's wide eyes. And I savored Anwen's smile as she laughed at some jest.

Georg sat across the fire, the flickering light sending jagged flashes of light across his sharp features. His eyes narrowed under his ragged eyebrows anytime Emeline's voice raised in a question or Josselin laughed at a joke.

Finally, about halfway through the performance, he stood up abruptly and stalked off through the village, toward the road up the mountain.

I started to stand and follow, then thought better of it. Whatever he planned, I couldn't follow him through the village shaped like a bear. And if he intended to harm my people, it would be better if I stayed with them.

Eventually when the fire had calmed to a steady crackle, a jongleur dressed all in white stood up and the crowd hushed. He walked to the fire and stood before it with his head bowed. The lead jongleur sat on the cold ground in front of him with his legs crossed.

"My friends," the lead jongleur said, gesturing to the crowd. "My family." He glanced at the troop of performers. "Let us remember why we celebrate. Let us remember the one who gave everything so we might be free to do so."

He raised his hand and all eyes returned to the man in white. The man made a great show of looking around, face open and curious and hopeful.

"The Almighty in his wisdom saw that His people were lonely and He became flesh and walked among us so that the people of Térne might know His love and generosity."

Several other jongleurs came up to the one in white to greet him with handshakes and hugs.

"But the enemy lived here already and had taken over the hearts of many people."

Two of the jongleurs spun, tearing away their outer clothes to reveal black costumes underneath. The crowd gasped. I rested my head on my forepaws, intent on the display below.

"The enemy's people wanted to destroy the Almighty's people. But the Almighty intervened."

The narrator raised his hand and the man in white spoke. "Kill me in their stead," he said.

"So the enemy's people took the Almighty." The two in black took hold of the man in white's arms. "And they killed him."

The men in black threw the one in white into the fire at the center of the green. The flames roared up and several people screamed. Emeline hid her face in Josselin's shoulder.

"And for that night Darkness reigned in the absence of the Almighty."

One of the jongleurs threw some kind of powder on the fire and the flames went out with a quiet wumph, leaving the village green in darkness. A round shadow crouched in the smoke and I stiffened, waiting for the best part of the play.

"But my friends, death is not the end. Darkness has not won. For we wait patiently for the Almighty's grace and light to return in the morning."

The narrator threw out his arms and behind him a figure rose from the ashes of the fire. The smoke cleared and a sigh went through the crowd as his white clothes flashed in the dark, a sign of the happy ending to the story. Tradition left it unfinished for now, but everyone knew what that sign represented.

Slowly, the narrator brought his arms together, then crossed them so each hand rested on the opposite shoulder, and he bowed his head. All the jongleurs froze, silent and still in the frigid night, not even a shiver marring the tableau.

Rustling began as the families and friends around the fire moved, but no one broke tradition by raising their voice.

They rose in silence to return to their homes as the jongleurs stood quiet and respectful. The older folks shushed the younger ones who didn't understand the significance of leaving without words. On LongNight itself they would return to their homes and light candles to ward off the darkness of the longest night of the year. The silence would turn to hushed whispers, the whispers would give way to soft laughter, and eventually families and friends would share stories from the year. In fellowship, they would wait till the sun cleared the horizon and the Almighty's grace returned to Térne.

In the morning it would be the head of the household's duty to tell the end of the story. To tell them how the Almighty had vanquished the enemy with his death and how he rose from the flames to join Térne again.

But that was for later.

Giles bid Fanny a silent farewell and the others left the green and followed the road into the trees. I lumbered ahead, keeping my ears open for anything disturbing the quiet night. Georg had disappeared this way not that long ago. He had to be lying in wait somewhere along the road, but I had plans to find him first. I couldn't wait to see the look on his face when a great big smelly bear snuck up on him.

I ranged up the side of the road, all the way to the gate without finding anything. I snorted in frustration, then turned around to check out the other side. Emeline was dragging her feet in the snow so I had time, as long as I was quick.

But a second pass left me empty-pawed as well.

I stood in the snow, flexing my claws. I knew he had to be out here somewhere, but I was also sure I hadn't missed anything.

I shook my head. There was nothing for it. Anwen and the others had moved on ahead, and I would have to hurry now if I wanted to get back to the manor before them.

As I passed the frozen waterfall along the road, I heard something that made me pause and hold my breath.

A voice.

I placed my paws as quietly as I could, moving so I could peer through the trees. A few hundred yards off the road, Catrin stood with her head high and her arms crossed as she confronted a man in a gold-trimmed blue cloak. I recognized the bald head and missing eyebrows of Anwen's patriarche.

What was his name? Jason? Justin?

"I know what you're playing at, Catrin," he was saying. "The vytl has been disturbed all over this mountain, and I recognize your hand in it."

A muscle in Catrin's jaw jumped. "Of course you do," she said. "I've been here for days, keeping an eye on Anwen. That's all."

"You think just because I'm more used to sitting at a desk, I'm not capable of tracking down a rogue enchanter?"

"There is nothing rogue about my actions," she said, hand slashing through the air.

"I will bring you before the Moot, Catrin. This can't go on."

Catrin jerked. "All I have ever done is protect this Family."

Her words were noble but when she spun around, her movements were quick with panic. She reached out, grabbed something invisible, and stepped up as if onto a step made of air. Then her cloak blew and the colors swirled. When I blinked, she was gone.

Saints, was Anwen's Family finally catching up to Catrin and her actions?

I didn't know how I felt about that. On the one hand, it would expose Catrin and her crimes. But on the other it would expose my crimes as well.

Justin's face creased with anger and concern as he whipped about, trying to find his wayward matrona.

I slunk back through the trees. As much as I wanted to see what Justin would do, I was late. I had to get back before Anwen and the others or she'd know where I'd been tonight.

I hurried through the snow and crossed the broken wall into the empty kitchen yard. I breathed a sigh of relief as I settled into my human form and there was still no sign of Anwen and the others. I'd made it.

A stack of clothes was where I'd left it, and I'd managed to get both legs into my hose when a footstep creaked in the snow behind me.

I whirled only to catch a fist across my jaw. Pain made me stagger, and I fell to the snow. I touched my jaw and scrambled to get my hands and knees under me but a weight landed across my hips and pressed me to the ground.

"That's right, you just stay human," Georg said in my ear.

I spat slush from my bleeding mouth. "Georg, you'll hang for this." I arched my back, trying to throw him off, but he didn't even budge. I had no hope against him on a normal day, but after a transformation and my near-death the day before I could barely breathe, let alone get out from under him.

"No one will care if I kill you. Not after that enchanter tells the King what kind of monster you are. I'll be getting rid of a public threat."

"I'm not—"

He pressed down harder, and I wheezed. My chest hurt.

Muck, if he didn't kill me, Anwen would.

Voices rang from the stone walls of the manor, and I twisted my neck to watch the others come through the gate. Emeline was the first to see me sprawled under her former guardian. Her eyes went wide.

"Léon!" She darted forward but Giles grabbed her as she sped by him. "Don't hurt him, Georg. Don't hurt him."

"I'm not hurting him," Georg said. "I'm just going to kill him a little."

Anwen's face twisted into an expression I'd never seen before, sending a shiver down my spine. She stepped forward, hands raised.

"You going to kill me first, mistress?" Georg said.

The words stopped Anwen in her tracks and she looked stricken. Her hands shook and they fell to her sides.

"No, put your hands where I can see them. Both of you," Georg told them.

Myrddin raised his hands and glanced at Anwen. She gazed off into the distance over my shoulder. Then she swallowed and shook her head at Myrddin as she held her hands out again.

What was wrong with her? She'd had no problem defending me from the mob the other day. She could budge this murderous oaf with a flick of her finger.

"See, she's too noble," Georg said in my ear. "I can kill you and all she'll do is ship me off for 'justice.'"

A little piece of me wished he wasn't right, that Anwen would blast him into the next kingdom. It was probably the really cold piece of me pressed up against the snow.

Emeline whimpered in the circle of Giles's arms. At the very least I hoped Georg wouldn't kill me in front of the children.

"Can I ask what the conflict is?" Myrddin asked as if they were having a reasonable conversation.

"I've been telling you all week he's not fit to rule us," Georg said. "He's a monster, a killer, and he stole my brats. My forge hasn't done half as well as normal without them to fetch and carry and pump the bellows."

"I can see your point," Myrddin said. "But is this the way to get what you want? It's a death sentence to threaten a noble."

I couldn't see Georg, but I could imagine his eyes narrowing to slits. "I'm not threatening a noble," he said. "I'm putting down a beast."

His big hands closed around my throat, cutting off my air. I thrashed under him.

Emeline screamed.

"Is every witness here going to see it that way?" Myrddin said, tapping his chin.

What the hell was he doing? He was going to get me killed.

"Hands!" Georg said.

"Georg, Georg," Myrddin said and clicked his tongue. "We don't need to use our hands. Though in this case I think it will be more fun to let the cat solve our problem for us."

Cat?

Something hit Georg and the shock went all the way through me before his weight disappeared from my back. I sucked in a painful breath and rolled so I was no longer eating slush.

Ten feet away, Georg lay trapped under a couple hundred pounds of snarling cat.

I struggled to my feet, coughing. "Georg, meet Brann," I said. "Brann, this is Georg."

"A pleasure," Brann said, flexing his claws into Georg's shoulders.

"Almighty save us," Georg said, eyes wide. "You're all monsters."

"A wolf always knows his brethren," Brann said. He must have flexed his claws again because Georg groaned and closed his eyes.

I limped toward them. "No more blood on the snow, please, Brann."

He glanced at me. "You object to this one's death?"

I examined Georg who stared back. "Only on principle," I said and lowered my voice. "And definitely not in front of them." I jerked my chin at Josselin and Emeline.

Brann considered me a moment before turning back to Georg. "Even as a monster he's a better guardian than you. Something to think about." He stepped back, not minding his claws.

I fixed Georg with my best lordly look. "I'll tell you one more time to get off my property. If I have to say it again, you get to go another round with Brann, and I won't ask him to spare you next time."

Georg stood slowly and glared at me while he brushed the slush from his tunic. With an arrogant tilt of his head he sauntered toward the gate.

Out of the corner of my eye I noticed Anwen's fists clench.

A gust of wind surged past me, catching Georg in the back and throwing him onto the road. The gate slammed behind him.

"Nice," Myrddin said.

Anwen fisted her hands in her cloak. "I hate bullies." Her gaze found my split lip and then dropped to my bare chest. "I'd mention the fact you're only half-dressed and explore the reasons why..."

I flushed.

"But I think you've been punished enough for the night." She turned and herded the group inside, leaving me to scramble for the rest of my clothes.

When I headed for the manor, I found Brann waiting to

walk with me. I smiled at him. A real smile. Without his help I'd have been dead.

"I thought you didn't like me," I said.

My tone invited him to share the joke but when he spoke his voice was filled with venom. "I hate you."

The shock of his words rocked me back on my heels. "God Almighty, why?"

Some of the vehemence went out of his stance and he swatted a clump of snow. "Because I used to be you," he said. "Shallow, arrogant. I showed the world a smiling face, hiding the selfishness, the rot underneath. I made everyone like me because it was easier to get what I wanted that way."

"What changed?"

He flashed a scowl at me. "How do you know it changed?"

"You speak in the past tense."

He shook his head. "My selfishness killed someone."

I jerked.

He bared his teeth. "Yes, that's right. My people feed on new experiences, memories. Withholding that sustenance from another is the most heinous of crimes. And when my actions resulted in another's starvation, I was exiled from our Realm. They named me Niobrann. Raven of doom."

"I didn't know that," I said quietly.

"Have you ever looked into my eyes?"

The question threw me off. "What? Why?"

"What color are they?"

"Blue," I said without thinking. They'd always been the bright blue of a flame's heart.

"Look closer."

I gave him a funny look before leaning over a bit and meeting his gaze head-on. They were blue, as I'd said, but now I was paying attention I saw the wide streak of orange marring his left eye.

"My kind change based on their choices in life," he said. "Those who choose good become Zevryn. Those who choose evil...they become the Vachryn. The Eaters. The moment I saw my eyes I knew what my choices were turning me into."

"A monster," I said. My stomach lurched. I knew the feeling well. I understood the full force of his gaze now.

"Then we arrived here, and I recognized myself in you."

I swallowed, desperate to pull some moisture into my mouth. "So you hated me."

"As much as I hated myself." His skin rippled in a shudder, but I didn't think it was the cold that bothered him. "Anwen changed it all for me. I was the one who decided to travel with her, but she was the one who accepted me and my past. She made me believe maybe one day I can go home. One day, maybe they'll let me bring back the memories I've collected here and make up for the damage I did before."

We'd reached the door, but I held it shut. He waited.

"Why did you defend me tonight?" I said quietly.

He met my eyes and the hatred had gone from them. "Because Anwen changed it all for you, too."

CHAPTER TWENTY-ONE

Anwen pushed out the kitchen door and tiptoed across the yard. The morning sun gilded the walls and snow with red and gold. A twinge of guilt plucked at her for slipping out without telling Léon, but she wanted a quiet moment away from his infectious smile and unnerving gaze.

He had this habit of looking up when she walked into a room, his smile spreading across his lips and his eyes resting on her face. When he gazed at her like that, she felt like he was seeing past her scars. Like they didn't matter. Like they weren't there.

Even Myrddin had trouble doing that.

And now she found herself looking up when he came into a room, too. She watched as the corners of his eyes crinkled and laughter lit up his face when someone made a joke. She watched as grief pulled down the corners of his mouth and his gaze flicked away when he was tired or lonely or afraid.

And she hated herself for watching. She had felt this

once before for someone who didn't deserve it and she'd sworn she'd never fall for a handsome man again.

She cracked the door to the stables, wondering if she'd have to wake Myrddin, but her freire sat in the open window talking to someone outside. Anwen recognized the voice before she registered the words.

Patriarche Justin stood under the eaves wrapped in his cloak with a wool scarf and hat covering his bald head. Myrddin wasn't nearly so bundled up even though he'd stayed the night in the stables in case Georg had come back.

She smiled and moved forward to greet them. Then she heard what they were talking about.

"And Nivianne de Fay?" Myrddin said, voice wistful.

Justin gave him a sharp glance. "She was fine the last time I saw her. But you know we're not speaking to them."

Myrddin flushed. "I know, but..."

Anwen expected a stab of pain at the mention of the Fays, but the girl's name only stirred a sense of sadness and a little embarrassment. The Emrys Family had cut ties to the Fays all because of Anwen. And Anwen's disastrous betrothal. Unfortunately, there were some innocents who had been caught in the crossfire. Innocents like Nivianne. And Myrddin.

"But what?" Justin's gentle voice prompted Myrddin's answer.

Anwen didn't need Myrddin to actually say it. As hard as he tried to hide his thoughts, she had grown up with him and could read every twitch and smirk.

Her eyes widened. "But you still love her," she said, advancing on the two of them.

Myrddin's head jerked up and she read the truth in his guilty face. Dread sank into her gut. Almighty, what had she done?

"Anwen, no. I'm not...I'm..." He gave up and hung his head. "I'm sorry."

She stepped forward and pushed him hard enough to make him stagger. "Why are you sorry? Don't apologize for being in love." She glanced at Justin. "Good morning, Patriarche."

"Good morning, Enfan," Justin said with a mild look. "Anything I can help with?"

"No, thank you." She turned back to Myrddin and planted her finger in his chest. "The only reason we're betrothed is because of Adrien. Which begs the question, why the hell are we betrothed if you're still in love with Nivianne?"

He opened his mouth, but she threw up her hands.

"I've been so stupid. Stupid and selfish. I thought you were protecting me from getting hurt, but really I was hurting you."

"I—"

"You should have told me," she said. Her shoulders slumped. "Why didn't you tell me?"

He leaned against the wall and crossed his arms. "Am I allowed to apologize for that, at least?"

She glared at him.

He held up his hands. "Look, I didn't tell you because I don't know if I love Nivianne."

She huffed.

"I care about her, yes. But I care about you, too. I don't want you getting hurt again. That's why I offered for you."

She clicked her tongue. "Yes, well, your offer is declined. I won't be marrying you now that I know your affections lie elsewhere." She raised her eyebrows at Patriarche Justin. "All right?"

"Catrin will be upset, but I only want what makes you two happy."

"Then wish granted." She paused then gave him a side-long look. "Matrona was looking for you, by the way."

"And now I'm looking for her. Seen her lately?"

"Not for a couple days, why?"

Justin dropped his gaze. "I'm trying to find the enchanter who cursed your lord. I thought she could help."

There was something in his voice that made her think that wasn't the whole truth. "Are you trying to find evidence for the Moot?"

"If they won't believe an enchanter's work was what hurt me, then I will find the proof and drag it back to them physically."

"Good," she said. "Do you need anything from me? Or Léon?"

"No. I got everything I need from the backlash reaction. Léon's curse bore a distinct signature I can follow."

"Anything I can use?" she said. "I still want to break his death curse."

Justin's gaze flicked away again. "I'm afraid Catrin was right about that. I don't have anything that will help you get around the binding on his heart. Just a trail I can use to find the enchanter."

"Good luck," she said. "I think this one is slippery as well as cruel."

"Thank you," her patriarch said. "I'll need it."

He followed his own tracks back to the gate while Anwen and Myrddin watched from the window.

"I'm not sure he's left the Refuge once since I've been there and now he's done it twice in the last month," Myrddin said, reminding Anwen he was still there.

She turned to look at him.

He frowned, then grinned, then frowned again. "Are you really mad at me?"

She rubbed the back of her neck. "I'm angry you let me use you for so long."

He sighed. "If you were using me, it was as a shield. And you don't rip away a knight's shield before he goes into battle."

She knew what he meant. The months after Adrien's betrayal had felt very much like a fight. She took a deep breath and her chest felt lighter. "I'm not in battle anymore," she said. "You can have your shield back."

Myrddin gave her a sidelong look. "You look relieved."

She fought down a grin. "Don't take this the wrong way but I kind of am. You?"

Myrddin laughed. "Me too."

"Thank you," she said. "For caring about me. But I guess I should guard my own heart."

He shrugged. "I'll still take up arms for you if you ask. So why are you up so early?"

She looked away, fingers twisting around one another. It seemed silly now to tell him she couldn't sleep. She'd kept seeing Léon lying sprawled and bloody beneath Georg. She'd come so close to blasting the blacksmith into another Realm. If she hadn't seen Brann stalking up behind him, Georg would have been a red smear on the snow.

"Do you ever want to punish someone?" She hadn't even realized she'd been about to say it out loud, and she flushed.

Myrddin's brows lowered in concern. "Like Léon was punished?"

She shivered. "Yes. Have you ever felt like you were justified? Like you understood why some enchanters might take things into their own hands?"

She clenched her teeth while she waited for his answer, feeling like a horrible person for even being tempted.

He shrugged. "Sure. People have made me mad before. But just because you think about pushing them off a cliff doesn't mean you're going to turn into a raging enchanter."

She sighed in relief. "It's just when I saw Georg sitting on Léon last night..." Her fingers clenched. "I thought I was going to kill him. I almost did. I've defended Léon before, but this time...I came so close to killing someone just because they threatened a person I..."

"I wondered why you froze," he said quietly.

"I was horrified. And then I couldn't be sure that I could do anything without accidentally—or not so accidentally—taking it too far. Am I a monster for wanting to smash him flat?"

"I've been talking to Georg all week and I've wanted to kill him on multiple occasions. He's a louse."

She huffed a laugh. "A louse."

"What?"

"Léon said something similar." Her smile faded. And why did she remember every little thing he said, the tone he said it with, and the way his mouth moved while he said it?

Myrddin smirked. "You falling for him or something?"

"No." She barely kept from yelling it as she whirled on him. "I'm not. I mean, I'm trying not to." She covered her face as he stared at her. "Saints, I can't fall in love with Léon. I can't."

He blinked at her. "Anwen, I was joking." His eyes narrowed. "Wait, are you really? Anwen, you know he might be a killer."

She laughed, a hair's breadth from crying. "I know. But I can't help hoping that he's not."

He pursed his lips and tipped his head.

"Don't look at me like that," she said, waving her hands. "I'm not some village girl with her head full of fluff because the lord looked at her twice. It looks bad, but he had no reason to kill those people."

"I don't think he was doing it consciously."

She paused. "What do you mean?"

"He spent a long time as a bear." Myrddin ran a hand through his hair. "You said yourself he was losing himself to it. I think when the bear takes over instinct might drive him to kill."

She shook her head.

"Anwen—"

"No. Look, there always has to be something underneath, right?"

"What?"

"The bear might be lurking under Léon. But when the bear takes over, Léon is underneath. And Léon wouldn't kill."

His gaze softened. "How do you know?"

"I have spent a lot of time with him recently," she said pertly. "He couldn't even hunt rabbits. Myrddin, he makes himself vulnerable in order to change for the better." She couldn't forget the shame that had suffused his face as he told her about the incident with his painting instructor.

"He recognizes his mistakes and learns from them. Behind the flirting and the bad flattery there's someone who cares even when it's inconvenient. Even when it makes him look bad." She laughed. "You didn't see what he did for Giles and Fanny..."

She trailed off as she realized what she was saying.

"Anwen," Myrddin said softly. "You may not have wanted to fall in love with him, but I think you did anyway."

She shook her head so violently her hair threatened to come loose from its braids. "No."

"Why not?" he said gently. "If you don't think he's a killer, why are you fighting so hard? Not because of me."

She covered her face with her hands and let her deepest fears bubble and break on the surface. "He's too much like Adrien," she whispered.

"Anwen." Myrddin's voice broke on her name and his face crumpled with guilt. He drew her into his embrace and held her against his chest. Within the safety of his arms she let the tears fall.

"I can't do it again. I can't trust Léon because of Adrien."

Myrddin stroked her hair. "I'm sorry I let him hurt you. But the man you just described isn't anything like Adrien."

She pulled away enough to blink up at him. "What?"

He raised his eyebrows. "You wouldn't hear anything against him at the time, but Adrien never had enough self-awareness to recognize his mistakes let alone learn from them. And he never had enough depth to care for anyone besides himself."

"I...I never noticed."

"Why do you think I never liked him?"

She frowned up at him. "You don't really like Léon either."

"Not true," he said. "I'm supposed to be neutral for this assignment, but you might be tipping me over the edge toward liking him."

She gave him a watery smile.

"But that'll only last as long as he doesn't hurt you."

Adrien's betrayal had left Myrddin as scarred as she was. She raised her hand to smooth the lines of sadness from his face.

The stable door creaked open and Léon poked his golden head through, a book and his leather painting case in his hand.

"Anwen, Giles told me you were in here. I thought we could..."

His eyes found her standing in Myrddin's arms in a shaft of light by the window. They widened in recognition before hurt filled his face. Ice spread through her chest as his gaze found her hand where it rested on Myrddin's cheek. She snatched it back but it was too late.

Léon straightened his shoulders, then his jaw clenched and he turned.

She felt like he took the light with him.

Muck, that sight hurt. Anwen in the arms of her betrothed. I swallowed hard and straightened up, hiding the shaft of pain the sight sent through me. I wanted to rub my chest but it wouldn't do any good.

And the jolt had come hard on the heels of my recurring dream. I'd chased Yasmina in my sleep, only this time she'd let me catch her. She'd turned, and Anwen's long hair had brushed my fingers. Yasmina's hazel eyes had laughed with me. I'd woken with the feel of her in my arms.

Muck on that. If she wanted to cuddle up with Myrddin the freire, I didn't have to stick around to watch.

I spun on my heel ready to flee from the sight.

"Léon!"

I closed my eyes tight at the sound of her distress. She couldn't be that upset. It had to be my imagination. I lunged for the door.

And ran smack into an invisible barrier that stretched across the corridor between stalls. I sprawled on the packed dirt, my leather case bursting, scattering my brushes and charcoal. The parchment bound into a rough book bounced on its corner and fell open, the precious pages open to the air.

I raised a hand to test the air in front of me and found a smooth surface, clear yet unyielding.

Magic. How dare she use magic against me? I whipped my head around to glare at her.

Anwen's brow furrowed in confusion. She had taken a

step forward and raised a hand as if to catch me. At least she had stepped out of Myrddin's arms.

She turned back to him and raised an eyebrow.

Myrddin crossed his arms. "Don't walk away when my sora is speaking to you."

A growl rose in my throat and I scrambled to my feet, brushing dirt and debris from my hose.

"It doesn't look like she needs to talk to me," I said. "You two seemed to be having quite the conversation before I interrupted. I'll get out of the way. Please continue."

Anwen flushed dark red, her scars standing out stark white.

I was such an idiot. But I couldn't regret my sharp words when I saw Myrddin step closer to her. Who knew jealousy could hurt so much?

"Keep a civil tongue in your head, lordling," he said, his voice lingering mockingly on the title. He turned to his sora. "Anwen? Do you want me to stay?"

I stiffened, but she shook her head. "No, I'll be all right."

He glanced from me to her and back again. He lowered his voice. "What about the Adrien thing?"

Her face hardened. "I haven't decided yet. But I don't need you hovering over me while I do."

His lips thinned and his eyes flicked to mine.

I don't know what he read there but he gave me a slight nod. "Very well. But make up your mind. It's not just your heart at risk anymore."

He kissed her cheek and left her in the back of the building. As he came even with me, his shoulder brushed mine, and he leaned in to whisper low and vicious, "If you hurt her, I'll blow you into the next Realm."

I couldn't help the shiver that started at the base of my spine and spread through my limbs. He was gone before I'd recovered from his threat.

Anwen stood in the shadows at the end of the stables hugging herself. Her face tightened as if she were steeling herself for a confrontation.

I threw back my shoulders. Fighting was the last thing I wanted but if it was the only interaction I'd get with her, I'd take it. Then I noticed her red eyes and the tear marks on her cheeks. The bear's protective rage and my own jealousy welled up.

Could I catch that thrice-damned Myrddin before he made it off my land and thrash him for making her cry? If I could do it while I was a bear, even better. Who cared if he could beat me into the ground with a flick of his finger?

But he was Anwen's freire, her closest family, and her best friend. If I did manage to hurt him, it would only hurt Anwen, too. Reluctantly, I let go of the idea.

I gestured to the book open on the dirt. "I bound some parchment for you. I came to ask if you wanted to start writing your history." I paused. "I'm sorry I barged in on you."

She shook her head. "Léon, what you saw was...nothing."

"It didn't look like nothing." I winced at my aggressive tone. Muck, this wasn't going well. "He made you cry."

She rolled her eyes. "I'm perfectly capable of making myself cry. I just needed someone to talk to."

I took a cautious step forward. "You can talk to me. Don't you trust me?"

"No."

Her calm answer made me jerk back. Why should she trust me? All I'd done was lie to, flirt with, and manipulate her.

I forced a smile. "When I'm working through a problem I paint. You want me to get you a brush? I'm sure we have a spare wall around here somewhere."

She gave me a weak grin, the scar at the corner of her mouth pulling tight. "I'd just end up painting you."

My breath hitched. "I'm your problem?" Maybe I should set her up in Josselin and Emeline's room so we'd be a matching set.

She scowled, but I got the impression it wasn't at me. "Handsome, charming men are my problem."

Somehow that didn't seem like the compliment I wanted it to be. I stepped closer. "I'm listening."

She stared at me as I settled myself against a stall door, hands crossed for comfort. How long would it take her to realize I wasn't going anywhere?

Finally she sighed and leaned against the wall next to me.

"I was betrothed once," she said, fiddling with the edge of her cloak.

"Myrddin?" I asked, fighting back the surge of jealousy.

She shook her head. "No. The Families arrange marriages between themselves. It's easier to have a spouse who understands what you've gone through. Someone who's shared the tragedy. I was betrothed early on to Adrien de Fay. Myrddin was supposed to marry Nivianne de Fay."

"But not anymore," I said carefully.

She swallowed, still not looking at me. "No. Not anymore."

"You didn't like him?" I said, striking a jocular tone, hoping it would make her smile.

"I loved him," she said, her face closing off in pain and memory.

I kicked myself but before I could think of how to get my foot out of my mouth she continued.

"We all grew up together. Adrien was wonderful. All the girls liked him. The boys not so much. Myrddin tried to tell me he was selfish and arrogant, but I defended him. Why shouldn't he think he was better than everyone else? He was."

Her voice had grown bitter. I'd never heard bitterness from her before and I didn't like it. Especially since it sounded like she was describing me.

"Everyone always told us we would be a handsome couple once we were old enough to marry," she said. "But when I was fifteen, I had an accident. That's where these came from." She touched a scar that ran across her cheek.

"What happened?" I asked, my voice hoarse. Did I really want to hear it?

Did I really want to stop her?

"A hunter and his dogs. He mistook me for his quarry. I don't remember any of it."

I tried to swallow but my mouth was dry.

"Matrona Catrin told me I'd never have to deal with him. I think...I think he's dead. And it makes me sick to think about. But sometimes at night, I'm glad he's gone. I'm glad I'll never have to face him and make the decision to forgive him."

My heart stopped beating for a moment, then pounded against my ribs. It was all I could do not to scream, "I'm right here. You're facing me now. Forgive me, please, forgive me."

But I kept my lips closed tight on the cries of my heart.

Anwen rested her head on her hands. "After that, he didn't want me."

I blinked and reminded myself to breathe. "The hunter?"

She raised her head and looked at me like I was an idiot. "The hunter is dead," she said. "I meant Adrien."

I winced. "Sorry."

"He came to visit me while I was at the Refuge healing. He took one look at me and he knew I would never be beautiful again. So he left. I remember that part well. He said, 'Beauty needs beauty. Not a beast.'"

My jaw dropped.

She glanced over and laughed at my expression. "I'm gratified you find it so horrifying," she said.

I shut my mouth with a snap and my face burned. I knew if she had told me this story years ago, my reaction would have been similar to Adrien's, and I fought down nausea.

"I don't blame him, really," she said thoughtfully. "That's the kind of person he was, and if I'd seen it sooner, I would have saved myself a lot of heartache."

"But you were in love with him, and he hurt you, and I'd like very much to hunt him down and hurt him back." A growl had crept into my voice.

Anwen gave me a sidelong look. "My Family had similar ideas. They broke Myrddin's betrothal to Nivianne and all ties to the Fay Family. Myrddin offered to marry me so I wouldn't be hurt again."

And how could I convince her to take a chance on me when all I could offer was another selfish bastard who would break her heart? "So when's the wedding?" I joked with a lump in my throat.

Her eyes studied me. "Never," she said.

My heart leapt.

She shrugged one shoulder. "I called it off. I realized I wasn't being fair to Myrddin. Though to be honest, he didn't tell me he was still in love with Nivianne."

"Then..." Saints, she was free. She was available.

I stopped the headlong rush of thought. She was wounded and vulnerable and deserved more than my clumsy joy.

"Then what are you going to do now?"

She sighed and rubbed her temples. "I don't know. Matrona Catrin isn't going to be too happy, but at the moment I can't bring myself to care. I suppose one day I'd like to find someone special, who answers the echo in my heart." She looked away and didn't meet my eyes.

I held my breath. Did I answer the echo in her heart? Did she answer the echo in mine?

When I dreamed of Yasmina, I saw Anwen. When I thought of my love and the most beautiful woman in the world, I saw Anwen. Is that what she meant? Was I the one she thought of? Or did she still think of Adrien?

I knew the answer to that. It was why we were having this conversation. It was why she'd been crying.

"You see that bastard, Adrien, in me, don't you?" I said stiffly.

I couldn't deny the comparison. Until recently I had been

every bit as bad as Adrien. How could I tell her I was different when I wasn't? I couldn't guarantee I wouldn't hurt her again.

Her eyes searched my face as I struggled. "There are differences," she said. "Important differences. I'm sorry it's taken me so long to see them. And I'm sorry you're the one to pay for his cruelty."

I knew what she was saying. It made my heart soar and twist at the same time. She wanted to love me, but I reminded her of the shallow, vain creature who had hurt her so much.

I reached out and cupped her cheek in my palm. "Anwen," I said, meeting her brown and gold-flecked green eyes. "He was an idiot if he thought your beauty is skin deep. You're so much more than your face. I wish I could put into words the way you shine in my sight. You laugh and I want to laugh. You smile and I find myself grinning. You cry and it's my eyes that tear up. Anwen." I breathed her name and leaned toward her.

Her eyes widened. "You were the one who wrote that poem for Fanny, weren't you?"

I groaned and pressed my lips to hers.

She didn't pull away and I shifted to deepen the kiss. She tilted her head, her pulse beating under my finger.

Muck on dreams and fantasy women, this was so much better. She didn't disappear, she didn't mock me with laughter as she ran from me. For that moment I swore I could fly if only she asked me to spread my wings and leap from the nearest cliff.

My fingers caressed the ridges of her scars, their thickness rippling beneath my skin. If only I could wipe them away as I wiped away a smudge of paint.

Finally, she pulled back on a sigh, but I only let her go a couple inches. I rested my forehead on hers. Did this moment mean as much to her as it did to me? I'd never have to be lonely again.

My breath shuddered on a ragged laugh. "Oh, Yasmina," I said.

She jerked under my hands and yanked herself away. Her eyes went so wide I could see white all the way around the hazel and my hands dropped to my sides.

"What?" I said, my heart thudding in my chest. "What is it?"

"I don't believe you," she said, her voice high and incredulous. She turned, shaking her head, and fled toward the door as fast as her limp would allow.

"Wait, Yasmina, what—?"

I reached for her arm but she spun and her palm cracked against my face. Pain blossomed in my cheek and I fell back a couple steps, watching as she darted out the door.

I slumped against the wall, my hand pressed to my burning cheek. What the hell just happened? Saints, I couldn't be that bad at kissing. Although, I hadn't exactly had a lot of practice as the bear.

I peeked around the edge of the door and made sure Anwen had made it into the manor before I started across the yard to the kitchen door. I peeked around that door, too. I may have loved the woman, but instinct told me I shouldn't pursue her before I'd figured out exactly what I'd done wrong.

The kitchen was empty, except for Giles who was clearing breakfast plates off of the small table.

He turned as I slunk into the room and folded my long legs to sit on the stool beside him. He glanced up and did a double take before staring at his hands, his lips twitching.

"I was going to ask if you knew what put Anwen in a huff, but given the hand print on your face, I think I can guess."

"Really?" I said sourly, reaching for some bread. "Then please enlighten me because I haven't a clue."

Giles tapped his fingers against the table, fixing me with a stare. It reminded me of the time he'd found our cook screaming about the rats in the larder when I was eight.

"Tell me what you did." He'd said that then, too.

I squirmed on the stool. "I told her I loved her." I frowned. "Or at least that's what I meant. And I kissed her."

He raised his eyebrows. "Obviously she didn't want to be kissed."

I shook my head. "No, I think she did. She didn't slap me till after." My jaw dropped as I realized what I'd said after our kiss. "After I called her Yasmina." I shut my eyes tight and groaned.

Giles made a strange choking sound and I looked up to see him muffling a laugh with his hand.

"It's not funny," I said. "I meant it as a compliment."

"You always were obsessed with that story," Giles said, composing himself once again. "I trust I don't have to explain what it seemed like from her point of view. Calling the woman you love by another woman's name is not on the list of things she'll appreciate."

"Saints, I have to tell her what I meant." I lurched off the stool. "I have to explain."

"Better talk quick," Giles said as I strode out the door. "Or you'll have a matching print on the other cheek."

CHAPTER TWENTY-TWO

Anwen's mood darkened with each satisfying thump of her steps on the flagstones of the manor.

By the Saints, she'd never been so mad. Not even with Adrien and that was saying something. Just when she was convinced Léon was different, he went and proved they were two sides of the same coin.

Adrien, the dark, moody one, and Léon, the fair, golden-haired flirt. Selfish, arrogant, smooth-talking bastards, all of them.

And she'd let them fool her again! Half the blame could be laid squarely on her. His words had been perfect, spreading a healing balm on her bruised heart. He knew exactly what she'd wanted to hear and had exploited it to perfection. All he'd wanted was a woman. Any woman would do.

Proven by the fact he'd called her the wrong name.

Candles blazed in their sconces as she passed, the vytl in

the air responding to her rage. Fitting considering this was LongNight.

But she was too much of a professional to let the power slip its leash. She needed to calm down. She needed to find a quiet place to have a good cry.

At least this time she wasn't betrothed to the man already, and the rest of her Family wasn't there to witness her humiliation.

Somehow that thought didn't help.

"Anwen!"

She managed to turn her startled jump into a hug as Emeline came hurtling out of their room.

"Anwen, Josselin says Mari can't be a hero."

Anwen took a deep breath and reined in her angry tears. Perhaps the children's fight would provide a distraction from Léon's betrayal.

When Brann and Myrddin found her there, she had a hand pressed to her temple while Emeline shouted that Mari was a better hero than Josselin would ever be.

"LongNight peace to you," she said, the irony in her voice strained.

"And also to you," Myrddin said. He glanced at the argument raging in the corner. "I don't think a hero has to prove their valor with words. Heroic actions should be enough."

Emeline's mouth snapped shut, Josselin's eyes went wide, and the fighting stopped.

"Of course they listen to you," Anwen said, rubbing her forehead.

Brann's eyes narrowed. "Are you angry? You're never angry."

"There's a first time for everything. Apparently I needed a suitable reason. A smarmy, golden reason with a fat head."

"Léon?" Myrddin's face darkened. "What did he do?"

"Nothing." She pointed her finger at him. "Wipe that look off your face. You don't get to go after him. That's my job."

"So he did do something," Brann said. He sat on his haunches, ears twitching.

"If he touched you..." Myrddin said.

Anwen rolled her eyes. "That's not why I'm mad. I liked that part."

Brann raised his eyebrows and she rushed on. "But then he called me by the wrong name."

Brann hesitated. Myrddin stared over her shoulder.

Neither reaction was what she'd been looking for.

"Are you sure?" Brann said.

"What do you mean am I sure?" She flung up her hands. "Of course I'm sure."

"Anwen," Myrddin said, voice distant.

"I just meant, I expected better from him," Brann said.

Anwen deflated. "You did?"

"Anwen, what's this?" Myrddin stared at the wall behind them.

Anwen spared a glance at the painting Léon had done for Emeline. She hadn't really examined it before now, only catching a glimpse through the doorway. But it looked the same as it always had. Why was Myrddin suddenly fascinated by it?

Emeline jumped up before Anwen could answer. "That's my princess. Léon drew her for me. He painted her face and hair and eyes. I did her dress. Léon made me special blue paint so she could have a cloak like Anwen's. Do you like her?"

"Anwen," Myrddin said, his voice soft. "It's you."

"What?" Anwen scrutinized the painting. The woman on the wall did wear blue, her brown hair flowed around her face, and her eyes could have been some kind of muddy green like Anwen's but...

She shook her head. "No, that's not what I look like."

Myrddin took hold of her shoulders and moved her closer to the wall. "Without the scars, yes, you do."

Her eyes narrowed, and she reached out to stroke the thick paint that colored the wall. The woman on the wall was beautiful. But Léon had only ever seen her with scars so there was no way he could remember what she looked like without them.

Her fingers jerked back and she shook her head again. "No," she said, putting some finality in her voice so the subject would be dropped.

"Her name's Yasmina," Emeline said, looking between Anwen and the painting. "The most beautiful woman in the world, Léon says. She does look like you, though."

Anwen's breath caught. "What did you call her?" she said, her voice a bare whisper.

Josselin piped in. "Yasmina. Leonides saves her from the sea monster and she marries him. Léon is named after him, you know?"

"Anwen?" Emeline said. "Are you all right? Your face is all white."

"That's what he called me," she said.

"What?" Brann said.

"He called me Yasmina, and I misunderstood. Saints, I have to talk to him."

I strode from the kitchen, Giles trailing behind me. I hadn't even stopped to take off my cloak.

"My lord," he said, holding out a dripping cloth. "You should put this on your face. It's starting to swell."

"What?" I touched my cheek and winced. He was right, the skin on my cheekbone was tight and warm.

"Here." He handed me the freezing cloth, and I realized it was wrapped around a handful of snow.

"Thanks," I said and turned into the great hall.

As I crossed the threshold, Brann and Myrddin emerged from the hallway across the room. Anwen followed them, looking troubled.

"Anwen," I called, racing across the flagstones. "I need to talk to you. I can explain—"

My toe caught something large and yielding on the floor of the great hall, and I fell across the bundle, the snow pack flying from my hand to splatter against the floor.

Giles gasped behind me and Anwen cried out.

Muck, could I humiliate myself any worse today? I pushed myself up to see what had tripped me and I bit my tongue. I scrambled backward and clambered to my feet.

A body lay in my great hall, blood pooling on the flagstones. Dark red stained my hands and knees from where I'd fallen on him.

He'd been mauled like the others.

I shuddered.

No one else moved so I swallowed down bile and stepped forward to turn the man over. Blood smeared his features but we all knew him at first glance. Georg, the man I'd threatened the night before, stared up at my ceiling with glassy eyes.

"Léon?"

I looked up at Anwen. Her eyes were wide in her white face.

I shook my head. "I didn't—" My voice cracked. "Anwen, please believe me, I didn't..."

"We know you didn't do it, Beauregard," Brann said.

I glanced sharply at the big cat.

"His body was not here when I came through earlier," Giles said.

"And he wasn't killed here," Myrddin added. "Someone must have dragged him into the hall after Léon left but before Brann and I came back in. Perfect timing, if Léon was our killer."

"Except they didn't know he was in the stables with Anwen, completely human at the time," Brann said, looking at Anwen, who flushed.

"Someone is trying to make it look like I killed these people," I said. Finally, someone believed I was innocent.

"Why else would they drag him in here? This is your lair."

This was my sanctuary. God Almighty, they'd been in my home.

"They've been making us think it's you all along," Brann said. "But now they've made a mistake."

"Yes, they have," I said, my voice dropping into the familiar growl of the bear. I let him claw his way to the surface and held him there. If I couldn't be rid of him, I might as well use him.

I stood and clenched my fists. The instinct to hunt and protect swallowed every other consideration. Brann's eyes narrowed, a predator recognizing another predator. Myrddin's jaw tightened.

I knew what I looked like, but what did they expect me to do? Roll over? Show my belly to an attacker?

My eye tracked movement over Anwen's shoulder. In one swift motion I tore off my cloak and laid it over the body before Emeline rushed past the others.

I couldn't hide the blood, though. Pools of it still soaked into the flagstones, and Emeline came to an abrupt halt, hands flying to cover her mouth.

"Léon?"

I stepped forward and swept her up into my arms, my free hand catching Josselin as he darted around me.

"What's that?" he asked.

"Nothing you need to worry about," I said. "I'm going to deal with it."

Emeline pulled back so she could look into my face. "You're going to have to be a bear again, aren't you?"

I nodded. The culprit was close. In the forest somewhere.

She took my face in her small hands and met my eyes with her serious blue ones. "But you'll come back."

I nodded again.

"You promise?"

A smile lifted the corner of my mouth. "I promise," I said.

She nodded seriously and dropped her hands so she could hug me around the neck.

"You're going to go with Giles now, all right?" I said.

Giles stepped up next to me. I handed him Emeline and met his eyes over her head.

"It's LongNight, my lord," he said.

"I'll be back for the vigil."

Too many emotions fought in his expression, but finally pride and worry won out. "Be careful, Léon," he said.

I nodded. He didn't have to say anything more.

My father had taught me nothing about being a lord. Giles had done it all. And for a long time my behavior hadn't done him justice. I didn't know how or when that had changed, but I hoped he didn't regret it.

He led Josselin and Emeline away, and I straightened my spine.

"Léon," Anwen said quietly behind me. "What are you going to do?"

"I'm going to defend my land."

"It's your right," she said. "But maybe you should let us do this for you. You're the one they're after. You're the one they want to hurt."

"They invaded my home, Anwen," I said, turning to her. She stepped back a pace and I couldn't stop to contemplate why. "This place is supposed to be safe. For Josselin and Emeline. For Giles. For me and for you." I took a breath. "If it's not, then I have to make it safe."

Anwen dropped her gaze.

"How are you going to find it?" Myrddin said.

"Track it. I used to be pretty good at that."

Myrddin and Brann both stared at me. Waiting.

I rolled my eyes, accepting the inevitable. "I wouldn't say no to some help."

Brann grinned. "Two noses are better than one."

I focused on Myrddin.

He gave a lopsided smile. "I'm sure I can come up with some way to be useful."

I glanced around the great hall and then my eyes found Anwen. "Giles and the children will be here. Would you..."

She nodded. "I'll keep them safe."

I opened my mouth to say something, I had no idea what, but Myrddin stepped up next to me and grabbed my chin. I tried to jerk away but he tightened his grip so I couldn't escape.

Muck on it, he was two inches taller than me.

"What are you doing?" I said through my teeth.

His lips twitched in a smirk and he glanced back at Anwen. "Nice battle wound," he said. "But in this case, you're undeserving."

He brought his other hand up and his fingers brushed my cheek. Gentle warmth spread from his palm and into my skin, soothing the sting from Anwen's blow. He drew back, releasing my chin.

I put my hand to my face and worked my jaw, feeling the ache subside.

"Now you say thank you," Myrddin said with a self-satisfied smile.

I scowled at him, still fingering my cheek. "I don't know. I kind of liked the reminder."

Myrdddin frowned. "Reminder of what?"

"To think before I speak," I said. My eyes flicked to Anwen.

She cleared her throat. "Um," she said. "Emeline showed me Yasmina."

A flush crept up my newly healed face. "Oh, that," I said. "You saw...?" She'd seen herself in the portrait?

Her lips curved in a gentle smile. "I saw," she said. "Léon, I'm sorry. I didn't understand..."

Didn't understand it was supposed to be a compliment. Didn't understand she was a piece of my soul fitting into place. I wanted to have this conversation—needed to have it, actually—but not in front of Brann and Myrddin.

I cleared my throat and took a mental step back from the enormity of what she might be offering. "We should get moving," I said, dropping my eyes to the body. "While the trail is still fresh."

Myrddin and Brann nodded, giving us both significant looks before moving off toward the kitchen. Before I followed them I let my eyes meet Anwen's, and I poured everything I was thinking and feeling into my look, hoping she would read it there.

Her own eyes seemed to soften and she gave me one last smile. "Be careful, Leonides."

Outside, it had started snowing. Big fat flakes drifted through the branches that hung over our heads as we crept through the trees. In the manor, I'd imagined racing through the woods, chasing the culprit before finally bringing him down where I could meet him face to face. I'd imagined myself a hero, confronting my villain, striding home to claim my heroine.

After two hours of walking, I growled to myself, coming to terms with a colder, wetter, slower reality.

Brann walked with his considerable nose in the air, jowls swinging with every movement. He'd changed into a bloodhound the moment we'd left the grounds. With new snow filling in any tracks we had to rely on scent to track our prey.

I couldn't voice my concern, but I knew this mountain better than anyone, and we'd been going in ever widening circles around the manor. Maybe the bloodhound's nose wasn't any better than the bear's.

Not that I was picking anything up either. Every now and then I turned, snuffling, catching the musk of something wild. The smell sparked an elusive memory I couldn't seem to catch. So without voice and without clues I continued to follow Brann.

My bulky shoulders caught between two tree trunks and I wrenched myself free, sending a wall of snow to the ground in a wumph.

I winced. Muck on this fat, plodding body. The killer would hear us coming and be drinking mead in Ballaslav before we got close.

Myrddin fell over a snow-covered log and cursed.

I grunted. At least I wasn't the only one with issues.

He grumbled as he climbed out of a drift, fighting with his wet cloak. "Brann, whatever we're following better be good because I'd hate to think we've been going in circles."

Hmph. Damn right.

Brann glanced back at us and then around at the miles and miles of shrouded trees.

Muck, he really had no idea where we were going.

Myrddin and I exchanged a look. He planted his feet and I jerked my chin and grunted.

"Brann," Myrddin said, drawing his name out.

Brann sighed. "You're right," he said. "We were going in circles."

"Were," Myrddin said.

"I wanted to follow the body. It's a strong enough scent I should have been able to follow it back to wherever he was killed."

"But?"

"But it wasn't dragged." Brann shook his head in frustration. "I lost it as soon as we left the manor. The circles were to try and pick it up again."

I nodded my massive head. That's how I would have done it.

"Did it work?"

Brann stared off into the trees. "Sort of."

"If you're holding out on us..."

"I think I've found the killer's trail."

Myrddin cast a swift glance around us as well. "Fantastic. That means we can find him, right?"

Brann hesitated.

"What's wrong."

"It doesn't smell human."

"That doesn't make sense. It has to be human. An animal wouldn't frame Léon."

"Look, I might have the nose, but I don't have the

instincts or experience to go with it. To me, it smells like Léon. Animal but wrong."

I growled at the implication.

"Hang onto your fuzzy little tail, Beauregard. I said it smells like you, not is you. This guy's got Georg's blood all over him."

I snorted in recognition. That's what I'd smelled the afternoon after I'd met with Catrin. And that's what I'd been smelling for the last half an hour.

The hackles along my spine rose. Was something stalking my woods with the intelligence of a man but the claws and teeth of an animal?

I mean, besides me.

Myrddin flapped the edges of his cloak, shaking the new snow off. "Something's wrong here, but I don't know what. Let's find the blasted thing before we imagine all sorts of impossibilities," he said as if he'd read my mind.

"Right," Brann said, glancing at Myrddin and I. "Between the three of us we should be able to keep from ending up mauled and dead."

Muck, I hoped he was right.

I followed them uphill, keeping to the bigger spaces between trees when I could.

A few minutes later, healthy trees gave way to bare, blackened trunks. A fire had raced through this area in my grandfather's time, but the forest had only just started to recover, sending up scrawny saplings. The trees stood like stark black-and-white poles rising to the gray sky.

The burned area had always made me shiver and I avoided it when I could.

Brann made his way over the snow-covered branches and sticks that littered the ground before stopping.

"This is it," he said.

Myrddin's eyes narrowed. "This is what?"

"This is where Georg was killed."

I scanned the area. It looked the same as the rest of the dead forest. But when Brann dug down through the fresh snow, he revealed bloody slush.

Claw marks made jagged pale slashes on the dark bark of the nearby trees. My eyes followed a line of them up and my gaze caught on an incongruity. A severed rope, its end slashed and bloody, hung against the trunk, swinging in the slight breeze.

What the hell?

I growled and jerked my head up.

Myrddin stared up at the grisly piece of evidence. "What the hell?" he said.

I rolled my eyes. I'd already covered that, Myrddin.

"What is it?" Brann said. "A noose? A net? Did Georg try to hang some kind of trap here before the killer got him?"

I pushed up onto my back legs and stood as tall as I could. The rope wasn't even tied. Just wedged and tangled in a fork of the tree. I shook my head and dropped back down onto all fours, snow cascading down my shoulders.

Whatever it was, Georg hadn't done much with it before he'd died.

The snow fell heavier, making a shushing noise as it came down.

"What can you smell, Brann?" Myrddin said, stepping

around branches to look at the tree from the other side. "Can we track it from here?"

Brann wandered in circles, his nose sweeping through the disturbed snow. "Maybe. I don't know. There are all sorts of trails—"

Myrddin yelped as he was swept off his feet and into the air by a hidden snare. His body slammed against the trunk of a tree.

Brann and I scrambled toward him, watching our feet for more traps.

Myrddin struggled upside down, his movements pulling the rope tighter around his legs. I glanced up and squinted, but I couldn't see if the rope was attached to the tree the same as the other had been.

"Muck on it, Myrddin, stop struggling," Brann said, absorbing a bunch of snow to become his usual snow leopard. "You're making it worse. Stay calm."

"You try dangling upside down," Myrddin said through his teeth. "We'll see how calm you are."

I caught movement out of the corner of my eye and whipped my head around. The space between the bare trunks remained empty.

My hackles rose and my breath came shorter and faster. A branch cracked and I spun to stare behind me.

There was nothing out there. The trap must have made me jumpy.

"Just blast yourself down," Brann was saying. He stood on his back legs, front end propped against Myrddin's tree.

"I'm not a shape-changer, you moron," Myrddin snapped. "If I lose my feet, I can't grow new ones."

"Now, now. No need for name calling."

A creak from above caught my attention. I raised my eyes and focused on the snow-veiled shape clinging to one of the trunks above us.

Tawny fur blended surprisingly well with the trees and big gold eyes stared down at me. Its gaze burned through me, down my spine to settle like a stone in my gut.

My nostrils flared, full of musk and blood.

I roared and launched myself forward as the feline shape sprang away.

"Léon!"

I left Myrddin and Brann behind, hoping they'd watch each other's backs.

I raced to keep the thing in sight as it sprang from tree to tree like a deranged mountain lion. I knew mountain lions climbed trees but were they supposed to be so fast? This one bounded from a trunk to the ground and across a stream. It was more at home among the trees and the rocks than I was, and I'd been born here.

We passed from the burned area, and I put on a burst of speed.

It darted away, far faster than it had been up to now.

My breath froze the air in a frustrated plume. The damn thing was playing with me.

It glanced over its shoulder and sprang for a snow-laden branch. In seconds I'd lost it.

I plowed to a stop, snow spraying up on either side of me.

I swung my head slowly from side to side, sweeping the area with my gaze. Where had it gone? There was nothing in sight but trees and snow. My hackles rose until the hair along my spine stood on end and a growl grew in my throat. It was watching me. Taunting me. Here on my land it still somehow had the advantage.

To the right, old snow showered down, swirling with the new flurries. Slowly, reluctantly, my gaze was drawn upward to the branches above me. I drew in a sharp breath, feeling the cold air slice my lungs.

It crouched there, on the black branches, its golden eyes pouring hate and rage down on me. Double handfuls of claws and a mouthful of teeth fell from the sky like a fallen angel turned demon.

CHAPTER TWENTY-THREE

The bear roared to the front of my mind, and I let him take control, giving myself up to him completely.

Teeth snapped. Too close.

Claws ripped, leaving searing pain. His breath came in great puffs.

A blur of razor claws and gold fur. Then a weight landed across his back.

He reared back, slammed his enemy against something solid, once, twice.

A yowl behind him, then the claws released.

In one glance, he got a good look at the thing's paw. Not paw. Hand. Hand covered in fur. Hand full of claws.

The bear didn't hesitate. He took the moment's reprieve and ran, sprinting through the trees in a straight line.

Toward the lights that meant safety.

Nothing followed this time.

Relief swept through him as he slid to the back of my mind, leaving me in charge of myself once again.

But pain and exhaustion muddled my thoughts, and I staggered in the same direction, looking for clarity and safety.

My feet sank into the snow that caked the road, leaving platter-sized depressions quickly filled with new drifts. I barely noticed the cold through my thick coat of fur, though my breath clouded the air in front of me. I could barely see through the veil of snow, so I let instinct guide me in the dark.

A branch above me creaked, and I jumped and peered into the branches, expecting golden eyes to be staring at me. But my gaze found nothing in the trees above but snow. I stepped forward once more, my left foreleg quivering and my chest aching. My elbow gave out unexpectedly, sending me face first into the powder. I lay there for a moment trying to remember where I was going and why I had to get there. There was someone I had to see.

Steeling myself against the pain, I levered myself to my feet. It wasn't far. I could make it. Three steps more. Two steps. Finally I stood at the gate, my limbs quivering with fatigue and pain.

Glorious light spilled from the manor, staining the grounds a comforting gold, giving me a guiding beacon. Every window, every ledge, every crenelation housed a candle or a lantern and the doors of the great hall stood open in welcome.

A figure stepped down from the doorway, her limp leaving a strange pattern in the snow behind her while a blue cloak swept around her feet.

Anwen, my mind whispered when my lips could not.

I stepped forward, the familiar fire creeping under my skin, burning away the animal, searing me back to the man underneath. I fell to my knees. Snowflakes bit into my flesh, and I bent over, shivering. Red blossomed on the white in front of me. Blood, that moments before had been hot in my veins, now froze in picturesque puddles as I heard feet hurrying toward me.

"Léon," she said, and I closed my eyes on the gentle caress that was my name on her lips.

Other voices made their way into my consciousness, but I clung to the feel of Anwen's hand on my uninjured shoulder.

"Changer's mercy, what happened? I figured he wouldn't have any trouble with...whatever it was he saw," Brann said.

"Giles, keep the children away."

"Come on, let's get him inside where it's warm," Myrddin said. "Hang in there, Léon. Here, give me that cloak."

Warm wool draped over my back but left the ragged claw marks that rent my shoulder and chest free. Hands helped me to my feet, taking most of my weight so I could hobble toward the door. My hand reached frantically for a familiar touch. Anwen's fingers clasped mine before I could panic.

The three of them managed to get me inside and to the kitchen where Giles hurried to set a stool by the fire. They settled me in front of the dancing flames. Gradually the warmth and comfort of home seeped into my limbs, and I blinked away some of the fatigue that had clouded my perception.

Anwen knelt beside me, my hand held tightly in hers, and I drew strength from her presence. I held the edges of the cloak tightly around my middle as Myrddin pulled the rest of it away from my wounds. I took one look down at the jagged edges of my flesh and turned away before I was sick. My own skin looked far too much like that of the other victims' right now.

"Can you heal him?" Anwen asked Myrddin.

"I can stop the bleeding and close the wounds easily enough," he said still examining me. "But more than that we should let nature take care of. It will heal better that way."

"What happened?" Brann asked as Myrddin laid a warm hand on my shoulder. "Last we saw you'd taken off after something."

"The killer," I said, my voice hoarse. My shoulder and chest tingled from Myrddin's work. "I saw it. Some kind of twisted mountain lion."

"What do you mean twisted?" Anwen said.

"I don't know. The way it moved, the way it thought. It was more than just an animal." I shuddered. "It had hands. Hands full of claws. And it used the trees. That's how it got me. I could never get it on the ground where I could overpower it."

Brann's eyes turned to slits. "Hands?" he said. "Could this thing have set those traps?"

"Yes," I said. "It could probably have moved the bodies, too."

"It was intelligent?" Myrddin said.

I shuddered. Insane was the word I would have used. "It was playing with us. It led us into that trap and it lured me off to try to kill me."

"How'd you get away?"

"I let the bear smash it into a tree. Then he ran. The bear protected me when I couldn't protect myself. I don't know what's wrong with that creature, but I would have died without the bear's instincts."

"It sounds magical," Anwen said.

"It sounds like a Zevryn," Myrddin said.

Brann shifted uncomfortably. "Vachryn," he said. "That's what we call the ones who go bad. But why does it want you strung up for murder?"

I shook my head. I had fewer answers and more questions than I'd had when we'd gone out hunting the thing. "I would have asked but I was busy trying not to die."

Anwen squeezed my fingers. "No one's blaming you, Léon."

From the beginning she had promised to stay and help me. And I had come to count on her, to look for her when I came into the kitchen in the mornings, to see her smile shining back at me when I felt like there was nothing to smile about. My Anwen.

"There," Myrddin said and the tingle in my shoulder and chest subsided. "Be sure to rest, and don't use your left arm for a few days while it continues to heal. But other than that, you should get off with nothing worse than some awe-inspiring scars."

I looked down at myself again but this time the skin was marred only by several wicked looking pink lines. The puckered skin hurt when I moved, but I no longer felt like my life was draining out with my blood. Myrddin fashioned a sling from a spare bandage and carefully immobilized my arm.

"It'll be back," I said. "If it really wants me hanged for murder it will come back."

"Let it," Anwen said, a light in her eye I'd never seen before.

Myrddin's eyes narrowed and he nodded.

"Going out to find it didn't work," she said. "So we let it come to us."

I surged up from my stool. "No. You didn't fight that thing. I did. It's not like anything I've ever seen. If it's cornered, who knows what it will do."

"If we corner it, it will be on our terms," Myrddin said. "You won't be fighting it alone this time. You'll have two enchanters and another large predator to help you. Between the four of us we can take down one scrawny ill-formed cat."

Anwen and Brann both nodded emphatically, fierce and competent.

I wanted to believe them, but I heard the echo of Brann's words in the woods. "Between the three of us we should be able to keep from ending up mauled and dead."

They didn't know what it was like to follow its lightning fast movements or know what it looked like as it fell on them from above. They hadn't felt its claws tear into their flesh.

I hoped desperately that by the end of this I would still be the only one to know those things.

Every candle we owned blazed in the great hall that night. While we'd been out hunting mad monsters, Giles and the children had set up our LongNight vigil. The candles stood in the center of a circle of light—tall and short candles, thick pillars of tallow and thin tapers lined up in rows. I sensed

Emeline's brazen personality warring with Josselin's thoughtfulness in the arrangement.

We sat on piled quilts and pallets, huddled together in a pool of light. Myrddin and Brann, Josselin and Emeline, Fanny and Giles, Anwen and I. Our fellowship would hold us through the longest night of the year until the Almighty's grace and love shone on us once again in the morning.

The others spoke softly, telling each other stories, encouraging the children when they would have laid down and slept the darkness away. I remembered several LongNights in my childhood where I had done the same.

Their voices warmed me, but I could not bring myself to join in.

"Léon?" Anwen's fingers slipped across the space between us and twined with mine.

I wrenched my attention around to face her.

Her lips rose in a smile. "It's going to be all right."

I tried to answer but my throat closed.

Muck, what was wrong with me? The most beautiful woman in the world sat next to me, curled on a worn quilt. She was the one I could imagine spending every LongNight of my life with. She knew my feelings, and I had a good guess as to hers. How could everything not turn out all right?

And yet something about the way she looked at me twisted my stomach, made me tap my fingers, pluck at my tunic. Restlessness tugged at me, urging me to some unknown action. If I loved her and she loved me, how was I still cursed? What else did I have to do?

Our family had always opened LongNight gifts in the morning, but tonight I wished I'd caved to Emeline's demands and brought out the gifts I'd wrapped in dull brown paper, if only to have something to distract me from the inside of my head.

I shifted as my thoughts turned to one of those anonymous packages, the one shaped like a book. A part of me couldn't wait to see Anwen's face when she drew back the paper to reveal the lovingly preserved leather binding. She would turn the cover and find Leonides's name scribed on the first page surrounded by delicate greenery and the occasional illuminated monster. Another more cowardly part urged me to flee the room while she examined my naked dream. Giving her the manuscript felt right but what evils would she see lurking among the pages of my soul?

I squeezed her fingers before standing. I mumbled something about keeping watch and retreated from the circle of light and friendship.

I stood in the doorway, everything I'd ever wanted behind me where I could feel the warmth and fellowship and still I stood here with my back to them, taking deep breaths of frigid air.

The night was quiet. Snow fell softly now, each flake a glittering star floating to the ground. But these stars wouldn't grant a wish. Which was too bad because I was doing a lot of wishing at the moment. I wished the night was brighter. I wished none of this had ever happened.

I wished I had a thicker doublet.

A flutter of movement caught my eye, and I stared hard at the branches of the tree opposite. An owl launched itself, and I stiffened. A shape-changer like Brann, like the Vachryn he'd mentioned could look like an owl if it wanted.

But the bird took off over the trees and disappeared quickly. I forced my shoulders to relax.

Anwen and Myrddin's magic surrounded the manor ready to trap whoever or whatever was brave enough to cross it. I didn't need to stand here watching for shadows, but it helped ease some of the tension in my gut.

I should go back inside and stand vigil with the people I loved. That was what LongNight was about. Anwen and Myrddin would know the instant the trap was sprung. I might as well be warm and useless rather than cold and useless. I turned to head back to the pool of light.

A twig snapped and I tensed. My eyes searched the frozen stretch of ground in front of me, but nothing came into view, either on the driveway or across the boundary of the forest. I forced my shoulders to relax, wincing as my damaged muscles unclenched.

Another rustle crackled in the undergrowth and this one sounded closer. My eyes strained, and I found myself holding my breath.

There. Across the courtyard and beyond the gate something moved between the trees. I tried to find golden eyes staring back at me or tawny fur flashing next to the bark. From this far away I couldn't see details, but something was definitely moving, coming closer.

Muck, where was the magic that was supposed to catch the damn thing?

I stepped back, an involuntary reaction that ran me into the door with a thunk.

A whispered voice rose in question and another answered it.

Voices? But that would mean...

A wash of magic sizzled against my skin and the voices rose in sharp surprise before falling eerily silent.

I breathed a sigh of relief as the door opened behind me, letting out a sliver of light from the candles.

"Léon?" Anwen said, her voice soft and worried. "Did you see it?"

Myrddin and Brann joined us. "Where is it?" Myrddin asked.

I pointed to the edge of the trees. "There."

Anwen held her hand aloft and a brilliant globe took to the air, lighting the entire yard as if it was midday instead of the middle of the night. "Well, let's see what it is we've caught," she said.

The four of us crept closer to the gate where I'd heard the rustling, taking the time to arrange ourselves defensively. Anwen's magic should have been keeping whatever it was immobilized but the memory of my injuries was a strong one.

I stopped at the edge of the boundary to my humanity and the others did as well. We didn't have to venture any farther.

Catrin de Emrys stood in the open gate, brushing her arms as if to rid herself of cobwebs. She raised her eyebrows at Anwen and Myrddin.

"Was that entirely necessary, enfani?"

Anwen sputtered. "Matrona? What are you doing here?"

Catrin raised her chin. "An errand," she said. "Speaking of, I'd appreciate it if you released my companion." She gestured to her feet where another man lay sprawled and rigid under the influence of Anwen's spell.

Catrin's eyes narrowed at Myrddin while Anwen dispelled her magic. "Myrddin," Catrin said. "I wasn't expecting to see you here."

Myrddin's shoulders straightened. "I'm on my own errand," he said.

The man with Catrin stood up and brushed the snow from his robes. My breath caught. He wore the shapeless gray robes of a Disciple of Createjoy. Not only that, but I knew his shaggy hair and patient blue eyes, narrowed now with some emotion I couldn't place. The last time I'd seen him, he'd been red with anger and covered in splotches of paint.

"You're the one investigating the lord's right to rule here?" Brother Warren said, glancing between me and Myrddin.

Myrddin cast me a look as I drew in a painful breath.

"It's not really a matter of his right," he said, carefully. "But that's close enough. Do you have something to say on the matter?"

"Here?" Brother Warren said. His eyes flicked to me. "In front of the lord himself?"

Myrddin raised his eyebrows at me.

I knew everything Brother Warren thought of me. The worst of the worst. A part of me wanted to rush forward and slap my hand over his mouth, but I wouldn't. I owed this man too much.

I swallowed. "You've nothing to fear from me if you wish to speak the truth."

He straightened his shoulders. "That's more than I expected." He turned to Myrddin. "I don't like to be the one to say it, master. But I don't think Lord Beauregard should rule here anymore."

I ground my teeth. I'd been an arrogant, self-obsessed brat when he'd left, but that was no different than most of the other lords ruling under the King's endorsement.

"Why not?" Myrddin asked.

"Because of the accident. I heard what happened after I left."

My lungs froze. He...he'd heard? God Almighty, I'd thought I knew the worst he could believe of me.

I'd thought wrong.

Myrddin studied my reaction. "I'm sorry," he said to Brother Warren. "You'll have to be more specific."

He looked between us. "The hunting accident," he said.

"What hunting accident?" Anwen's voice sent a shudder through me, and my hands started shaking.

Her eyes. I couldn't meet her eyes. I wanted to cry out "Forgive me!" before the crime was uttered. But even that would be too late. It had been too late for a while now. I'd been desperate for something that could never be because I'd sealed my fate three years ago.

If I didn't speak and the truth came out, I would lose Anwen forever. Damned if I did, damned if I didn't.

Would I rather lose her because I'd done the wrong thing? Or lose her because I'd done the right one?

"He's not going to tell you," I said around the knot in my throat.

Brother Warren's head came up sharply and Myrddin glared at me, the shape of the truth forming in his eyes. "Why not?"

I clenched my fists at my sides, forcing myself to continue. "Because I'd rather tell you myself."

Bravery was meeting Anwen's eyes. Bravery was hiding the way my whole body had seized in refusal of my decision.

All of that bravery couldn't make up for the cowardice of my original lie all those days ago when she first showed up at my door.

"Three years ago, I made a mistake," I said. "I left the manor to hunt a stag. Instead, my careless anger nearly murdered a girl."

I raised my trembling hand to Anwen's face. "It was my crime that caused this," I said, tracing a scar. "It was my arrogance and cowardice that left you bleeding out your life on the forest floor three years ago. It was my fault Adrien left you. I am the source of all your misery. I am the hunter."

Anwen's gaze fixed on me, wide and open. Shocked, not horrified. My betrayal hadn't sunk in.

I'd thought it would be better to meet her understanding face on, but I couldn't bear to see the haunted look creep over her beloved features. I shut my eyes. Except then I saw her lying on the leaves of the forest floor, bleeding and mangled. I saw Yasmina staring up at me with accusing eyes, and that was worse. Saints, what had I done?

Anwen shook her head. "No," she said. "No, the hunter is dead." She turned to her matrona. But Catrin's gaze was fixed on me.

She'd brought Brother Warren here knowing what he had to say would break Anwen's faith in me. Our truce had only lasted until one of us betrayed the other, and she'd acted first. What had changed?

An image of Justin, confronting Catrin by the frozen waterfall crossed my mind. I wanted to curse the man for sending Catrin into a panic, but the original fault was still mine.

A short spike of vengeance stabbed at me. I could reveal Catrin's part in all this, but who would I be if I repaid one betrayal with another? Anwen deserved to trust someone right now, even if it was Catrin.

"They let you believe I was gone because it would hurt you less," I said.

Anwen's mouth hardened, and I felt her pull away from me as surely as if she'd taken an actual step. With her went her mercy and then my heart, as though it had been torn out by a clawed hand.

"I'm sorry." I reached out to her, the words pouring from me, and I made no effort to stop them. "Saints, I'm so sorry. Forgive me, please. I wasn't...I'm different now. Different because of you. Please believe me. I can't lose you. Anwen... my Yasmina. I love you."

I ignored her look and stepped forward. She lunged back from my reaching hand, and Myrddin blocked me hard enough that I staggered back and fell to my knees.

I stayed there, not because Myrddin made it clear he'd knock me flat if I tried to reach her again, but because I belonged on my knees begging her forgiveness.

"You really did kill those people."

That made my head snap up. "No! I wouldn't..."

"How can I believe you?" She raised her hand to her cheek.

"The mountain lion," I said, looking between Brann and Myrddin.

Brann tilted his head. Myrddin's lips tightened. "Neither of us saw it."

"The wounds," my voice lost its resolve.

"Self-inflicted, I'm sure," Catrin said.

"You've maimed before. Is it that much harder to kill?" Anwen said.

And I couldn't respond to that. Because she was right.

But she was wrong, too. Almighty God, everything was wrong.

Anwen's mind spun, and the world spun with it. She staggered and Léon raised his hand as if to try to catch her. She recoiled.

Her chest hurt and her stomach wrenched. She didn't want to think or act, she just wanted to curl in a ball until the pain went away. Or put her fist in Léon's face. A face that had gone tight with distress and pleading.

Her instinct was to soothe that hurt, tell him everything would be all right. But her own hurt twisted the compassion everyone else valued and her mercy died bitter and sour in her throat.

Anwen's hands shook as she crossed her arms over her stomach. "I always imagined facing you," she said. "I always wondered what I would say. How I would feel. I guess now I know."

She stared down at me, the look on her face making my chest hurt, and I knew the once beating, pumping center of my soul had shriveled into a cold, hard stone.

My hand, red and chapped from the cold, dropped to the snow to support my sagging torso.

Anwen stepped around me, and my gaze lifted to watch the hem of her blue cloak sweep over the ground as she disappeared into the manor. Myrddin stepped up beside me, a silent bodyguard, emanating barely controlled violence.

He didn't have to worry. I'd begged and pleaded. I'd debased myself on my knees, sacrificing my pride for love. And I had my answer. She wouldn't have to refuse me twice.

Minutes later Anwen appeared in the doorway with a pack over her shoulder, holding Josselin's hand and carrying a sleepy Emeline. Giles appeared behind her, meeting my eyes anxiously. I returned his look with a blank one.

She was taking the children. Of course she was taking the children. I wasn't fit to be their guardian. I was a beast, fit only to scrounge for food and struggle for existence. Catrin had been right.

Anwen stopped in front of me, but I refused to raise my eyes from the hem of her tunic.

"I leave you in a better state than I found you, Léon Beauregard. We are done, you and I."

She walked to the end of the drive, and stepped across my boundary without a backward glance. Myrddin, Brann, and Catrin followed her.

Emeline twisted in Anwen's arms, staring back at me,

realization creeping across her face. "Léon!" she cried. Josselin didn't cry out. He watched with dark, silent eyes, accepting the upheaval as he always did.

My chest contracted with a silent sob. Dammit, my heart was already dead in my chest. It couldn't possibly hurt more, yet somehow the little girl's cry stabbed deeper than any knife or claw.

"I'm...I'm sorry, Lord Beauregard." Brother Warren's voice was laden with hesitance.

I'd loved that voice best of all things in the world once. I'd respected it. I still respected it.

I shook my head. "You don't need to apologize to me, sir. I've spent too long hoping to apologize to you."

Giles's footsteps crunched beside me. "My lord?" he said, voice low and uncertain.

"It's over Giles. She knows the truth."

Fanny trudged over to us and I winced away.

"Go, Giles," I said. "Go with them."

Brother Warren was already turning, but Giles stood fast. "My lord, you don't mean that."

"Don't I?" I glared up at him. "I'll never be free, Giles. I won't ruin another person's life as well. Go back to your scholarship. Marry your love. Just go." I wanted to shout but my voice trailed off into a whisper. "Please."

Giles stared at me for a long moment before he took Fanny's hand and led her away. He stopped at the edge of the woods and gazed back at me. I refused to meet his eyes and after waiting for a goodbye I couldn't give, he and Fanny slipped away.

What was it to love someone selflessly? Was it telling

them a truth that would hurt them because you knew it would hurt them more to stay silent? Was it letting them walk out of your life because that was what was best for them?

Telling Anwen the truth and letting her walk away from me was the most selfless thing I'd ever done, but the bear still prowled restlessly behind my thoughts.

CHAPTER TWENTY-FOUR

Sick dread curled in Brann's stomach as he paced up the road, the new layer of snow muffling his footsteps. What kind of welcome would he get after that scene in front of the manor two nights ago?

He'd left his sworn companion, best friend, and merciful redeemer back in the village, busying herself with anything and everything that could distract her. But he was making the trek up the mountain for her sake. And for Léon's.

Brann had followed Anwen for over a year because of her unwavering compassion, and he knew better than anyone that when her heart had healed enough for her to look back, she would wonder about the lives she had left behind. He went now to make sure her absence hadn't shattered the bear lord she'd poured so much of herself into.

And he needed to see Léon for his own sake as well. Anwen had changed him for the better, just like Brann. He couldn't leave the man without speaking to him at least once.

Much as he loathed what that man had done in the past.

Nothing stirred on the grounds beyond the gate as Brann padded across the snow to the front door.

On the threshold, the Zevryn took a deep breath. He didn't worship the one god the Valerians did but he considered praying to the Almighty just this once. *Please, please don't let Léon have taken the final way out of his curse. Please let him be sulking in some corner, alive if not well.*

The door creaked as if he'd been gone for years instead of days, and he slipped his lithe feline shape through the opening.

The quilts and blankets they'd used on LongNight still lay in wrinkled heaps in the middle of the great empty hall. The candles had long since burned down into puddles of wax and tallow, solidified where they had seeped across the flagstones.

Brann's anxiety grew as he searched the manor, room after empty room, until he stopped outside the open door of the chapel. Discarded jars of paint and brushes lay scattered on the floor.

He'd expected it to be dark and deserted inside like everything else, but he blinked in the sudden light. Sun streamed through the expensive windows and every sconce bore a blazing torch, washing the chapel with gold.

He took a step forward before the walls caught and held his awed gaze.

A fortune in paints colored the walls. No white remained. The vivid greens and blues, the wondrous browns and reds, coalesced into a realistic landscape and Brann stared.

New depictions of the Saints' pledges covered old faded

paintings. Even with no other experience, Brann could see the painter's style had changed. His strokes were longer, broader, the base designs larger. The originals peeking through had been impressive, but Changer's mercy, he'd never seen anything so wondrous. So holy.

Dittany, lady's mantle, vervain, and a hundred others crowded the space in a garden worthy of the Almighty.

His eyes trailed along the painting, finding lifelike creatures peering at him between the flowers and trees. He savored it all, storing it in his memory so he could one day share it with his people. This. This sight was worthy of his return. This was worthy of his redemption.

At the end of the chapel, Léon sat on a stool, a brush in one hand and his palette in the other. His head remained bowed. Had he even noticed Brann enter?

Behind him on the altar, a long-stemmed rose lay, petals dry and brittle. The dead blossom, brown with decay, filled Brann with a cold, quiet dread.

"Léon?" Brann said, creeping toward the quiet painter.

Léon didn't turn, but he finally heaved a great sigh. "I've run out," he said, sounding lost and plaintive, like a child.

Brann's eyes narrowed as he came even with Léon's stool. "Run out?"

"Of paint. I...wasn't finished. But now..." He gestured to the wall.

Brann followed, then squinted and bit down a gasp. Here at the end of the garden the lord had painted a tall, well-built man beside a bower full of roses. The sunlight glinted from his gold hair and armor, and his blue eyes flashed with realistic feeling. He held a sword protectively and his free hand reached out across the room to another figure at the other end of the wall.

Anwen. Dressed in her blue cloak and tunic, a crown of wildflowers woven through her hair. Her face was uncolored but the lines of charcoal made her expression clear. And it chilled Brann. She recoiled from her rescuer with fear and loathing, her beautiful face marred by the look she wore.

"It's my dream," Léon said, his eyes focused on the figure of the woman. "I thought by painting it I could make it go away. I should have known what would happen. It told me. I've always chased Yasmina, and she's always disappeared just as I've caught her. I should have known I wouldn't get to keep Anwen."

The brush and palette dropped from his hands, and he raised them to cover his face. Brann waited quietly while Léon's shoulders shook with sobs or laughter. At this point, Brann would have believed either.

Finally Léon rubbed his face and looked up. This time he met Brann's eyes with a clear blue gaze.

"Why are you here, Brann? Come to gloat? Or keep an eye on me and make sure I don't follow her?"

"There's nothing to gloat about," he said. "And no one sent me to make sure you don't follow. I came to check on you."

Léon gave a bitter laugh. "You mean you wanted to see if I'd killed myself."

Brann clenched his teeth. "It must have occurred to you. It's your last chance to escape. If you're dead, you're human."

"It occurred to me," Léon said in a faraway voice. "I sat in the snow for hours, trying to convince myself that it was the next best thing. But if loving Anwen enough to let her go isn't enough to break my curse, then I'm not sure I want my freedom. Maybe this is better."

"You're not sure?"

Léon shook his head.

Brann didn't know if that was the answer to his question or just general denial, but he decided to go with the former. "At least you're still alive," he said.

Léon gave him a sharp look. "Now you can run off and tell your mistress she's not responsible for my death."

"Anwen doesn't know I'm here."

Léon's nostrils flared.

Brann glanced away. "I didn't want her to have to decide to let me come or not. She's not ready to care if you're all right. But she will be one day."

"Just because I'm alive doesn't mean I'm all right," Léon said. He gestured to the walls. "Witness my madness."

Brann glanced around at the painted splendor. "Léon, if this is madness, we should have driven you over the edge a long time ago."

Léon jumped off his stool and stooped to pick up his brush and palette, his face pulled in a pained frown. "This is the benign side of it. If I don't get some more paint, you'll see the violent side."

Brann stepped in front of him, blocking his escape. "Did you love her?"

Léon reached out to the altar, touching the dry petals of the dead, withered rose. "No, I didn't love her. I do love her."

"It wasn't just a ploy to get her to stay here and free you?"

Léon's face crumpled. "Even if it started that way, that's

not how it finished. Brann, you have to believe me, I would give anything to go back and keep myself from hurting her three years ago."

"You knew who she was," Brann said. "You recognized her, but you never said anything."

Léon clenched his fists. "I thought if she knew, she would leave. At first, I needed her to stay to break the curse. Then I just wanted her to stay because I couldn't bear it if she left."

"Why don't you go after her then? If you love her..."

"Do you think she would forgive me?"

Brann paused. "I don't know."

"Would you?"

The snow leopard regarded him carefully. "No," he finally said.

Léon rubbed his bandaged arm. "I wouldn't either. That's why I can't go after her. I don't deserve her, Brann. If I begged her forgiveness and she gave it, I could never guarantee I wouldn't hurt her again."

"You've changed," Brann said.

"No, I haven't. I'm still selfish. I want her forgiveness even if that's not the best thing for her. But if I stay away from her, then I can't ever hurt her again."

"Seems like the coward's way out, Léon."

"Why do you care so much?" Léon said. "You believe I'm a killer."

"I don't know what I believe," Brann snapped.

Léon cocked his head.

Brann growled and paced the flagstones. "Up on the mountain I smelled something different. I thought it must have been our killer, but Léon, you smell different. Like human and animal all mixed up."

Léon's jaw clenched. "I can't explain what you smelled. But I'm not a killer. I can stand it if Anwen left me because of the truth. But not if she left me because of a lie."

"If you didn't do it, why aren't you out there looking for the one that did?"

Léon pulled his lip back as if the bear inside him was growling. "Get out, Brann," he said. "Leave me to my madness in peace. If you want to help, bring paints, not arguments."

Brann's feline teeth weren't meant for grinding but he did it anyway as he walked away from the manor. If the moron wasn't going to rise to the challenge Brann had given him, then he deserved to rot alone.

Brann stalked back down the mountain, grumbling about snow between his toes. He had to alter course to go around a large stone shaped like a horse's head and the wind shifted.

Brann's nostrils flared. Human. Musk.

Blood.

He froze, his ears swiveling to track sounds.

Nothing moved. The forest was still.

Every animal, even a shape-changer, knew what that meant. His hackles rose, sending a prickle down his spine.

"Whatever you are," he said to the forest. "I'll bet I'm bigger." He absorbed the dirt and snow under his feet until he swelled to unnatural proportions.

A wind stirred the leaves but nothing answered him.

"Léon?"

A low growl rolled down from above him and his head tilted toward the sound as his claws flexed.

He stared up until he found the gold eyes hanging in the branches.

Changer's mercy.

Two days hadn't blunted the jagged edges of Anwen's anger, though she kept her touch gentle as she gripped the borrowed quill and added another line to the history she was writing. Myrddin cast her a glance under lowered brows from his place across the room as he helped an older man sit up and take a sip of water.

Anwen's plan had been to take the Byways back to the Refuge of Saint Redemption immediately, but she hadn't wanted to take Josselin and Emeline away from the mountain they called home. So they'd settled the children with the Disciples of Saint Innovate for the time being. And when she and Myrddin had seen how many people the Disciples had taken in for the winter months they'd lingered to help the ones they could.

Innovate was the Saint of Craftsmen, but the Disciples took in anyone who was in need before they made their way to other more suitable Refuges. The man beside Myrddin was destined for the Saint of Healing as soon as someone could make the trip with him. The woman Anwen had spent the morning talking to would return with them to the Refuge of Redemption.

Anwen tried to ignore Myrddin. Without a patient to

tend she had to keep writing. She hadn't intended to bring the book of bound parchment Léon had made for her, but it had already been in the bottom of her bag. And when she'd found it, it had been a needed distraction. Now she dared not stop for fear she'd never get started again. The confusing feelings roiling under her skin fed the words of a history that spanned what she knew of the fall of the Vemiir Empire to the problems enchanters faced in the present day.

She reached the end of the page and set down the quill to stretch her aching hands.

Catrin took the opportunity to step up to her and place a conciliatory hand on her shoulder.

"Are you all right?" her matrona asked.

Anwen exchanged an exasperated look with Myrddin. Her freire was just as worried about her, but he had the decency to leave her alone. Only Catrin asked her constantly, reminding Anwen that there was something to be upset about. She was used to Brann being a buffer between her and her matrona, but the Zevryn had disappeared hours before without explanation.

"I'm fine," Anwen said shortly. "You can stop asking."

Catrin crossed her arms. "I think it would be better for you if we didn't linger here."

Anwen blew out her breath and tried to recapture the thought she had been chasing so she could write it down. "I have to finish this."

Catrin eyed her work dubiously. "I'm very confused by this new hobby. Why would words on a page change anything about the way the world works?"

"It will bring understanding. I hope. I'm writing this so

people will understand enchanters better and not fear us or our power."

Catrin's lips thinned. "Fear is power. If you would learn to wield it—"

Anwen set aside the book and headed for the door, cutting Catrin off. The thought she'd been following was lost now, and she needed to breathe. Away from those who meant well.

Outside, the cold air filled her lungs. Along the edge of the village between the buildings and the woods, men and women hurried about, building a solid wall to keep out any beast that might come to call.

That had been Anwen's suggestion. She might have left the manor with a clear conscience, but she couldn't leave these people defenseless against the man they had once called Lord.

Her gaze caught on Emeline, playing on the ground beyond the wall, her brother beside her.

Anwen winced and turned away before they could see her. Why did they look like they'd been kicked? She'd already explained to them they were better off far away from the suave killer she'd lost her heart to.

She passed a hand over her eyes. She did not miss him. That was absurd. His carelessness had disfigured her, and worse than that, he'd lied to her about it. She still couldn't believe how smoothly he'd turned aside any question about his past. She'd been wrong about him being the same as Adrien; he was worse.

The door of the Refuge opened and she looked up, eyes

searching for gold hair and blue eyes before she even realized what she was doing.

Muck on it, the man had ruined her and she didn't have the sense to forget him. She couldn't help remembering the regret in his expression alongside the guilt. And when she'd taken the children with her, she knew she'd broken him.

Hands she knew as well as her own took her shoulders, and she tilted her chin to acknowledge Myrddin. She'd been too busy looking for someone who'd hurt her that she hadn't even seen her freire. Myrddin didn't say anything, but he didn't need to.

A familiar voice raised in pain made them both turn. Patriarche Justin came around the end of the new wall. He had Giles's arm over his shoulder and blood dripped from a sizable gash in the manservant's left leg.

Anwen gasped then limped after Myrddin as he stepped across the cleared road, passing Josselin and Emeline where they played.

"Giles?" Myrddin said. "What happened?"

"Master Myrddin," Giles said. He didn't even try to smile at them. "Crosscut saw. Got me in the leg."

"Set him here," Myrddin told their patriarche. "We can get him walking again, then he can rest in the Refuge." Justin helped him sit against the base of the wall where the snow had been cleared.

"Where have you been?" Anwen asked Justin as Myrddin bent to examine the wound.

A muscle in Justin's jaw jumped. "Tracking down the rogue enchanter," he said. "I was still looking for proof. Now

I've found it, but the man who provided it was hurt." He gestured down at Giles.

"What were you doing?" Myrddin said, frowning at the slice.

"Helping cut the lumber for the wall," Giles said

Anwen glanced up in surprise. "You're not at the manor anymore?"

Myrddin winced, and she could have kicked herself for saying it out loud.

Giles met her eyes deliberately as Myrddin laid his hands over the slash on his leg. "No, he asked me to leave. He said he didn't want to ruin another life."

Anwen jerked. That demanded response, but she didn't want to think about the implications of it. "So you came here to help defend against him?"

Giles shook his head violently enough to make Myrddin frown and adjust his grip on the man's leg. "My lord didn't kill those people," he said. "But something else did. This wall is to protect against that."

"Giles," Anwen said with a sigh.

"Anwen, you need to hear what he has to say," Patriarche Justin said.

She paused. Justin nodded to Giles, who frowned.

"My lord didn't kill those people," he said again. "He may have been careless and selfish but you changed him, mistress."

"I broke him, you mean."

Giles raised an admonishing eyebrow. Léon had been right; the man really could kill you with a look. "That too," he said. "It's hard to forgive you for that part."

Anwen's mouth dropped open. "Forgive me?" she said. "Did you expect me to stay after he lied about what he did?"

"Justin." Catrin's voice rang against the rough unfinished wall. She strode up to them, her face creased with anger and fear. "What are you doing?"

"Following the evidence," Patriarche Justin said, his expression like a slab of granite. Anwen had never seen him look so serious. Or angry. "I said I found proof. Giles continue."

Catrin stopped in front of them, her lips pressed tight. Giles stared up at her, his normally open face closing off. Anwen glanced between them, a sense she was missing something growing in her chest. Giles raised his chin and turned back to Anwen.

"You didn't break him by leaving," he said. "We knew you would when you learned the truth. I think you broke him because you left with her."

Myrddin's hands stilled, the cut beneath closed and pink with new skin.

"Anwen, you aren't needed here," Catrin said, her voice rising, but Anwen ignored her.

"What do you mean, Giles?" she said quietly.

Giles noticed Anwen's baffled expression and Myrddin's cautious one. "They still don't know, do they?" he said to Catrin.

"Don't you dare speak," Catrin said, raising her hands in an unsubtle threat.

Justin lurched forward to grab her arms. "You can't hide from this, Catrin."

For once Giles's eyebrows didn't move, and Anwen found

that more intimidating than all the times he'd used them to cow Léon.

"Here's the thing, mistress," he said to Catrin. "I'm not frightened of anything you can do to me. You've already done the worst." He turned his disappointed gaze on Anwen. "Didn't you wonder why she dislikes him so much? Or who transformed him?"

Anwen sucked in a breath, fighting the tightness in her chest.

Myrddin pressed his palms together. "I'd wondered."

Anwen flushed. She hadn't wondered. She'd been too busy storming around, thinking the worst of him. She shook her head. "It's not possible."

"I was there, mistress," Giles said, his eyes returning to Catrin's face. "The day he hurt you and the day she cursed him."

Anwen turned to her matrona, gaze horrified. She didn't have to ask if it was true. She could read the truth in Catrin's face. Then Catrin yanked herself from Justin's grip and crossed her arms, contempt and self-righteousness covering any regret Anwen had seen in her expression. The woman who'd raised her was gone, replaced by a ruthless enchanter.

The damn cat had been right, not that I would ever tell him that. The walking talking fuzzball would never let me forget. That is, if I ever saw him again.

I stared up at the rope hanging from the snow-burdened tree and ground my big nasty teeth. Traps littered my mountain, some sprung and bloody where the victim had died, some waiting for someone to walk into them. I was sure I hadn't found all of them in the hours since Brann had prodded me into action, but I'd disabled the ones I could.

This one was just off the road to the manor, fifty feet from the gate. How had I missed it in all the times I'd roamed the woods in the last week? The night Anwen had left with my heart, I'd wondered if I really was the killer. If maybe I'd imagined the crazed mountain lion.

But that creature was setting these traps. It hunted my lands, and I'd catch it, even if there was no one to prove my innocence to. I'd catch it because I had to keep it from killing again.

I turned back to the manor and lumbered along the road. So many times I'd grumbled and moaned about all the people who had invaded my sanctuary and now the manor felt empty without them. I hated facing its echoes. The chapel was the only place where I didn't feel like I rattled, so I spent most of my time there. The mural had been empty comfort at first, but it filled the room as if someone stood over my shoulder waiting politely to speak until I was ready to hear. A few months ago that would have been creepy. This morning I had almost spoken over my shoulder to ask if anyone wanted anything to eat.

At the gate I stepped across Anwen's boundary, welcoming the fire and the memories it brought. A cloud drifted across the sun as I rose on two feet and slipped into my hose and boots.

I pulled my doublet over my head and stepped away from the gate. The hair on the back of my neck rose as I realized something was wrong. Footprints that I hadn't left marred the snow leading to the door.

My eyes followed the prints to a darker mound beside the front steps.

The mound stood up, and I rolled my eyes in exasperation.

"Beauregard," the snow leopard said.

Damn cat. He was the last one I wanted to see right now. "You're not welcome if you didn't bring paint, Brann," I said, striding past him to the door.

"Léon." The harshness in his voice stopped me, and I paused, foot halfway to the next step.

He leaned against the wall, as if he couldn't stand upright without the support. The cloud shifted and the sun shone down, bringing his coloring into sharp relief. Shadows turned into bright red stains on his pristine fur and my heart thumped in my chest.

I scrambled back down the steps and reached to help him. "Almighty take me for a fool, what happened?"

The big cat shook his head and made more of an effort to straighten himself. "Some of the blood's mine," he said. "Some of it belongs to that foul creature."

My hands stilled on his shoulder. "The mountain lion? You saw it."

"Mountain lion from hell," he said with venom. "I couldn't kill it. I only survived by changing into a tree and hiding. Léon, it's headed for the village."

Ice flooded my veins. "Josselin and Emeline," I said. "And Giles." They were all in the village.

"I had to get you. I can't take it by myself, nearly ripped me to shreds the first time."

Brann hadn't finished speaking by the time I turned and sprinted across the driveway. I'd kill it this time. I'd tear it apart and scatter its remains across the mountain. I'd protect my people whether they wanted me to or not. *God Almighty, help me protect them.*

I leaped across the boundary and welcomed the fire rippling beneath my skin. I landed, shook myself, and roared, the echo of my deep voice ringing through the trees.

CHAPTER TWENTY-FIVE

"What did you do?" Anwen said, voice shaking.

"I protected you, like I always do," Catrin answered, all regret and guilt gone from her posture. Whatever she had done, she had justified it to herself.

"You lied to me," Anwen said. She spun around to Justin. "And you knew. When we talked to you in the stable, you knew who you were hunting, and you didn't say anything."

Justin met her eyes squarely. "I didn't want to disillusion you until I was sure of the truth. Anwen, you believe the best in everybody, and you believe it so deeply no one wants to hurt you by shattering that belief."

She staggered. This feeling of betrayal was all her fault, then. She'd been so idealistic that the people she trusted wouldn't even be honest with her.

"I'd rather know the truth," she said. "I'd rather be able to trust. God Almighty, does everyone lie?"

"Can you blame us?" Catrin said. "This idealism you have is impractical. Sometimes people need to be protected."

"And sometimes they need to be punished," Anwen said, echoing the words a golden man had once said to her. The anger she'd felt for the rogue enchanter who'd cursed him came crashing back down on her, mixed with fierce satisfaction. The combination made her nauseous.

"Why didn't you go to the King?" she said. "When he first hurt me. He could have been brought to justice through the courts. Legally."

"That wasn't enough," Catrin said, leaning forward. "Anwen, he didn't care about what he did to you. I had to make him care."

"Congratulations," she said. "You succeeded. Now release him. He doesn't deserve to remain cursed."

Catrin stepped back, jaw slack. "You can say that after what he did to you?"

Anwen swallowed back her automatic response. It would be so easy to say the words "I forgive him," but would she really mean them?

Someone let out a cry and Anwen spun to see what was wrong.

Leaves rustled at the edge of the woods and Anwen tensed. A couple branches cracked as a huge furred shape pushed through and stepped out into the cleared area before the wall.

"Léon!" Emeline cried, and she leaped up to run to the bear.

A niggling suspicion caught the edges of Anwen's mind, and she grabbed the little girl as she darted past. "Emeline, wait."

Something was wrong. Léon's gold eyes didn't stray to

Emeline. They didn't stray to Anwen. He stalked toward the group, head low, gaze fixed on Catrin.

"Léon?" Anwen said. "Léon, don't do this."

Still he came and Catrin paled.

Anwen pushed Josselin and Emeline behind her. Myrddin helped Giles to his feet, the manservant staring at his former lord in disbelief.

"Léon, I will stop you," Anwen said.

Léon took one last step and paused, ten-feet away, muscles bunched, yellow gaze locked on his quarry. A low growl made the very air around them rumble.

It took Anwen too long to realize it wasn't Léon's growl.

A golden blur fell from the top of the wall, and Léon shot forward to knock it from the air. A rangy mountain lion twisted on the ground and yowled, making her hair stand up.

"Samuel," Catrin gasped.

It sprang once more at Catrin, but another shape, white smudged with black intercepted it with a snarl.

"Brann!"

"Get everyone to the Refuge," Brann said as he tried to gain a handhold on the slippery predator under his claws. "Muck. Léon, grab him."

Léon roared and lunged for the mountain lion, but it hissed and sprang to the top of the wall. It turned once to glare balefully at Catrin before it leaped away and disappeared into the forest.

"Catrin," Justin said, voice flat. "What was that?"

Catrin shrugged uncomfortably. "A crazed mountain lion?"

"You called it by name," Anwen said.

Catrin's shoulders twitched. "Are you questioning me, enfan?"

Myrddin straightened and glared at her as well. "We both are."

Justin's heavy hand came down on Catrin's shoulder.

She glanced between them. "Fine," she said. Anwen expected her shoulders to slump in defeat, but instead she straightened her spine. "Samuel once asked me to marry him. After everything I'd been through to earn my power, the fool had the audacity to demand I leave my magic for a life with him. It would have made all my suffering worth nothing."

"So you turned him into a mountain lion," Justin said.

"There's something wrong with it," Brann said. "That's not just a mountain lion."

"That is Lord Beauregard's fault," Catrin said, glaring at Léon. "I tracked Samuel here. To the mountain." She glanced at Anwen. "You were with me. I only left you for a moment, but when I was halfway through the casting, I heard you scream. By the time I reached you, the damage was done. And Samuel had escaped, half-changed."

Anwen's mind couldn't contain her horror. "Saints," she whispered. How many lives had her Family destroyed? "What have you done?"

"That was years ago. Why is he here now?" Justin said. His voice remained quiet but the undercurrent of menace was unmistakable.

Catrin's face paled in anger, but one look at Justin's expression and she spilled the rest of the story. "I lured him here. He's been trying to kill me for years and when he's thwarted he goes into a rage and slaughters anyone nearby. I assumed if he followed me here, he would resume his murderous ways and Anwen would blame Lord Beauregard."

Léon growled, but Anwen held up her hand. He quieted immediately, his gaze on her.

"Samuel might have been a fool," she said quietly. "But you were the one who made him a murderer."

Leaves rustled in the trees, making them all tense. The villagers that stood on the half-finished wall, gripped their makeshift weapons.

"Myrddin, can Giles move?" Justin said.

"Yes, carefully," Myrddin said.

"Then let's get him and the others into the Refuge. Catrin, you will be confined there as well."

Catrin's eyebrows went up. "Are you placing me under arrest?"

"Yes," Justin said simply. "If the Moot won't keep you in check, then I will."

Catrin drew herself up like she was about to protest or bolt, then surveyed her Family arrayed against her and wilted.

A snarl rolled out from the forest.

"Go, now!" Justin yelled to the villagers as Myrddin helped Giles toward the Refuge.

Léon jerked his chin at Brann and the two raced to put themselves between the villagers and the threat.

Anwen couldn't help noticing Léon didn't even cast her a second look.

✳

A golden blur shot from the trees, and I stood on my hind legs to meet it. The lion hit my chest, and I wrapped my arms around him, taking him to the ground. I tried to get my teeth around his head, but he twisted, raking me with his claws.

I bellowed in pain and let go, trusting Brann to pick up where I left off.

The lion tried to spring away, but as I'd hoped, Brann leaped on him, breaking his trajectory. I ranged around them, keeping myself between Samuel and the wall. Sounds of moving villagers reached us, and I recognized Justin's voice, calling them into the Refuge.

We just had to keep the cursed lion distracted until the villagers were safe.

At last a door slammed.

Samuel sank his teeth into Brann's foreleg. Brann snarled in pain and shook himself free. The lion rolled to his feet, hissed, and launched himself at the wall. I lunged forward to stop him, but the lion's claws hit my shoulders and pushed off, using me as a ladder.

I roared and my teeth snapped shut inches from the lion's flank.

"Muck, I wish he'd stop doing that," Brann said, wincing.

I hesitated, but he growled at me, "Go. I'm coming."

I couldn't spring over walls the way Samuel could, so I thundered around the unfinished end and skidded to a stop in the road, claws leaving furrows in the layer of ice under my feet.

Myrddin trotted up beside me, coming from the Refuge. "Where is he?"

"You didn't see him?" Brann said, limping into view.

"Should we have?"

"You have eyes, don't you?"

Anwen stepped between them and quelled them with a look. "We know he's here. We just have to find him."

"And kill him," Myrddin said.

"No." She took his arm. "He's a man, Myrddin. The same as Léon. He deserves to be free."

"You know how long that will take. He won't sit still, even if we ask nicely."

"Then we trap him. I mean it, Myrddin. I won't let you kill him."

I'd been avoiding her gaze deliberately but that made me swing around to look at her. She couldn't be serious.

"She's right," Justin said, coming up beside us. "If we kill him, we're no better than Catrin."

"There," Brann said and jerked his chin at the Refuge.

A lithe shadow leaped to the roof. The figure stood illuminated by the winter sun, and Anwen gasped beside me. This was the first good look at our enemy the enchanters had gotten. Tawny fur covered long powerful limbs and slitted golden eyes stared out of a narrow head. Its body was vaguely feline but with a twisted quality that reminded one of a man. It crouched on hind legs, its forelegs barely touching the ground. Its hands were tipped with wicked claws that already dripped with blood.

"Almighty, Léon, you were right," Anwen whispered.

I didn't have time to enjoy the rush of vindication. Its eyes locked on mine before it casually reached down, grasped the lantern on its hook by the door and smashed it over the shingles. Flames raced across the roof.

Screams rose from inside.

Anwen gasped. "It's flushing out its prey."

"Still want to trap it?" Myrddin said.

"Yes!" She shot a bolt of energy at the creature, which dodged and hissed, before bounding across the roofs.

I took a step, ready to chase the thing down, but cries of fear came from the Refuge. My heart tugged me in two directions before I growled and chose to rush toward the flames.

Scaffolding leaned against the wall above the door, swaying dangerously with the heat. Even as I moved, the structure collapsed in a heap against the doors. Someone pounded on the other side.

"They're trapped," Brann said behind me.

"Split up," Myrddin said, already heading off down the street. "We'll take Samuel. You two get the people out of the Refuge."

I sped toward the side door in the end of the dormitory, the same one I'd come through the night I met Anwen, but it was boarded shut. I lowered my head and rammed my shoulder into the wood. Once, twice. And not even a crack formed. It would take too long to break through.

I stepped back. There'd been one other option when I'd been trapped myself that night.

I didn't stop to second guess myself but ran around the corner to the wall that faced the quarry.

Createjoy forgive me.

I put my head down and launched myself through the beautiful stained glass. My thick fur kept the razor edges from cutting me as I landed behind the altar inside.

Smoke drifted through the air as white faces with wide

eyes peeked around to see a bear in the chapel. Only the crackling from above and a couple of gasps and sniffles greeted me.

Saints, I hadn't thought this through. What if my appearance caused a panic and they trampled themselves in their haste to get away?

"Léon!" Emeline shrieked, and I turned my massive head toward the sound. She sprang from Fanny's arms and threw herself at me.

I sat on my rump and put the bear's arms around her. Josselin joined us a moment later.

Giles stood from his place with Fanny and gave me a desperate smile. "Come to rescue us, my lord?"

"I thought you liked this window, Beauregard," Brann said, front paws hanging over the empty window frame. "This way, folks. The coast is clear for now, but you'll want to hurry."

They stared unblinking in the murky light. It wasn't until I lumbered to my feet and led Josselin, Emeline, Giles, and Fanny through the broken window that they stirred themselves and followed.

Between myself, Brann, and the crazed mountain lion, they probably thought nature itself had risen against them.

I gave myself only a moment to make sure everyone was safely out and to cuddle against Josselin and Emeline one more time. I savored their easy affection as my heart slowed its staccato beat. But who knew where the creature was and how long they'd have to make their escape?

I pulled away and nodded to Brann, who still had a voice.

"Take them all back to the manor," he said to Giles.

"Along with anyone else you can convince to flee. You can barricade yourselves in there until this thing is dead."

Or we were. I was starting to doubt the creature's mortality.

"Not you, Catrin de Emrys." Catrin had been lurking in the crowd, set apart only by her blue cloak. "You can help clean up the mess you've made."

Catrin drew herself up with a haughty look, but she stayed behind as Giles limped away, herding a reluctant Emeline and Josselin. The group scurried across the street and into the woods. I watched anxiously, convincing myself they'd be all right.

From the other end of the village Anwen screamed.

Brann jerked beside me, and then we were running down the street, snow flying under our claws. I couldn't spare a thought as to whether or not Catrin followed.

At the end of the village, too close to the cliffs of the quarry, Myrddin lay under the tawny shape of the mountain lion, its lithe form disguising the power of its muscles.

I put on a burst of speed, and with an echoing roar, I struck the creature in the side. I'd taken it by surprise and we flew through the air, our limbs tangled. Our bodies skidded along the icy ground. The creature scrabbled for purchase while I struggled to get my jaws around its neck. It snarled at me, its teeth snapping inches from my face, and its claws raked down my shoulders, parting the fur as if it weren't even there.

I growled in pain but I still clung to it, knowing the moment it got away it had the advantage. My size was the only thing it couldn't match. It was faster and more lethal with its unnatural weapons.

"Catrin, free him. Turn him back," Justin called.

"You know I can't when he's running around like this."

My grip didn't loosen, but Samuel gave a mighty heave and slithered out from between my claws. How did he do that? One moment I had him, the next he was springing away onto a roof. I heaved myself to my feet, blood dripping from my shoulders.

The thing snarled at us from the rooftop. I roared back, feeling frustrated and clumsy. I glanced around. Brann stood over Myrddin. The enchanter lay gasping, but I didn't see any blood. I remembered the wall of air he'd used to stop me in the stable and hoped he'd done the same thing to Samuel.

But I'd heard Anwen. Where was she?

"Léon, don't kill him," she said from behind.

I growled. Compassion was one thing, stupidity was another. She and the three other enchanters could have finished this an hour ago if she wasn't so intent on saving him.

I turned to give her a look but that was when the creature chose to strike. It leaped high in the air with its powerful back legs, arching over us. He slammed into me broadside.

I let him take me to the ground, but I wrapped my arms around him and latched onto his throat. He planted his back claws in my vulnerable belly and tore. I rolled away to avoid being gutted.

The thing was blasted slippery. Every time I got a hold of it, it got a hold of me, too. I couldn't disable it without killing it, and there was no way I could kill it without getting torn to shreds.

Another snarl made me whip around, shaking the blood and slush from my eyes. My heart stopped when the creature leaped at Anwen. I was too slow. There was no way I could get there in time and Anwen wasn't moving. She didn't try to dodge. She just watched as a misshapen mountain lion flew at her with claws outstretched...

And then hit an invisible wall. It fell to the ground, stunned.

"Now, Léon!" Anwen cried.

I didn't hesitate, but I wasn't going to trap him like she wanted. This thing was too good, too slippery to ignore any advantage we might have. And it was lined up perfectly. Feet from the cliffs.

I ran, and as I ran my eyes found Anwen's face. She was my reason. She was my life. Without her I was worth nothing. I couldn't let anything live that might threaten her. And if that meant this was the last time I would look at her, so be it.

The creature stood, shaking its head and I hit it full on. My arms wrapped around it, my jaws closed on its throat...

And my momentum took us over the edge of the cliff.

CHAPTER TWENTY-SIX

Anwen watched in horror as Léon struck Samuel and they both plunged over the edge of the quarry. She gaped silently, too shocked to scream.

Her hands crept to her mouth, then she scrambled to the edge and fell to her knees, leaning as far out as she could. The wall of the cliff dropped straight below her, the layers of rock in stark relief to each other in the evening light. A forest of scaffolding and equipment blocked her view at the base of the cliff.

Slowly she became aware that she was whispering Léon's name over and over again. Brann crept up beside her and sat, staring over the cliff with his large blue eyes. One of her hands stole over to clutch Brann's fur while the other flexed on the icy rocks in front of her.

"Is...is he gone?" Myrddin said from behind them, voice husky and strained.

"It is done," Catrin said. Anwen couldn't help noticing how shaken she sounded.

"No," she said, ignoring the way her own voice wobbled. "No, no, no. It's not. He can't be. Come on, we've got to find him."

She spun around to find Myrddin. "Are you all right?" she said.

Justin helped Myrddin struggle to his feet, face white, his arms clutching his middle. "I think he cracked a rib."

"Here, I can help." The faster they could get him moving, the faster they could descend into the quarry.

Myrddin pushed her hands away. "Save it. If he's not...I mean, maybe..."

Anwen knew she should argue, but she wanted that maybe to be true as well.

She expected Catrin to argue but their matrona set her shoulders and followed them. Maybe she wanted to see the end of it all, too.

They set off down the sloping slippery ramp that led to the base of the quarry where the workers cut stone out of the mountain. Ice kept them from running and Myrddin had turned a shade of gray by the time they made it to level ground.

The cutting face stood abandoned, everyone having run to protect the village. As Anwen limped around the tools and carts, she realized she wasn't even sure what she was looking for. Fur? Blood?

She swallowed down nausea and picked up her pace.

"Look," Brann said.

The big cat pointed, and Anwen saw a path of broken scaffolding leading from the cliff edge to the ground. Her eyes traced the path of wreckage until she found the two figures sprawled on the bare stone.

One lay across the edge of a cut block, back broken by the fall. His human features reflected the shape of the mountain lion's face, and his throat had been ripped out.

Samuel's curse had been a death curse as well, then. When his heart had stopped, he'd turned back into the man he'd been. His face was blank and peaceful, bereft of the madness that had haunted him in the end of his life.

The second figure was Léon.

Anwen's heart seized in her chest when she saw his human form spread out limp beneath the scaffolding. His gold hair fanned out against the ice and a trace of blood colored the corner of his mouth. His bare skin was as pale as the rock he lay against.

She ignored the tears streaming down her cheeks as she stumbled toward his body. Her legs collapsed, and a sob escaped her throat as her knees hit the ground. She wanted to clutch her chest where it hurt like her heart was dying, but instead she reached out both hands and pulled Léon to her.

Justin's hands gripped her shoulders, steadying her. Her fingers hovered over the lacerated skin where Samuel had clawed Léon's chest. The fight and the fall had somehow left his beloved face unmarked.

Her throat closed while she studied his features. Brann and Myrddin stood behind her, flanking Catrin. But how long would they let her sit here mourning a corpse?

Léon's chest moved under her palms, and she gasped.

He inhaled again, and she sobbed aloud with relief, searching for his heartbeat against her hands.

"He's alive. Myrddin!"

He stumbled forward and dropped to his knees beside her to survey the damage. She held her breath as he noted the broken bones and lacerations.

"I don't understand," Brann said, moving to sit across from them. His voice shook. "How is he human if he's not dead?"

They looked up at Catrin, who crossed her arms over her chest as if hugging herself and refused to answer.

Anwen shook her head, too relieved to question it. Who cared why the curse was broken? He was alive and well, or would be if they could get their act together.

"Myrddin?" she said. "How bad is it?"

"I can manage it if you feed me power."

Instead, Justin took Myrddin's wrists while the younger man laid his hands on Léon's chest. Normally an enchanter didn't need help drawing power. But if Léon's wounds were bad, Myrddin would need all his concentration to tend to them.

She closed her eyes and shoved down her fear and worry, her love and anguish, then she opened them to watch. Justin drew vytl in and sent it into Myrddin, who used it to seek out the pain and damage and heal it.

It took a very long time for the skin of Léon's shoulders to close and the blood to stop flowing.

Almighty, please. Please.

Finally, Myrddin drew his hands away, and Anwen dared to breathe again. She watched Léon's face anxiously.

His golden lashes fluttered and opened to reveal the deep blue eyes she'd missed so much in the last two days.

When they met hers, she sobbed and leaned over to kiss him. Yasmina coming home to Leonides.

I remembered the fall from the cliff, the air rushing past me and my stomach lurching like I'd left it behind. Blood filled my mouth as the mountain lion struggled in my grasp. Then pain ripped through my chest the same way it had when Myrddin had tried to break the curse but this time it twisted and stopped as suddenly as it came. Fire burned along my limbs, like it did when I crossed the boundary. I lost my grip on the mountain lion in surprise as cold air rushed against my skin.

And then I hit the scaffolding.

I didn't expect to wake up. I didn't want to wake up. But the sight of Anwen pulled me to consciousness faster than the cold or the pain.

While I blinked in confusion, her eyes teared up and her mouth parted. She gripped the sides of my face and suddenly her lips were on mine, warm and soft, coaxing me back to life. Salt and blood mingled on my tongue but it was sunshine and roses that I tasted.

I brought my own hands up to cup hers, closing my eyes and savoring the feel of her palms against my skin.

She kissed me with a fierceness I'd never seen in her before, her lips and touch and warmth dragging me from death, back to life.

I wanted it to never end, but eventually she pulled away, her eyes full of emotions I couldn't begin to sort through at the moment. I let my fingers linger on hers as I finally allowed myself to take stock of my hurts.

I became aware of several things at once. I was alive. I was human. And I was naked. Again.

Between the cold and Anwen's kiss, certain parts of my anatomy were complaining vociferously. I flushed, but Myrddin unclasped his cloak and laid it over me before Anwen could turn and see anything too dramatic.

"I don't understand," she said. "I mean, I'm grateful, but how are you alive?"

"I think the scaffolding broke his fall," Justin said from my other side.

Beside him, Brann glanced up at the broken structure. "And I don't think he was a bear for most of that fall or he would have splattered at the bottom, instead of bouncing."

My stomach heaved, and I fought to keep my breakfast down. The effort made my head throb.

"But how?" Myrddin said. "I thought it was a death curse."

I glanced at Catrin, whose lips were thin and pinched. She knew exactly what was going on, but she wasn't saying.

I sat up slowly and took a deep breath. And another. My lungs moved freely as if a band had been compressing them for so long I'd forgotten it was there and now it was gone. I hadn't realized how weighed down I'd been by the bear.

That was when I knew, too.

"My heart changed," I said. I frowned up at Catrin. "It was supposed to stop and then the curse would be released. But it changed enough the magic no longer recognized it."

Anwen had said it before, but even she hadn't believed someone could change so fundamentally.

"But why now?" Anwen said. "You've been changing since I met you. What's different about today?"

I didn't meet her eyes. "I was thinking something very specific when I went over the cliff."

"What was it?"

I flushed and shook my head. Every moment with Anwen, every thought I'd had of love before today had come with something to gain. Anwen's love in return, breaking the curse, even never being lonely again.

It had always been about me.

"It wasn't supposed to work that way," Catrin said, voice tight. "Only becoming the complete opposite of the selfish boy you'd been would have been enough."

I met her blue eyes. She knew exactly what I'd been thinking as I went over the cliff.

For the first time, loving someone hadn't been about me or what I could gain. It had been about Anwen, and the village, and giving everything for the people I loved without thought of what I might get in return.

That was what it looked like to love someone selflessly.

I swallowed. "That was it?" I said as lightly as I could manage. "That's all it took?"

Brann rolled his eyes and took the bait. "You say that like it was easy. Do you know how hard we worked on you, Beauregard?"

I fought off a smile and focused on Anwen. "So...I'm free now."

Her beautiful lopsided smile spread over her face. "Yes, I'm afraid you are."

My heart sank. For one bright bursting moment I'd thought maybe I could keep Anwen now. But I had to keep thinking about what was best for her, not what was best for me. And I'd hurt her so much already.

I rolled to my knees, clutching the ends of the cloak around me.

"Whoa there, lordling," Myrddin said. "You just fell off a cliff. Take it slow."

"Your healing was excellent as always," I said, smiling at him.

A quick glance at my torso under the cloak told me that I was going to be crisscrossed with scars. The bright red lines were fading thanks to Myrddin's healing touch, but I would be marked for life. If there had been any justice in the world, it would have been my face.

I levered myself to my feet, swinging the cloak over my shoulders and holding it closed in front of me. I stopped and leaned over, breathing hard, my head swimming. Anwen reached out to help me, but I waved her away and stood on my own. I had to be sure my knees would hold me.

I took a couple steps toward the still figure I had taken over the cliff with me, trying to hide the way I stumbled. The man lay limp in the snow, his eyes closed in his pale face, a lock of his dark hair laying across his forehead. In death he finally looked peaceful, so long as you ignored the unnatural bend of broken bones and the bloody swathe where my teeth had torn out his throat.

I swallowed down bile and rubbed my mouth with the edge of the cloak.

"Catrin," Anwen said quietly but with a bit of steel underlying her tone. "Is there anything you'd like to say to him?"

I thought she was talking about me, but when Catrin stepped up beside me, she was looking at the dead man.

"I'm sorry, Samuel," she said and she sounded like she'd rather choke on the words. "For everything I did to you."

My jaw clenched and I turned to face the woman who'd done so much more than ruin my life.

"Did you set him on my barony?"

She raised her chin but a flash of fear lit her wide eyes. "I thought if people started dying, Anwen would know you for a killer and leave. And if you were any kind of lord, you would protect your people."

A growl rose in my chest and that startled me enough to keep from lunging at her. Was the bear still inside me somewhere?

That thought didn't frighten me as much as it should have. I'd learned to work with him and it was comforting to think he was still with me.

I huffed and turned my back on the enchanter. "As you can see, I did. Now all that's left is to protect them from you."

I expected Anwen to rush forward to defend her matrona, but she and Myrddin stared at me, waiting. Brann studied his forepaw before licking it thoroughly.

"What are you going to do to her?" he said as if in afterthought.

Even Justin waited, his lips pressed together.

Then I realized I was the law around here. I could kill the manipulative witch and the King would support my decision.

I glanced at Anwen, still waiting for her to show the mercy that had made me love her so much.

Nothing.

"You don't want to say anything?" I said, quietly. Even while we fought the monster, she'd been spouting nonsense about not killing it.

She raised her chin. "No. She's a killer and a rogue enchanter. I cannot deny her guilt and you have the right to do whatever you wish with her."

I just kept my mouth from dropping open.

She saw the look on my face and sighed. "Compassion is one thing," she said. "But I've recently realized just how important the truth is. I may believe the best of people, but if my naivete is going to hurt more people then it's a weakness I can't afford anymore."

A dull ache filled me at her words. It sounded like wisdom, but it was also the breaking of something that had made Anwen who she was. She'd believed the best of me, and yes that had blinded her to the truth, but that was also what had changed me. I wouldn't be standing here in my own form without her compassion and belief.

My brows lowered. "It's a weakness you can't afford to lose," I said. "And it's one that I must take on." I straightened my spine and let go of the need for revenge which gripped my gut.

Then I met Myrddin's eyes. "Myrddin de Emrys, as the King's closest representative, I remand her into your custody. She should face royal justice. Justin de Emrys,

Niobrann, if you would help him to make sure she doesn't escape."

Myrddin nodded and Justin raised his chin. Brann stopped licking his paw and focused on Catrin with a predator's stare.

After a moment's hesitation I added, "And if the King would like my recommendation, I think her punishment should be dealt out by her peers." I met Justin's eyes.

He nodded solemnly. "I think he will agree."

My shoulders sagged in relief. That was done. "Now I have to go check on the village. And find Giles and the children."

"But wait," Anwen said as I started to walk away. "What about us?"

I paused, willing my heart to stop aching at the sound of her voice. "You may come with me," I said. "I'll return Myrddin's cloak when I find some clothes. Other than that..." I swallowed. "Your obligation to me is fulfilled. There is nothing left to tie you here."

Anwen's mouth dropped open. It looked like outrage, but I didn't know why she'd be angry at me. I was setting her free. I drew the edges of the cloak closer around me trying to keep out the sudden chill. It felt like more than just the wintry air.

She opened and closed her mouth a time or two until finally she settled on a resounding, "Nothing left?"

I closed my eyes, unable to watch her face anymore while I tried to let her go. "I love you too much to keep you here with someone who hurt you so deeply. I know you could never love me enough to forgive me for what I've done to you, and I can't stand being this close to you without that. So please...please go."

Instead of hearing her footsteps walking away from me, I heard her voice, shrill with emotion. "You stupid, arrogant man."

My eyes snapped open as she stabbed me in the chest with her pointed finger. She glared up at me and something inside me rejoiced to see I had stirred so much emotion in her.

"How dare you say I can't love you enough to forgive you? That's for me to decide, you twit. Saints, I can't believe you."

She spun away, but I lunged after her, my heart in my throat. Did she mean what I thought she meant? I had to be sure. I would not hurt her again, I would not assume. I would know.

"Wait, Anwen." I gripped her wrist and she stopped, casting an annoyed glance over her shoulder.

I caught my breath in familiarity. Her expression might have been different, but the movement was so much like my dream when Yasmina laughed at me by the garden gate.

"You love me," I said. We might as well make it perfectly clear.

"Yes," she said, the word escaping a breath of exasperation.

I reached for her other hand, and pulled her back toward me. "You forgive me."

Her fierce gaze met mine, her lovely mouth drawn into a serious line. "Yes. Do you forgive yourself?"

I jerked. I didn't want to. But who was I to hold onto my

guilt when my victim stood in front of me offering my salvation in her hands? All I had to do was reach out and take it.

Even while I'd lied and manipulated her, I'd wanted to earn my redemption. But how could I earn something freely given?

"I do," I said.

I tipped her face up toward me, and Yasmina's features settled over hers seamlessly.

"You are made better by your journey," she said, breath soft against my lips. "It's one of the many reasons I love you, Leonides."

At last, at long last, she drew my head down and let me kiss her. My arms slid around her waist. No more lies. No more pain and betrayal. Myrddin's cloak and her tunic were the only barrier between us now.

I didn't try to harden my heart for the day she would leave me. I let go of my fear and trusted her.

"I guess this means our engagement really is off," Myrddin said with a smirk.

I drew away from Anwen and pulled my lips back in a growl that had become second nature.

"Careful, Myrddin," Brann said. "Don't provoke the beast."

"Why?" Myrddin said. "The curse is broken."

"Humanity's more than the skin you wear," the shape-changer said. "The bear is probably still in there somewhere."

2 Corinthians 3:18

ACKNOWLEDGMENTS

I'll be the first to admit that as introverted as I am, there are many, many things I can't do alone. Launching a book is one of them. So many thanks are owed to all of these people and more:

Mom and Dad, for their unwavering support in the face of four creative daughters.

Arielle, Miranda, Lacey, Betsy, and Alison, for what I'm now calling the *Skin Deep* summit. Thanks for catching those plot holes before anyone else saw them.

Darby, Todd, and Chris and so many others in the Pikes Peak Writers, for your constant encouragement and lovely words. It really is constant.

Wendy, Janet, Ralph, Don, Bruce, Apryl, and Paul, for many Tuesday nights which only made the book better.

Kim Killion, for an amazing cover design. *Skin Deep* wouldn't have been nearly as beautiful without you.

Fiona McLaren, for copy edits. And for your diligence and unending enthusiasm for making me grumble.

Sasha Grossman, for your promptness and eye for commas. Those sound really boring, but they are qualities I appreciate more than anything twice as flashy.

And Josh, for putting up with the crazy while we learn all the fun things like taxes and deadlines.

ABOUT THE AUTHOR

Books have been Kendra's escape for as long as she can remember. She used to hide fantasy novels behind her government textbook in high school, and she wrote most of her first novel during a semester of college algebra.

Kendra writes familiar stories from unfamiliar points of view, highlighting heroes with disabilities. Her own experience with partial paraplegia has shown her you don't have to be able to swing a sword to save the day.

When she's not writing she's reading, and when she's not reading she's playing video games.

She lives in Denver with her very tall husband, their book loving progeny, and a lazy black monster masquerading as a service dog.

Visit Kendra at:

www.kendramerritt.com
www.facebook.com/kendramerrittauthor
www.twitter.com/Kendra_Merritt
www.goodreads.com/kendramerritt

ALSO BY KENDRA MERRITT

Mark of the Least Novels

By Wingéd Chair

Skin Deep

Mark of the Least Shorts

When Quiet Comes to Call

Aria at the Opera

Don't miss a new release! Sign up for Kendra's newsletter to receive updates, book recommendations, and exclusive excerpts future projects.

www.kendramerritt.com/mailing-list

CPSIA information can be obtained
at www.ICGtesting.com
Printed in the USA
FSHW022006090820
72833FS